Crucible
Along the
Mohawk

Johnny T. Rockenstire

First Paperback Edition

Cover Photo: *Schenectady Massacre* by Samuel
Sexton

ISBN-10: 1-5323-9323-5 (paperback)
ISBN-13: 978-1-5323-9323-5 (paperback)
ISBN-13: 978-1-5323-9267-2 (ebook)

For my family

ACKNOWLEDGMENTS

Writing *Crucible Along the Mohawk* was an amazing, fun, experience. But it was also a long, and at times, difficult road. From inception to publishing was roughly five years. This includes all the research, lectures, writing, editing, and going using the backspace on my keyboard more than I care to admit. I would not be where I am today without those I love. So first and foremost, I would like to thank my family for your love and support.

My brothers Jay and Jerry, my sister, Jill, thank you for encouraging me to keep writing and helping to keep me motivated. My dad, John, thank you for always being there when I needed help with practical tasks while my idealistic mind was somewhere else. And my mom, Jean, the hidden, steady hand in all my writing, thank you so much for all your advice, encouragement, and feedback in every crazy idea I've ever had. I love you all.

I'd also like to thank my wonderful girlfriend, Lauren, for always believing in me, and encouraging me to keep pushing through this long project, and of course by insisting to be the first to read my novel. I love you, babe.

A quick special thank you goes out to Lauren's mom, Diane, for helping me pick my editor. I had several individuals who submitted samples of their writing, and without her help, it would have been much more difficult to pick a good editor.

On that note, a huge thank you to goes out to my editor, Danielle, and the Rising Phonics Literary Service team. As any author knows, editing is the most costly, time-consuming, and nerve-racking part of writing a book. Danielle was very understanding of my requirements, budget, and timeline, and was not only able to work with me on all of it, but was very informative and encouraging throughout the process. I can honestly say *Crucible Along the Mohawk* would not have been published when it was, without her assistance.

I can't believe I forgot this mention in the first round, but every author knows the value beta readers bring in feedback and changes needed to the story before it's ever published. On that note, I'd like to thank my friend Greg, who was the only beta reader to give me feedback that helped me make some much-needed adjustments. So, thank you Greg.

Historical fiction requires a complex gathering of research and documentation, and in this note, I cannot list every numerous source that assisted me in this process. However, there are a few organizations and individuals I would like to mention specifically.

First, the Schenectady County Historical Society and the Grems-Doolittle Library, where some of my initial research took place many years ago. And to that unknown librarian who assisted me the day I asked for every scrap of documentation regarding the events described in this novel. They brought out a heap of papers for me, and let me pour over them, recording everything I needed to get started.

The next thank you must go out to the Iroquois museum and the numerous individuals of Iroquois descendancy, from whom I learned a great number of things about your history, culture, and legends. It's great to see the stories are still alive and being passed down generation to generation.

As a historical fiction author, I have to thank the nonfiction authors who have come before, documenting the history, sometimes in such detail that I can honestly say, it was as thrilling to read about these stories as I hope it will be for my readers.

Professor Jonathon Pearson, author of *A History of the Schenectady Patent*, Lawrence H Leder, author of *Robert Livingston and the Politics of Colonial New York*, John Henry Brandow, author of *The Story of Old Saratoga and History of Schuylerville*, Nelson Greene, author of *History of the Mohawk Valley: Gateway to the West, 1614-1925*, Charles McLean Andrews, author of *Narratives of the Insurrections, 1675-1690*, Nellis M. Crouse, author of *Lemoyne d'Iberville: Soldier of New France*, John Andrew Doyle, author of *The Middle Colonies*, and finally, the talented author and ethnographer, Adriaen van der Donck, author of *A Description of New Netherland*.

All their works of nonfiction contributed to the writing of this novel in one way or another. Without their hard research and thorough documentation, this novel would never have been able to be written. A collective thank you to all these authors, past or present.

And finally, I'd like to just thank all my family and friends who read my first book, a little-known fictional action/adventure novel titled *Forty Feet Below*. I was still an amateur author at the time, and wrote it more for my own entertainment than anything else. But like all authors, I wanted it to be widely published. When that novel was not the success I had imagined it to be, it was a sobering wake-up call. There were some hard years of struggling with whether to keep at my passion of writing, and it was all your support and encouragement that tipped the scales, and here I am today. I hope you enjoy *Crucible Along the Mohawk*.

Thank you!

Crucible Along the Mohawk

Part One

1688

The world stands on the brink of war. Under the indomitable rule of King Louis XIV, France is the most powerful empire on earth. An alliance of nations, led by Prince William Henry of the Netherlands, stands against him. Only England has not yet chosen a side in the coming war.

France's expansion has been unstoppable everywhere, except one place – the New World. There, the French and their Indian allies have been locked in a bitter decades-long war with the most powerful native empire of the New World – the Iroquois Confederacy.

It has been 14 years since the Netherlands have surrendered their colony in the New World over to England. The small Dutch communities in the New York colony, live under a tenuous rule. They struggle to keep their alliance with the powerful nations of the Iroquois, and stay loyal to their new English overlords.

Prologue

1688 - Quebec

The governor general dipped his pen in the ink and returned to the letter at hand. By the dim-light of a flickering candle, he inscribed each character with precision and care. He took great caution as to not present anything less than absolute perfection. He had reason for concern. The letter, after all, would be read by the King of France.

As Jacques-René de Brisay de Denonville transferred his long thought-out plans onto the letter, his heart raced with pride and fear. Pride for France, for the title of Governor General was a great honor that had been bestowed upon him. Fear, for he knew his plans were far more ambitious than any in the King's court could have conceived. While his plans could reap great rewards for king and country, he knew they could also go awry, and spell the end of French rule in the Americas.

Denonville was an aging man, now fifty years old. He had been Governor General of New France for only four years, but they had been long years for Denonville. Under his authority, New France had seen its trade suffer and its settlements routinely raided by Indian parties of the Five Nations in the Iroquois Confederacy.

There was a sudden knock on the door. Before he could respond, the door swung open and a man of strong appearance stepped inside. Had it been anyone other than Louis-Hector de Callières, he would have lashed out in anger. Over the past few years, however, he and Callières—the governor of Montreal—had become close friends. Callières was his second in command, a military man like himself, competent and intelligent, but ruthless and cunning. "Come in, Louis," Denonville said, as he walked over to greet him, as if his friend needed the invitation. "Are you packed for your journey?"

"Yes, Monsieur," replied Callières. Louis-Hector de Callières was an ideal commander – mid-forties, but sharp. In his mind, was the fiery spirit of youth and action. He was raised in the small coastal area of Normandy but had long yearned to join the inner-circles of government. He joined the army at age sixteen and had fought in numerous campaigns in New France, mostly against the tribes of the Iroquois Confederacy. "It still saddens me to leave the colony for so long, but as you stated, it is for the best."

Denonville nodded. "It is." He sighed and walked over to a chair, dropping into it as if his legs had suddenly lost their strength.

"Are you feeling well?"

Denonville closed his eyes for a moment. "I inherited a mess. You know that, don't you?"

"Sir?"

"Quebec," the governor general replied. "Montreal, the settlements – New France. All of it was in ruin from the savage's raids and disease outbreaks. My predecessor lacked the foresight and strength to accomplish anything. He was foolish for spreading our citizens out in the wilderness, scattered and helpless. Our towns had no defenses whatsoever. The English mocked us, and the savages slaughtered us. I tried to fight the way I was raised to – with a sense of honor. Make the savages stand and fight like men, not disappear like cowards in the night. For months, we tried to bring them to battle, but they just wouldn't fight like Europeans."

Callières brought up a chair and sat next to

the governor general. He understood Denonville as if he had known him for a lifetime. He had grown to respect him, not only because of his desire for social reform and higher civil standards in the colony, but his burning patriotism and loyalty to the King and to France.

Denonville had a glassy-eyed stare as he spoke, "It seems like just yesterday we were out in the wilderness hunting down the savages. And damn it Callières, we tried. With the Lord Almighty as our witness, we tried."

"We sure did," Callières agreed. "But we lost, monsieur."

Denonville bowed his head. He knew his friend was right. The Iroquois, using their hit and run, lightning fast attacks, had drained the French and their Indian allies of the will to carry on a prolonged campaign. They fought the way they were trained and were soundly beaten with little loss to the Iroquois. The natives had continuously dealt blows to the glory of France, both militarily and economically. They had driven a wedge between the French-Canadian colony and its Dutch inhabitant neighbors to the south, where there was a complete dominion of the fur trade by the Iroquois. Although the two French commanders had been raised on certain principles regarding the fighting of a war, their campaign taught them a hard lesson about frontier warfare.

"I'm tired," Denonville finally said, breaking the silence in the room. Callières listened quietly. "I don't know how the others lasted so long in this unforgiving post. It is a blessing and a curse to oversee the colony in the Canadian territory." His tone was somber and Callières could see the pain in the governor general's eyes.

"I don't follow you."

Denonville looked to his trusted friend. "I am requesting to be relieved of my position."

Callières was stunned.

"At this moment in time, when France needs you most, monsieur – you would leave it?"

"It's not that simple," Denonville rebuked. "War is brewing between France and the rest of Europe. The king's expansion has fueled the resentment of our kingdom; no doubt perpetrated by Protestant English spies. This so-called *League of Ausburg* will not keep the peace for long. The king wants me to command forces out in the field in the coming war. Furthermore, I need respite from this heaven-forsaken frontier. You and I are both soldiers, Louis. But you understand how to fight the natives. I do not." Callières opened his mouth to speak but Denonville cut him off. "It was you after all, who originated the plan you will now take directly to Versailles."

Callières smiled. "It was both of us who devised this expedition," he stated humbly. "So what happens now, monsieur?"

Denonville stood up. "You will travel back to France. There you will give the king my letter of resignation personally. You will also present our well-laid out plan to the court and seek approval. The king will send you back with my replacement most likely." He rested a hand on Callières' shoulder. "We cannot beat the Iroquois savages in a conventional feat of arms. But the English settlements in the New York province are encouraging the Indian raids on our land. The blood of our countrymen is on their hands as much as it is the savages. This alliance of the natives and the English will be our downfall unless we do this. We *must* strike!"

Callières' eyes glanced downward to a map on

the governor general's table. It outlined the English settlements to the south and a line traced around the area. The label read *Dominion of New York territories – 1688*. The map bore red lines and arrows that snaked out from Montreal and Quebec like weeds that grew out of abandoned frontier homes.

"Only a complete takeover of the New York province will ensure the English hold on the fur trade and their alliance with the savages is broken," Denonville continued. "And as we have learned, there is only one way to get rid of the English and Dutch settlers."

The governor of Montreal nodded grimly. Both men had learned the barbarity of frontier warfare from their Iroquois adversaries.

Denonville eyed the English territories on the map. "We are outnumbered on this hostile continent, with only one way to fight. There can be no mercy for the English when war inevitably comes between our nations. How long will a Catholic monarch last in a kingdom dominated by Protestants? King James will not live forever. We may wish he is succeeded by a ruler who is sympathetic to fair France. But we must inevitably be prepared for a king who is hostile to us. We must strike the hardest blow, and we must strike first."

Callières took one last look at the map. His eyes followed the Hudson River up from New York City – the jewel of the entire New England territory. It was an ideal port and whoever controlled it, controlled the Hudson as far north as Canada. His eyes fell upon the town of Fort Orange. A place that, like it was written on the map, the English called *Albany*. It was situated just south of where the Hudson met another river, named for the Mohawk tribe of the Iroquois. Albany was a lucrative target and the first objective of the plan he and the governor general had drawn up. He followed the Mohawk River west several leagues where another small circle had been colored in, symbolizing another settlement. It was a small town, with only a few hundred—mostly Dutch—colonists, fur traders, and farmers. To Callières, he knew its name as *Corlear*, named after the founder of the settlement. On the map, however, the town's name was written as the locals called it – *Schenectady*.

In June 1688, the line of succession to the English throne was thrown into chaos when England's Catholic monarchs, King James and Queen Mary, gave birth to a son. This removed their Protestant daughter, and wife of Prince William Henry of The Netherlands, from ascension to the crown.

Protestants in England, feeling the oppression of their king's rule, pleaded with William to usurp the thrown of England. William gathered the largest fleet ever assembled to that point, nearly twice the size of the Spanish Armada, and in November 1688 – invaded England.

Within a month, King James II fled to France and William became King of England and The Netherlands. The League of Ausburg welcomed the new king, but the move was strongly resented by France.

War had broken out on the continent the previous autumn, and when Louis XIV gave sanctuary to the deposed king and supported his invasion of Ireland, King William III brought in the combined armies of the Netherlands and England, and in the spring of 1689, declared war on France.

From the moment the first cannons were fired, there was a race to get word of the war to the New World colonies. What had previously been little more than sanctioned raids on rival frontier outposts, would lead to open warfare between New France and New England; as well as drawing in closer, their Native American allies. It was a race against time and each other. Fate would have it that word of the war reached Albany before Quebec...

Chapter 1

May 18, 1689

The boy sat on a flat boulder by the riverbank, watching the gentle flow of the river in total silence. In his mouth, he twiddled a piece of straw between his teeth. His bare feet pressed into the dark, wet dirt. No boats could be seen on the river. Sounds of insects and birds filled the air. The sky was bright blue, and the sun's rays shone through the leaves, reflecting off the shimmering water. The serenity was perfect.

He was of average height and a slimmer frame than other boys in their late teens. His hair was dark and long, nearly touching his shoulders, and his face was clean-shaven; adding to his youthful appearance. Wearing simple trousers and a plain linen shirt, he matched the look of other hard-working commoners from the colonies.

Of all the small things that gave him pleasure, few could beat the natural beauty of being out by himself in the middle of a forest, or by the river. He glanced down at his book, a feeling of accomplishment spilling over him. He finished reading it in record time. The town's reverend, Peter Tassemaker, told him it would take him a month to read. He finished it in two weeks.

"Johannes, there you are," a gentle voice said from behind him. A slender girl in a pale, blue dress and white bonnet strolled up. "Mother wanted to know where you were."

"Hey Angie," Johannes replied. "I just needed a quiet place to finish my book."

His sister, Angenietje walked up beside him.

"I know," she replied. "It's hectic at home, especially with father gone."

"He's supposed to be returning tomorrow." Johannes sighed. "I wish he would choose to not take me trapping. It is not my favorite career. I was never good at it."

Angenietje laughed. "Oh Johannes, it was never your favorite thing to do. You hate it, admit it."

He smiled. "That's not true. I know it's important and I love spending time in the wilderness. I just want to enjoy it a little more."

"Well we have work to do and Mother will be looking for both of us." Johannes grabbed his book and stood up.

"I need another book," he said as they headed back up the riverbank. "I need something different to read."

"You should ask around the village. I am sure someone has one book that you have *not* read yet."

They cleared the trees and came to a dirt road. Johannes threw on his shoes and they started off down the path, with the warm morning sun beating on their backs. Flies buzzed around, and their feet kicked up dust on the road. Angenietje turned to him. "Johannes, when do you suppose Samuel will visit again?"

Johannes thought about it. Neither of them had seen their eldest brother in weeks. "He's a busy man, Angie. He still has the spring harvest to worry about, let alone checking the traps. Then of course, there are the normal repairs and maintenance to his home. I doubt we will see him until summer."

His sister's head dropped. "Yeah," she said, dragging it out. "I just miss him."

"I'm sure he misses you too. Father said he would stop by Samuel's house and help him out if he had the time. I wouldn't worry about him, sis. He knows how to handle himself."

"I know," she said. "But what about the Indians?"

"What about them?" he asked.

"Well – what if they come raiding?"

Johannes couldn't help but chuckle. "Angie, the Mohawks have been our friends since before we were born. They aren't going to raid the settlements. And the Algonquians are too far north to venture this way. Trust me," he said, "you have nothing to fear."

Angie smiled. "Oh Johannes, you're always so knowledgeable about everything."

"Well I like to read," he said. "Even the French have never ventured south to attack the colony."

"Okay, okay, I get it," she giggled. "We're safe."

"The only thing I am concerned about is Father returning," Johannes admitted. "I really don't want to go back out there with him. He always chastises me when I don't know some trick of trapping or if I make a mistake when setting one up. Albert feeds off it and just makes it worse."

"I know, Johannes. Albert can be a real jerk sometimes," she said. "He's lucky he is strong enough for manual labor, because he's not smart enough for politics."

"Yeah, but he knows trapping," Johannes said. "And that's all that father seems to care about; how good his sons are at trapping and trading."

Johannes heard a rapid gallop approaching. He turned and instantly grabbed his sister, pulling her to the side of the road. A rider on a horse bolted past them, the courier riding towards for the village.

"Oh no, is there trouble?" Angie asked.

"I don't know," Johannes said, shaking his

head. "I suppose we will know when we get home."

Sweat dripped from Johannes' forehead. The spring was in full blossom and the heat of the day was intense. Only a steady breeze kept the air slightly cooler today than the last few in the week.

Eventually, the forest on either side parted, and the wooden palisade wall came into view. Outside of the stockade, small patches of farmland dotted the surrounding landscape.

In one of the fields, a man was resting his horse. "Hello Mr. Potman," Johannes called out.

"Hello Johannes," Jon Potman replied. "You're not avoiding your chores now, are you?"

"No, sir. Mother gave us the morning off and our brother Arent is taking care of Corset."

"Well it's past noon now," Potman reminded them. "You two best be getting back now."

"Yes sir, we are," Johannes said. "Say, was that you who rode past us on the road?"

"No. A rider came in from Albany bearing dispatch. I don't know what type, but he seemed excited by my account."

Johannes nodded, and thanked Potman before carrying on their way.

Shortly after, they approached the gate to the village. Johannes glanced up and saw a face peering out from the window of the village blockhouse.

The blockhouse was a mini fort and—other than the guard tower at the opposite corner—was the only real defense within the village. It functioned as the armory, powder storage, and at times, the village jail. The rest of the stockade itself was no more than a sturdy 10ft tall palisade square of pine logs, enclosing their home and the rest of the village of Schenectady. As Johannes had heard the Mohawks comment from time-to-time, the stockade walls were of no use against any healthy warrior, as it could be scaled without difficulty.

Passing through the north gate, they walked down Church Street towards their home. The village was laid out in a simple cross with Church Street running north to south, intersecting with Union Street, running west to east. Other roads ran around the interior of the palisade wall. The Vedder home, being in the northeast quadrant, was just a short walk from the village square and the intersection of the two roads.

Any important news was usually read aloud from the church steps.

And today, there was news.

"What's happening?" Angie asked Johannes as they walked up to the huddle of townspeople. The people seemed flushed with joy and celebration.

"I don't know," he replied.

A man burst out from the crowd and shouted "Revolution!" at the top of his lungs.

"Revolution?" Johannes asked. "Whose revolution?"

Johannes tapped a man on the shoulder.

"What's happening?"

"You haven't heard, boy?" the man asked surprised, as if the news was already old. Johannes shook his head. "A message has come from Albany. William the Third of Orange landed in England and disposed King James."

Angie held her mouth to hand and gasped, "Oh no! Is there war?"

The man howled with laughter. "There's no telling either way, child."

"So, what does this mean?" Johannes asked.

The man grinned. "It means we have a new king, lad – and he's a Dutchman."

Chapter 2

Johannes stood outside leaning against the wall of his home, watching the festivities. It was already being called the 'Glorious Revolution' and word spread swiftly throughout the village. Traveling locals informed the neighboring homesteads, and jubilant crowds came from all around. As the summer sun set, the evening was rife with drinking and celebration in the village. A large bonfire was erected in the crossroads. The Dutch settlers of the Mohawk valley took great pleasure in knowing a new king of Dutch-descendancy was on the throne of England.

Johannes turned as he heard the front door open behind him. His elder brother, Albert, having finished his dinner, stepped out, rubbing his belly with a wide grin. "I believe I am ready to partake in this celebration." He punched Johannes on the arm, just enough to cause Johannes to take a corrective-step to control his balance. "Are you coming, brother?"

Angie joined her brothers outside. "There is such joy tonight!" she exclaimed. Albert wrapped his massive arms around each of them and laughed.

"Let's go mingle and drink and celebrate the demise of that Catholic monarch."

"Oh no!" Angie replied. "I'm not drinking. Mother would disprove."

"And I'm not going to talk politics with you and your friends," Johannes added with a light laugh. "I cannot for the life of me understand how you find such matters to be entertaining."

"Entertaining?" Albert inquired. "It is not entertainment. There are important matters to be discussed. But don't worry, you children wouldn't understand them anyway. Leave it to us adults."

"I am not a child," replied Johannes. "I am only a year younger than you."

"But you're immature," Albert said mockingly.

Johannes pushed him away. "Oh really? We shall see about that."

Angie tugged on both of their arms. "Would you two quit your quarrelling and let's go already."

With that, they stepped off from their front steps and headed for the town square.

Around the bonfire, men and women sat on benches brought out from homes and taverns. There was extensive drinking and laughing. Two girls rushed around waving the tri-color Dutch flags. Occasionally someone would fire their gun into the air or set off some fireworks, illuminating the night sky in a bright, colorful spectacle.

Over a smaller fire, some men roasted two hogs. Women of the village walked amongst the crowds with baskets of bread and apples, offering them freely to anyone who wanted some food to balance their drink.

"Albert, Johannes, get over here," a voice called out from amongst the noise. Johannes and Albert looked for a second before seeing another villager, Johannes Teller, waving them over to the hogs.

"How are you Mr. Teller?" Johannes asked shaking his hand.

"Good, good, and yourself?" Teller asked, not waiting for the reply. "Here, try this."

He handed Johannes a piece of roasted hog. Johannes took a great bite out of it, slowly eating it, savoring the juicy pork and crispy skin.

"This is so delicious," he said, his mouth watering.

17

"Hear, hear," Teller said, eagerly giving a piece to Albert. "Angie, do you want a piece?"

"Oh, no thank you, Mr. Teller," Angie said politely.

Johannes grabbed her and edged her closer in. "Sis, you need to try this."

She eyed Albert who nodded, his mouth stuffed. Teller gave her a small piece and she took a bite.

"Wow, this is so good," she replied. "Truly a master chef."

"Thank you, thank you!" Teller said. "So, what do you think about this?"

"This, as in?" Johannes said questioningly.

"The revolution Johannes, what else?"

Johannes shrugged. "I don't know, what will it change here?"

"Who knows?" Teller shrugged. "That's what makes it so exciting. We have been under a veiled threat since the English took over the colony. But now – now we will be secure in our way of life here. We could not have been blessed to be born at a better time in history, lads."

"But aren't the English still in control?" Johannes Vedder asked.

"Yes," Teller went on, "but there is a world of difference between a Catholic Englishman being on the throne, and a Protestant Dutchman, who ascended to the throne via his wife, the daughter of the now-deposed king." Teller laughed. "It's really quite complicated, the intricacies of the royal chain of succession. But it matters naught. May the oppression we have suffered be a thing of the past."

Johannes tried to take it all in but could see Angie was itching to get away, and Albert was already moving in another direction.

"Well thank you for the pork, sir," Johannes said.

He politely made his leave, and no sooner had he done so, he found himself amongst another group of men discussing the revolution.

The men spoke enthusiastically about the events across the ocean.

"When did it happen?" one of the men asked.

The town surgeon, Reynier Schaets, spoke up. "I hear William and his army landed last November. Apparently, they were invited by a group of nobles and laymen."

"So William truly is our king now?" Albert asked.

"It seems that is so," Schaets replied. "I for one will not miss that Catholic monarch. They have suppressed our people since returning to power after the civil war. We should have remained with Cromwell."

Another man spoke up. "We should have fought harder to keep the English out of New Amsterdam. But Peg-Leg Pete couldn't rally the people to defend the city in 1664."

Schaets—who was well versed in history—responded sharply, "The English sailed into the port with no warning, with four men o' war and six-hundred men-at-arms. There was no option for resistance. Stuyvesant made the only call he could and surrendered the colony."

A moment of silence drifted over the circle of men, until Albert broke it.

"Well," he said, "we can all agree that we are finally moving in the right direction again."

"Hear, hear," a few men cheered, raising their cups. The conversation continued, and Johannes Vedder found himself walking away. The politics of it all held little interest to him. He wandered around, drifting through clusters of people eating, drinking and laughing.

"Here come the Wilden!" a man cheered, holding up his cup of ale. Johannes turned and saw a group of Native Americans walking up the street. He noted them as Mohawks, most likely of the Wolf Clan, from the great castle at Tionnontogen. The Mohawk frequently visited to trade or engage in drinking and politics with the men of the village. One man whom he was familiar with, led the group. Known simply as Lawrence, he was a common traveler between the Dutch and Mohawk lands, and well-liked by all who knew him.

Lawrence smiled as some of the Dutch children rushed up to him. He reached down and hoisted one girl up onto his shoulder, using his powerful arm like a chair, as if she were his own daughter. The father of the little girl patted Lawrence on the back as they spoke and laughed.

Lawrence set the girl down as he neared the bonfire. "Joy!" he shouted to the villagers of Schenectady. "What is the cause of your celebration, my brothers and sisters?"

With that, several of the prominent men of the village crowded around him to tell him the splendid news.

Johannes continued roaming around the crowds, smiling at the view. He had never seen such a celebration before. The night sky was lit with the bonfires and occasional shots into the air. His eyes looked over the masses but stopped when he saw an unfamiliar face.

She too walked alone in the crowded street. Her stroll was careless, yet graceful, and her smile showed Johannes that she was just as mesmerized as he was about the occasion. He could not quite tell her age from a distance but she appeared neither young nor old. Her hair was veiled with a white bonnet and her figure was covered with a white and dark blue dress. She was a bit of a mystery, but something about the girl struck him as remarkably attractive.

Johannes took a deep breath, and approached the girl. "Good evening, Miss," he said, polite as he could muster. He tried to keep his bearings, but his small smile betrayed him.

The girl dipped slightly and replied with a warm, "Good evening, Sir."

Up close, he could see she must have been of a similar age to him, and strikingly beautiful. They stared at each other for a moment, in total silence. Johannes thought to speak but the words fell from his mouth. She raised an eyebrow. "How are you enjoying the festivities?" she finally asked.

He smiled again. "I have never witnessed something like this before. The word is we have a new king."

"I know," she said, as if his statement was an affront to her intelligence.

"I didn't mean it to be offensive, Miss," Johannes said, embarrassed. "Of course, you know. I haven't seen you before. Did you just move here?"

The girl paused, looking at him. "Are you not going to ask me my name? Or is where I am from of more interest to you?"

Johannes' cheeks flushed. "I am truly sorry. My manners have not…"

"Just ask me," she said, sighing.

He bit his lip and paused a moment. "What is your name?"

The slightest smile crept over her face. "I am Maria. Maria Vandervort. Who are you?"

She spoke in a manner that left Johannes bewildered. This girl's tone seemed so direct as to be almost impolite. She did not act like the other women he knew. Her accent too, was eccentric, though he could not place where she was from. "I'm Johannes Vedder. My father is Harmen Vedder."

"I see," Maria Vandervort said. "I know that name."

Johannes raised his head a bit. "He was a magistrate, and one-time schout of the village. He got away from it and is a fur trapper now. And your father?"

"He is a laborer in Albany," she replied. "He works when and where he can, mostly on the dock or in the warehouses with the furs bound for New York City."

"I am afraid I don't know him," Johannes said. "I know a lot of the families, from my father's business with them, but I don't recall meeting a Vandervort."

Maria glanced around, leaning in ever so slightly. In a low tone, she spoke, "Well my father isn't Dutch. He is French."

"French?" Johannes nodded slightly.

"His name was Jean la Fort," Maria explained, "but changed it to Jean Vandervort to fit in."

"Interesting," Johannes mused. "The French are not exactly our friends. How did he end up here?"

"He wanted to practice his faith like everyone else, without fear of harassment and persecution." She sighed. "Persecution is everywhere."

"I suppose it's a difficult time for him now, what with the war starting."

"Our family are survivors," Maria stated.

Johannes could not help but be enthralled by the beautiful girl. "What brings you to Schenectady?"

"I came to visit a family friend. My father is somewhere amongst all these drunkards."

Johannes laughed. "So is my brother." He paused watching her for a bit. "I don't mean to be forward, but are you promised to any man at this time?"

Maria sighed. "I knew it," she said aggravated. "It's all men think about, isn't it?"

She started to walk away, but Johannes jumped in front of her.

"Please, Maria, I didn't mean any offense."

"You never do," she whispered in a cynical tone.

Johannes threw up his arms. "I was trying to make conversation. You are new to me and seem like a woman who might be looking for companionship." He bit his lip the moment the words left his mouth. Maria's jaw dropped, and she stared at him for a moment. "I did not mean marriage or – what I meant to say was…" he gave up. "Never mind. Sorry to bother you Miss Vandervort. Have a pleasant evening."

He turned, heading back towards the crowds.

"Johannes?" He twisted back. Maria let out a slight smile. "When you are in Albany next, I hope we cross paths again." Her lips opened slightly, as if she meant to speak again, but she caught her tongue, and without another word, turned and disappeared into the crowd.

His face lit up. "I hope so too, Maria."

Chapter 3

Late that night and into the early morning hours, rains from the west rolled in and poured down on the village. By the early dawn, any signs of the previous day's celebration were washed away, save for a small, blackened fire-pit. Though news of the revolution was exciting to the villagers, England was simply too far away to have a notable impact on their daily lives.

As the morning sun rose, concealed by a thick overcast, the village of Schenectady began to stir. Unlike other days of the week, the men did not grab their packs and head off to check their beaver traps and plots of farmland. The women got busy feeding their children but refrained from many of the daily chores of the household; such as washing laundry, scrubbing the floors, and making soap. On days of the Sabbath, there remained a strict no-work policy.

Johannes' mother, Anna, woke her children promptly at sunrise. "Though your father is not back yet, do not think you are free to do as you wish," she said to Johannes and Albert, both who were still in their beds. "We still need to feed the livestock, and I want the bottom boards on the pantry replaced. They are moldy, and we need to ensure the food stays fresh."

Albert sighed. "But the Sabbath ..."

"The Lord Christ was a carpenter," his mother retorted with a sign of the cross. "He will understand."

Anna was forty-seven years of age, and a strict but caring mother. Her adult life had been spent bearing children and raising them to the best of her ability. Her wavy brown hair was graying, and she always concealed it under a bonnet. Though usually soft-spoken, neither Johannes nor any of her other children dared to question or disobey her.

Anna set up a simple breakfast of bread and butter, milk, and nuts and berries for her children. "Hurry and eat," she said. "We must be ready for services."

As usual, Johannes and Angie were the first downstairs. They were followed by their two youngest brothers, Arent who was twelve years old, and Corset, who just turned three last month. Albert was last to enter, still rubbing his eyes, moving sluggishly while trying to wake himself up.

Angie looked around. "Is father coming home today?"

Anna looked to her daughter and shrugged. "I don't know, Angie. He was supposed to be back yesterday. Perhaps he was held up at your brother's house. The Lord knows Samuel needs a helping hand maintaining the plot."

"He ought to find himself a wife," Albert said. "That way at least he doesn't have to do his own cooking." His mother and Angie both scolded him with looks. He smiled. "I am just saying, he has a lot else to do. He's ready for marriage."

"And you are ready to move out and build your own estate," Anna replied. "Once your father returns, perhaps I will have him arrange a land lease for you to go out and build a new home."

"Well once I do, then I can find myself a wife," Albert said. "Unlike Samuel, I will not wait so long. I have more than one admirer in the village."

"You've been staring into too many mirrors," Johannes commented, causing Angie and Arent to burst out laughing.

"Shut it!" Albert growled.

"I did not see any girls swooning over you last

night," Johannes continued.

"Well I was busy talking politics with the other men. If you were a real man, you would have been there too."

"Enough of this," their mother said with a stern voice. "Finish your breakfasts and get dressed. We shall not make jokes nor talk about politics on the Lord's day. This is a day of worship and giving thanks for how good of a life you all live."

The church was filled with townspeople. The reverend took the pulpit and opened his thick, worn-out Bible. In his late thirties, Peter Tassemaker was an intelligent and vivacious man of the cloth. His sermons not only brought comfort to the people, but also hope and strength when times were hard. His short, brown hair, dark eyes, and strong jaw made him an impressive figure. It was no secret why several single women of the town would often show up to services early, so they could get an upfront seat to see Tassemaker up close.

"Let us pray," he said beginning the morning sermon. "Lord, we have been given proof of your mercy yesterday with news of the ascension of William the Third and his lovely wife, Mary, to the throne of England." Several of the townspeople nodded their heads in prayer. "Religious freedom is a sacred right, and now may we enjoy it even more in our little town. But let us not forget that no earthly king will ever match your almighty power, Lord, for you are the bringer of life and light, and you are our guide in this uncertain world. In your name, we pray, Amen."

The people sat, and he continued.

"That was some celebration last night," he said, much to the laughter of the people. Tassemaker smiled. "Truly, the news brought yesterday was cause for celebration. I will be the first to admit this glorious revolution will surely lead to a greater deal of liberty from the tyranny of King James, though may we never speak that name again."

"Amen, Reverend," a man shouted out.

Tassemaker laughed. "Yes, amen to that." He waited for the church to quiet. "First though, I would like to remind you of two things. The first is that in your celebrations, you must always remember, it was the Lord's will that William ascend to the throne. So, before you throw your arms up in celebration, you should drop to your knees and give thanks where it is truly due."

Several of the congregation nodded their heads in agreement. Tassemaker paused for a bit. "And second," he went on, "let us not forget that our home country of the Netherlands—to which William was king and many have longed to return under its just and holy protection—has been at war with France for some time. This glorious revolution has united England and the Netherlands. Therefore, by sworn allegiance, we have also now joined into the fray."

Tassemaker leaned over the pulpit, staring down at his congregation. "War is never something we should look forward to with joy. It only brings horrors and misery unbeknownst to most of you. Those of us who are older may remember the war of King Philips over a decade ago in New England. Innocents, both Christian and heathen alike, were slain, many while they begged for mercy. Living under the protection of our friends of the Iroquois, we are fortunate to have thus far been spared such terrible events, but I stand before you today, not just as a minister but as your fellow citizen, to tell you that with this war, we may yet be subject to a crucible of such terrible power, that it will test our faith and will to its very limits." He raised his arms above his head. "Heed my warning my friends, we may have storm clouds on the horizon. Let us trust that the Lord will guide us all through the coming ordeal, and to his paradise on the other side."

Four days had passed since news of the Glorious Revolution had reached Schenectady. Anna and Angie were busy washing laundry in the backyard. They duly scrubbed the clothes on the washboard, dunking them in the warm, soapy water, made warmer by the morning sunlight beating down. After scrubbing the garment clean, they then rinsed them in clean, cool water, before twisting them tightly, draining the water back into the bucket for the next article of clothing. Finally, the two women strung the clothes out on a clothesline and let them air dry for the day.

It was a tedious and time-consuming task, made ever more difficult by the size of the family. As the men would typically leave early to tend to the fields or trade work, or hunt and trap, the daily chores were left almost predominantly to the ladies of the household. although, at times, Anna volunteered one of the boys for additional labor. "Put that one back in," Anna said, pointing to the shirt in her daughter's hand. "You call that clean?"

Moaning, Angie dropped it back in the soap bucket then placed it on the washboard and repeated the process. "These stains aren't coming out, Mama!"

"Serves you right for playing in the woods with your brothers all the time," her mother snapped. "You get that clean or I'll make you wish you had."

Angie doubled down on her efforts and scrubbed away in silent obedience. Anna finished ringing out a pair of trousers and hung them on the line. "You really need to start learning how to behave like a proper woman, you know. I won't always be there for you."

Angie looked up. "What do you mean, Mama?"

Her mother walked over and knelt beside her. "You'll be expected to marry in a few years, as will other girls your age. And when you do, you'll be expected to take care of your husband and future children just as I take care of all of you." She smiled and grabbed her daughter's hand, interrupting the laundry washing. "I like to think I did a good job raising you, Angie. But there will be things you will need to learn about being a grown up that cannot be taught so easily."

"Like what?" Angie asked curiously.

"Well," Anna said, "for starters, to find a suitable match for a husband, you need to be more – ladylike." Angie looked on in confusion. "What I mean is, you need to present yourself in a more formal manner around town. When a man sees you playing in the dirt with your brothers, he says to himself that you're not ready for marriage."

Angie almost laughed. "But Mama, I'm not ready to be married. Why do I have to be married so soon?"

"You cease that at once," her mother growled. "Now, there are plenty of fine, young men in this village and in the surrounding areas, especially Albany. Your father and I were talking and…"

"And what, Mama?"

"Well, your father and I are looking for matches for you."

"*What?*"

Anna gave her daughter a stern look. "Don't get an attitude with me, young lady."

"But – Mama…"

Anna cut her off. "I did not say you were getting married, my dear. I said we started looking.

There's still plenty of time but I would like, in the next few months, for you to start getting out more and being noticed, that is all. We can talk about formal introductions next spring, but for the moment, I only want you to start preparing mentally for the idea of marriage. Do you understand, Angie?"

Angie nodded sadly. "I understand," she whispered.

Anna rested her hand on her daughter's shoulder and leaned in. "We're doing this for you because we love you. I would rather we prepare early and find a man suitable to marry our daughter, than have you rushed into marrying someone who can't take care of you. We both love you more than the world and want you to be happy."

"I know, Mama."

"My baby girl, all grown up."

"Stop it, Mama," Angie laughed.

Anna stood up. "You're right, dear. Plenty of time for that later. Finish up with the laundry out here. I'm going to start baking the bread. When you're done, come inside and get some water."

"Okay, Mama," Angie said, going back to her washing. After a moment, she glanced back over her shoulder to make sure her mother had indeed gone inside. Seeing no one behind her, her false happiness disappeared and she dropped the bar soap into the water. Staring blankly at the ground, her blood raced throughout her body and the hair on her pale, thin arms stood up.

I'm not ready, she thought to herself. *Please God, I'm not ready yet."*

Chapter 4

Johannes' father returned that afternoon. Harmen Vedder strolled up the road, leading his horse by its reigns, being greeted by many of the men and women he passed. His clothing was made of brown leather and wool, and his cavalier boots were caked in mud. His graying hair and rough skin told a tale of a man forged on the hard frontier life. As former Schout and one of the original settlers of Schenectady, Harmen was among the most respected men of the village.

When he got home, Anna called out their children who rushed to see him. "Where have you been, Father?" Albert asked eagerly. "Is there anything wrong with the trapping grounds?"

"Or with Samuel?" Angie added.

"Samuel is fine," Harmen said wearily. Never a man to joke, Harmen rarely entertained even so much as a smile. "The roof on his barn gave out. I had to spend two days repairing it."

"You were gone for a lot longer than usual," Johannes commented.

"Do you think I don't know that, boy?" Harmen barked. Johannes instantly stepped back. Harmen took a breath and calmed himself down. "The waterways from last season showed no presence of beaver activity. I had to travel another day to the west before I found more suitable trapping grounds. They are moving further away from us."

"What does that mean?" his wife asked.

"It means we'll be gone a little more than last year, that's all." He turned to Johannes and Albert. "Make sure you are packed for tomorrow. We are leaving at dawn."

31

"Oh Harmen," Anna said, "you aren't going to stay a single day? There's so much that needs to be done here."

"The season is perfect for trapping," Harmen replied coldly. "We cannot wait. If we get a good catch, we will return and barter them for some healthy livestock and goods." He clenched his fist. "Those aristocrats in Albany still refuse to drop their regulations on the trapping. They're all thieves," he muttered.

"Can you at least help repair the pantry?" Anna asked wearily. "Your sons have been cutting wood all day for the new boards. They could use some help."

"They are both strong and healthy men," Harmen replied. "I need a bath and a meal."

With that, he led his pack-laden horse around to the small stable. Johannes glanced at his mother. She just stood in the front of the house shaking her head. She looked to him.

"Well, you heard your father. You and Albert get back to work on those boards."

Harmen woke up Johannes and Albert while it was still dark outside. They moved quietly through the house, trying not to wake their mother, Arent, Angie, and especially young Corset.

"Eat a hardy meal," Harmen advised them quietly.

The two brothers sat in silence, devouring bread and some salted meat. Though not normally eaten at breakfast, Harmen made them eat the meat.

"You will need all your strength for the trip," he said. "Hurry up, I want to be out of here before the others wake and follow us."

They exited the house just as the first glimpses

of light were touching the sky. The air was cool and breezy. They loaded up the horse, using it not for riding, but as a pack animal. They made their way to the south gate, still shut from the night before. A militiaman halted them at the gate.

"Good morning, Vedder," the man said. "Heading out a little early, aren't you?"

"Just getting a head start on the day," Harmen said. "Please open the gate."

The man nodded and opened the wooden gate, creaking as the hinge bent.

"Might want to get that fixed," Harmen noted, leading the horse and his boys through.

The road stretched out before them. The east would lead to Albany. He turned his horse right, and headed west, into the wilderness. Aside from a few scattered farms and cabins, Schenectady was the last outpost of the English colony.

Harmen led the boys through the thick woods, west of Schenectady. It was a land rarely disturbed, save for the occasional trappers, traders, or settlers who wished to brave the very limit of colonial settlement. On more than one occasion, Harmen had pointed to the west, stating that to venture further would be to go into the lands of the Iroquois.

Johannes understood the warnings well enough. The western-most of the Iroquois nations— the Mohawk—were close allies of the Dutch, but they were finicky about incursions onto their land. Battles had broken out in the past, as one side or the other pushed too far into the other's lands.

"Why do you lay your traps out so far from the village?" Johannes asked.

Harmen grunted at his son. "You should know by now," he grumbled. "I have taught you more than once." Johannes' head drooped slightly. "The other trappers swarm the local wetlands closer to the stockade. The beavers have all left that area or been killed already. That's why many have such ill fortune in their trappings."

"They're bad trappers then," Albert stated. "Not in their trade, but if they don't know where to look, then they clearly don't know their business."

"Precisely, lad," Harmen said. "Pay attention to your brother, Johannes. He's clearly got his head in the right place. That place would be on this good earth where it ought to be."

"Yes, Father," Johannes whispered. He shot a glance to his older brother. Albert smirked and turned to Harmen, following closely in his footsteps.

"The borderlands are still rich," Harmen said to both boys. "Many trappers fear the Mohawk. They've heard stories, about what happened to others in the past."

"What stories?" Johannes inquired.

"Men being scalped, tortured, even eaten by the Wilden." Harmen paused for a moment, wiping the sweat from his forehead. "Of course, they are true – well, most of them are."

He turned to Albert and Johannes. "But you never hear what happened beforehand. Many of our countrymen ventured uncalled for, deep into Iroquois land. They ate their food, stole their game, both fish and meat. They mocked the Wilden and even raided settlements. The Wilden have a simple philosophy and so long as we do them no wrong, we will not incur their wrath."

"Let them try," Albert said. "Do we not have firearms to shoot them all dead? Do we not have discipline and strength in numbers? I have never heard of a Christian force being defeated by natives yet."

34

Harmen approached Albert. "You are a skilled trader but dammit if you ain't one stupid boy when you open your mouth. The Wilden outnumber us four-to-one and that's just the Mohawk." He paused. "The Mohawk are just one of the Five Nations of the Iroquois. Their territory stretches hundreds of miles into the interior. They have conquered many powerful adversaries, and if we go to war with them, they could wipe us out. Never underestimate the Wilden. They are smart and ruthless."

Johannes chimed in, "Why don't they?"

"Why don't they what, boy?"

"Why don't they attack us?" Johannes saw that his father and brother weren't following his words. "If they have the numbers, why don't they take over the entire valley? Surely they would benefit from such a domination."

Harmen shook his head. "You boys are both brainless. I swear, how are you my kin? We have fought the Iroquois in the past. Both they and us have found it more profitable to trade and barter, than shoot and club each other. They are useful to have guarding our western gate, protection from their hated enemy – the French. They respect us, and we respect them. Let us leave it at that. Daylight is burning."

Harmen passed the first two traps. If he was disappointed by their emptiness, he did not show it. Climbing down a slope and into a thicket, he let out a roar. "Oh, he's a big one. Down here boys, quick."

Johannes and Albert rushed up. Inside the trap, the brown fur of the dead mammal filled the cage. Harmen dragged it out with an effort, heaving it into the muddy ground.

"That's the biggest one I think I've ever seen," Albert commented in awe.

"I think this is one of the biggest I've ever

caught." Harmen beamed. "He must be nearly three feet without the tail. Barely fit in the trap, easily sixty pounds."

Johannes smiled and took a knee. The fur was wet and stiff. The body was bulky, and the tail was flat and massive. "How much would this pelt get us?"

Harmen ran his hand across the back fur. "Pelt prices grow exponentially when it comes to size. This one will get us a few shillings for sure." He examined it further. "Good size testicles too. They'll fetch a good price as well."

Albert grabbed the beaver and heaved it over his shoulder. "How many more traps do you have out this way, father?"

"Just a few more," he said. "Three more and then we will head back home. Albert, give the beaver to Johannes. He needs to build his muscles."

"With pleasure."

Albert grinned, handing the beaver off to Johannes who grunted as he threw it over this shoulder.

"Get used to it, boy," Harmen said. "Once you start trapping on your own, you'll be carrying them regularly."

It took the rest of the day to check the other traps. That night they camped in a small clearing in the forest. Harmen made sure his boys did most the wood-gathering, igniting and maintaining the fire, and preparing the meat for dinner. In the dim firelight, Johannes munched on rabbit and jerked venison. In his own solitude, he thought about the girl he met the other night in Schenectady. *Maria Vandervort*, he remembered, seeing her glowing eyes and sly grin, and he found himself smiling in the dark.

The next morning, they resumed their hunt, checking further traps, before heading back to the last one, before the trail back home. Harmen clasped Albert on the shoulder when they saw that trap full, though the beaver was much smaller.

Harmen stopped the boys on the trail back. "Look at these felled trees."

"Beavers," Johannes commented at the sight. The trunks were pointed like a palisade log, as if someone hacked their way through.

"We know they were beavers," Albert said.

"Quiet you fool," Harmen hissed. "Look at the diameter of this trunk it ate through. I don't think this little beaver did it alone." He studied the ground. "No, I bet there's at least one more in these parts. Probably bigger than this runt as well."

Johannes was first alerted by the noise behind them. "Father, someone's coming!"

Harmen grabbed his rifle and gathered his boys behind him. They stepped off and crossed through the trees to a narrow, overgrown path. A large group of Indian men stopped when they saw the three white men. "Greetings, friends," Harmen said. "What brings you east?"

Several of the men looked at each other, not understanding his words. Then a voice called out from behind the group. "Greetings, friends. We are on our way to Albany."

"For what purpose?" Harmen asked wearily. He looked at the men. They had no pelts to sell. This was not a trading expedition.

The group of Indian men parted, and one man stepped out in front. Harmen studied the man. "Do I know you, friend? You look familiar."

"You know me, Harmen Vedder," the Mohawk replied. "I am Lawrence, of the Mohawk."

Harmen lowered his guard and approached. "I remember now. It's been a year."

"At least," Lawrence said. "You strike a hard bargain with us."

"My father strikes a hard bargain with everyone," Albert commented.

The Mohawk burst out laughing. "Your God be praised; these must be your kin."

"They are," Harmen said.

"This is my boy, Morachalwo," he said, wrapping his arm around a younger boy. "He is only fifteen but a remarkable hunter."

"I killed many deer and bear," Morachalwo proudly stated.

"And he knows English very well," Lawrence added.

"I wish my boy was as skilled," Harmen said. Johannes tried to pretend his father's public insult did not cut into him as deep as it did.

"I am with Tahajadoris, our chieftain. We are on our way to meet with brother Quider and the men of Albany," Lawrence said.

"You mentioned that, but you did not say to what purpose, my friend."

"A messenger arrived bearing news. We are told you have a new king and that the English hold you down no more."

"It's true we have a new king," Harmen said. "But the situation is more complicated than you may have been told."

"Then tell us," Lawrence prompted. "We have a long journey ahead."

"We are on our way back to Schenectady," Harmen said. "You may join my family for dinner if you would like. My home belongs to those who found Christ, whether Dutch, English, or Wilden."

Lawrence nodded. "Then we will follow you to your home. The others will find lodging in that place and carry on to Albany when the sun rises."

That evening, Lawrence dined with the Vedder family. The conversation was polite, though Lawrence tried a few times to tell a joke or funny story to the children. Johannes and Angie enjoyed the company of the Mohawk as he was friendly and spoke impeccable English.

Harmen kept his usual strict composure and focused on matters of trade and business. "The beavers are all but gone from the land between here and Albany," he stated. "Every year we have to venture to new lands to trap."

Lawrence swallowed a spoonful of porridge and licked his lips. "What will you do after the beavers have disappeared from these woods?"

"I don't know," Harmen said, shaking his head. "How is the trading to the west of Canajoharie?"

The Mohawk paused for a moment. "There are streams and creeks which branch off the Tenonanatche. The beavers still populate those waters in great numbers. To the north and west they grow fewer as we approach the great lake of the Erie. The French traders have been hunting those parts for many seasons." He paused, and Johannes saw the Mohawk was considering his next words with caution.

"Now, we will fight them," Lawrence said suddenly. "They have taken much from us, so we will take much from them."

Johannes eyed Lawrence. The Mohawk's smile had faded, and he was quite serious. Hoping to ease the mood, Johannes spoke up. "How big is the lake of the Erie?"

Lawrence leaned into the table. "It is so big you cannot see the other side. You cannot sail across it, for you would lose all sight of the shore, and become lost."

"No way," Johannes said. "What's it like?"

"Johannes," Harmen grunted. "That's enough."

"Quite alright," Lawrence replied. "The lands of the north are old. The forests are not as dense, for the dead trees have long fallen and the old trees grow tall and wide. You can walk for days and never pass another man. The land is rich for planting and hunting and fishing."

Johannes marveled at it. "I want to see it someday."

Lawrence smiled. "I am sure you will. But to visit only." He leaned back, looking more towards Harmen. "Not every Iroquois is pleased with the new settlements of the white man."

"How so?" Harmen asked. "We have kept the integrity of the borderlands for decades. How dare the Wilden accuse us of violating the treaties?"

Lawrence raised his hand. "Easy, my friend. We know the Dutch as our friends and brothers. But we do not trust the English. We have heard of many treaties they broke with other tribes to the east.

"Our people have suffered greatly from the French in recent years. Their raids have devastated our lands. They have murdered many of our kin and carried more off to slavery. The English claim to be our ally, yet they stood by and did not help us fight our common enemy. Can you trust an ally who does not pick up the hatchet and march with you?"

"I suppose not," Harmen replied. He downed his drink. "Unfortunately, that's not our call. We can only go to war if the king says so. But with our new king, it appears you may have gotten your wish."

Lawrence stabbed a piece of meat and looked at it with his knife. "This will be a red year indeed."

Chapter 5

Pieter Schuyler walked steadily up the street to the gates of Albany. Passing the townspeople, he could feel every set of eyes on him. They were uneasy. If Schuyler was nervous, he hid it well from the people. The stakes were too high to appear vulnerable.

Schuyler was a man who was born to lead. He was tall and had dark, curly hair that rested on his broad shoulders. He dressed in fine attire, and whenever he spoke, his voice would echo through the streets and chambers. His colleagues often said he was always the smartest man in any room. But on that day, he had a question he could not – but one that demanded, an immediate answer.

He arrived at the gate to find that, yet again, he was not the first to be aware of the coming Mohawk delegation. "Mr. Livingston," he said, extending his hand. The man shook it, but continued to stare attentively at the closed gate, as if it were about to burst. "I should have guessed you would be here," Schuyler said. "Robert, the whole city and indeed, the whole country, is looking to me to answer the question that I am asking you. Will the Iroquois continue to stand with the English colonists in New York? Will they stand with us?"

Robert Livingston faced Pieter Schuyler. It was indeed the question on every colonist's mind. It had been discussed since the moment news of the Glorious Revolution had arrived. Every member of the governing council knew such a momentous shift in power brought forth by the revolution could have unforeseen and potentially devastating consequences.

"We will know when they arrive," Livingston said.

"I was hoping you wouldn't say that," Schuyler muttered.

Livingston knew better than anyone what was at stake. As head of the Commission on Indian Affairs, he often transcribed the sachem oratories and meetings of the Iroquois Confederacy. He was well-versed in their politics and innermost goals. And most important of all, he knew the strength that the Five Nations possessed.

He spoke with Schuyler, not as a subordinate, but rather as an equal. As Schuyler's half-brother, Livingston was allowed some informalities. He was a head shorter than the mayor, but of similar age and appearance. Though originally from Scotland, he had moved to Albany at a young age, and quickly immersed himself in the aristocratic class of the *handlaers* – the Dutch merchants who ran the colony virtually unopposed.

"Wilden emissaries approaching!" came a shout from the soldier atop the wall.

The gates opened, and the procession of Mohawk Indians walked through. Some wore nothing more than a deerskin loin covering their genitalia, and a sash over their chest. Others wore shirts and leggings, likewise from deerskin, decorated with blue and white wampum beads, porcupine quills, and painted symbols of their nation. They all wore moccasins on their feet. Tahajadoris walked at the head, sporting a bright red and blue sash across his chest, and a feathered kastoweh hat atop his head. The others had feathers in their hair, and some wore earrings of bone. Each had a tomahawk or war club, with two warriors in the back, wielding muskets.

Though the emissaries were peaceful, and

their decorations suggested peace, every settler could see that the Mohawk were nonetheless a force to be reckoned with.

"Welcome, brothers, to our humble city." Pieter Schuyler shook hands and embraced Tahajadoris and the other Mohawk chieftains. "Our home is yours, as always. The Council will convene in three hours. We are still waiting on several of our officials who are making their way here with all possible haste."

Tahajadoris nodded. "We understand and apologize for our own late arrival. Our hosts in Schenectady fed and sheltered us, otherwise we would have arrived sooner."

"I would have expected nothing else of them," Schuyler laughed. "Please, in the meantime, make yourselves at home here. Grab some food or drink if you wish. We will have plenty of time for politics."

Tahajadoris thanked him and the Indians dispersed to the local shops or to find old friends in the city. Some headed for the lodges that had been set up to house the Mohawk during the fur trading season.

As Pieter Schuyler walked away from the gate, towards his city mansion, he was joined by Robert Livingston.

"I do not like this situation," Livingston stated plainly.

Schuyler knew the gravity of the topic but continued to smile at townspeople as they walked. "What don't you like? That they did not give us an immediate answer? It's simply too early to tell, Robert."

"But we need to know soon," Livingston pressed.

"Robert, you will have your answers in the council meeting," Schuyler said. "You said it yourself."

Livingston nodded and took a breath, maintaining a calm demeanor. "We need the Mohawk, and you know it."

"I know," Schuyler agreed. "But I have been given no indication they will choose another course. Have you?"

"Well, no but —"

"Then what are you worried about?" he asked. "Calm down, my friend. They know they need us if they want their domination in the fur trade to continue."

"I have my reasons to be concerned," Livingston said. "I've heard rumors that the French and several Wilden tribes are secretly negotiating a truce that will see the French paying better prices for the fur. If the furs go through Quebec instead of New York, it'll be a disaster." Livingston moved his arm in front of Schuyler, stopping him in the road. "We need to be cautious, here."

Schuyler gently lowered Livingston's arm. "I have known many of them for decades. I mean, personally known them. If any of the other Five Nations conspired with the French, the Mohawk would have surely told us." He stiffened up and his natural smile faded. "Besides — *you* of all people should know not to trust rumors, right?" He stared at Livingston a moment longer. "Get some rest. We have a busy afternoon ahead of us."

He turned and walked away.

Livingston stood in the center of the street, his face red with not only anger, but embarrassment as well. He looked at residents passing by, their every glance in his direction piercing his mind, as if they knew every incriminating detail of his life. He straightened his jacket and regained his composure.

I won't give them the satisfaction or an excuse to talk

about it anymore.

He headed off to organize his papers. It would be a long afternoon indeed.

City Hall bustled with activity as the Mohawk delegates arrived. The magistrates were all gathered in the room, but few had yet to take their seats. Men were standing in small clusters, talking quietly among themselves, engaging in more than the usual political banter. Occasionally, a man would leave one group only to join another, whispering something into someone's ear.

Another secret deal had been made.

Pieter Schuyler stood at the center of the largest cluster of magistrates. Right by his side was Robert Livingston. Another elderly gentleman, even taller than Schuyler, stood in the group as well. Gabriel Thomase was another juggernaut of the fur trade. Other men included the City Alderman, Livinius Van Schaick, and Sheriff Richard Pretty - an Englishman who had established himself well with the Dutch after the English takeover. All the power players were present in the circle.

Except one.

Standing beside his own table, another man had a smaller, albeit undoubtedly more loyal circle of town officials gathered around. At just twenty-six years old, Kiliaen Van Rensselaer was the rising star of the province. By age twenty-one, he had inherited the deed and title of the family manor. Five years later, he had carved out an empire in the Albany area. Unlike his counterpart, Pieter Schuyler, Van Rensselaer was not invested into the fur trade. He set his sights on, and made a fortune in, property, church, and government.

Van Rensselaer glanced over and Robert Livingston glared at him. Van Rensselaer pretended not to notice and went back to his localized discussion. Suddenly a voice spoke up. "Gentlemen, please have your seats."

The magistrates and City founders took their seats.

Livinius Van Schaick stood before the City Council as he made his announcement. "The delegation from our Native allied nation – the Mohawk and representing the Great Iroquois Confederacy."

He stepped to the side as Tahajadoris and the other chieftains walked to the center of the room.

Tahajadoris stood before the Council, his bare shoulders were broad, his arms strong. He had a strong jaw and deep, commanding voice. "We stand before our Dutch brethren, representing all clans of the Mohawk Nation. We have come in friendship and rejoice at the news of the transition of power that has taken place in your homelands.

"We regard now, as we have regarded always, that the Dutch are our friends in peace, and brothers-in-arms in war. We stand here to renew the sacred covenant we forged with the Dutch, before the invasion of English soldiers." Several of the Albany magistrates grinned slyly. The Mohawk have long been the protectors of the western and northern flanks of the province. "We also stand ready to join forces with you to dispel the English from your forts, towns, and lands."

There was a quiet murmur amongst the magistrates. Sheriff Richard Pretty leaned forward in his chair. "My friend, you misunderstand the situation. The Province is bound by oath to the King of England. Though he may also rule in the Netherlands, we still abide by English law here."

Tahajadoris paused for a moment. Finally, he spoke, choosing his words more carefully. "As we understood, a Dutch king now sits on the throne in England."

"That's correct," Van Rensselaer said. Livingston muttered some words of contempt to the man next to him, before taking a quick glance at Rensselaer.

Tahajadoris continued, "You are Dutch, though? Why do you suffer the English soldiers in the fort? Expel the English from your lands that rightfully belong to you." He took a step forward, his voice rising with passion. "Before the arrival of the English, we Mohawk held a close bond to the Dutch settlers who laid the foundations of this very house. They welcomed us in with open arms and we slept under the same roof. The English do not see us as allies and as such we sleep outside, not under their roof but under the roof of the Sky Woman.

"The Dutch respect us as equals, but in the English, that respect is lost. We seek to reestablish the strong bonds which we held with Brother Jacob in years long since passed. Only united, will we be strong enough to drive the French out of Canada and into the sea. We stand ready for your reply."

Pieter Schuyler leaned over and talked quietly to some of his closest companions. He stood up slowly, using his hands to help him up. "We have always respected the Mohawk and to this day regard them as our closest ally. We will welcome the renewal of the covenant and embrace you as friends in peace and brothers-in-arms in war. As you may not know, the Dutch have been engaged in ongoing warfare with France." He looked at Tahajadoris for a reaction but saw none. The Mohawk stood in silence, listening.

Schuyler licked his lips dry before continuing. "This Province—formerly New Netherland and now New York—is bound by oath to England. When King

William took the throne, England inherited from the Netherlands its triumphs, and its debts." Schuyler looked about the room to ensure everyone heard these next words. "We are now in a state of war with France, all her colonies, and all her territories."

On the inside, Tahajadoris processed the information, but on the outside, he remained emotionless as he spoke. "The French are sworn enemies of the Mohawk people and all Iroquois people. They have invaded our lands, burned our crops, killed our men, women, and children, and sent many of our chieftains into slavery. We have been at war since they first murdered our kin. We welcome the inhabitants of Albany and Schenectady, and together may we be blessed in our victory over the French in the north."

"And we will join you in this war," Pieter Schuyler replied. He could feel the eyes of everyone in the room bearing down on him. These were momentous times and he had to tread carefully. "I know you may not trust the English, but please trust in this. We must look to the future. We cannot underestimate the strength that English arms will bring to the coming war. If we stand united—the Mohawk, the Dutch, and the English—we can and *will* defeat the French."

There was a loud uproar. The men slapped the tables repeatedly with their hands or banged the floor with their staffs in approval at Schuyler's words.

"Hear, hear!" some of the men shouted.

After settling down, Schuyler directed the scribe to rewrite the covenant so that the magistrates and Mohawk could sign it.

While waiting for the copy to be finalized, the council room again broke apart into talk among the gathered parties. Tahajadoris and Pieter Schuyler talked privately. "I will take word to the other nations to bring word of the covenant renewal and stress the importance of them coming to renew it also."

"That would be a great help to us," Schuyler replied satisfactorily. "We will need the Iroquois united behind us on this one. How to do you think they'll receive you?"

Tahajadoris did not need to think about it. "Favorably," he stated. "The Seneca particularly have much bad blood with the French. The others will be convinced to join us as well."

"The Seneca," Schuyler said quietly. "Good men in that lot, I've met a few in my travels. And I know all the clans of the Mohawk stand behind you."

Tahajadoris tilted his head in thanks. "As your people stand behind you, my brother. You command a great deal of respect and love from your countrymen, like children to their father."

Schuyler chuckled. "Not all of them, I think. Albany has become a viper's pit in recent times." Tahajadoris looked on, confused at the reference. Schuyler shook his head. "There's so much politics and whispering. Everyone is out for themselves now. Nobody is looking to the future of the province. I try to keep the powerful families from going to war with each other.

"We have had multiple land disputes, accusations of infidelity, and anonymous death threats, to name but a few. With a new king, the balance of power will likely shift again, and everyone will want to be at the top."

"Everyone wants your position, you mean?"

"Well – some do," Schuyler admitted. "But I'm not going anywhere soon. Albany needs me, you see? All of New York needs me. I think, as long as I can still do some good as Mayor, I should stick to it."

Tahajadoris rested his hand on Schuyler's

shoulder. "The leader who sees himself as the servant will always be the truest and most just man for the job. Your countrymen should be grateful for your vision and strength."

Schuyler held out his hand and Tahajadoris shook it firmly. "And the same for you, my friend."

The covenant was signed by the early evening. There was a great round of applause and thanks spread around the room.

"And now we must return to our homes," Tahajadoris said.

"Nonsense," Schuyler blurted. "You will come drink with me and dine later with my family." He spoke loud enough for everyone to hear. "First ten men who follow us to the tavern will have their drinks paid from my pocket."

There was laughter and cheering as Schuyler and Tahajadoris led a column of men out of the closed-in, and equally hot, council room into the streets of Albany and down to their favorite pubs. The mugs were filled with ale and the men were soon drunk in celebration, for nobody could underestimate the victory which was won that day in the City Council chamber.

Chapter 6

Johannes Vedder entered one such tavern with his father. Harmen, upon hearing about the gathering council from Lawrence, had elected to follow closely behind the Mohawk emissaries. Albert had come down with a severe cough and could not travel. So, Harmen decided to introduce Johannes to the politics of the land and took him to Albany.

"I thought I'd find you here," Harmen said to a young man sitting in a small group. The man looked up and smiled. He turned to the others.

"We can finalize the details later." They understood the reference and cleared out, making room for Harmen and his son. "Please, have a seat. It's been a while."

"That it has," Harmen said. "I do not believe you have met all my sons. This is Johannes. Johannes, this is Kiliaen Van Rensselaer. He is one of the wealthiest men in the entire province."

"It's a pleasure to meet you, sir," Johannes said, shaking his hand.

Kiliaen looked at him. "You are definitely your father's son. How are you finding the family business?" Johannes opened his mouth, but Van Rensselaer stopped him. "Wait! Let's get another round of ale, first."

Harmen slapped Van Rensselaer on the shoulder. "That's a good idea if I ever heard one."

After the maid brought them three mugs, filled to the brim with the dark, warm liquid, Kiliaen turned back to Johannes. "So, how do you like beaver trapping? Does it suit you well?"

Johannes knew what he wanted to say. But

even if his father were not sitting beside him, he would not say he disliked trapping. Not only would that inevitably get back to his father and he would surely get a beating for it, but there was something else. It would be a source of shame, not following in his father's footsteps. So, Johannes said the only thing he could say.

"Very much so; I believe I've learnt a lot about the work and am ready to trap on my own if I need to."

Kiliaen Van Rensselaer turned to Harmen. "Good lad, you have there. You must be proud."

"He's not ready yet," Harmen said, much to the chagrin of Johannes. "But almost. By next year, he'll be trapping with the best of us. And it'll take more skill than ever before. The beaver populations are declining all around. Some trappers are pushing out west and it has created some tension with the Mohawk. I've been seeking out smaller streams nearby that haven't been tapped yet. And of course, there's the question of what do we do in the long run? Any decent economist would see clear as daylight that eventually we'll just run out."

Van Rensselaer leaned back. "Well if there's any man who can find and trap them, it's you."

Harmen took a long sip from his ale. "It'd be easier to turn a profit if the regulations of selling furs that the Albany Council created weren't in place."

"I told you, there's only so much I can do," Van Rensselaer replied humbly. "Schuyler, Thomase, and Livingston control the Chamber. Together they're too powerful. You don't know how hard it is, even for a man of my *influence*, to make any real change there."

"You *must* try," Harmen insisted. "The prices the traders in Schenectady are getting are not sufficient. Your money is tied to land and government, so you don't know how bad it is, but we need help, Kiliaen. Otherwise I may have to have my sons find other fields of work to get into. You force us to sell in Albany at a higher price, like a tariff for foreigners."

"Well, there's always more land," Van Rensselaer said. The answer only annoyed Harmen.

"I'm serious."

"So am I," Van Rensselaer replied. "The English are greedy. I have no doubt we will renegotiate land treaties with the Iroquois soon, as well as push further north."

Harmen set his cup down. "And if the Mohawk don't want to give up any more land?"

Kiliaen did not want to answer the question directly. "I will do my part to make sure all land claims are dealt with fairly and diplomatically. But we both know how the English lack diplomacy." He thought about it, his face grim as if the future was a foregone conclusion. "Whether it's next year or twenty years, I don't see our friendship with the Mohawk lasting – though I honestly hope it does," he added. "God knows we need them now more than ever." He finished off his mug and ordered another.

Johannes tried to follow the conversation as his father and Van Rensselaer talked about the specifics of the unfair trade practices regarding the fur trade, and the who's who of the wealthy and powerful. *Politics*, he thought to himself.

Some bread rolls in a basket were brought over by a young maid, who set them on the table and smiled at Johannes, before returning to the counter. He grabbed a roll, ate it in record time and washed it down with a second mug of beer. He realized he was hungrier than he thought.

As the two other men grew deeper into their talk, Johannes glanced up at the window. Whether by luck or fate, he saw a girl walk by the window outside. He knew her face instantly. He turned to his father.

"May I be excused, sir?"

Harmen leaned back and looked him over, as if wondering the reason for the sudden request. "Okay, but don't wander too far. We'll be heading back soon."

"Thank you, Father." He turned to Van Rensselaer. "It was an honor meeting you, sir."

He quickly made his way outside, looking down the street. "Maria," he called out, jogging the distance between them and ignoring the curious glances of the townspeople he passed.

To his surprise, she turned around eagerly.

"Hello, Johannes," she said politely.

Johannes could scarcely contain his happiness at seeing her there. "I was hoping I would see you before I head back to Schenectady. I wanted to say..." he started, before clearing his throat. "I wanted to say it was really nice meeting you the other week and I had a lot of fun."

Maria laughed lightly and her face flushed red. He felt his heart melt just looking at her. She looked like she wanted to speak but could only manage to giggle a little more. He took a step closer. "I'm sorry if that came off wrong or anything. I was just ..."

"No, that was very sweet," she said. "Thank you. I had fun too." Johannes tried everything to think of something clever or funny to say but his stomach turned to knots. She looked at him and couldn't help but feel the need to help him out. "Will you be coming back soon?"

"I hope so," Johannes said dreamily, "if only to see you again." *Uh oh!* He froze, thinking she be taken aback.

"Well you better come back for me," she snapped back. Then a slight grin touched her lips.

Johannes was surprised if not aroused by her reply. "I mean, I'm sure there will other reasons to visit Albany," he began, "but I'd really like see you again. Maybe we can walk down to the river and have lunch."

Maria looked disappointingly at him. "You know our fathers must approve first. My father is talking to another man who wants to court me."

Johannes instantly felt a tad of jealousy creep up inside him. He swallowed. "Oh, I see. So – do you like this man?"

Maria rolled her eyes. "I barely know him. And he's much older than me, nearly thirty-three. He's not handsome at all."

"Not like me?" Johannes joked. His jealousy turned to sympathy for the girl. "Nobody should have to marry someone they don't love. That's something myself and Angie always talk about. How do you spend your life with someone and lie about how you feel about them? The Lord, I would think, would want us to follow our heart."

Maria looked down at the dirt road. She ached to reach up and embrace him but could not. "I think you're right," she said, barely above a whisper. She looked back up and her eyes caught his. For a moment she seriously considered it, regardless of the consequences.

Johannes could see it in her eyes. He started to reach forward to grab her hand, but she suddenly jerked hers back and he swiftly retracted, embarrassed by the moment. "I'm sorry," he said quickly.

"No, it's not that," Maria said. "I like you, Johannes. I really like you. But my father would hurt me if he knew. Or he would hurt you."

"I can defend myself," Johannes declared, straightening up as if the challenge was already thrown at his feet.

"Don't be stupid," she said. "Ask your father

to ask my father for permission."

Johannes thought about what she said for a moment. "Are you saying you'd accept my hand in courtship?"

She did not hesitate. "Of course I would. You're a lot better than a man twice my age and not as ugly."

"Wait, what?"

"I'm kidding," she laughed. "But ask him." She looked around. "I must go. Come back soon."

Before Johannes realized it, she was gone, leaving him standing there, unable to stop smiling no matter how hard he tried.

"I will," he whispered to himself.

* * *

In the tavern, Harmen Vedder and Kiliaen Van Rensselaer were deep in conversation. "You are sure?" Harmen asked.

Van Rensselaer shook his head. "I can't prove it – but yes, I am sure."

"That *bastard!*" Harmen leaned forward. "And what does Schuyler think of this affair? It was his sister that also committed this heinous act?"

"I don't know," Van Rensselaer said plainly. "My uncle took Livingston into his care, giving him honest work when the other handlaers laughed at him. And how did he repay my uncle? By going around and sleeping with his wife. But make no mistake about it, when she married Livingston after my uncle Nicholas died, and they conspired to seize our entire patroonship, they made a terrible mistake and a powerful adversary." He paused, shaking his head. "It's no wonder they married so soon after his passing."

Harmen shook his head in disgust. "But you

won that battle."

Van Rensselaer took a long drink from his cup, finishing it off. "Damn right," he said, almost with a smirk. "My family kept the patroonship and Livingston only kept my uncle's land. Pieter knows his sister was in the wrong, but he certainly wouldn't have objected to bringing in all my land into his family fold via his sister. But I am trying to look beyond past transgressions. I see this city about to tear itself apart if Schuyler can't reign in his partners' monopoly on the fur trade. What I need to know is if I should make a move, will the Schenectady fur traders back me? Will you send men at arms to my side?"

"Will you need them?"

Van Rensselaer nodded. "Livingston is powerful and ruthless. With the Schuyler and Van Cortlandt families backing him, they are too strong for my family alone."

Harmen picked his words carefully. "The English way is force. The Dutch way is to negotiate. I believe – I must believe," he said tapping the table, "that the rule of law will prevail and keep our province united as it always has been. But if the aristocrats strike first at the merchants, many of the fur traders will back you. They're tired of the bad deals they get coming from Albany."

"But will *you*?" Van Rensselaer asked. "Will you back me?"

Harmen checked the rusty clock hanging above the bar. "I must start making my way back home. Anna will not be happy I am late."

"I understand," Kiliaen Van Rensselaer said reluctantly. "Please pass the news to the others of the village that I am trying."

"I will, my friend." Harmen stood up. Kiliaen braced his hands against the table, and stood up, swaying slightly.

"The celebration has gone to my head," he said with a warm smile. "Oh, one last thing. Don't travel to New York City anytime soon." Harmen looked at him questioningly. "We had a rider come up here this morning. He said there's a lot of tension building in the city between the English garrison and the local militia. We'll have to keep an eye on it for sure."

Harmen nodded and grabbed his hat. "Take care, my friend. I will see you again."

He left to go find his son, disappointed that he had not stuck around to listen to the real business the men of the province dealt with. Someday, he promised himself, he would make sure Johannes learned the art of politics. The thought drifted away as he walked out into the sunlight beaming onto his face from the setting sun. He found Johannes patiently waiting outside. "Come, boy," he said sternly. "Let's get back home."

Chapter 7

May 30, 1689 – New York City

It was a hot and humid day in the jewel of the New World. Formerly New Amsterdam—as it was named under Dutch rule—the city bustled with activity. The docks were crowded with merchant vessels of the Dutch West India Company and independent vendors; each trying to get ashore with their goods to sell to the wealthy aristocrats and businesses. Trade was booming and the driving economic force in the colonies, and New York City was the central hub with many goods passing through its harbor.

On one dock, a group of slaves from West Africa stood in chains while the slave drivers awaited a ship to take them to the North Carolina colony. Two more were being sold to a land owner who resided up the Hudson Valley. A family of French Huguenots departed a ship with their slim belongings. With no money to pay the captain for the voyage, they too would be bound into the slavery of indentured servitude. The smell of fresh fish and crab filled the air with fishermen selling their abundance of catches from the Atlantic. Dutch fur traders and even some Mohawk Indians were also present, negotiating the trading of their beaver furs for rum, wampum, coin, or for the Indians the most important articles of trade – shot, powder, and muskets.

Horse-drawn carriages carried the elite Dutch aristocrats through the city, driving past the poor, who were struggling in the alleys, begging for food. Many Dutch merchants had accepted the English takeover of New Amsterdam with open arms and profited immensely from trade deals struck with the English, most notably the monopoly on bolting meal – the process of sifting out bran and making flour. They held little concern for the farmers who were financially hurt from these trade agreements.

While the city stirred, one part remained like a statue. Situated on Manhattan Island, Fort James looked out upon the harbor, protecting the city from those who would do it harm. The fort, named after the King of England, was still the most dominating structure in the rapidly growing city. Its walls and cannons were manned by English soldiers. They were few in number and supplemented regularly by soldiers of the New York Militia.

Francis Nicholson, Lieutenant-Governor of New York, approached the fort with an advisor and two English soldiers. He was there to check on the powder supplies. Unbeknownst to the city people and even the militia, Nicholson had been keeping tight track of the supply of gunpowder in the fort. And what he knew caused such concern to him that he visited the fort on a weekly basis to ensure it remained as it was. On most days, the position was manned by a professional soldier who would recognize him and let him pass. As it was on this day, the gate was guarded by a soldier of the militia.

"State your name and purpose," the guard said, stepping in front of the Governor's entourage. The soldier, Nicholson noted, was a just a young lad, probably no more than seventeen years old. Still, he was annoyed by the question. After all he was now the most powerful man in the Dominion after the arrest of Edmund Andros in Boston back in April.

"Get out of my way, boy!" Nicholson demanded. But to his surprise, the young soldier stood his ground.

"I'm sorry, sir, but I cannot let you pass until

you state your name and pur…"

"Do you know who I am, dammit?" The boy took a slight step back but refused to acknowledge his apparent lack of name recognition. "I'm Governor Nicholson dammit. Get out of the way or I'll have you flogged."

"What's going on here?" Lieutenant Henry Cuyler of the militia walked briskly up to the gate from inside the fort.

"Lieutenant," the Governor said. "Get this *boy* out of my way or else."

Cuyler looked at the guard. "It's alright lad, stand aside." The boy snapped to attention and backed off to the side, freeing the path into Fort James. The lieutenant turned to the Governor. "My apologies, sir. This is the lad's first time on gate duty. He didn't recognize you. That's my fault."

"He doesn't recognize the Governor and his own Commander?" Nicholson raged. "You're with de Peyster's company, are you not?"

"I am, sir."

"What the hell is he doing with my company? Doesn't he know how to train his own men – *my* men?"

Lieutenant Cuyler had known the Governor to be a hardheaded and stern man, but he was always fortunate to avoid direct confrontations in the past.

"Sir," he breathed deeply, struggling to keep his composure as the Governor lost his. "Sir, he was doing his job. His job was to guard the fort and protect against entry of unknown persons. You were unknown to him. He stopped you per his orders. He was only doing his job."

Nicholson stepped closer, barely a foot from the lieutenant. By now, other members of the militia had congregated to see what the commotion was about. "Don't you dare lecture me on duties," Nicholson said.

"Why is militia even guarding the gate? Why isn't a soldier – a *real* soldier, on post here?"

Cuyler had heard enough. "You stupid, arrogant sonofabitch," he suddenly shouted. "Who do you think is in charge of this fort *and* the city *and* the whole province? We're the only ones protecting this province while people like you scheme away to instill your Catholic popery on us. These English soldiers are loyal to King James who, if the rumors are true, isn't even our king anymore."

Nicholson glanced down and Cuyler saw fear in the Governor's eyes. Cuyler followed the Governor's gaze down to his own belt. Without realizing, the lieutenant had reached for the hilt of his sword and was gripping it tightly, ready to draw. The English soldiers with Nicholson had stepped forward, ready to draw their own sabers. The men at the gate stood in silent tension for a moment before Nicholson broke it with his commanding voice.

"You will remove yourself from this post at once. You will remove yourself from this fort and by my honor if you so much as take one more step in here I will have your head."

Lieutenant Cuyler weighed his options for a moment before realizing he had none. His body straightened up and he let go of his sword. He turned and stormed off, knocking his shoulder into one of the English soldiers as he left. After Cuyler left, Nicholson also immediately dismissed the young sentinel, but finding no available soldiers of the English garrison, replaced the guard with another man of de Peyster's militia company.

The fuse was burning.

Two miles away, a middle-aged captain of the New York militia sat in a pub with a few of his fellow officers. His name was Jacob Leisler.

Well known to the people of the city, Leisler was popular with the poor and middle class for his stance against the aristocracy. Born of Huguenot parents in Germany, he had immigrated to the colonies in 1661 and since then, made a name for himself as a deacon of the Dutch Reformed Church, a wealthy merchant, and finally as a captain in the militia.

"How much longer must we wait?" he was asked by fellow captain, Charles Lodwick.

Leisler finished off his mug of ale and set the cup down. He looked at the others around the table. They included other officers of the militia and a prominent merchant. "Like I said before," he began. "I don't want to risk moving before we know for sure what the situation is in England. We move the moment we know for sure that William is on the throne."

"But how will we know that?" asked Gabrielle Minvielle, another militia captain. "I'm not for sure about this whole plan. It still seems a bit rash."

"I agree," Leisler replied. "We have the word of a single courier, several months old. We need confirmation." He looked at his lieutenant and good friend, Jacob Milborne. Milborne nodded silently. Leisler turned back to the others. "If you get me confirmation that William is on the throne, then by right, Andros and the whole lot of Catholic oligarchs must be taken from power."

Lodwick leaned in. "And will you lead the men? Demeyer is with us, but let's be fair, he doesn't have it in him." The captain was speaking of Major Nicholas Demeyer, second in command of the New York Militia.

"Doesn't have what in him?" Leisler responded. "He is a German-born immigrant much like myself. He didn't take long in reaching out to us as a friend and ally."

"He is nevertheless a timid man, always indecisive and passive as a commander of men."

Leisler remained stern but knew the question remained. "Yes, I will lead – if I must."

Lodwick sat back, resting in his chair. He smiled. "Good," he said plainly. "The men are ready. We have the numbers both inside the fort and in the city."

"What kind of numbers?"

"Given the changing of companies within the fort, on any given day we have a five-to-one advantage over the English."

"Milborne, what of the powder?" Leisler asked.

Milborne cleared his throat. "There's barely any left. Dongan sent too much away with the men we sent northeast to deal with the Abenaki tribes. There hasn't been a shipment of powder in months."

"Which adds truth to the story that the king has been dethroned," Lodwick added.

Leisler nodded and leaned back, his mind deep in thought. The other men watched him, waiting like a loyal dog waits on its owner.

"So," he began. "This city is almost defenseless against a French invasion and our only defense is a fort without the powder necessary to defend it? That's what you're telling me?"

"Well, we have Albany and the Mohawk to our north," Minvielle replied. "Surely they would stop any invasion down the river valley."

"That is true, you are correct," Leisler said. "But if the French seize Albany and the Mohawk switch their allegiance…" There was no need to finish the sentence. The militia leaders knew well the fighting skills of their Indian allies. "But…" Leisler continued, "it also means this city is defenseless from forces within." Milborne smiled. Leisler rested his hands on the table. "We're in the perfect position to take the fort from behind. All we need is the support of the populace and of the City Chamber."

"We have the people," Lodwick stated. "Not the City Chamber, but do we need it?"

"It would give us a level of legitimacy," Leisler replied. "Popular revolution would work but only if there was no king at all. We have a king; we just don't know who it is. Therefore, I believe we need the Chamber to legalize our holding of the fort and arrest of Nicholson."

Lodwick was disappointed. "We'll never get them to do that," he said. "Bayard has them in the palm of his hand. Half the Chamber is in his debt for loans."

Leisler knew Lodwick was right, but hesitated to say so. He took a look at another of his captains, Nicholas Stuyvesant.

Stuyvesant seemed not to notice, and his eyes never looked up from the table. Leisler stood up. "Let us meet again a week from now and we will discuss these matters further."

The officers' council dismissed and left the tavern, dispersing back to their daily routines. Milborne stepped beside Leisler and lit up a tobacco pipe.

"What should we do about Stuyvesant?" Milborne asked.

"I don't know what you mean."

"Oh yes you do." Milborne took a puff from his pipe. Overhead the sky grew gray as the storm clouds rolled in. Thunder rumbled in the distance. "He's Bayard's cousin. He's family of Peg-Leg Pete for Christ's sake."

"He said he was with us before," Leisler replied. "I have no reason to believe his position on the matter has changed. Why, do you?"

Milborne grumbled, "I don't trust him."

"You don't trust anyone."

Milborne could not help but laugh a little at his friend and commander's remark. "You're right, I don't. I don't plan on starting now, not at a time like this." He looked to the sky.

*   *   *

The smell of hot porridge filled the house, bringing a comforting feel to Johannes. Outside, ferocious storm winds pounded the windows and the roof. The dirt streets of the village had been turned into canals of mud.

Anna grabbed his bowl and poured the ladle of steaming porridge into it. "Eat up," she said, "then I want you to go check the animals. This storm is frightening."

"Yes, Mother," Johannes said.

She disappeared into the pantry, leaving him alone at the table. He listened to the torrential rains coming down in silence. After a few bites, he picked up a book he had read before, and opened to the first page.

"What are you reading?" his sister said, walking into the room.

"Nothing," he said, setting it down. She nodded and poured a small bowl of porridge and took a bite. Johannes sighed. "Do you ever feel that need to just – leave?"

Angie swallowed and looked up. "What do you mean, Johannes? Are you leaving us?"

"No, I just …" he trailed off. "I don't know. Sometimes, I just think there's so much more we're missing. I read these stories of these people who go off on great adventures, and I wish I could be in one of them. I've never been west of Samuel's house, east of the Hudson river, more than a league north of the Mohawk river, and south of Rensselaerswyck. I feel like I'm missing out on so much."

"But this is where we live. This is our home."

"I know," he replied. "But if I left to see the world, of course I would return eventually. I just want to see what else is out there."

His sister breathed easy. "Well promise me that wherever you go in your travels, you won't forget about us."

Johannes nodded. "*If* I ever leave, I won't ever forget you all. I promise."

Chapter 8

The rain continued well into the next day. That morning in New York City, Lieutenant Cuyler was summoned to the Council Chamber. Captain de Peyster—having been informed of the previous day's events—decided as Cuyler's commanding officer, he too should be present at the Council meeting.

The Council Chamber rested on the second floor of City Hall. Three long tables were constructed in an arc-like form.

Francis Nicholson himself sat in the center of the middle table. He was flanked by Colonel Nicholas Bayard – commander of the New York Militia, and Frederick Philipse. Beyond being Nicholson's eldest council and close friend, Philipse was also the wealthiest man in the Province; rich off the trade monopolies imposed by the Dominion on the people of New England. Other members of the Council included Joseph Dudley and Stephanus Van Cortlandt – a former mayor of the City, who happened to be married to one of Pieter Schuyler's sisters.

The Chamber room was almost unbearably hot. The windows were shut against the storm and the men in the room could hear the rain pound against the glass. De Peyster and Cuyler stood rigid before the Governor's Council. Both were finely dressed and de Peyster wore his saber at his side. Cuyler too had arrived with sword in sheath but at Nicholson's order, had been disarmed before entering the Council Chamber. It was an act of shaming and Cuyler boiled inside.

Colonel Bayard stood up and read aloud the charge. "Lieutenant Henry Cuyler, you stand here today on this thirty-first day of May in the year of our Lord sixteen-hundred and eighty-nine, charged with sedition and attempted mutiny."

The words pierced the lieutenant like a dagger. De Peyster too was shocked. "Sedition and mutiny? What is this nonsense?" he said stepping forward. He had expected some charge but nothing serious. "Cuyler attempted no such actions."

"Calm yourself, Captain," Bayard responded before resuming his seat. De Peyster stepped back, biting his tongue.

Nicholson straightened up in his seat. "How do you plead, Lieutenant?" Without any hesitation Cuyler claimed he was innocent. "Very well," Nicholson continued. "You are confined to Fort James until further notice. You will be notified when to return before us for a *fair* trial. You are relieved of your commission as an officer in the New York Militia, pending the outcome of this inquiry."

Colonel Bayard looked at the accused. "You are dismissed. Report to the fort at once."

Cuyler had scarcely believed his ears. *I have done nothing wrong*, he thought. Slowly, he turned to his officer. De Peyster nodded, grimacing. The Lieutenant snapped to, and exited the Chamber, taking one last glaring look at Nicholson before leaving.

Once his subordinate officer had left, De Peyster exploded in a rage before the Council. He was furious at Nicholson's decision and treatment of the young officer. Unlike Cuyler who was rasher by nature, de Peyster was a man hard to anger. But above all else, his deepest respect was for legitimate authority which he believed Nicholson did not possess. The two men yelled back and forth, with the Captain standing his ground against the belligerent Governor.

"The militia will never follow an appointee of

the deposed king, and mark my words, liberty will reign in New York as it now reigns in Boston."

"As it reigns in Boston?" bellowed Nicholson. He stood up and walked around the table, standing off a few paces from De Peyster. "Boston is in open rebellion to the crown. And mark my words Captain, New York will not fall to the chaos of revolution. I would sooner set fire to the town."

There was silence in the chamber. Even the council was too shocked at the Governor's words to speak. Eyeing the room, Nicholson sensed his words had hit a chord. He could feel that something, in that single moment, had changed everything. He stiffened up. The die had been cast.

De Peyster had heard enough. "Governor," he said. "You have made a terrible mistake, making yourself the usurper of a free people, and instituting your tyrannical law on them and there will be hell to pay." He stormed out, leaving the Council Chamber deathly silent, save for the sound of the falling rain and wind outside.

Stepping out into the rain, Captain de Peyster was met by Sergeant Jost Stoll of the Militia and several other men.

"What's happening?" de Peyster asked the sergeant.

"Sir, Lieutenant Cuyler filled us in on the goings on of the Council meeting."

"Where is he now?"

"Reported to the fort," Stoll said. "But not for confinement." De Peyster did not respond. "Sir," the sergeant said. "We're ready; the men are ready. Your orders, sir."

De Peyster exhaled, his heart beating faster. *The time has come*, he thought. He wasted no time. "Stoll, get word to Leisler and his company of men. The rest of you men come with me. Stoll, tell Leisler that I want his company and mine to rally at noon."

"And then, sir?"

"Then," de Peyster said. "Then we march on Fort James and we'll take the whole lot of them."

* * *

"Mother," Johannes said, walking up to her in the garden.

"Heavens, you startled me," she said, leaning back on her knees, wiping sweat from her forehead. "Do you see these little flowers, growing here?"

Johannes leaned in, not quite following his mother. "I do," he said.

"That means that it will grow tomatoes," she said. "It will be a few months, but I imagine four or five on this plant. It's a good year for planting."

Johannes wiped his hands nervously on his pants. "Mother, I have something to tell you."

Anna glanced up. "What is it?"

"Well – uh…"

His mother stood up. "Oh just tell me," she said.

"Okay," Johannes said, slightly smiling. "I met a girl a while back. I ran into her at the celebration of the Glorious Revolution and again in Albany. I like her, and she likes me too."

Anna wiped her hands with a rag and smiled. "You know, I think your father was as nervous as you are when he first met me."

Johannes grinned. "Really? I can't imagine father being like that."

"So, tell me about her," his mother insisted.

"There's not a lot to tell," Johannes said. "I mean, there is. Her name is Maria. She's unlike any girl

71

I've ever talked to. And she's so pretty." He sighed. "But there's a problem. She isn't Dutch. She's French."

His mother squinted her eyes. "And you met her here?"

"Her father changed names, long story," he said. "But, I don't know what to do. I want to ask father if he can ask her father for permission…"

"…for courtship?"

"Yes!"

Anna sighed. "You're afraid he won't approve? Well, he is definitely more traditional, but if you really like this girl, I will talk to him, and smooth it over."

Johannes' face lit up in excitement. "Really? Thank you, mother," he said and reached over, embracing her in a tight hug. "Thank you so much."

"I'm glad to see you met someone who makes you this happy. You've seemed rather down this past year. But do not play with this girl's heart. If later you don't feel the same as she does about you, before you commit to it."

"I don't think that will change," Johannes admitted. "I can't stop thinking about her."

Anna smiled. "Alright, well I will talk to your father. And in the meantime, I will give you enough chores to take your mind off this pretty girl you're obsessing over."

Chapter 9

Clive Anson—a ranking English soldier of the garrison—stood on the north wall of Fort James. He was the first to spot the mass of men moving down Broadway towards the fort.

They were not marching in formation, but they were clearly armed with muskets and pikes. At first, he merely watched in curiosity at the procession. It was not the first time an armed mob formed. In fact, it was getting to be almost common. It was when, through the foggy air, he saw several definitive men of the militia, however, he sounded the alarm.

"To arms, to arms," he shouted. Other soldiers and militiamen within the walls, rushed from the barracks or their daily activities to the walls of the fort. There was commotion as the fort's gunner ordered two of the cannons loaded and directed at the mob - who now numbered more than seventy men. Others were streaming in from all over the city in small clusters. At Sergeant Stoll's order, a dozen or so men formed a hasty firing line at the vanguard of the militia. The line soon stretched the breadth of the entire fort, the opposing sides staring each other down at the end of a hundred gun-barrels.

Anson leaned out from the parapets. "By order of the King, I order you to disperse."

Sergeant Stoll stepped out in front of his firing line. "Which king?"

The English soldier paused. It was well known that the throne had been contested and possibly even replaced. For a moment, a clever reply popped into his mind. "The King of England," he said. He glanced from side to side. The other soldiers and militiamen within the fort were staring at him, waiting for his call. He turned back to the men outside. "King James the Second," he shouted.

There was an uproar from the men outside – as well as the militia inside. Instantly, Anson knew he'd made a mistake. There were yells from all over.

"Hang the traitor!" someone cried. Shouts to storm the fort were heard from the walls.

Below, Sergeant Stoll tried to quiet the men so they could all hear him. He called up to Anson and the English garrison. "By proclamation of the free people of the New York Province, lay down your arms, open the gates, and surrender all arms and powder immediately."

Anson froze. "Shit," he whispered. "Shit."

He turned to the other English on the walls. They stood ready to fight and he knew he could count on each man to hold his own. *But what of the militia?* The men did not take kindly to Anson proclaiming James to still be king, even after the persistent rumors of his demise. Many had begun to relax their stance as if there was no imminent threat. Others glared at the English beside them, hatred in their eyes. Even their company commander, Captain Lodwick just sat there on a supply crate in the interior, reading a book and clearly not concerned with the situation outside.

"Lieutenant, you better come see this," said one of the militiamen inside the fort's barracks. Lieutenant Cuyler stepped out his room, dressed in full uniform and armed with a pistol and saber. "There's militia forming outside the fort."

"And…?"

The man appeared hesitant. "I think they mean to *attack* us, sir."

"Well then," Cuyler responded with a smile. "I

think we need to go stop them. Follow me." Cuyler left the barracks and headed for the wall, striding with his head held high. "You men with me," he called out to several others of the militia company. A squad of ten men soon formed behind the lieutenant. Pausing briefly, he turned to Lodwick. Lodwick gave him a silent nod. Cuyler saluted and carried on. He approached the fort's gate and was met by an English soldier.

"I beg your pardon but what do you think you're doing?" the soldier demanded to know.

Cuyler looked around. There were three other English soldiers by the gate. The rest were on the wall. "Open the gates," he said to the soldier.

"Are you bloody mad? There are a whole lot of men out there meaning to take this fort."

"Captain Lodwick would like me to negotiate with them." The soldier hesitated and Cuyler grew impatient. "Move or I will move you myself."

The soldier tried to locate Anson or another English officer, but they were too occupied on the wall. He gave up and stepped aside. Several militiamen unlocked the great gates of Fort James and the wood creaked as they opened.

Anson heard the doors opening. He ran down along the parapet closer to the gate. "What are you doing? Close them immediately!" When the militia failed to respond, he yelled out to the English soldiers by the gate. "Close them now." Four soldiers started to converge on the gate until Cuyler's squad blocked them, pushing them up against the walls, and forcibly holding them there.

Enraged, Anson climbed down from the parapets. Immediately, Captain Lodwick stood up and intercepted Anson. "He opened the gates on my order," he said.

"But why?" Anson admitted he failed to know the entire situation, but could not fathom why anyone in their right mind would surrender the fort to a mob.

"To negotiate," Lodwick stated.

Cuyler watched from the gates and as soon as he saw that Lodwick had Anson under control, he stepped out, standing in the open gates. Sergeant Stoll and several men approached the fort. The two men saluted and faced off for a moment. The English soldier at the gate listened in. Cuyler spoke first. "What took you so long?"

"Had to assemble the men," Stoll replied.

The English soldier could not believe his ears.

"And you've come to seize the fort?" Cuyler asked.

"Yes. Captain de Peyster is marching twenty men on City Hall now and sending for others to seal off the City to the north."

"Will Colonel Bayard join our ranks?"

Stoll shook his head. "The Colonel stands with Nicholson."

"Well let me see what I can do," Cuyler replied. He turned and walked back in the fort. He approached Lodwick and Anson. "He wants us to surrender the fort."

Anson was appalled that such a demand would be made. "How dare he ask us to turn over the fort," he said. "What kind of nonsense is this?"

Cuyler was unimpressed. He looked at Lodwick. The Captain gave a nod. Cuyler turned back to the gate.

Lodwick stepped out for all to hear him. "Stand down," he ordered. Anson turned in horror.

"What? Are you mad?" The militia within the walls—the few who were still pretending to be concerned with the militia outside—backed away from the walls. Others turned their guns on their English counterparts.

Cuyler arrived at the gate. Sergeant Stoll stood there casually. "What's the verdict?" he asked the lieutenant.

Cuyler did not say a word. Rather he stepped to the side, extending his arm inward to the fort. Stoll grinned and turned back, waving his arm. There were rebellious shouts and cheers. The men broke from the firing line and stampeded towards the gate. As Stoll passed Cuyler, Cuyler patted the sergeant on his back. "Welcome to Fort…" Cuyler paused, catching himself. "Welcome to Fort William," he said with a grin.

The militia stormed the fort without a single shot fired. The English garrison, heavily outnumbered and completely unprepared, did not have a chance and capitulated in an instant. They set down their arms and were led to the barracks under guard. Lodwick assembled a small council of officers and sent couriers to Leisler, de Peyster, and the other company commanders of the Militia.

The men, still rapturous with victory, were a rabble and the sergeants struggled to restore military discipline within the ranks. Eventually, the gates and walls were manned. Lodwick ordered one cannon on each of the four corner bastions to be manned as well. Slowly, the fort resumed its military appearance.

Outside the walls, word had spread. Throughout the city, dozens of inhabitants flocked to the fort in celebration of the demise of the Dominion of New England. What had sparked in the Massachusetts colony, had spread throughout the Dominion until only New York remained loyal to the old order. That too, had now fallen and the masses of Dutch citizens and immigrants from across Europe could not be happier.

Jacob Leisler had just finished getting dressed when he heard the knock. Milborne entered without waiting for his lieutenant to answer. "Jacob?"

"In here," came the reply. Milborne went to the bedroom, a note in hand.

"We have word from the fort. It's been taken. There are no casualties. Lodwick is in command and de Peyster marches on City Hall." Milborne looked up. "Where's your uniform?"

Although armed with his sword, Leisler had seemed forego the wearing of his uniform. Only the Militia officers wore uniforms as the enlisted could rarely afford such commodities. Leisler faced him. "We must be seen not as aristocrats and nobles, but as one with the common people. It's the only way we can gain their unwavering support."

"But we have their unwavering support," Milborne noted.

"Yes," Leisler replied. "But having a good image can't hurt either." He smirked. "If this is shown as our revolution, the people may sway allegiances, or they may not. But if they believe they are the ones having the revolution, they'll support anything we do."

Milborne could not help but admire the man's genius. "You're too smart for your own good." He threw the note to the floor. "Come. Let us take our place in history."

Leisler tugged on his jacket, and looked himself over one final time, ensuring he fit the profile he wished for. He exited his home to find a small contingent of his company outside. Others, civilians, were congregating around him as well. With a roaring, "Let's go!" he set out for the fort with his rapidly growing entourage.

"Lieutenant," he called out to Milborne over

the cheers and other noise. "Walk with me."

Milborne pushed his way through the crowd to Leisler's side. "Glorious day for a revolution, eh?"

Leisler looked up. The rains had stopped, and the clouds had begun to fragment, sending scattered rays of the setting sun everywhere, reflecting off the windows and pools of water in the streets. The fog too had departed, leaving a fresh, clean air. He had to agree with Milborne. "So," he said, "let's get back to the details."

"You mean the politics," Milborne replied.

"Well," Leisler admitted. "You're the expert."

"Demeyer hasn't been located yet," Milborne said. "Rumor has it that he took his nephews north, to stake out land or something. He probably won't be back in the city until nightfall at the earliest."

"That's good," Leisler replied. "He's a weak officer. Too timid and doesn't command the slightest bit of respect from the rank-and-file militia."

Milborne nodded. "And with De Peyster at City Hall, there's no chance of Bayard turning up. You are the senior captain. That puts you in charge of the militia and the fort."

"What of the other captains? Have we received word from them yet?"

"The courier who delivered the message said the rumor is that Captain Minvielle showed up at the fort outraged that we seized it and then left. No word on Captain Stuyvesant either." Leisler cursed under his breath. Milborne shrugged. "I told you before and I'll tell you again, no matter how much you don't want to hear it. I don't trust Stuyvesant. He's Bayard's cousin."

Leisler gritted his teeth. "What am I supposed to do with him? He's well-liked by his company and a good officer. I can't arrest him like the others."

"We can reassign him," Milborne suggested.

"Meaning what?"

"Send him to Albany, or somewhere well outside the city."

Leisler shook his head. "If I can't trust him here, I certainly can't trust him up there with that damn aristocrat Pieter Schuyler. No, I want him close where I can keep an eye on him. What about de Bruyn?"

"Oh, Captain de Bruyn is on board all the way. In fact," Milborne pointed, "there he is now."

Leisler looked down a side street where de Bruyn marched with the entirety of his militia company. Unlike the rabble of de Peyster and Leisler's companies, the men of de Bruyn's marched in order, their bearing and discipline a testament to their company commander.

"Now there's a solid officer," Leisler said. "Almost every other officer in the militia, I've doubted at least once. The two exceptions are yourself and de Bruyn." Leisler looked behind him. Already he was at the head of a parade of over two-hundred militia and civilians with still more joining. *The entire city must have turned out*, he thought. "Run over to de Bruyn. Have his company fall in behind the people and keep order back there. I don't want this revolution to become a riot."

"Right, sir." Milborne smiled. "Glorious day for a revolution," he said again. He saluted Leisler and headed off to de Bruyn's company.

Leisler continued down Broadway towards the fort. Outside the walls there was a great deal of celebration. The crowds who had been exuberant before, became even more so when they saw Jacob Leisler arrive. Flags of the Province, the Netherlands and the Dutch West India Company waved through the crowd. One man thought it wise to run around with a flag bearing the Cross of Saint George, the symbol of England, but was harassed and threatened until he left.

Kegs of ale were brought forth from taverns and mass drunkenness soon ensued. As the sun set, torches were lit, and muskets were fired into the air.

The atmosphere was jubilant. Leisler himself found it difficult to make his way through the mass of people. Finally walking through the gate, he felt the hair on his skin rise. It was awe-inspiring to see so many of the militia in celebration at the seizing of the fort and indeed the city at whole.

Once inside the fort, he was met by Lodwick, Cuyler, and a gathering of other officers. Milborne and de Bruyn joined them shortly thereafter. "Well gentlemen," Leisler said, flushed with relief. "We just carved our names into history, but the hard part is still to come. We must form a new government and restore order to the entire province." They all agreed. "Okay then," he continued. "The first order of business is the most important. It may take a while for the council to be replaced, so in the meantime we need to choose a leader. Now, Colonel Bayard is in the Nicholson camp and Demeyer is God knows where, doing God knows what."

The officers chuckled. It was becoming quite the common theme, Major Demeyer's noticeable absence when anything of importance was taking place. Leisler took a breath. "In light of that, I am asking for your informal support to affirm my role as temporary commander of the New York Militia and defender of the common people." One by one each of them agreed to the appointment. "We'll draw up a more formal charter in the days ahead, but we have three priorities first."

"What are those?" Cuyler asked.

"First – to keep the peace. There may be a backlash and we must be ready for it. Captain de Bruyn, you have the finest company. Your men will watch over the city tonight and my company will relieve yours tomorrow at noon." De Bruyn nodded silently. "Second – we need to do a full inventory of the gunpowder supply here. Nicholson has been keeping it under lock and key. Captain Lodwick, take a squad to City Hall, where de Peyster is holding the City Council. Get the keys to the fort's powder magazine."

"Very good, sir," Lodwick stated and started to march off.

"Hold it," Leisler said. Lodwick stopped. "I want you to hear this last part. Third – and most importantly, we need couriers to get to Boston and the other colonies, to verify the situation in England." He paused, the joy of the moment vanishing in a dark reality. "If we heard wrong and James is still the King of England, then we just declared war on the throne." He looked to each of his officers. "We do not have the manpower to oppose England for long and will need to act swiftly or every last man here will lose his head to the executioner's axe. This is the most important task. I want men sent out in every direction immediately. Are there any questions?"

"Just one, sir."

"Lieutenant Cuyler?"

"What of the English soldiers in the barracks? We have them confined there, under guard of course."

Leisler thought for a moment. In his mind, he knew that although they had sanctioned his leadership, he was not yet in a position of total dominance. They were still needed. "What do you all think we should do?"

De Bruyn spoke first. "Keep them there until we get word from England. If James is King, we can use them to barter a deal with the Crown."

"And if William is King?"

"Execute them." De Bruyn spoke firmly and

without hesitation. Leisler looked to the others.

"Well I don't share his view," Lodwick said. "Let them go, send them back to England or another colony for the time being. It'll buy us good favor with whoever may be king, and we'll be seen as merciful and just." Leisler glanced to his loyal lieutenant. Milborne tipped his head in Lodwick's direction.

"I agree," Leisler said. "We'll hold them for now, but ultimately I think it best to release them." De Bruyn grunted and Leisler set his hand on his shoulder. "We can't kill everyone, my friend. Even if they are English," he said. "Let's get to it, gentlemen. Lodwick, fetch the keys."

Chapter 10

Captain Stuyvesant was summoned to Jacob Leisler's office. Stuyvesant was expecting the entirety of the military council—now the governing council of New York province—to be present. In the three weeks since seizing Fort James, Stuyvesant could feel the council's distrust of him through his lack of meaningful assignments. Instead, he had been largely assigned to administrative or policing duties, not worthy of his rank. When he entered the room, to his surprise, only Leisler and Milborne were present.

"Please, take a seat, Captain," Leisler said, offering a chair.

"Thank you, sir."

"Do you know why you have been summoned?"

"I have several suspicions, sir."

Leisler smirked, impressed at his honesty.

"You are by blood and relation, connected to several of the aristocratic families that have dominated, and from time-to-time, oppressed the people of this fair province."

Stuyvesant gave not an inch. "I cannot speak for the actions of others, no matter their relation to me."

"Of course not," Leisler said, lighting a pipe. "No son shall be punished for the sins of the father." He took a seat on his desk, facing Stuyvesant. "But surely you have heard whispers."

"Whispers, sir?"

"Rumors, hearsay, whatever you would like to call it. That is why you are here."

Stuyvesant shifted in his seat, the first sign of

unease. "I'm afraid I don't understand, sir."

"I trust you, Nicholas. Truly I do. I believe you see what is wrong with this province and will do what you believe to be right to correct the injustices the people have suffered at the hands of the aristocracy."

Stuyvesant tilted his head in acknowledgment. "Good," Leisler replied. "Nicholson and the English garrison were just the beginning of our own glorious revolution."

Stuyvesant glanced at Milborne who stood with his arms crossed and grinned.

"Nicholas," Leisler continued. "I need you with me on this one. You could be our most valuable asset in what is to come."

Stuyvesant started to sweat. "And how can I accomplish that, sir?"

"Where would Bayard hide? Where would the other criminals hide? Will Pieter Schuyler yield to the revolutionary council we established, or must we force them to yield? How are the defenses at Albany organized?"

"You want me to spy?" Stuyvesant asked. "That's not honorable of a soldier's duty, sir."

"Listen to me, Nicholas," Leisler pushed, his voice rising. "Sooner or later, I'm going to march on Albany and finish what I started. I don't want a war, but we cannot have this colony being divided at a time like this. I have risked everything before and will do so now. If we seize enough of the aristocracy, the others will give up without a fight."

"You would go to war with your fellow countrymen?" Stuyvesant asked.

"Yes," Leisler replied without hesitation. He stood up and walked behind his desk. "But it does not have to come to that. You can find out where your cousin and his friends are hiding. After we deal with them, we'll send you to Albany where you will report back to me directly on their defenses. We'll seize their fort just like we took the fort here.

"Now, Captain," Leisler said, straightening up. "Can we count on you?"

Stuyvesant sat in his chair for a moment before rising and coming to attention. "You can count on me, sir. I'll bring the traitors to justice."

* * *

Johannes Vedder rose earlier than usual to begin the work his father had set out for him for the day. He dressed quickly and rushed downstairs to eat, filling his mouth with porridge and bread, barely stopping to breathe. Upon finishing, he raced to feed the animals in their pens, move more food stock into the house for his mother to cook, and finally set about checking the nearby traps that his father had recently set up, after discovering a hidden stream south of the village.

He returned to the village by mid-morning, a wide grin flashing across his face. Slung over his back were three beavers, each fatter and larger than the last. "The Lord has blessed us today," Harmen said as Johannes laid the beavers on the bench behind the house. "The other traps were empty?"

"Yes Father," Johannes replied. "I checked them all."

Harmen scrutinized each beaver, feeling its pelt and Johannes sighed as he knew Harmen was looking for any excuse to criticize the catch. "These will do," he said, finally giving into the good fortune. "Get your brother and get these pelts ready. Perhaps we can sell them this week if we work fast enough. I want all of this cleaned up before I get back."

"You're leaving?" Johannes asked.

"I must head up to Niskayuna for a few visits. I'll be back by this evening."

Johannes took a breath. "Father, once I finish, I was wondering if I could visit Samuel and take Miss Vandervort with me."

Harmen set his tools down on the bench but refused to face him directly. "So, you like this girl?"

"She's very nice," Johannes replied casually. "I could show her the trap I have set up and then Samuel's farm. The journey is quite safe."

"It's not your or her safety that concerns me," Harmen said, finally turning to his son. "I will not allow my son to be the cause of rumors of immoral behavior outside of marriage."

Johannes straightened up instantly. "Father, I assure you, I will show her the utmost respect and would never dishonor you or the family."

Harmen crossed his arms, thinking it over. He glanced at the beavers on the bench. "Finish these, and then you may go. But I say if you dare lay an inappropriate hand on that woman, I will beat your rear mercilessly."

"I would never do that," Johannes said, trying to avoid smiling. "Thank you, Father."

* * *

"You must leave now." Stuyvesant felt like his words were falling on deaf ears. "Cousin, listen to me, please. They're searching the city for you."

"Let them find me," Nicholas Bayard grumbled in misery, sniffling. "I will not run from them."

"You already have," Stuyvesant said. "You ran from the City Chamber when de Peyster's men came for you."

The two men stood in the claustrophobic wine cellar, where Bayard had been in hiding for several days. His clothes were foul and his face bore a heavy stubble.

"That was different," Bayard argued.

"Yes, it was. If they captured you then, it would have been in full view of the public. You would have been guaranteed a trial."

Bayard paused. "What are you saying?"

Stuyvesant grabbed his cousin by the shoulders. "If Leisler's men find you here, at night, no witnesses. Who's to say what conspired?"

Bayard was appalled. "He would not dare. I am …"

"Nobody," Stuyvesant said. "You're nobody to them, a scapegoat for the anger this city has for the aristocracy; an anger that Jacob Leisler has tapped into magnificently. They will kill you and throw your body in the Hudson River without a second thought."

"Jacob Leisler is a coward," Bayard roared.

"Then tell that to Pieter Schuyler and the Albany Council. They will listen to you." Stuyvesant paced over to the window and peaked out the curtain. He scanned the street for observers.

Bayard considered his options carefully. "How sure are you that they will kill me?"

Stuyvesant walked back.

"Positive," he said. "If you stay in New York City, you will be dead before the week's end. Leisler may not have appeared to want his position, but it was merely a show for the others. He is not a reasonable man. I saw it in his eyes. The man is mad, and he will drag New York into a civil war. But that may be preferable to allowing him to become the de facto king of the province."

Stuyvesant produced a letter from his jacket and handed it to Bayard. "Give this straight to Pieter Schuyler. It's from myself and Stephanus Van Cortlandt. Tell Schuyler that he must organize Albany to resist this usurper, or else we will lose everything."

Bayard grabbed the note and sighed. "How will I escape?"

"I have two trusted men who will ferry you past the wall. Once you are past the defenses, there will be a horse waiting for you."

Bayard nodded. "It will be hard leaving my son and wife here."

"They'll be safe," Stuyvesant promised. "You have my word. You have to go now."

"And what of you?" Bayard asked, suddenly worried about the captain.

"Leisler trusts me. I will stay here and report his movements to Schuyler. My loyalty does not belong to a usurper. It belongs to my family, and to King and Country."

Chapter 11

Kiliaen Van Rensselaer looked down at the letter he had been handed by the courier just moments before. He thanked the young boy, gave him a coin, and sent him off again. Unsealing the envelope that was personally addressed to him, he found himself staring at a mostly blank page except for a few short words in the center.

Van Rensselaer checked the time and seeing he did not have much, he headed for the address that was written in the letter. He arrived at the home of a fur trader, not well known in the city. The elderly man who answered the door, directed him to the storehouse around back. When he opened the door, he was met by the city's mayor, Pieter Schuyler. Schuyler was sitting on a chair against the back wall and acknowledged Van Rensselaer with a smile.

"Unusual location for a town council meeting," Van Rensselaer remarked.

"I'm glad you could make it, Kiliaen," Schuyler said. "This is not a council meeting though."

Van Rensselaer nodded. "Then may I inquire as to the reason for such - obscurity?"

"In a moment," Schuyler replied. "We're waiting on one more individual." They heard a knock on the front door and the fur trader go to answer it. "And he's here." Within a moment, the storehouse door opened once more.

Van Rensselaer immediately regretted coming. "What is *he* doing here?"

Robert Livingston walked in, the look on his face betraying his own loss of words at the company in the room. "Pieter, what's this about?"

Both men looked to Schuyler for answers. Slowly, he stood up and took a few paces forward. "I have summoned you two here today so that we can move forward. As you know, the rebellion in New York City several weeks ago, was led by a German merchant named Jacob Leisler. He led several militia forces in the capture of Fort James and took over City Hall, along with other government buildings." He produced a letter from his pocket. "This arrived today from Stephanus Van Cortlandt."

"The mayor?" Livingston inquired.

"Yes, and my sister's husband," Schuyler added. "The news is not good. Leisler said he was just going after government officials belonging to the Dominion of New England; those loyal to King James. This letter tells a different story. Van Cortlandt has confirmed that Leisler intends to overthrow the aristocracy of the entire colony.

"Since the time of Eelkens, Stuyvesant, and Van Curler, our people have dominated the trade of this colony. And under our rule, this colony has flourished for decades. Dutch landowners - people like you Kiliaen and myself, have taken the Hudson and Mohawk valleys from a few scattered settlements, and made them into viable communities and centers of trade and wealth."

"I'm sorry," Van Rensselaer said, "but what does this have to do with us meeting in a storeroom?"

Pieter Schuyler tried to find the right words to tie it all together. "There's a lot of people - the poor, traders and merchants, many in New York City, Schenectady, and elsewhere, who believe they've been given misfortune by us. They blame us for holding all the trading rights and land deeds. Leisler is convincing them that there's no difference between Nicholson's Dominion, and ourselves - the ones who built this colony in the first place."

Schuyler held up the letter. "Van Cortlandt says Leisler intends to spread his revolution to Albany and the rest of the colony. He intends to instill a new government, one that would see us lose everything we own."

"It's Oliver Cromwell all over again," Livingston commented.

"It would seem that way," Schuyler replied.

"He won't succeed," Livingston sneered. "We are far more powerful than whatever ragtag force he has in the city."

"I wouldn't bet on that," Van Rensselaer replied.

Livingston glared at him. "Was I talking to you?"

The rage Kiliaen Van Rensselaer had bottled up finally boiled over. "You tried to steal my land," he barked. Livingston opened his mouth to speak but caught himself. "You *did* steal my uncle's land," Kiliaen continued. "You conspired with my uncle's wife to marry her when he passed and rob my family of land that belonged to us for generations. I can only guess at what indiscretions took place in my uncle's home between the two of you when he was not home."

"How dare you accuse me, sir?" Livingston snapped, stepping closer to Van Rensselaer.

"I know the rustlers who tried stealing my horses last year were paid for from your pockets, Livingston."

Robert Livingston leaned in. "I answered every aggression from the Van Rensselaer family with equal force. You will soon learn that I do not forget and every man who made themselves my enemy has fallen."

"Here I am, sir," Kiliaen challenged. "You

tried your best. And I am still standing."

Livingston smirked. "We shall see."

Schuyler interceded. "Please, gentlemen. No more." Van Rensselaer and Livingston took a step back. Schuyler cleared his throat. "Kiliaen is right, Robert. Leisler has the support of many in the city, and when he took Fort James he acquired whatever stores of arms and powder were there. When word gets up here about his intentions, he'll garner even more support in Schenectady among those that feel they have been wronged by us."

"Then fix it," Van Rensselaer said. "You and the council have placed regulations on the bolting of flour and the trading of furs for them. They aren't wrong to be upset. Change the laws."

Livingston crossed his arms, staring in disbelief at what he had heard. "You are on our side, right?"

Van Rensselaer ignored the tone of the question. "Yes. I am a landowner as well, no thanks to you, and I do not want to see this colony stagnate because we believe we should control everything. Trade and business are more important than making war."

"I agree," Schuyler said. "But that change will not come easy in the city council. It won't pass a vote and we have more pressing matters." He started to pace around. "The government of this colony is gone. The magistrates are gone. We don't know if or when they will return. Word will only reach us from New York or Boston.

"Leisler intends to capitalize on that gap by seizing power. If we let that happen, we will lose everything. I intend to create an Albany convention - a government of the people, that will not recognize any authority not expressly coming from the king. I intend to resist the usurper Jacob Leisler's government with every means at my disposal." He paused, letting the words sink in.

"And I want you two with me."

"I am with you," Livingston declared.

Schuyler turned to Van Rensselaer. "Well?" Kiliaen did not speak. Schuyler took a deep breath. "We will need all the families of the Rensselaerswyck patroonship united behind us in order to resist the usurper. We will need every good man in the upper colony the Lord knows.

Van Rensselaer thought for a moment. Finally, he said, "I'm with you, too."

"Good," Schuyler said. "All matters of quarrel or feud between the two of you, of both business and family matters, must cease. Whatever happened in the past must be forgiven and forgotten. I know it will be hard, but it must be so. From this point on, we stand united against Jacob Leisler. We stand for Albany."

* * *

Emotion swelled up inside Johannes Vedder as he took in the scene before his eyes. In front of him, Maria Vandervort sat, leaning back on her elbows, her chest pushing upwards, and her head tilted towards the branches overhead. The sun shone on her face, glistening off her auburn hair and her snow-white teeth glowed when she laughed. Butterflies fluttered past, bees buzzed around the tall grass, and birds seemed to call out from every tree. The river shined with the sun's reflection, the heat touched his face with a gentle heat, and the wind was but a light breeze at the riverbank.

Truly, it was heaven.

He sat up next to her, noting every curve of her body with rising tension in his muscles. He could not focus on one single facet of her that made her beauty incomparable to any woman he had ever seen before. The way she smiled whenever he talked, even if he had nothing interesting to say, or how her eyes would light up with enthusiasm when she mentioned what she wanted to do with her future. The way she gently moved her hand through the long, green grass with such a gentle touch that the blades barely moved, as they would in the wind.

It was certainly better than the way their trip started. Albert, when hearing their destination decided he would tag along for the short journey. Although out loud Albert insisted he was making the journey to see their elder brother, Johannes knew his motive was to upset Johannes' plans of spending an afternoon with Maria. Albert would constantly turn the conversation to as many embarrassing memories of Johannes' past that he could conjure up; exaggerating many of them to the point where Johannes was showing outright anger towards his brother. Only when Johannes insisted on bringing up why Albert was following them, instead of courting a young woman himself, did he suddenly remember he had more work to do and turned back to Schenectady.

As soon as Albert was gone, the awkwardness disappeared in a flash. Maria, who had been quiet most of the trip now opened with jokes and stories, and even at times humor that to Johannes would have, in formal company, been inappropriate to say the least. "I did not take you to be such an adventurous lady," Johannes commented with a laugh.

"I'm adventurous, am I?" she asked hintingly, with a sly grin as they walked along. "What else am I?"

Johannes blushed. "You're charming," he said to her. "You're intelligent – very intelligent for a woman."

Her eyes narrowed. "Just what does *that*

mean?"

He swallowed hard. "Nothing, I swear. I mean men are better educated but you put many of them to shame. I have conversations with men about things that matter, and I feel like I'm talking to a horse. I might as well actually be talking to a horse," he laughed. "But you understand *and* are intrigued. I just never met a lady like you before."

She smiled and looked around. Johannes could see the smile crossing her face. "It's nice," she said. "It's nice to be considered something more than a future wife and mother and nothing more." She glanced up and caught his eyes. "Thank you."

Having shown her the trap he had constructed and watching her light up with joy, even though he sensed it was not something she was particularly interested in, he decided they should stop for lunch at the riverbank.

Having eaten a light meal, they rested in the grass and he was consumed by her every move and word. The temperature rose in the summer afternoon and Maria leaned up, removing her cloak to reveal a light blue stay, and under it a white shift which was low cut around the neck. Johannes could not help but glance down at her deep cleavage, not caring that she noticed.

His eyes traced a path from her breasts up her neck to her face where she bit her lower lip. He leaned in closer, throwing his arm over her waist so that they were more intertwined in the grass. His arm felt up and down her side, and his pulse quickened as he moved his hand lower, to her hips and leg. He could smell her scent as he leaned ever closer in.

For the briefest moment, he held himself still, looking her in the eyes. Then he went in and their lips touched. Sensation shot through him as they kissed.

Suddenly he backed off feeling her body shake. She burst out laughing, rolling around in the grass. "Oh, you killed the mood," he said throwing up his arms but still smiling.

"I'm sorry, I'm sorry" she said. "I couldn't help it."

He chuckled lightly then regained his composure at some almost unseen sign from her and once again they embraced and started kissing in the grass. Johannes dug his fingers in the earth, and then reached up, placing his hand on the side of her head, steadying it as they kissed.

As they broke apart once more, he whispered to her. "My father is going to kill me. He told me not to do anything immoral outside of marriage."

They glanced around and giggled. "I suppose you need to ask my father for my hand," she said, half serious.

Johannes leaned in. "I will. I will ask him tonight."

"Don't be a fool," she said leaning up. He sat up and grabbed her hand.

"That was the first time I ever kissed a girl. And you're the only one I want to spend my life with."

For the first time that day, Johannes saw a change in Maria's tone. She spoke with no sign of humor. "I want to spend my life with you too, Johannes Vedder. But if you ask now, my father will deny you and your father will wallop you for trying. It is better we wait until you have a place of your own."

"What if you're promised to another man before then?" Maria shrugged. Johannes' heart sank. "I don't think I could endure to watch you with another man without maintaining my composure and pride."

Maria leaned in and kissed him. "I promise you won't have to," she whispered. He smiled and went in to kiss her when he heard what sounded like a heavy rustle in the forest beyond the riverbank.

A sudden alertness overtook him. "Wait here," he ordered, adjusting and brushing off his shirt. Maria straightened herself up but ignored his request and followed him as he snaked precariously through the trees and brush, trying to make as little noise as possible. They made their way inland and the noise grew louder but never more than a rustle of trees and occasional breaking branch.

Johannes rounded a tree and nearly bumped into the massive chest of the warrior who stood before him. Johannes backed away in fear, gripping Maria as she took her place behind him. The warrior standing there was tall and muscular. His bare chest bore several smaller scars and one running diagonally across the whole of his body. His skull was shaved except for a black strip down the center. His face was painted red and black. On his waist, the warrior had a hatchet and large knife, as well as several smaller buckskin pouches. He carried a war club more than two feet long and was the most fearsome man Johannes had ever seen.

The warrior looked them over and then without a word, turned and walked away, towards the river. Johannes' eyes followed the man until Maria spoke. "Look at them all," she said. Johannes turned his head. Stretched out in the woods as far as he could see, lines of Mohawk warriors streamed through the woods, all headed to the river. They filled the forest and yet, as they marched, they made such little noise and not a man among them spoke aloud.

"Where are they headed?" Maria asked. Johannes gripped her hand tightly, hearing the fear in her voice. He wished he had some answer for her, but his own mind was blank. His father and the other village men had long said the Mohawk were their dearest allies. Surely it could not be a strike against Schenectady or any of the settlements. Maria hated his silence. "Are they going to attack us?"

"I don't think so," he said. "If they were, they would have killed us."

He watched as more and more warriors crossed their path, all around them, all heading in the same direction. Not a single one paused to talk to them. Only a few even glanced briefly in their direction before continuing. "There must be hundreds – thousands of them," he said to her. "They're headed north. I can only think of one place they are going."

Chapter 12

The fort at Albany filled as men streamed in from all over the territory. Pieter Schuyler had called for the meeting to be on the first of the month of August. He sent word for every landowner, merchant, and prominent citizen to assemble for the momentous gathering.

Though the air was thick and muggy, it was even worse inside the cramped fort's buildings. So, Schuyler directed the gathered men outside where they waited in the intense heat and sunlight.

To many men who were familiar with the politics of the area, they were shocked to see Kiliaen Van Rensselaer and Robert Livingston casually speaking to each other. When the mayor passed by them, they both acknowledged him without hesitation. The balance of power had shifted. To what end, few knew.

"What are we waiting for?" one man demanded to know.

"For him," Schuyler said. The man turned and saw a rider on a horse trot through the gates. "For those of you who aren't familiar with Captain John Alexander Glen, he is the commanding officer of the Schenectady Militia. I wanted him here for this announcement."

Schuyler greeted Glen warmly. "You must be exhausted from the ride."

"My horse could use some rest," Glen replied, patting the mane. "I am honored by your invite. Your letter was most persuasive."

Schuyler stepped up on a raised platform at the center of the fort. "Welcome gentlemen, to Fort

Albany. I have asked you to be here because we have an important decision that must be made."

"We have confirmed that William of Orange is now king in both the Netherlands and England." There was a roar of applause. He raised his arms to quiet them. "The last bastions of King James have been extinguished from our glorious empire. However, in New York City, a crisis remains. A usurper by the name of Jacob Leisler has taken control for himself and instituted a military regime in that place. Landowners are having their property seized and are even being arrested."

Schuyler held up a folded piece of paper. "I have a letter from him asking that we recognize his legitimate authority." The crowd watched him closely. He tossed it to the ground. The crowd stared in silence. Schuyler continued, "He is *not* appointed by the King or any magistrate and has no authority. I submit to you that we institute new government here and now. We shall govern *ourselves* until a duly appointed magistrate arrives.

"Jacob Leisler claims his loyalty lay with the crown, but his actions speak otherwise. He has overthrown and imprisoned the English soldiers who guarded the fort. He has forged new laws and imposes them with an iron will. That is not the will of the king.

"We must bond together, gentlemen, and form a convention. We will unite New York under our common leadership and protection. Our loyalty remains with King William and Queen Mary – the rightful rulers of our empire. We will resist by all means, any usurper who wishes self-government and separation from our righteous kingdom."

The men of the crowd applauded in acceptance. Schuyler raised his hand, quieting them. "We have drawn up a declaration and wish all those who are willing, to sign it. The Albany Convention will become the beacon under which the colony will unite, in these perilous times. And may God keep us safe in our venture."

The gathered men crammed around to read the document. The overwhelming majority lined up to sign it with enthusiasm. Livingston kept a close eye on those who refused to sign the accord.

One man who surprised him by not signing was Douw Aukes. He had been the first innkeeper of Schenectady, but since turned to other businesses in trade. He was wealthy and well-liked. He married Mary Viele, the daughter of Aernout Cornelisse Viele, who himself was the most experienced and respected Indian translator in the colonies.

Livingston approached him. "Your decision surprises me, sir."

Aukes turned to him.

"It is no surprise that a man will follow his conscience in times of great upheaval."

"Your conscience tells you that we should bow to a usurper?"

"I did not say that," Aukes growled. "Some of us from the village do not believe you Albany aristocrats have our best interest in mind. We have seen your policies that restrict our trading rights and force us to pay you to support your merchant empire. Perhaps you are right about Jacob Leisler. But I think I shall wait until I meet the man in person, before I make an opinion of him and his decisions."

Livingston could not formulate an intelligent reply, so he simply nodded his head and moved on. A few others from Schenectady had heard Aukes' statement and they too refused to sign. It was no secret that trading rights between Albany and Schenectady were deeply divisive, and it burned Schuyler to know

Leisler would soon find out about the rift – if he did not already know.

* * *

Johannes walked up to Reverend Peter Tassemaker who was on a stool, cleaning the windows of his church. "Good day, Reverend."

"Well good day, Johannes," Peter replied. "What can I help you with?"

"I was wondering if you had any new books I might read. I'm afraid I already read all mine."

Peter smiled and stepped down, wiping sweat from his forehead. "Now let me think. What are you looking for?"

"Nothing fiction," Johannes said. "Looking for something more educational."

"I see," Peter mused. "Well, I don't know offhand what I have, but I know that Barent Van Ditmars has quite the collection of scientific and otherwise educational books in his house. In fact, he and his wife turned one of their upstairs rooms into a study, with shelves full of books. You should go ask him. And give him my regards."

Johannes thanked the minister and strolled towards the Van Ditmars house.

It was larger than most houses in the village. The siding was painted dark green, with white shutters and a white door. To most villagers, Barent Van Ditmars was no prominent citizen. He was merely an elderly citizen who had made smart choices about his investments, becoming wealthy in the process.

Johannes knocked and waited for a full minute before the door opened. An elderly gentleman appeared in the doorway. His hair was a light gray and his skin was wrinkled. "Can I help you, son?"

Johannes cleared his throat and introduced himself. "Father Tassemaker said you might have a few books I'd find interesting."

"Come in, lad," Barent Van Ditmars said, opening the door wide.

Johannes stepped inside. The house was graceful in its modesty, but elegant nonetheless. European furniture, vases, and paintings decorated the dining room.

"Now tell me, what are you looking for?" asked Van Ditmars. Johannes opened his mouth, but the man held out a finger. "How much do you know about where you live?"

Johannes thought about the question. "I am not sure I understand."

"It's quite simple, lad," Van Ditmars said. "Do you know the rivers of our illustrious colony? Do you know about the soil, and the birds and beasts? Do you know about the Wilden and the beavers? Do you know about the trees and flowers?"

Johannes shrugged. "I know a bit about beaver trapping. My father ensured that. Beyond that, not much."

"Well, that is a problem, is it not?" Johannes guessed that the old man was not trying to be insulting, regardless of how his words came out. "Wait here," the man said. He disappeared in the back and reappeared moments later, holding a brown-covered book. "I suggest you start with this."

He handed the book to Johannes.

Johannes looked at the cover. It read 'A Description of New Netherland' written by Adriaen Van Der Donck. "But New Netherland fell," Johannes said.

"Oh, it did," Van Ditmars said, "but the land remains the same. The soil, the forests, the plants and vegetables, mammals and fish, all of it remains as it did in 1656 when Van Der Donck first published this work. It is a fitting place to start if you wish to understand your world better."

Johannes nodded. It was not what he was expecting. If nothing else though, hopefully it would be different from other novels he had read. He thanked Barent Van Ditmars and headed back home.

Chapter 13

August 4, 1689

"Hurry up with the crops," came the shout from the doorway. Aubert Boutin nodded without looking back at his mother. He knew her gaze would be the same as he dug up the last of the peas – yet another measly harvest yield. Although he was young, Aubert knew they should have planted more wheat. But his step-father had made it clear they would plant peas. The seeding happened too late. Aubert had argued for an earlier planting, but nobody had listened to him.

He shook his head, scooping up the last of the peas. It was no land for farming. It was rough and dry. The grass was more brown than green, devoid of nutrients by years of overplanting. Each year the crops failed to reach last year's yield. He looked around to his neighbors and saw their meager wheat crops.

At least there was maize. There was *always* maize. Maize for lunch. Maize for dinner. Every meal. He sighed thinking about it. The meals were never what he remembered as a child in Quebec.

He could never understand why, after his mother remarried, they decided to leave the city to settle in the barren westerly province. Since the move, they'd scratched their living out of the hard earth in the outlying settlements of Montreal – a small, desolate village called Lachine. French for *Chinese*, Lachine was so aptly named because the explorers who settled there had been seeking a route to Asia when they turned back and colonized instead.

"The storm is almost upon us," Aubert said, pointing to the menacing clouds bearing down on them. He stood up with the basket and felt the strong wind blow against him, causing him to take a step back to regain balance.

"Well get inside," his mother said harshly.

Aubert sighed again. He gripped the basket tightly, gazing into it. *How can we expect to survive off so little food?* he wondered. He cleared it from his mind. They would manage. They always had before. He took one last look at the dark, hanging clouds as they rolled in. Lightning flashed, and the low rumble of thunder sounded in the distance. The first drops splashed on Aubert's face as he took the last few steps and passed under the roof. Safely inside, he watched as the storm came.

That night, rain poured down upon the Saint Lawrence River Valley. The French inhabitants of Montreal and its surrounding settlements closed their doors and windows as the storm hit with a fury that frightened even the hardiest settlers.

Aubert ate his pea and maize porridge in silence, listening to the rain mercilessly pummeling the roof over his head.

In the midst of his dinner, he realized that he had not tied up the two sheep. Nevertheless, they would be there come the morning sun, he thought to himself. He finished his meal and was soon asleep, knowing tomorrow would bring another day of toil in his hard world.

While the inhabitants of Lachine slept, and the rain fell in the dark of night, the southern bank opposite Montreal Island began to stir. Dark shadows crept up to the water's edge – warriors of the Mohawk. They crouched in total silence, watching the glow of candles fade until the village on the far side of the river disappeared in the black night.

With the eastern sky changing shade from

black to gray, the warriors knew it was time. The storm had nearly passed and only a light drizzle remained. The morning fog crept along the banks of the Saint Lawrence as the warriors—whose discipline remained perfect throughout the ferocious night—rose as one. Teams of men rushed forward with canoes, dropping them in the water. Warriors jumped in without a single verbal order given. The Mohawks, experts at surprise and concealment, had planned the entirety of their raid before having ever laid eyes upon the homes of the settlement. The rain had dampened the black powder of the muskets. Many men opted instead for their traditional weapons of choice, the tomahawk and the war club.

As dawn approached, hundreds of warriors set off across the river in dozens of canoes. The current was calm, and the rain shielded the sound of the paddles. It also obscured the view of anyone who would gaze out into the river. Luck was with the Mohawk as Lachine had little in the way of defenses. The houses were scattered, and no walls protected the settlement. The local Canadians slept peacefully, believing themselves to be safe, while boats approached the southern shore of the island with little noise.

The warriors clenched their axes and clubs, some bows, and a few still holding their muskets in hopes the powder would be dry enough to spark.

While the riverbank swelled with warriors, several Mohawk rushed ahead to the line of trees on the outskirts of the settlement. Ever increasing numbers of warriors swiftly moved around the edges of Lachine, keeping to the woods to avoid detection by dogs or farmers who arose earlier than usual.

The Mohawks swarmed into the village at the break of dawn. No sun shone through the rainclouds however, and the light was still relatively dim. The warriors slipped in between the houses of the settlers as they slept in their beds.

Initially having planned on raiding the main town of Montreal, the Mohawks realized that they had brought an excessive number of warriors for the raid on the tiny village of Lachine. The elders in command directed several men to the doors of each home in the village. They followed orders and waited at the front doors, ready for the signal.

A chief made his way to the center of the village. Taller than all the rest, with broad shoulders and a bare chest, his body bore scars of countless battles past and his face was steady. His eyes raced back and forth like an Eagle stalking its prey and watching over the land.

Clutching his war club tightly, the chief let out an ear-splitting war cry. Then raised his club high in the air and cried out again.

The army of warriors let out a roar of similar cries. Then the chaos began.

The Mohawk smashed through the doors and all at once swarmed the homes of the French settlers, even before they were awake. Some of the inhabitants had barely opened their eyes before war clubs crashed into their skulls.

Others were luckier. A few Frenchmen managed to get out of their bed in time to be cut down by spears and tomahawks. The women were not spared either.

Aubert woke from bed when he heard the thunderous roar outside. He had barely climbed out from his bed when the door smashed open, the hinges coming undone, sending the door crashing to the floor.

Three terrifying, painted-men burst in. The first warrior jumped at his step-father, hacking him down before he had barely stood up.

Aubert grabbed the first object he could, wielding a hoe like a pike, trying to force back the shorter Indian who approached him. As the warrior tried to rush in, Aubert swung too wide, the blade missing the warrior, but the wooden handle struck the assailant in the head, knocking him down. The big Indian had not seemed to notice him. Instead, he yanked his mother from the bed and dragged her by her hair, over her husband's slain body and out the door. He threw her into the muddy ground and let out a ferocious yell.

A scream forced Aubert to turn back inside. He watched in horror as the third Indian—a man with a cruel face and scarred body—raised his club, bringing it hard down onto Aubert's younger half-brother, Pierre. The thud was sickening, and he could hear the skull cracking. The warrior struck again and again until the boy lay still, smothered in blood.

In rage, Aubert charged the man, swinging the gardening tool like a madman. The sheer speed and force of the attack, forced the warrior back, stumbling and crashing over a stool. Aubert screamed and cursed, stabbing at the man, watching as lines of red opened on the warrior.

He did not feel the first stab. Nor the second. Only when the third blow cut into a nerve in his back did he know he was being butchered from behind. The tall warrior who had killed his father was behind him, stabbing into him over and over. Aubert dropped the hoe, the loss of blood going to his head. He did not react as the blade moved in front of him and passed just underneath his eyes.

There was little pain, even as he knew in his mind that his throat had just been slit. His gaze swept across his father and brother's mangled bodies and turning, he stumbled outside and fell into the mud. The last thing he saw was the terrified look in his mother's eyes as she cried.

Like Aubert's mother, most of the inhabitants, unable to fight back at all, were dragged from their homes and thrown to the muddy ground outside. They huddled in fear as hundreds of Mohawk warriors swarmed around them, torches alit. Within a few minutes the first homes were set ablaze.

It was not an attempt to capture the settlement. It was a raid. With all raids, the aim was to cause death and destruction and nothing more.

Scattered resistance was met in only some parts of the village. In one home, a fur trader and his two sons barricaded themselves and killed two Mohawks before their home was set on fire. When they emerged from the burning wreck, they were shot and had their heads scalped. In another corner of the village, an elderly man shot a warrior as he broke down the door but he too in turn was hacked to death by several more Mohawk.

The initial attack was over in the space of minutes. Dozens of the inhabitants of Lachine lay dead inside their burning homes, or sprawled out in the mud, many with their scalps removed as trophies by frenzied warriors.

Others were rounded up and surrounded by fierce, heavily armed Indians. They watched in terror as most of the homes and buildings in the village were put to the torch. A few Mohawks carried out handfuls of plundered goods – the spoils of a perfectly executed raid.

Some inhabitants though, had managed to escape and fled northeast to Montreal.

The chief of the raid, stood in silence. His own brother had been one of the Iroquois tricked by an offer of peace from the governor general of New France. Witnessing the destruction his warriors exacted in revenge, filled him with satisfaction. He thought hard about how he could take his warriors all the way to Montreal and burn it all to ash.

His dreams were soon dashed, however.

His warriors had looted all the alcohol from the homes before burning them and set about getting drunk in victory. The chief could do little but order smaller raiding parties to set out from the scorched ruins of Lachine and ravage the surrounding land. He knew the French had seven hundred well trained soldiers inside the walls of Montreal, and if brought to bear against his drunken force, the French could very well pull off a stunning victory and his men would be annihilated.

At night, his warriors tortured several of their captives, mostly burning them to death in fires that were made visible to the sentries atop the walls of Montreal. Other parties roamed the surrounding area, burning out homes and killing the inhabitants. Every French man and woman not already dead or captive, took refuge behind the walls of Montreal. They watched from the ramparts every night as the fires spread to new areas – seeing the flames of their homes and farms light up the dark sky.

After three days of absolute devastation, the chief became convinced that the French were amassing their forces for battle. His warriors were drunk and preoccupied with their loot and prisoners. He called a quick council and after a brief meeting, decided to withdraw. The huge Mohawk force slipped away in the night, just stealthily as they had arrived, leaving the island of Montreal decimated. Almost everything south of the town itself had been burned, and most of the inhabitants had been taken prisoner and tortured to death or had been outright killed.

Louis-Hector de Callières visited the settlements after the scouts confirmed the Mohawk had withdrawn across the river. He rode with a small contingent of men, surveying the utter ruin of the farms and villages, especially Lachine. He climbed down from his mount at one burnt-out home. Outside what looked like the doorway, the body of a young man lay sprawled out. Flies buzzed around, and the stench was overpowering. Callières covered his face and continued the gruesome survey. With every new dead body discovered, he swore vengeance on the savages responsible for each atrocity committed.

Chapter 14

The summer of 1689 was long and hot. Intense heat lasted for days on end, baking the earth. Occasional rain cooled it back down, but much to the relief of the villagers, did little damage in flooding.

The crop yields were much as expected and the village flourished in the trading and bartering of grain, flour, meat, fish, berries, nuts, peas, corn, and too many to name.

Boats sailed east from Albany, so heavily laden with goods, they barely stayed afloat. Canoes sailed in from the west, where Mohawk trappers traded pelts for muskets, iron stove pots and other trinkets.

For Johannes, it was perfect.

He had made several more trips to Albany, in which he was learning more of the business end of trading. He also made it a point to see Maria Vandervort on every possible occasion. Much to his surprise, in mid-August, his father informed him that he had spoken with her father and they had agreed that he could accompany her in courtship.

Though the rules of courting a lady were strict and Johannes struggled to obey protocol, they took every opportunity to sneak away from the public and get closer to each other. Such was the case when Johannes found himself free the entire afternoon and took her west.

"Where are we going?" Maria asked eagerly. He could see her excitement but refused to cave.

"You'll see in a few minutes."

"That's what you've been saying for ages." She laughed.

"It's just around this patch of trees," he said.

He gripped her hand and nearly ran, eager to show her his discovery. "I found this a week ago."

They rounded the corner and Maria found herself staring at a mill. She looked confused. "Who owns it?"

"Nobody," Johannes smiled. "I checked. It belonged to an old couple who died without children. It just sits here abandoned by the world. I actually fixed it up a little the last few days."

"No you did not," Maria shouted.

"I did," Johannes replied. "Come, I'll show you." Johannes led Maria inside. The mill was two stories tall, and littered with hay, old tools and barrels.

"You cleaned this up?"

Johannes looked around. "Trust me, it looked worse." He grinned. "Follow me."

He turned and climbed the ladder up to the top floor. Expecting her to hesitate, he was surprised to see her eagerly right behind him, up the ladder. Up top, Johannes pointed out the window.

"This is a beautiful view," Maria said, staring out the small window.

The meadow before them bristled with flowers and buzzed with bees. The sounds of insects and bugs echoed everywhere. A fish jumped out of the water in the distance.

"It is," Johannes said. "I wanted to show you this since I first saw it."

Maria turned back and embraced him in a passionate kiss. They fell onto the hay pile that was laid loosely on the floor and one by one, articles of clothing came off. Johannes watched as Maria loosened her undergarments and he took a breath as she revealed her breasts to him. She giggled as he held them, and he wasted no time removing the rest.

She let out a light scream as he entered her,

and in the hot summer afternoon with the heat already cooking them, they made love in the haystack of the old mill.

When they were finished, they lay in the hay, covered in sweat, kissing each other gently.

"We committed a terrible sin," Johannes said aloud.

"It wasn't too terrible," Maria replied with a grin.

Johannes felt his heart soar. He looked at her in the flesh and knew he had fallen completely and truthfully in love with this woman. "I guess it's not so bad," he said with a smile.

Maria raised her hand and gently ran it down Johannes' body. "Nobody saw us but God. And if he disapproved, I believe he would have stopped us. We were meant to be together," she said, lowering her hand until Johannes gasped at where she put it.

"It's far too warm in the day to go again, my love."

She glanced down and back up with a grin. "Are you sure?"

He was taken aback and swiftly turned her over and they began again in the summer heat.

Washing up in the meadow, Johannes and Maria were soon back on the road to Albany, talking and laughing modestly as if nothing more had transpired. "When will I see you next?"

Johannes shrugged. "When I come to Albany next. I hope soon."

"Me too," Maria said. "Though I think we should stay somewhere public, so as to not get carried away."

Johannes could not take his mind off the mill and smiled. "I agree, let's keep it respectful. Still, I wonder how soon I can ask your father for your hand in marriage."

Maria stopped in her footsteps. "Do you truly mean that?"

Johannes turned to her and said, "Of course I mean it." He gripped her by the hand. "I would rather lose an eye than spend my life without you."

Maria embraced him, not caring who saw them. Fortunately, there were few travelers on the road. "I love you," she said.

"I love you too," Johannes replied.

*　*　*

When Johannes returned home, a tall man was outside his house, speaking with Harmen. "Boy, come here. I want you to meet someone." The man was a head taller than Harmen but not as muscular. "This is Symon Schermerhorn."

"How are you, lad?" Symon asked, extending his hand.

Johannes shook it firmly. "I am fine, sir."

"Symon is moving to Schenectady," Harmen explained.

Symon nodded. "My brother, Ryer, has built a new homestead outside the palisade. I will be buying his home within the village. He is expanding his holdings with the fortune he is amassing in timber."

"Timber?" Johannes inquired.

"For shipbuilding," Symon replied. "Ryer has been sending timber down the Hudson to New York City for construction. Make no mistake gentlemen," he grinned, "the fur trade will pass into twilight sooner or later. The real money is to be made in timber. Just look at the forests to the north and west, stretching from horizon to horizon. This land is rich with resources, and for those that can harness it, there are great riches to be gained."

Johannes eyed his father. Harmen clearly was not amused by Symon saying the fur trade would diminish, but Johannes guessed his father knew Symon was correct. Each year, finding the beavers was more difficult than the year before.

"Did you sign the Albany Convention?" Harmen asked, changing the subject.

"No," Symon replied, "but not out of love for Leisler. He has a point for sure when it comes to free trade, but I believe any division of the colony is bad for business. We need unified action and security at a time like this." Symon paused. "My brother on the other hand, he is adamant about opposing the convention. Ryer is passionate about Leisler's policies making their way up to the Mohawk river valley. He believes Albany has too much control, and I can't argue with him. So long as it does not resort to violence."

"And if it comes to that?" Harmen asked.

Symon shifted uneasily. "If it comes to that, I will follow the Lord and my conscience. That's all any man can do."

Harmen rested his hand on Johannes' shoulder. "He is one of the most hardworking men of the colony. You pay attention to Mr. Schermerhorn. I have a feeling he will make history someday."

Chapter 15

The third day of September brought Tahajadoris and several Mohawk back to Albany. Pieter Schuyler was conversing with Harmen Vedder and other traders and aristocrats when the Mohawk arrived.

"Welcome, brothers," Schuyler said with open arms. They embraced. "What brings you back to Albany?"

Tahajadoris wasted no time explaining his purpose. "As you know, we have won a great victory over our enemy at Montreal. They will clean their wounds for many days to come. We have taken this opportunity to prepare a move of our castle at Tionnontogen. We must prepare for the next year's harvest and our victory gives us time to do so."

"Move a castle?" asked one fur trader. "How do you move stone?"

"Their castles are not stone," Vedder explained, "they're wooden. They're palisaded much like our own villages."

Schuyler turned to the Mohawk. "You picked quite a year to move."

"We decided we must move," Tahajadoris said. "Each year the earth yields less crops than the previous and the soil cannot maintain our presence any longer."

"I see," Schuyler said. "So you came here to tell us you're moving? How far?"

Tahajadoris thought for a moment. "Not far, less than half the distance from Schenectady to Albany. The soil there is rich, and ripe for the harvest next year. With many warriors still in the north fighting our enemies, we ask, brother, if you may spare some strong men to assist with our move?"

"Of course," Schuyler said without hesitation. "I can give you a dozen men and a few oxen teams. I'll appoint Robert Sanders as head of the team."

Tahajadoris nodded in approval. He knew the old statesman and interpreter from years of negotiations and alliance-forging.

"He is an honest man and will do well."

"Good," Schuyler replied clasping his hands. "We'll have them leave tomorrow. They'll reach the castle within four days." Tahajadoris thanked him and left. Schuyler turned to Vedder. "Harmen, I know it may be asking a lot but if you don't mind -"

"I can go," Vedder answered firmly.

"Thank you," Schuyler replied. "I want a good man at the front, someone who knows the land and has dealt with the Mohawk regularly. Robert Sanders is capable as well, but I have doubts about his handling of a working party."

Vedder stood up. "If you get me a dozen good men, I will keep them in line and get the job done. I'll take my son Johannes along as well. The Good Lord knows he needs some hard labor in his life."

Schuyler chuckled. "Troublesome?"

"You could say that," Vedder said. "His imagination gets the best of him."

"Well if he's your son, he'll be raised right. That's a fact." Schuyler stood up. "I'll have the volunteers start off to Schenectady tomorrow morning. And obviously, any men you find willing to go from the village is okay as well."

"That will work for me." Vedder shook Schuyler's hand. "Just please, nobody who is lazy or a liar. I will work them to death if they are."

* * *

The working party set out in the hot afternoon. Fortunately for the men, clouds shielded the worst of the heat. The dirt road continued for another mile west of the village before it faded into a series of beaten paths taken by the fur traders and settlers who dared the very frontier of English settlement. The oxen and carts rumbled slowly over the dirt paths that were fraught with rocks.

"Can we stop already?" asked a man from Albany. "We've been walking all morning. My legs are killing me." Some grumbling of agreement rose from two others. Harmen Vedder ignored the men and pushed the working party forward. "We're all a bit tired," the man called out.

Vedder cursed the man's weakness under his breath. "We will stop when I say we stop. Save your breath for the march."

Johannes was both impressed and intimidated by his father's firm leadership. He had known his father to be a stern and, at times, harsh man but had rarely seen him display it among strangers. Even the interpreter, Robert Sanders, whom Schuyler had selected to lead, soon found himself following Vedder's orders.

Johannes had heard Sanders' name mentioned before when Indian matters arose, but this was the first time he had ever met the man. Although only a few years Harmen's senior, Sanders looked a lifetime older. His short hair was gray, and wrinkles crossed his face. But despite his somewhat fragile appearance, the man proved to be in far superior physical condition than many of the younger men making the trip. He bore the weight of his pack without slouching or dropping pace.

Walking alongside Robert Sanders was a boy

who looked to be Johannes' age. Johannes had seen him before but couldn't recall his name.

"I'm Arnout Viele," the boy said as he and Johannes got to talking. "Did you volunteer for this working party?"

"No, that's my father," Johannes said pointing to Harmen. "He insisted I go to learn more about the Wilden and get some hard work. How about yourself?"

"I'm an interpreter," Viele replied. "Well interpreter in-training you could say. My father got me an apprenticeship with Mr. Sanders. I'm learning the art of diplomacy and statesmanship."

"That's neat," said Johannes, genuinely impressed. "Do you know Mohawk?"

"A little," Viele said. "I know French, English, and Dutch well enough. Mohawk is difficult but I'm getting there. I just wish they had books to read in their own tongue. But for all the hassle, I like translating."

"I need to find a trade skill I can enjoy," Johannes replied. "My father has been teaching me the fur trading business for years and I have yet to find it to my liking. Not to say I'm not good at it, but it certainly doesn't offer much inspiration."

Viele stepped over a log in the path. "I know what you mean," he said, adjusting his pack's straps. "But sometimes we just have to follow the path that the Lord set for us."

"Even if that path has rocks and logs in it," Johannes commented.

Viele laughed. "Sure, why not? Maybe it's a test. Not every road traveled can be laid out. However, if we could stop soon for a break, I wouldn't mind that either. Albany is a long way away now."

"My brother's cabin is up ahead. My father said we will stop there for the evening."

* * *

Samuel Vedder wiped the sweat from his forehead, brushing his auburn hair away, and set another block of wood on the chopping block. He pushed up his sleeves again and raised his axe and brought it down, splitting the wood in two. Immediately, he grabbed another piece and sliced that cleanly apart.

The voices and sounds of moving carts coming from the forest alerted Samuel. He grabbed his musket which he always kept close by, and sidestepped to partially conceal himself behind a tree. The working party emerged from the forested road into the clearing by his cabin.

When Samuel saw his father and brother, he relaxed and came out, waving his hand. "Father. Johannes."

Johannes was elated to see his eldest brother and headed over to him. Johannes went to hug his brother, but Samuel held out his hand instead. Johannes nodded and shook his hand. Harmen came over and greeted his son.

"How are you, Sam?" Johannes asked.

"I've been great," Samuel replied. "Just restocking the firewood. The work never ends. Got a turkey this morning so I had to clean it up."

"You need a wife," Harmen said half-serious. "And kids of your own, to help you around the house."

"They are hard to come by on the frontier," Samuel said, glancing at Johannes with a smile. Johannes laughed. "But I would like to soon. Maybe some pretty girl will come by my house someday."

"It would help," Harmen reiterated. "You shouldn't be all alone out here, this close to Wilden territory. Any traders come by recently?"

"All the time," Samuel replied. "Last one was a few days ago, three of them. Another two the day before that. I think one of them was John Schuyler, the mayor's brother."

"Interesting," Harmen murmured. "They strangle our own fur trade, then bypass us to go straight to the Wilden."

Samuel wiped his face with a rag. "That begs the question, what's all this?" he said, pointing to the men of the working party, who were relaxing in the grass.

"We're headed for the Mohawk," Johannes said.

Samuel's eyes narrowed. "Why?"

"Schuyler's request," Harmen replied. "Request for volunteers to help them move their castle."

"Christ," Samuel said, looking shocked. "Where are they moving to? Any further east and our lands will be damn near touching. We won't be able to go any further west."

"I believe north, actually," Harmen said. "And perhaps more to the west. They are taking great caution not to upset the borderlands. If it's alright with you, I would like to stay here tonight. Then it will only be two more days until we reach their castle."

"Yeah, you can stay. They can set up camp right where they are," Samuel said. "Besides, I missed my little brother. Johannes, what's new?"

Johannes shrugged. "Just the usual work, and learning." As their father walked off to tell the men to set camp, Johannes grinned. "I met a girl."

"Don't believe it for a second," Samuel laughed. "No way you met someone before me or Albert. What's her name?"

"It's true," Johannes said. "Her name is Maria Vandervort."

"Vandervort? I don't know them."

"Let's just say her family is a bit different," Johannes said, without revealing too much. "She's not like any other girl I've ever met. She is not one to obey the rules, that's for sure."

"So complete opposite of you?" Samuel joked.

"Funny, but no you're right. Very much opposite of me. Probably why I like her so much."

"Does father know?"

"He knows what he needs to know. Lately though, he's been obsessed in work and politics. The war is on everyone's mind."

Samuel grunted. "Sometimes I think it would be better to move back to Schenectady. I'm too exposed out here on the frontier. If the Mohawk ever turn on us, I'll be one of the first to go."

"Don't talk like that," Johannes said. "If anything, you're probably safer here than you would be in Schenectady. There is some tension between the Albany Convention and supporters of some merchant captain in New York City named Jacob Leisler. A lot of people think Leisler should be charge, and a lot are against him. I don't think it will get better anytime sooner."

Samuel stood in silence, contemplating his brother's words. "Well," he said finally, "we can only hope for the best and work our asses off in the meantime. Want to help me with the wood?"

That night, Johannes dined with his brother and father as the men sat by the fire outside, having some of Samuel's beer and singing songs.

"This isn't for the boys outside," Samuel said returning from the cellar with a small keg. He poured two cups, handing them out. As Johannes gulped it down, he found himself coughing.

"That's quite strong," he said. "You make it yourself?"

"Van Slyck himself gave me the recipe," Samuel replied. "I had to pay a shilling for it, so enjoy it."

"I'll take another cup," their father said, letting out a belch.

It did not take long before Harmen and his two sons were laughing, talking trade, politics, and every topic imaginable. Johannes watched in amusement as it was the first time he had seen his father drunk and merry. What intrigued him the most was that he talked to Samuel not as father and son, but man to man - like they were of no relation, only good friends and business partners. He silently wished Harmen would someday talk to him like that, and not like a child.

Johannes was soon nauseous. "I have to retire," he admitted.

"There's a cot in the back room," Samuel said. "Remember, this is as good as it will feel. Tomorrow will be a different story."

Once Johannes had left to go to bed, Samuel turned to his father. "You need to stop treating him like a child, Father."

"I treat him like a man, same as you."

"No, you don't," Samuel said. "I can tell. He wants you to recognize his accomplishments. He needs to be encouraged or else he will resent you for the rest of his life."

"I want him to grow into a strong man, not a wild idealist who buries his head in books and daydreaming."

"Father," Samuel said, shaking his head, "knowing where I am now, I wish I'd read more when I was his age. I wish I daydreamed more. He has so much creativity sparking in his head. If I were you, I would send him to Amsterdam where he can learn things I could only dream of." He paused, taking a long drink from his cup. "Don't get me wrong, I love the frontier life. It's hard but self-rewarding. Johannes would have more trouble than I, or Albert even, being out here. But he is not a fool nor is he lazy. He keeps a clear head, is very intelligent, and has an open mind. Father, let him cultivate it. It will pay itself off, I will promise you that."

Harmen stood up and paced around. "Once he has proven himself a man, I will honor any commitment he wishes to make towards his future. Until that time, as he stays under my roof, he will do what I tell him to do. I won't treat him any different than I treated you or Albert."

Samuel got up and refilled his cup. "But he is different, Father. Let him show you what he can accomplish. That's all I ask."

"I will see how he behaves in the company of the Wilden," Harmen said. "Albert runs his mouth too much to take on this trip. We'll see how Johannes handles himself."

Johannes awoke with a pounding headache. He immediately rushed outside and vomited in the grass. Harmen was already awake, washing himself with a bucket of cold water out back. "Grab a quick snack," Harmen said to Johannes when he noticed him. "We'll be moving all day today."

Johannes grabbed a few bread rolls and an apple from Samuel, then downed them with an exorbitant amount of water. The men assembled, and Harmen took a quick head count to make sure nobody had wandered off or perhaps shirked their duties and returned to Albany. Satisfied, he turned to Samuel who came out to see them off. "Take care, son."

"Take care," Samuel called back. "You too, Johannes. Keep an eye on the old man. Don't let him get you into trouble."

Johannes smiled but said nothing, and just waved goodbye. The column started off, and swiftly vanished down the road to the west.

It took another day of hard trekking to reach the western borderlands. Some of the men had volunteered for the journey because of their respect for the Natives, or opportunities to see what trade might be possible. Others, however, had never been west of Schenectady, and Harmen Vedder knew to keep them under strict control. He stopped them on the road.

"Gather around." The men formed a semicircle around Harmen. "Listen up," he said. "Before we reach their village, I will lay out some rules, and every man here will follow them without question. Do I make myself clear?"

A few of the men spoke up that they understood, and others nodded. He continued. "Nobody is to disturb their living quarters or go anywhere without their permission, understand?" The men acknowledged without hesitation. Harmen's tension eased a bit, but he continued to speak. "The Mohawk Indians are our most valuable ally, and this is our opportunity to thank them for their generosity and show them how Dutchmen act – with integrity and selflessness. Do *not* preach the Gospel here to those who wish to remain true to their heathen Gods. I will not be the man responsible for starting a religious war over their beliefs.

"You will respect their traditions and their women. They live in a matriarchy. That is to say, their women are more often the heads of a family."

There was a murmur from some of the men.

"What odd people they are," someone commented.

"Do not worry yourselves with the reasons for their strange societal structure. Though it is alien to us Christians, it is not for us to pass judgement upon them.

"This is a diplomatic mission, gentlemen. By helping the Mohawk move their homes while their warriors are away, we show them that we can be trusted with their women and children's safety. That holds weight with them and our alliance will be greatly strengthened. Gentlemen," Harmen declared, standing tall before them. "Work hard, work well. The Lord guides us on this journey and if we lead these Wilden families to their new home, the Lord will surely keep our own families safe from harm."

"Well said, brother," a voice came from behind, startling Harmen.

The Mohawk Lawrence appeared calm, leaning against a tree as if he had been there the entire time. He and Harmen shook hands, sharing quick words of reunion. Lawrence turned to the Dutchmen gathered up. "Your leaders and your God send you as a gift to us, to help move our castle to better land, so that our people may know a more bountiful harvest and feel safer from attack. For that I thank you, and I welcome you to the land of the Mohawk."

Chapter 16

Johannes felt the sweat drip down his forehead. He followed Lawrence and his father at the head of the column. When asked how much further the town was, the tall Mohawk would only reply "Not much further."

By his own count, Johannes guessed they must have walked another four miles since entering Mohawk territory.

He humored himself at the thought of the actual boundaries between the two peoples. Nobody could tell for certain where English lands ended, and Iroquois lands began. Even in the north, some marked New France at the Saint Lawrence River, while others claimed it was over a hundred leagues south or farther.

At long last, the Mohawk let out a call and Johannes could hear it answered by several voices, all in the foreign tongue. The column of men sent by the Convention and their Indian guide found themselves no longer on the rough trails in the forest, but rather in a vast opening, staring at a wooden palisade. Unlike Schenectady and Albany, the palisade was not solid. Many small gaps breached the wall, allowing one to look inside, but none wide enough to allow even a child to slip through.

All about them, women moved around, some with baskets of maize or grain. Children raced around, only stopping when the strange white men from the east arrived. Lawrence led them through the open gate.

"Like you," Lawrence began, "during the day we keep our gates open. We close them at night."

"Have you already begun to tear down?" Harmen asked Lawrence.

"You are quick with your eyes my friend," the

Mohawk stated. He walked up ahead of the working party to greet his children who rushed to embrace him.

Johannes leaned to his father. "What did you notice, Father?"

Harmen halted the group in the village center. As the men sat down to rest, or take in their strange surroundings, Harmen turned to his son. "Normally, all Mohawk villages have more elaborate paths to get inside. Not quite a maze, but several layers of palisade walls. Notice how we just walked right in? They're already tearing down the village."

"They are indeed a strange people," a volunteer said as two young boys rushed past them, devoid of all clothes.

Some of the children ran up to one of the men, staring in awe at his massive size and reddish beard.

"I bet they never seen a man as big as you, Connor," one of the men said with a laugh.

Connor McDowell responded with a smile that stretched ear-to-ear. A recent immigrant to the New World, he had almost leapt at the opportunity to volunteer for the expedition. Schuyler noted the man's sheer size and agreed without hesitation.

"I only see women and children," he replied. "Where are the men?"

Lawrence turned to the big man. "A few are around. Many are raiding in the north. A man's number one priority is to take care of his family. For us, the French are the biggest threat to our families. So, we fight them far from our lands. This way, they do not disturb our homes and our families."

McDowell nodded, laying his massive hand on a small boy's head and rustling his hair. The boy laughed and ran away. "You are a friendly people," he said to the Mohawk. "I am eager to help you."

"We thank you and bless you for your gesture of friendship," Lawrence replied.

Others in the party were not so enthusiastic about the forthcoming job. From early on, a small faction had formed amongst the men. They talked amongst themselves, glancing at the Natives, and either pointing in mockery, or shaking their head in disgust.

Harmen made no attempt at confronting them. He knew the importance of being seen to be in complete control of the working party, and internal strife would do more harm than good. Besides, a few hours of sweating in the heat and they would forget all about the Natives' culture.

"Where would you like us to start?" Harmen asked.

Lawrence was taken aback. "You have journeyed far today, my friends," he said to the men from Albany. "We will not work this day for it is almost at an end. Join us in meal and let us give thanks for our good fortune. This year has been kind and the Great Mother has rewarded us with bountiful food from the earth. Tomorrow, we will move our homes."

Having spent time with the Natives before, Harmen graciously accepted Lawrence's offer, knowing it would be considered offensive to refuse. Further, he knew that Lawrence was right. The long day of walking had worn out the men. They needed a good meal and a good night's rest.

Lawrence led Harmen and the others towards one of the houses. Johannes marveled at them. He had read about the great longhouses of the Iroquois but always imagined people exaggerated their size. He was thrilled to have been wrong.

The massive house stretched more than two-hundred feet, and it reached over fifteen feet high. It was as massive as even the largest buildings in Schenectady.

As they approached, Johannes was awe-struck by how sturdy the building was constructed. Though made only of wood and bark, strewn together with rope, it had a permanent feel to it. "How did you build this?"

Lawrence rested his hand on the walls. "We build a frame using poles, mostly from hickory saplings. These are bent and set into place. Other beams are then laid upon those until a solid frame is in place. We then cover it with bark, stripped and peeled down, of course. This, we lay several layers deep, until it is solid from the rains in the warm seasons, or the snows in the winter."

"And there are six houses," Harmen commented, himself amazed at the size of the village.

"This is the largest of the castles."

One of the men spoke up. "How many savages reside here?"

Harmen subtly shook his head at Lawrence, urging him not to answer. But the Mohawk turned and answered the man directly.

"In times long past, the Mohawk roamed over the land in numbers like all the beasts of the land. War and famine have taken their toll on our men and women alike, but we are strong still. When the warriors return, this village will number over a thousand."

Some of the more resentful men from Albany were unnerved by that number of Indians so close to their own settlements, in a number they could not match.

"Well I hope all of your warriors return to their women and children before the snows arrive," Harmen stated aloud.

Lawrence nodded and directed them inside the longhouse.

They pushed aside heavy blankets that blocked the entrance. Stepping inside, Johannes couldn't help but think how different these people were from his own. There was not a single wall the entire length of the longhouse. Bunks stretched along the side as far down as he could see. More skins were stretched out. The beams holding up the roof were adorned with the antlers of great deer and other beasts.

Centered and evenly spaced throughout the longhouse, were cooking fires. Women knelt beside them, stirring the food. The pots of porridge filling the air with a savory smell. The smoke rose and disappeared outside through ventilation holes in the ceiling. From what Johannes could observe, the longhouse was superbly built. Every detail was carefully crafted to maximize the central space of the building, while sacrificing nothing in heat or comfort.

One of the sachems, an elderly man with graying hair, approached Lawrence. He whispered some words and then disappeared outside. Lawrence asked Harmen's men to sit. Women passed around bowls of porridge. Bread and fish were also served. The sachem returned with a few of the men from the tribe who joined in the meal.

Johannes leaned over to Lawrence. "Is he your king?"

Lawrence stopped chewing and looked at him. His face was like a stone for a moment. Johannes thought about apologizing. Suddenly the Indian burst out laughing, causing a few to quiet their own conversations, as he spoke.

"He is an elder and all elders must be respected," Lawrence said. "He is wise in his old age. You can think of him as a spiritual leader and father to us all." Lawrence paused, thinking of the right words.

"Our customs are strange, no?"

Johannes smiled, almost embarrassed at his own ignorance. "In some ways, they are very different. You have no public buildings. You invited us – strangers, into your home and fed us without asking payment."

Lawrence nodded. "Yes, in our land, a man's ability to eat should not be determined by his wealth. A hungry man who comes in peace will never be refused food or water. No man is more privileged than another. No man will receive the best parts of the bear or fish, while another only receives the rotten meat of a beast that has spoiled."

"And yet you have no desserts," Johannes continued. "No cakes or baked goods, no sweets."

"I have had English baked desserts," Lawrence replied, "and though delicious, I have also seen many men and women among your people of shall we say, larger statute. You will rarely see such men or women among the Haudenosaunee. Our people are healthy and able-bodied."

Johannes nodded, having witnessed that himself. "But a sweet cake on occasion cannot be bad for the body or soul."

"And that is why I visit you English so often," he said, laughing.

"And we always welcome the company," Johannes added. "I cannot argue that."

"I hope you all will join us this evening," Lawrence announced to the guests. "We will eat more, smoke the tobacco pipe, and tell the story of our origin. It is a fascinating history of how the Five Nations of the Haudenosaunee came together to form the Great Confederacy."

Harmen stood up. "It would be an honor to join you in hearing this tale."

Chapter 17

The chill of the night was swept away from the fires of the Iroquois, inside the walls of their great village. The bonfire sent sparks soaring into the air.

Lawrence had gathered what Englishmen were willing to listen, to the fire where the sachems and mothers of the village sat in silence. Most of the men accepted, though a few elected to confine themselves to their makeshift shelters on the far side of the village.

The sachem that had eaten beside them earlier, stood with Lawrence by his side. He spoke in his native tongue. His voice was deep, but carried by the winds so that all present could hear him. Lawrence translated the sachem's words for their guests.

"Brothers, welcome," he began. "We have come to another turning of the Great Mother. Tomorrow we will uproot our homes and travel to a new patch of rich soil. There we will seed the earth with the three sisters – corn, beans, and squash. And we will begin again in our new home. And as we grow in strength, we feed into the power of our brothers in the Five Nations. Together, we are strong. But it was not always this way."

The sachem ceased, and everyone looked up from the fires to see two strong men helping a third to the fireside. He was old; far older than even the sachem who was speaking. He moved carefully, his body appearing so fragile that he would fall from the slightest breeze. His gray hair was long and thin. Wrinkles covered his face and his hands trembled.

He took a seat, and Lawrence spoke to the Englishmen. "This is Teeyotago – the eldest of the sachems. He is grandfather to us all and watches over

the people, as he has for many sunrises and sunsets."
The tone of Lawrence's voice led Johannes to the
understanding that the Mohawk held more than respect
for the old man; they revered him.

"As a boy, Teeyotago witnessed our tragic
defeat on the shores of the great northern lake, at the
hands of our blood enemies – the Huron and
Algonquin nations, and the French warmonger who
went by the name, *Champlain*."

"Impossible," one man whispered.

Johannes added up the years. "That was the
Battle of Sorel," he said to his father. "I read about it."
He gasped. "That means he must be almost ninety."

Harmen ignored his son, and sat motionless,
listening to his Mohawk friend speak. Johannes glanced
at the old sachem. The fire's glow shone in the old
Mohawk's eyes. They bore the look of a man who had
seen a lifetime of trial and tragedy.

The orating sachem continued, and Lawrence
went back to translating. "During the time before the
white man came to us, the Haudenosaunee were
broken. The Five Nations made war with each other.
Blood was spilled, homes destroyed, crops burnt. This
went on for many years. And it nearly destroyed us.

"Among the many warriors, was Hiawatha of
the Onondaga. Hiawatha became disgusted of the
bloodshed and wished for peace. But the Onondaga
sorcerer Tadodaho, relished war, and instigated it.
Tadodaho was wicked and snakes ran through his hair.
He was twisted, and Hiawatha saw this. Hiawatha
gathered some loyal warriors and led a revolt against
Tadodaho, but the sorcerer saw them coming.
Hiawatha failed and fled his lands.

"It was then that the Great Peacemaker,
Skennenrahawi of the Huron, and born of a virgin
mother, appeared from the foggy waters to Hiawatha."

"This is blasphemy," hissed one of the men. "Only Christ was born of the Virgin Mary."

"This is their tradition," Harmen replied softly. "Hold your tongue out of respect for their story, even if the words are heresy. Few of their people have been redeemed in Christ."

The man scoffed but spoke no more.

Lawrence continued, "Skennenrahawi drove the hate from the heart of Hiawatha. And together, the two men walked many miles to the lands of the Mohawk. They brought a new message – a message of peace and unity. And the Mohawk joined. Next came the people of the standing stone. This was the Oneida. Then came those of the Great Swamp. They were the Cayuga. They continued to where the Seneca – people of the Great Hill, joined.

"Finally, there was only the Onondaga. And the Peacemaker and Hiawatha confronted the sorcerer. They spoke at length with Tadodaho. For a time, he would not walk away from the path of violence. But in a miraculous event from the Great Mother herself, there was a great eclipse of the Sun, that they convinced Tadodaho that peace was the way forward. The snakes fell from Tadodaho's head, and he chose to lay down his arms and join his brothers in peace."

Lawrence held up a single arrow, high above his head. "Hiawatha said to Tadodaho that one arrow is like one nation, easily broken." Lawrence snapped the arrow and threw it into the fire. He reached down and picked up a bundle of 5 arrows, strewn together with twine. "But together, the Five Nations are unbreakable."

His muscles strained, and the bundle of arrows bent.

They did not break.

"The men and women of the Five Nations

buried the hatchet between them on that day. They signed the Great Law of Peace, and from the earth rose a tall, white elm tree – a symbol of peace."

Lawrence paused for a moment. "And that, my brethren, is how the Five Nations became as one in the Iroquois Confederacy. Remember – in unity, there is strength."

* * *

Jacques-René de Brisay de Denonville welcomed Louis-Hector de Callières back with open arms. "I trust your journey to Paris was not too perilous, my friend."

"No, monsieur," Callières replied somberly.

"What news do you bring? I sense something is amiss.

"A rider came in from the west." Callières handed Denonville a dispatch. He watched as Denonville' s heart sank. He fell back into his chair and wiped his face, reading the letter again.

"Another village has been laid waste by the Iroquois. Forty-two men, women, and children are dead or missing." Denonville let the letter go and watched it float to the floor. "We are in dire need of help, Louis. Our numbers are depleted. Our winter crops have largely been erased. I am sure you have heard news of the massacre at Lachine?"

"I have," Callières replied.

"The savages have made this the bloodiest summer in the history of New France. They have wreaked destruction over hundreds of miles. Most of our western settlements are gone. The truth, my friend, is that we are hanging on by a thread."

Callières handed Denonville another letter. This one bore the seal of King Louis XIV. The governor-general straightened up and took the letter. He took great care unsealing it, as if it had been touched by the Lord. "I have spent many sleepless nights praying for the day this arrives."

Callières stood in silence until Denonville finished and set the letter down. He stood up. "Louis-Hector de Callières, my resignation has been accepted."

"Monsieur?"

"I am to depart for France post-haste. My replacement should arrive next month. Until then, I leave New France in your care."

"You honor me. I will defend our lands to the death. For king and God."

The pair shook hands.

Denonville sighed, and appeared as if the long, hard years in the New World had finally caught up to him. "I think – I think I will go for a walk," he said.

He gathered a few documents, a ledger, and stuffed them into a leather satchel. He hesitated in the doorway, briefly glanced back over his shoulder, and then disappeared.

* * *

The workday started just before dawn. Much to Harmen's delight, the Mohawk fed them again, a good meal of porridge, fish, poultry, grains, and nuts. They were even offered juice squeezed from plush grapes, to accompany the hearty breakfast. Johannes was startled to find that the Mohawk had no concept of fermenting the juice and making wine, as was common in the Dutch world.

The breaking down and moving the massive longhouses and the rest of the village, began after breakfast. The path to the new location had been pre-scouted and cleared of much of the underlying growth that would have slowed movement.

The Englishmen were astounded at the speed the women cleared the longhouses of possessions and interior decorations. While their own women were certainly no strangers to hard labor, some of the Mohawk squaws were making quick work of what should have taken hours. Embarrassed and not wanting to be outdone, the men took heart in their work, and rapidly disassembled the tall wooden beams that made up the frame. Before their eyes, the longhouses disappeared into piles of poles, ropes and bark.

The critical items, those that would be needed at the future village, were piled into sleds and carts. The Mohawk—being unfamiliar with wheels in a transportation role—were awed by the ease of moving heavy weights on the Dutch oxen carts. By early afternoon, the first men and supplies departed for the site of the new village.

Johannes Vedder trudged along the beaten path. The undergrowth had been trampled into dirt. He and Arnout Viele pulled a cart with baskets of corn, furs and trinkets, which one of the squaws had piled on before they departed.

"What do you think of the Wilden?" Johannes asked.

"I think they are an interesting people," Viele replied. "Did you notice there are so few who have physical deformities, and like Lawrence said, there are so few who are overweight?"

"I did," Johannes acknowledged. "But is that within their hereditary traits or do they discard the ones who are at birth?" Viele looked at him shocked. Johannes shrugged. "I don't know the answer myself. I admire their work ethic and their strength. They don't complain nearly as much as our own people."

"In that sense, they remind me of your father. He must like being around them."

"He doesn't like the Wilden," Johannes disputed. "He respects them, but only so far as to be good allies and trading partners."

"I want to learn as much as possible about them," Viele admitted. "I think it would be best for both the Wilden and the colonists. We need to have mutual understandings and respect, or this could all fall apart. One thing I learned from my father is just how precarious relations with the native tribes can be. He told me all the stories from the early days in Massachusetts and Plymouth. Just a few misunderstandings and fears started King Philips War. I do not wish to repeat their mistakes."

"Do you think we will ever go to war against them?"

Viele sighed. "Possibly, but I hope not. They are a remarkable people. From their culture to their system of democratic government, they are more sophisticated than most of us would give them credit for." He looked ahead and watched a Mohawk man wearing nothing more than a loin and moccasins, carrying a basket and a hatchet. "They are a paradox."

"What do you mean?" Johannes asked.

"Think about it. Their culture is advanced, though we may not recognize it. Yet, they are also a primitive people. In a hundred years, they may not even exist. They could be wiped out by disease or driven away by either the French, or even by our own hand. As things stand now, if they were our enemy, they could lay waste to the whole Mohawk valley. Schenectady, even Albany, would not have a chance against the full might of the Iroquois Confederacy."

The two walked in silence for a moment. Finally, Johannes spoke. "I wonder if they know that."

Viele looked at him questioningly. "What way the winds are blowing," Johannes explained. "I wonder if they see their fate as clearly as we do."

"I believe they do," Arnout said. "But here and now, they are our allies. Truly, there can be no better friend or worse enemy than the Iroquois."

The following day, work started on reassembling the great longhouses of Tionnontogen. The beams soared into the air, with some women, petite yet strong, sitting atop, binding the poles together. The men began the laborious task of rebuilding the defensive palisade. The new location was situated in part on a plateau. A steep embankment provided protection to one side, and the other would be well-guarded with towers and loopholes in the palisade, to shower any attacker with arrow and musket.

It would take another three days before the castle was complete, but when it was, the English men stood in awe before it. Smoke filtered from the enormous longhouses as women cooked food for their families. Warriors stood looking out from the towers and walked about the camp, sharpening their tomahawks and arrows, or cleaning their muskets. Baskets of food, deerskin hides, beaver pelts, and piles of wampum beads could be found everywhere.

"This is a place of extreme wealth," Harmen admitted, with Johannes by his side. "They are fine people, and a great ally."

Johannes stood in silence but could not agree more with his father. The week spent with the Mohawk had opened his eyes to a world alien to his own; primitive yet graceful in all its conduct and lifestyle.

As Harmen turned the working party east, back to Schenectady, Johannes was a little saddened to leave such a life-changing experience. But as soon as the great Mohawk castle was out of sight, his thoughts soon reverted to Maria Vandervort and his glorious homecoming.

Chapter 18

Tahajadoris and Pieter Schuyler spoke out of earshot of the men in the room. As before, when they spoke in private, all formalities were cast aside, and they spoke as friends.

"Brother Quider," Tahajadoris spoke quietly. "The Five Nations have not risen to greatness through war alone." He rested his hand on Schuyler's shoulder. "Neither have you Dutch, my friend. We must choose our fights carefully and weigh all options before sending our warriors to die away from their wives and children."

"As do we, my friend," Schuyler replied. For all their friendship, at times Schuyler swore sometimes he could not understand the Natives. One moment they pledge their complete and unwavering support and in the next moment they seek other options.

"We have not had war on the Eastern nations of the Plymouth area in a generation," Tahajadoris said. "They remain our allies so long as they do not intrude on Iroquois lands. They are of no threat to our people."

"But they are a threat to *our* people," Schuyler insisted. "King Philip's War devastated the population of our brethren in Massachusetts and Plymouth."

"It devastated the Wampanoag also. And the Narragansett. Many other tribes, too. It was your brethren that stood victorious and now they ask you to assist in killing a beaten people. It is not a wise move my friend, especially while more powerful enemies remain."

Schuyler paused, taking in his friend's words. "What would you counsel?"

Tahajadoris straightened up. "Make war on

the French." He saw Schuyler's eyes and knew immediately he was considering it. "They are our most dangerous enemy, yet we have dealt them a devastating blow at Montreal."

Schuyler nodded subtly. "Lachine?"

"Yes," Tahajadoris replied. "They now lick their scars like a wounded beast. If we allow the scars to heal, they will emerge a stronger foe. But if we strike now…" the Mohawk trailed off and Schuyler contemplated his words. There was a wisdom in Tahajadoris' words which could not be denied.

"Will the Mohawk fight side-by-side with us if we move on Quebec?"

The strong Mohawk nodded sternly. "I have met in council with the Five Nations. If it is your decision to remove the filth of France from these shores forever, to erase their seed in this world, the Five Nations will stand to walk and fight beside you." He leaned in closer. "And if the fire goes out, and the Five Nations no longer stand as one, I give you my word, the Mohawk *will* fight. We will live and die together."

Schuyler held out his hand and Tahajadoris gripped it tightly. "Then it's settled, brother. When we've figured out what to do about the usurper in New York City, we will marshal our armies here and march north and strike the French a blow they will mark as the darkest chapter in their history."

A commotion diverted their attention to a messenger. "What's this?" Schuyler said to himself. There was worry and sorrow in the faces of the men nearest the young boy. "What news do you bring, lad? Is it the French?"

The young boy did not move or look Schuyler in the eye. Kiliaen Van Rensselaer stepped forward. "I'm so sorry, Pieter."

The houses and stores, the people and the carts, all of it was a blur to Pieter Schuyler as he ran as fast as his legs could take him. He took on tunnel vision, narrowly missing an oxen and an angry merchant who cussed as him as Schuyler darted in front of his cart. His legs felt weightless, but his heart was heavy, and his mind was filled with terror. Tahajadoris and several others raced behind him, the Mohawk's strong leg muscles carrying him ahead of the others but still behind the mayor.

Schuyler threw open the front door and a servant pointed upstairs and bowed his head. Schuyler swallowed his saliva and suddenly lost his speed. He took each step up the narrow dark wood staircase with dread. With his heart pounding and eyes watering, the mayor stood at the top and saw the door ahead, partially closed but open enough to allow him to see a candlelight flickering inside. He took a deep breath and pushed open the door.

Engeltie Schuyler, Pieter's wife, sat in an old chair and leaned over the small bed. She raised a damp washcloth and dabbed the forehead of his baby daughter. A sickening feeling overtook him as he stepped inside and saw the baby, her skin so pale and still. He crossed to the opposite side and knelt beside the bed. Up close, he could not hold back his tears. He raised his hand and shivered as he touched her cold forehead.

"Doesn't she look so beautiful?" Engeltie said. He looked up and saw her smile.

"Why are you happy, woman? Our child is dead."

Engeltie waved her hand at him. "Nonsense dear. She is just sound asleep. She looks so peaceful." Pieter watched as Engeltie moved the blanket up further, tucking in the baby as she did every night. "We are blessed my love. We are blessed to have the Lord bestow two beautiful daughters upon us."

Pieter stood up, looking over the bed in shock. "She's dead, Engeltie."

"How dare you say such a horrid thing," she hissed. "Our baby is asleep, and you wish her dead."

Pieter glanced up. Tahajadoris and Kiliaen stood in the doorway. Kiliaen, who had heard Schuyler's wife's delusions, slowly approached and took Engeltie by the shoulders. "She is sound asleep. We should go get something to eat. You look tired yourself."

She smiled gently at him. "Yes, yes I suppose we should leave her to rest."

Kiliaen choked up. "Yes, let her rest in peace."

As he guided her out of the room, Tahajadoris entered and stood beside Schuyler who dropped to his knees.

"I am sorry, my friend."

He knew better than to tell his Christian friend that no soul truly dies, as he'd learned many times, that comfort is the only gift one can bring in times of grief. Arguing over whose God was real and what happened after life, was moot.

"We will bury her, and we will mourn for your loss. Nothing is harder than losing a child."

Pieter folded his hands, not hearing a word of what Tahajadoris said. He bowed his head in prayer and cried until numbness overcame him.

* * *

Gabriel Thomase tapped impatiently on the table, whilst Kiliaen Van Rensselaer stood at the window. The other members of the Convention grew restless, and after a moment, Robert Livingston finally spoke up.

"We cannot wait for the mayor."

Van Rensselaer turned from the window, walking back to the others. "We should wait for Mr. Schuyler."

The city alderman, Livinius Van Schaick, leaned forward in his chair. "I agree with Mr. Livingston. The day's business must be addressed."

Van Rensselaer looked to him. "He's mourning his daughter – your niece's passing."

"I too feel the loss," Van Schaick stated "However, we have a duty to administer this city and this province."

With reluctance, Van Rensselaer conceded and took his seat.

"Gentlemen, we have a problem," Livingston said, standing up. All eyes focused on him as he spoke. "For too long we have worried about the threat from the usurper Jacob Leisler to the south. We have ignored the far greater threat to the north from the French and their Wilden allies. As you well know, last month the Mohawk struck a most terrible blow against them at Lachine. They were weakened by this attack, but by no means have they been destroyed. Strong forces remain at Quebec, Montreal, and in the wilderness."

Kiliaen Van Rensselaer guessed what Livingston was about to ask. He spoke up. "We cannot launch an invasion into Canada this late into the year. Winter is coming, and we cannot risk being trapped north in the deep snows."

There were murmurs as several men agreed with Van Rensselaer.

Livingston held up his hand. "I do not propose we invade Canada. By spring we should have word from the new king – as well as reinforcements. Surely, England knows the war has spread to her colonies and will not leave us to fight the French alone. But spring is a long way away and I propose we look to our defenses."

"Our defenses are solid," said the city sheriff, Richard Pretty.

"I do not speak of Albany," Livingston said. "The village of Schenectady continues to ignore the perilous situation we are in. They have not even begun the most basic and necessary of preparations for siege and war. We must send a delegation to that village to oversee their defensive measures." He paused, thinking. "I also propose we send for more men to strengthen both Schenectady and Albany. Twenty-five to thirty more to shore up our walls."

"And where will we these men come from?" Van Rensselaer asked.

Livingston took a breath. He knew it would be controversial. "Ulster County."

The room erupted. Several members of the convention shouted their disapproval. Kiliaen stood up, his arms extended.

"Friends," he shouted, "friends please." The room quieted. He turned to Livingston. "I share the view of some of these men. Taking that number from Ulster County while not leaving them defenseless, would leave them drastically weakened. They are our closest ally to New York City. If Leisler gets word, which he eventually will, and if he moves against Ulster, we cannot protect it. If Ulster falls, Leisler will march straight up to the gates of Albany itself. It's a dangerous gamble you suggest Mr. Livingston."

Robert Livingston nodded. "Aye, it is Mr. Van Rensselaer, but the alternative is slaughter at the hands of the French. Leisler seems content with strengthening his position in the city. After Lachine though, you can bet the French will seek revenge. They are coming for us, sooner rather than later. We will not stop them; not by ourselves."

"We have the Mohawk," Van Rensselaer retorted. "They are our closest allies."

"Yes, yes we do," Livingston said. "Do you trust them to come to our aid at the drop of a dime?"

Van Rensselaer paused. "Yes," he shouted.

Livingston shook his head. "I don't. I know them better than anyone here. They are key allies to be sure. But they are also suspicious of us. They worry that we will not stand by their side if the French attack them instead of us."

He looked around the room. "Albany is the center of power for the Convention. We must focus our strength here." He felt the mood in the room shift in his favor. "We will *ask* Ulster if they can spare the men. If they can, our position will be greatly strengthened. All in favor say aye."

Across the room, one by one, every member of the Convention voiced their approval. Even Van Rensselaer hesitantly agreed, not wanting to be seen opposing the majority decision.

"Then it's decided," Livingston said. "I have one last request. As our dear friend, Mr. Van Rensselaer, said earlier - the Wilden are also our allies. We all know how they fall to madness and drunkenness in the face of our alcohol sales to them. They are reckless and drink themselves into foolishness without reservation. We must forbid the sale of alcohol to them until the crisis passes."

There was more grumbling at this request, as several men in the room guiltily admitted to themselves that they used alcohol to dull the wits of the Natives in trading negotiations. However, in the end, they too came to a consensus of a ban on alcohol sales.

* * *

When death came for Engeltie Schuyler in early October, she felt no pain. One night she fell asleep, never to wake again. The fever is what killed her, but Pieter suspected she died of a broken heart from the loss of three of her four children. First Philip, who was taken by a nasty disease which had torn through his body, blackening his skin and causing him to vomit. Then Anna who had succumbed to malaria just two summers before. Pieter recalled, with tears, how Anna showed the same delusional behavior as his wife, before her own passing.

But baby Gertruj appeared to be the last hope Engeltie had. Both she and Pieter were so sure that the Lord had taken two of their children and two would be allowed to live. Certainly, it was God's will that Gertruj live. Her death came so fast and unexpected, that none could have foreseen it. When she died, both parents grieved. But while Pieter accepted the hard fact, Engeltie lived in denial, even claiming Gertruj was staying at her brother's while the dirt was thrown upon the tiny casket at the funeral.

Pieter sat outside of his house while men carried the body off to be prepared for burial. Margarita walked up and without a word took a seat next to her father. She carried flowers and as he saw them, he forced himself to smile.

"Papa, is Mama dead?" Margarita asked innocently.

Pieter's heart shattered into a million pieces. He looked into her light brown eyes, noting how much she looked like her mother. How could he tell his only daughter—who had already suffered the loss of her three younger siblings—that her mother was dead?

"Mama won't be coming back," he said finally.

Margarita's head dropped, and she curled in closer, resting her head on her father's chest. He wrapped his arm around her, looking outward. *How was this God's plan?* he wondered. How could some families pass from generation to generation without loss, and yet his family be devastated like this?

Margarita looked up, seeing a stream of tears make its way down her father's cheek. "Don't cry, Papa" she said. "Mama has gone to look after Philip and Anna and Gertruj. And I have you to look after me."

Pieter nodded, wiping away his tears. "Yes, my dear. Mama can look after your brother and sisters."

"Can you believe it?" Margarita continued. "Next week, Philip would have been six."

"Six?" Pieter laughed. "My God, time flies." He grabbed her, hoisting her up on his lap. "You must be eight then, my sweet angel?"

"Of course I am, Papa," she laughed.

He smiled genuinely, for the first time in weeks. Time had indeed passed faster than he realized. "Of course you are," he whispered back.

"How old are you, Papa?" Margarita asked.

Pieter laughed aloud.

"Too old, dear. Up," he said standing up with her sliding off his leg. He looked to the house, seeing that the men had left with his wife's body. "Go change the sheets on all the beds. And then we shall decide what to eat for supper."

As he sent her inside, he looked around. Though his daughter had temporarily comforted him, the reality of loss returned to him and he sighed in despair. Unlike many of his companions who had traveled from the Netherlands and England to settle there, Pieter had been born and raised in the colonies. Yet since the loss of his wife, he felt foreign to the land. How could he call such a desolate and sorrowful place his home? He tried to suppress the thoughts and went inside to help young Margarita. It was all he could do.

Chapter 19

Harmen watched the darkening sky. The sun's light was shrouded in the overcast afternoon. The river was gray and waves splashed against the narrow sloop, which was uneasily tied to the docks. "Hurry up with the provisions."

Johannes climbed aboard the sloop, stowing the last of the food. Though they would be back in the village by first light, the owner, and de facto captain of the vessel, made it a rule to leave with a minimum of seven-days water and rations. He also ensured there would be spare tools, firearms, and powder. There were too many tales of boats being stranded up river or disappearing, never to be found again.

"All aboard," the captain shouted.

He was a sturdy man, his hardened face shrouded in a short, dark beard and large brown hat which cast a shadow over his eyes. Just as the last two years, he made it abundantly clear that he would take his passengers up-river as they requested, but during said time, his orders were law.

Echoing the captain's call, Harmen yelled out from the deck of the sloop. The ladies who had been watching the activity patiently, picked themselves up from the grass and approached the flimsy wooden dock at the river's edge.

Maria Vandervort picked her steps carefully. She looked down, seeing the gray water rush by through the gaps left between the planks. It made her uneasy and she was relieved to be helped aboard the vessel.

Once all the passengers were safely on-board, two boatmen tossed off the rope anchors and the wind slapped into the sails.

"This will be a bugger of a trip," the captain grumbled. "This westerly is stronger than I had hoped."

Harmen looked out to the choppy waves that resisted their trip. "Will we get far enough downriver by nightfall?"

"With luck," the captain answered. "And skill."

He took the helm and spun it, sending the vessel at an angle to the straight course originally plotted.

Never one to miss an opportunity, Harmen motioned his son closer. Johannes, gripping the sides, made his way up to the helm.

"Boy, I want you to pay strict attention to Mr. Wessing here. He has a lifetime of experience on the water and can teach you anything about sailing."

"Yes, Father."

He stood in silence, wondering if he should ask a question. For all his curiosity about handling a sloop, he truly only wanted to go back down where Maria sat with Angie and Maria Glen, whom Albert was excited to have, as they began a courtship only two weeks prior. Captain John Glen—of the Schenectady militia—was quite accepting that his daughter was seeing the son of a prominent citizen who, thank the Lord, was not a Leislerite.

Mr. Wessing grabbed the helm and turned it, sending the sloop on a starboard course. After a few moments, he wheeled it to port.

"Why do you turn the boat so much?" Johannes asked. "This part of the river is relatively straight east to west."

Wessing pointed to the sails. "That is a fore-and-aft rig. Rather than a square sail that runs perpendicular to the boat, these run along the keel. But sails alone aren't enough," Wessing explained. "You have to tack the boat. Do you understand?"

"What's tack?"

"Tacking is how we sail upwind," Wessing explained. "We can't sail straight into the wind. We wouldn't get anywhere. So, we sail diagonally, neither into nor against the winds. But the air is picked up at an angle into the fore-and-aft sails and takes the boat upwind to either side, depending on if you're facing port or starboard."

Johannes nodded. "So, you basically zig-zag the boat to gain a side-wind?"

Wessing, who seemed so stern, laughed aloud. "Well it's a bit more complicated than that, but basically yes. Are you looking to pursue a sea merchant career?"

"No," Johannes answered honestly. "I just like to learn new things."

"Well I can instruct you on the seafaring trade all day long," Wessing said, "but all you really need to know is waiting for you there."

Johannes turned to see what Wessing was looking at. Maria had stood up and was leaning against the railing. Mist from the river sprayed her face and she laughed. Just seeing her having fun made him smile.

"Young Mr. Vedder," Wessing continued. "You will often hear sailors and merchants referring to our boats as 'she' or 'her'. It's because we fell in love with the oceans and rivers, and we have developed a bond with the vessels we sail aboard. But for all its joy and fulfillment, at the end of the day, when the sun has passed beyond the edge of the world, nothing and I mean nothing replaces the comfort a good woman can provide."

Johannes thanked the captain and headed forward to the others. The sloop continued its course, picking up speed as the strong westerly faded in strength and changed direction.

Remembering what his father had taught him on a previous trip, Johannes turned to their new guests. "We are now beyond the borders of our own lands," he commented. "This is Iroquois land."

"Isn't it dangerous being out here?" Maria Glen asked. "What if they attack?"

Harmen replied to the girl, whom he regarded as a bit naïve. "We're not in dangerous waters. The Iroquois are our friends."

They sailed to a point some twenty miles upriver where a small outlet formed a natural harbor. Wessing knew the area well and directed the sloop right towards the shore.

The boat drifted into a fog.

"Isn't this dangerous being out here?" Maria Vandervort asked aloud. "I thought this was the Wilden Indian's territory."

"They will not bother us tonight," Johannes replied. Maria eased up next to him.

"Can you be sure?" she whispered.

Johannes smiled. "They are busy on the riverbanks preparing for tonight."

"What happens at night?"

"You will see," Johannes said. "And you will be glad you made the trip."

It was another two hours before the call came out. "Smoke!" Arent called out. "There's smoke downstream."

Maria rushed out from the cabin, her worry showing. "What is happening?"

Johannes laughed. "This, Maria, is why we are here."

"What do you mean?"

The boat drifted further on, the fog becoming a thick smoke. Several on the boat coughed as the smoke drifted all around them.

"I see a fire," Angie called out.

Downriver, a flicker of a bright orange light soon gave way to a building fire, increasing as it consumed the brush and dead woods. Soon, another fire was spotted on the opposite bank. In moments, the boat was drifting gently into the wind, fires burning on both banks.

"What is happening?" Maria asked Johannes.

"It's the autumn burning, by the Mohawk," he replied. "Like I said, you just have to see it."

Maria leaned over the side and her eyes widened.

Both sides of the Mohawk river lit up in a terrifying and fascinating light. The fires burned brighter than Maria had ever seen. She could feel the heat being emitted from a hundred yards offshore, almost to the point of being unbearable. Glowing embers could be seen shooting off the tallest of the dead pine trees as they tumbled to the forest floor, their crashes heard from the boat.

"Why are the Indians burning the forest?" Maria asked.

Johannes rested his arm over her shoulder. "It's customary to burn the forest in the autumn. It clears the forest of all the undergrowth and dead branches that have built up over the year. This makes it easier to stalk prey in the winter hunting months. As strange as it sounds, it makes the forest healthier and able to grow stronger."

"It's fascinating," Maria said.

Johannes' heart melted when he saw the ear-to-ear grin on her face. "You know, I read about this in a book given to me a while back. It talked about the autumn burnings. But you know, as amazing as it was described, the words do it no justice. This—" he gestured to the vision before them "—must be witnessed in person."

"Some sights cannot be beaten," Maria muttered. Johannes looked at Maria; her face glowing, and the fire reflecting in her eyes.

"No, some sights cannot be beaten," he repeated quietly.

Chapter 20

The cold, crisp air of the coming winter swept around Louis-Hector de Callières' fur coat. He stood atop a cobblestone platform just above the docks of Quebec – the bustling capital city of New France. He gazed upon the horizon where the sun's rays reflected off the snow-covered banks along the Saint Lawrence River. But through the glare he made out two distinct masts of the approaching ship. It was a barque longue class ship, weighing some fifty tons.

The ship had been expected for over a week, but Callières knew that even slight navigation errors or rough seas caused delays in ship schedules. The icy wind did little to calm his anxiety for he knew that somewhere on that vessel, was the King's newly-appointed governor general.

Crewmen spilled the wind from the sails and the ship slipped up to the docks, gently swaying back and forth in the churning river. They then helped the dock workers to toss ropes and tie down the vessel.

Few noticed a unique figure standing tall on the ship, watching them.

The man stood on the forecastle of the barque, looking down at the dock workers moving about their regular duties. One worker, a young man of no more than twenty years, lost his balance and plunged into the freezing waters of the river. The man screamed and kicked his legs frantically while the others rushed to his aid, throwing ropes into the water and yelling at him to grab one. The man on the deck shook his head in annoyance. It would surely delay his departure and every minute he spent aboard the godforsaken ship, he grew more impatient.

After a short delay the worker was brought out of the water and the ship safely docked. There was a line of travelers and colonists, soldiers and traders, ready to depart the boat, but they waited patiently so they didn't get in the way of the ship's VIP.

He came ashore. The black bucket-topped cavalier boots he wore glistened in the daylight. His armor breastplate had been polished to a mirror over a Persian blue jacket. A bright red sash crossed his chest and a rapier hung at his waist. On top of his curly, white wig, he wore an elaborate black cavalier hat with a red lace band. The man was slightly overweight but to no degree less intimidating. His mustache was thick and graying, and his face was one of hardship and anger.

He stood on the wet docks for a moment before he was approached by Louis-Hector de Callières. The governor of Montreal removed his hat and bowed to the visitor. "Welcome back to New France, monsieur Frontenac."

The man grunted. "You may call me governor now," he sneered. "The King has taken note of the lack of progress here and has sent me to take command of Quebec once more. I have also been sent to speak to monsieur Callières, governor of Montreal. Do you know where he may be?"

"Well I suppose I should," Callières chuckled. Frontenac barely blinked. "I'm Callières, Governor."

Frontenac looked over the more casual appearance of his fellow governor. "My mistake. I thought a representative of the King would be more prestigious in his appearance; not looking like a common aristocrat, wrapped in the hide of a dead animal because he cannot tolerate the cold of his own land."

Callières fumed inside. *Who does this man think he is to talk about me in that manner?* But he knew better than to openly challenge Frontenac. His reputation was well known. He was unforgiving, harsh, but above all, brutally efficient. As much as he hated the man, Callières knew the King sent him for a reason. Frontenac was the right man for the job. Still Callières could not help but wish they had met in Versailles, so he could have pleaded with the king to send someone else.

"I keep warm, so I may continue to serve the King as he wishes," Callières said finally. "Have you been detailed on the plans I have drawn up, concerning the New England colonies to the south?"

"Yes, and I believe I have some much-needed changes to make concerning them," Frontenac replied. Suddenly the two men heard a thud and turned around. A boy who was helping unload supplies had tripped on an uneven plank on the dock. "You stupid bastard!" Frontenac growled.

He walked over to the boy and raised his hand. The boy cringed as the governor brought it down, back-handing the boy across the head. He struck the boy three more times, cursing and threatening him until the boy had picked himself up, collected the bag of supplies, and rushed off.

Callières felt uneasy about the abuse done to the boy. "Well that was done …"

"Do not dare question my means to which I accomplish the King's directive!" snapped Frontenac. "If it were not required to lead New France by brute will, the King would surely have sent a weaker man as Governor."

Callières' eyes fell to the earth. He knew Frontenac was right. Even so, doubts crept into his mind that he had made a mistake in recommending Frontenac return to command the expedition, without first meeting the man face to face.

"Nevertheless, I am here now, and I would like to discuss the plans after I am settled into my quarters. I thank you for your welcoming and look forward to your visit in say…one week?"

Callières nodded in agreement. Without another word, Frontenac walked off towards his new office, trailed by a column of men with his personal effects. Callières looked across the river to the south and sighed. He knew Frontenac would unleash a trail of blood throughout the territories of fur traders and farmers. *At last*, he thought, *France will meet the English on the field of battle in the New World.* Looking south, it was as if he could see straight through to the colonists of New York.

"God help them," he whispered.

The next time Callières and Frontenac met, there were little formalities to be had. Frontenac had maps strewn all over his office, showing lines of advance into the New York, Massachusetts, and New Hampshire colonies. Callières was taken aback by the plans on the maps. He noted immediately the change Frontenac had laid out, and studied it carefully. The governor general barely even looked up. Callières had seen enough. "Monsieur?"

"What is it?"

"I'm afraid I'm a bit lost on your plan here." Frontenac shook his head in disgust and Callières felt a little sheepish, questioning the plan. "I don't see a plan to take the harbor or city of New York, only the town of Fort Orange and other smaller villages. Has the King abandoned the plans?"

"No – I did!" Frontenac announced. "Your plans were inadequate and stupid."

"I beg your pardon!"

Frontenac stepped up to Callières, looking

down upon the Montreal governor. Frontenac collected his words. "If we gather all the men of New France and put them in arms, which alone we cannot accomplish, and we gather all our savage allies which we also cannot do in the time available, we still would find it costly to take the harbor and city of New York. You have fought wars before and should know the numbers are greatly at our disadvantage."

Callières nodded. The governor general had a point. The English colony was particularly strong at the harbor and the French forces in Canada were insufficient to capture it indefinitely. "What is the new plan, monsieur?"

"We avenge Lachine." Even as the words left Frontenac's lips Callières knew what that meant. "Our women and children were dragged out of their beds and butchered. Their women and children must also be dragged from their beds and put to the sword. We have enough Canadian militiamen and savage allies to raid up and down the New England settlements. We will strike a fear in them that will force them to the protection of the coastal forts. This will break their trading agreements with the Iroquois and we can arrange new trade agreements, all while occupying the northern areas of the New York colony."

Callières grinned slightly. He had little in the way of respect for the pompous French aristocrat, but the plan had a certain appeal to it. Callières remembered only too well the brutality of the Indian fights, and the fate of Lachine at the hands of the Mohawk. "Will you be leading the expedition?"

Frontenac looked insulted. "I have to attend to the colony. I leave the details to you." Frontenac crossed the room to his bed. "Don't forget to take the maps on the way out."

Callières was dumbfounded. *That's it?* He

thought to himself. Frontenac had already removed his boots and was lying down.

"Do you wish to discuss it further?" Callières asked, and when he received nothing but silence, he added, "Have a good night, sir."

He collected the documents and maps, and quietly headed for the door.

"Governor Callières," Frontenac called out from the bed. "Who will you pick to lead the expedition to Fort Orange?"

I haven't even begun to plan it out, Callières raged in his mind. He could only feel resentment and apathy for the lazy governor general. *It's a miracle the entire province of Canada didn't collapse under your rule, you fat, crude bastard.* But Callières knew he had to give an answer. Suddenly he had a moment of enlightenment. "I think I have just the men for the job, monsieur. I will let you know within the week."

"Very well," Frontenac said, yawning. He waved his hand, as if brushing Callières out the door.

Under the burning oil of a lamp, Callières got to work. He studied the rivers, mountains, settlements, and trails of the New York and New England colonies. He had only a limited time to prepare a complex campaign against the English. He paused for a moment and looked out the window.

Outside, the night sky was a little brighter as the moonlight reflected off the falling snow. Callières sighed. *Yet one more complication.* He went over the timeline in his mind many times. There would be no possible way to avoid the raiding expeditions taking place in the dead of winter, which would put extreme pressure on the militiamen and natives assembled for the raiding parties. They would have to carry everything they needed from Montreal, to their objectives in the south, and back.

Callières planned on the expeditions leaving in mid-January. By then, the snow would be deep, the temperature below freezing, and all the rivers frozen over.

The mind of a soldier in Callières began to spin. He concocted plans to use the winter to his advantage – something he believed the Canadian militia would do well against the English to the south. From gear to food, weapons to transport, the governor went to work on transforming Frontenac's raiding plan into cold, hard reality.

* * *

Jacques Le Moyne de Sainte-Hélène walked through the streets of Quebec, holding his horse's reigns in his hand, and smiling at the women he passed. Though a married man, at only thirty years of age, he was a strikingly handsome figure and few women failed to blush when he passed.

He was dressed in rough knee-high boots, pants of deer hide, and a gray woolen overcoat. His attire was typical of the coureurs de bois – the Canadian woodsman, skilled at trading, trapping, the outdoors, and battle. Only his clean-shaven face and short-trimmed hair made him stand out from the others.

As he walked, he marveled at the growth of the town. Though he had made the same journey just a few months prior, it seemed as though every time he returned, a new home was being built, a new family moving to the area, or a shop being opened for business.

He tied up his horse in front of a tavern and went inside. Sainte-Hélène was met with praise and cheers.

"Safe return for a hero!" someone shouted as a few men raised their cups.

"God bless the Le Moyne brothers," another cheered.

Sainte-Hélène smiled and embraced old friends. He welcomed the praise and carried his head high. His brother, Pierre Le Moyne d'Iberville, walked in moments later and was met with equal praise.

The Le Moyne Brothers were well-known in the colony. Charles le Moyne de Longueuil et de Châteauguay was a man of many talents. He was a soldier, a trader, an interpreter, and apparently, a man with a talent for fathering sons; eleven to be exact.

Although Charles had passed away several years earlier, his sons were rapidly garnering a reputation for being patriotic Canadians who emboldened the spirit of exploration and embraced the dangers of unconventional warfare.

With Sainte-Hélène and d'Iberville back, there was new reason for celebration. D'Iberville grasped his brother's shoulder and set a foot on a wooden chair. "My brother Jacques finished a journey from Quebec to Hudson Bay in less than forty days. We have brought back over three-hundred fresh pelts for the Paris markets and opened new lines of trade with the savages to the north."

There was a roar from the men of the tavern. D'Iberville continued, "May Canada and her native country prosper forever!"

From the corner, an elderly man stood up. Sainte-Hélène and d'Iberville turned their attention to the man as he spoke. "We can only pray that the almighty be with us during these perilous times."

Sainte-Hélène took a step forward. "What peril do you speak of, sir?"

The man's voice trembled. "My wife and children were slain by the savages of the south. The Iroquois laid waste to the provinces around Montreal."

The Le Moyne brothers eyed each other.

"Surely, you are mistaken," d'Iberville responded.

Tears rolled down the man's cheek. "I held my son's body in my hands. Had I not left so early for Montreal, I too would have been murdered by the savages."

Sainte-Hélène could hardly believe it. "I grieve for your losses, sir, and I promise you, you will find the justice you seek." With that he turned to his brother. "I must go to my wife and make sure she is safe."

Sainte-Hélène rode hard for two days before arriving in Montreal. Though Quebec seemed to be prospering, the town he called home appeared as though under siege. The walls were manned by armed soldiers and clusters of militia and Indian allies patrolled the forests nearby.

Inside the town itself, Sainte-Hélène was horrified to find masses of refugees from the outlying farms and territories huddled near fires and under makeshift shelters. Those men not on guard duty were busy building new houses for those whose homes and farms were burnt during the summer raids.

Riding up the road, he grew anxious to see his wife and children. He barely finished securing his mount before bursting through the door. The cold air swept in and he heard a tiny voice call out, "Close the door."

Just as he looked down, his son saw who it was and leapt up into his arms. "I missed you, Papa."

"I missed you too," Sainte-Hélène said, giving him a kiss on the forehead, and setting him down. "Where is your mother?"

"Upstairs, Papa. Would you like porridge?"

"I could eat a whole pot right now," he replied before rushing up the stairs. He opened the bedroom door and inside, a very young woman sat motionless in a chair, knitting a scarf.

"You're back?" she asked meekly.

Jacques did not reply. He simply walked over and knelt next to her. He removed her cap and gently brushed his hand through her dirty blonde hair and down her soft cheek. Through the long months in the wilderness, he often forgot the beautiful wife he left at home.

Though not a *filles du roi* – or King's Daughter, Jeanne Defresnoy Carion was a young bride by any standards. Married to Jacques at the age of twelve, she was told from the outset her purpose was to bear children for the thriving colony and be a faithful wife to her husband.

At seventeen years old, Jeanne had grown into a strong, yet somber young mother. Jacques rarely stayed at home. For all his faults, she could not fault him for cowardice. He was always volunteering for extra hazardous duties when others would sheepishly dodge them. His assignments had carried him to the very boundaries of the Canadian colony and beyond.

With her husband gone, Jeanne was left to raise their three children almost exclusively by herself. Her days were spent in back-breaking labor, cleaning the house, gardening, and feeding her children. By night, she read them stories until they slept, before she herself collapsed on the bed, exhausted, only to do it all again the next day. Winter gave some respite from the gardening and allowed her more time with the children.

"Will you be going again soon?" she asked her husband.

Jacques wrapped his arm around her. "I don't know. The enemy is upon us."

Her eyes dropped to the floor.

"Is it me?" she asked in her quiet voice. "Do you not love me? Is that why you will not stay?"

Jacques could not conceal his own shame. "I love our children," he said, side-stepping the question. "As their mother, and my wife, I will take every step to ensure you are safe."

He knew that was not the answer she wanted to hear, but it was the only one he could faithfully give her.

She sighed and stood up. She began disrobing and stared at the bed, sorrowfully. "I know my duties as a wife."

Jacques slowly stood and closed the bedroom door. Though never around to show his young wife the love and affection he knew he should, Jacques never hesitated to enjoy the pleasures of being a husband. He took off his shirt and took her into his arms.

Chapter 21

Jacob Leisler stood on the parapets of the newly renamed Fort William in New York City, looking out upon the Atlantic Ocean. The autumn breeze chilled him to his bones and he gripped his great fur coat tightly around him. For a moment, he thought back to simpler times when he was a simple merchant and naval officer, sailing across the world.

He closed his eyes.

His mind brought him to the hot and humid waters of the Mediterranean, off the coast of Morocco. The year was 1678. The blinding sun scorched the bodies of the sailors. The wind had died down and spilt from the sails, bringing the vessel to a near stop. In the space of two hours the Moorish pirates had found them and swarmed the merchant ship with two dozen men. Some of the crew were ran through with scimitars and spears, or simply pushed overboard. Others suffered a different fate.

Leisler gripped his wrists where he and three others had been bound by rope following their capture. They went on to spend nearly a year in captivity along the Tunisian coast, while the pirates waited for an answer to their demand for ransom. During those dark days, he had but one goal – to survive. He grimaced at the thoughts of what he had done to ensure he stayed alive.

Finally, one day, he was brought outside the Moroccan jail. He was sure it was the end, but to Leisler's surprise he was escorted to a Dutch West India Company ship. He fell upon the deck in tears, thankful to have made it. He was shocked to have learned his ransom was paid by none other than

Edmund Andros – the very man who threw him in jail three years prior. Apparently, to Andros, the capture of a prominent and popular—not to mention wealthy—merchant was something not to be tolerated.

Leisler's mind returned to the cold Atlantic air blowing in his face. He wondered for a moment if Andros had regretted his decision to pay Leisler's ransom. *Simpler times*, he thought.

Jacob Milborne ascended the steps and walked over to him. Leisler looked over. "What's the word?"

Milborne handed Leisler a letter. "The Convention stands firm. Albany will not capitulate."

Leisler crumpled the letter in his hand. "Those insolent bastards have no right to oppress the commoners of Albany and Schenectady." He cursed them and threw the letter down on the stone battlement. "We have no choice," he said with a deep anger in his voice. "They have forsaken any peaceful resolution by their refusal to recognize the people's government."

Milborne straightened up. "I agree," he said. "What shall we do?"

Leisler thought for a moment. "How many men do you think it would take to storm Fort Albany with no warning?"

"If we were over the walls before they were ready, no more than forty, I would guess."

"I'll give you fifty," Leisler said. "You take fifty men and you sail up the Hudson River. We have many who are sympathetic to our cause within the city walls, even the Albany militia itself. Once you're over the wall, they'll surrender. They'll *have* to surrender."

Milborne grinned. "They won't have a chance."

Leisler continued, "Once they surrender, the people of Schenectady will follow, and then Ulster.

They've been a thorn in my side for too long. Arrest Schuyler, Livingston, and every other papist aristocrat you find. Then send word to me when it's done." Leisler paused, as if reflecting on his own plan. "If the fort falls, the city falls."

"Just like here," Milborne noted.

"Precisely! But if they force a battle, then let them bleed. I *want* that city," Leisler growled. "You hear me? I want it."

"When do I leave?"

"Today," Leisler replied instantly. "Gather your men, provisions, the boats, ladders to storm the wall if necessary, and then get moving. The sooner we seize Albany the better."

"I'll get ready," Milborne said as he prepared to leave.

Leisler held up his hand. Milborne stopped. Leisler looked back out to sea.

"I was just thinking about my capture by the Moors," Leisler said. "And as hard as my time in captivity was, I must admit it was easy; if not preferred to all this. Politics sickens me, Jacob. If it was up to me I'd march two hundred men straight to Albany and destroy every bastion of resistance. My will alone would be enough to carry any battle, but maybe we can do this without too much bloodshed." He glanced at Milborne who remained silent, listening. Leisler shook his head. "Just reminiscing," he said, sighing. He held out his hand. "Good luck, my brother."

Milborne shook it and headed off. Leisler faced back to the ocean. A gust of wind blew against his face that almost felt warm and for a moment he imagined it having traveled all the way across the ocean, from that hot shore off the African coast. He sniffed, returned to his stern demeanor, and headed back to the City Hall.

* * *

It was mid-day when Jacques Le Moyne de Sainte-Hélène arrived at Callières' residence in Montreal. He galloped in on his horse, his grayish-blue Lieutenant's uniform catching the attention of those he passed. Though the Governor's house was modest compared to the government quarters in Quebec, it still stood out as the largest building in all the town.

Outside of the governor's place, standing on the porch was another man. This man was dressed in the attire of the coureur de bois - the Canadian woodsmen and fur traders. He had a strong body and stiff face, emotionless. Jacques dismounted and tied up his horse, staring up occasionally at the man on the porch.

"You must be Sainte-Hélène?" the man on the porch said aloud.

"I am, sir," Jacques said with a grin as he ascended the steps. "My reputation precedes me." Jacques glanced over the man's attire. "And who are you?"

"I am Lieutenant Nicolas d'Ailleboust de Manthet," the man said, bowing slightly.

"You're a soldier?" Sainte-Hélène said surprised. "I am sorry, without a uniform, it is difficult to notice."

Manthet smirked, trying not to dig too deep into the insult. "The governor insisted I wait for your arrival before he receives us. Thank you for not taking too long in getting here." Manthet opened the door and motioned for Sainte-Hélène to follow him inside.

Upon stepping foot into the governor's parlor, Sainte-Hélène he felt a rush of warm air originating from the stone fireplace. The parlor was bright with ambient light shining through the windows. It was modestly decorated with red carpet and delicate furniture and dishes. A servant offered the two men cups of red wine. Jacques downed his serving in one swift gulp. He failed to notice the disdain on Manthet's face at his apparent breach of hospitality.

"I'll refill your glass, monsieur," the servant said, taking the glass away. The two men stood in silence for a moment before they heard a door opening. Callières stepped out from his bedroom, a warm smile crossing his face.

"Welcome to Montreal, gentlemen. I am Louis-Hector de Callières, governor of Montreal."

Sainte-Hélène and Manthet snapped to attention and bowed before snapping back to attention. Callières approached the two officers. He looked over each man carefully, nodding as if approving of his own choices.

"I'm sure you're wondering why I summoned you here. Follow me." Callières led the men over to a large table with maps and charts. "The governor general, on orders of the King, has instructed me to take the war directly to the English frontier settlements. We will attack on three fronts, striking deep into English territory. You two are among our finest military leaders. You will lead the main thrust against the town of Orange in the New York colony."

Manthet looked at the map, eyeing the vast distance between Montreal and Orange. "Monsieur, I didn't know we had that many troops in New France for such an invasion."

Callières sighed. "We don't, lieutenant. We are expecting one-to-two hundred troops, mostly militia, and an additional hundred or so from our Indian allies."

Jacques was shocked. "Is this a joke?"

Callières glared at him.

"No, it is not a joke, and you will not use that tone with me. I don't give a damn about your family name. I will have you punished for insubordination."

Manthet stepped in. "Monsieur, I'm sure Jacques meant no disrespect, but please, three-hundred men cannot capture Albany – or six-hundred for that matter. We would need a thousand or more."

"I will leave the decision to attack Fort Orange to you two when the time comes," Callières replied. "But this is not an occupation. It's a raiding party." Callières pointed to the map. "Three prongs, each independent of the other two will strike deep into the English colonies. Now, do not concern yourself about the other two columns. You two – you will be leading the main attack against Orange. Get in, lay waste the town, kill the inhabitants, take prisoners at your discretion, and make your way back to Montreal."

Manthet eyed the map. "That is quite a distance to march such a small force, Monsieur. Surely the Mohawk will find us."

"Wait!" Jacques blurted out. "That's our advantage – our size."

"Precisely," Callières said. "You will likely go unnoticed through the mountains and the rivers are frozen, so you won't need boats. They won't be expecting anything until spring."

Manthet exhaled deeply. "Monsieur, not to be overly-prudent, but if we have prisoners, the Mohawk will catch up to us before we reach Montreal." Callières rested his hands on the map table, a look of annoyance crossing his face. "I'm sorry Monsieur, but it is the truth."

"Are you afraid of a little battle?" Jacques asked. Manthet turned and the two lieutenants stood facing each other, a mental battle of dominance ensuing.

"I fear no enemy," Manthet boldly stated. "But I learned the hard way, how the Iroquois savages fight, and never to underestimate their ability to wage war. I lost many men to the Seneca because of that error."

"Well then," Jacques began, pointing to Manthet's heavy coat, "perhaps you should have taken your soldierly studies more seriously."

"*How dare you!*" Manthet shouted, resisting every urge in his muscles to strike the arrogant, young man before him. But even he knew that only trouble would come from attacking a Le Moyne brother.

"*Enough!*" Callières yelled. "I will not have you two at each other's throats for the duration of this expedition." He looked to Jacques. "Do you want to avenge Lachine?"

"Of course," growled Jacques through his teeth. Callières eyed Manthet.

"Do you want to avenge Lachine?"

"Yes, Monsieur," he said, breathing deeply, calming himself.

Callières straightened up. "You will be in charge," he said pointing to Manthet. Jacques stepped forward, opening his mouth to protest but Callières held up his hand, silencing him. "However, you will cooperate with Jacques on all matters regarding the expedition. Final authority will rest with you, but you will take his counsel first on every instance. Is that clear?"

Manthet nodded. Callières glanced at Jacques who also agreed.

"Now, we do have another who will be leading. His name is Athasata and he is a leader of the Caughnawaga."

"Caughnawaga are Mohawk," Jacques said. "How can we trust him?"

"Mohawks who converted to Catholicism," Callières countered. "He will lead the entire native contingent, but he will report to you two and you will make sure he does so." Callières paced around the table. "There is one key decision you must make."

"What's that?" Manthet asked.

Callières pointed to the small village west of Fort Orange. "If the defenses of Orange are too strong, the garrison too well defended, you may divert the attack to this village – Corlear." The three men closed in around the table, looking at the map.

"What are the defenses here?" Manthet asked, looking at the map.

"A stockade, a blockhouse on the northwest corner, maybe a few dozen soldiers or militia, a few Mohawk allies. A much smaller force than any that would be at Orange."

"We can take Orange," Jacques boasted, resting his hand over the town.

Callières sighed. "I hope so, but do not risk a pitched battle. That is the last thing you want. If you can get over their defenses before they are ready, then make it happen. But a pitched street battle will hamper you down, the relief forces will cut you off, and the entire expedition will be annihilated."

Manthet nodded. "I agree, monsieur. Orange is a bigger prize, but the risk is much greater." Jacques seemed disappointed but out of respect, chose not to discuss it further. "Nevertheless," Manthet continued, "we will be triumphant in seizing Orange and making that place as inhabitable as Lachine."

"We will plan out the details of the offensive in the coming weeks," Callières said to his officers. "Every detail, down to the men's provisions and arms, will be decided before departure. History will reward our professionalism, and the English will know our cruelty." Jacques grinned at the last part. "At stake," Callières added, "is the future of New France. God willing, we will prevail."

Chapter 22

November 5, 1689

The harvest was in for the year. Johannes Vedder stood with his father in the pantry, recounting the food stock. Harmen silently made notes in his book, as Johannes read off the amount of wheat and grain, beans, corn, and dried meats. After finishing the count, Johannes looked at his father. There was worry in his eyes as checked and rechecked the figures.

"You kids are growing up so fast," he muttered, almost to himself.

"Is everything all right, Father?"

Harmen glanced up. Seeing the concern in his son's look, he slapped the book shut and straightened up with a slight smile. "It's fine. It'll just be a little lean before the spring harvest." Not trusting himself to say more, he turned and left.

Johannes thought about the look his father gave him. He never smiled. He looked back to the pantry. Maybe it was him growing taller, but it did seem less than last year. How much less, he could not tell.

When Johannes returned, Harmen was speaking to Anna, whispering quietly, as to not disturb the house. But one glance at her face, and Johannes could tell the news was not good. He took a deep breath and went outside, trying not to think of the food problem. The snow had yet to fall and the air was calm and almost warm. Perhaps it would be a mild winter and the spring harvest would come early. Perhaps their weak food storage would be enough to shield them through the cold months.

Of course, the main concern of every household was the harvest. Would it be enough? Would it hold the family through the winter? In every house, pantries were scrutinized, and calculations were made. It was critical to make an honest count. As the winter months waned and spring was just around the corner, the food stocks would shrink to depressing levels. It was not uncommon for families to run out and be forced to beg for food from others, many of whom were hesitant to share what little they had left.

Johannes had to shake his head free of the worry. The day, after all, was a day of celebration.

Additional supplies were reserved for special days. The traditionally-accepted end of harvest, meant a great feast, thanks, and well-wishes for the coming winter. The politics of the day, the Leislerites and Convention, even the war against France, were all put aside for one day. Thus, allowing families to gather together and celebrate.

As Johannes looked at the effigy which was to be burned later, he could only think that it was strange that the night's celebrations would be far different in tone than the day's feasts.

All around the village, preparations were underway for the night's festivities. At the center of town, men were busy building a great effigy and surrounding it with logs. Smoke rose from every home; the smell of cooking hams and turkeys and bread filled the air. Some of the children played outside, working up an appetite for the feast to come. The men did the same, engaging in more than the usual manual labor.

Working parties of volunteers were set to repairing a section of the west palisade. Heavy rain had caused the ground to give way and collapse a ten-foot section of wall. Other men led by the Reverend Peter Tassemaker, had set about making repairs to the church roof. Tassemaker gave Johannes a friendly wave as he passed by.

Anna had set the table exactly the way she wanted it. She blew out the candles, not needing them as the late-morning sunlight poured in through the windows, illuminating the table in a beam of light that presented the food in an almost heavenly manner. The turkey lay at the center; its dark brown skin glowing. A basket of neatly sliced, warm bread, lay beside it. Corn, cranberries, raspberries, nuts, and cake all lay mixed in with the plates.

Anna hung up the apron and looked over her masterpiece, flushed with satisfaction. It was one of the days she cherished the most, looking forward to the feast and more importantly, the chance to sit and enjoy the meal with her family.

"It smells delicious," Angie said as she entered the room.

"Did you wash your hands?" her mother asked.

"Not yet."

"Then go wash, child. And call your brothers and father. Hurry before this food gets cold."

Angie rushed off to spread the word. Anna watched as her daughter disappeared, and a thought occurred to her. *This may be the last time she's with us. This time next year she could be married and providing the harvest meal for her husband and maybe even a newborn child.* A tear streamed down her cheek as she clenched a towel, admitting to herself that Angie was not ready yet.

Suddenly an almost strange voice spoke from behind. "Is there room for one more?"

Anna turned and her heart warmed.

"My dear," she said, opening her arms. "How I missed you."

Samuel Vedder embraced her, his huge arms wrapping all the way around her body. *Harmen was right,* she thought. He was so much bigger than she remembered him last.

"When did you get here?"

"Just now," he said in his deep voice. "I apologize for my appearance, but there was little time to clean up." He motioned to his dirty jacket and trousers, and his grubby face. "I've been busy with many, many things. I will tell you all about them when we eat."

She smiled. "Well clean yourself up, take off that dusty rag of a coat, and pull up an extra chair from near the hearth." Looking at him, she sighed. "It's so good to see you again. I have one more thing to be thankful of today."

The table was soon filled as the family piled into the room; creating a lively, active atmosphere. Harmen made sure everyone was seated, and then stood up with a cup of ale.

"My boy, rise." Samuel grabbed his cup and stood up. To Johannes' surprise, Samuel was not much bigger than his father, perhaps only by an inch or two, and slightly more muscular. Nobody could mistake the blood relation. "Welcome home, Son." Harmen rested his hand on Samuel's shoulder. "We're all very proud of the man you've become."

"Thank you, Father – and Mother," he said with a motion to Anna. "My work has occupied much of my time. You haven't heard from me because I have been in New York City."

There was excitement at the table. Angie leaned forward. "How big is it? Is it grand?"

"Little sister, it is eye-opening," he said. "The piers are even now loaded with merchant ships and every street corner there is someone selling and two more buying."

Johannes smiled. *Now that sounds like a place to*

carve out your future, he thought to himself.

Samuel continued, "They have a wall running across the entire peninsula, separating the city from the north."

Harmen took a gulp from his cup and smacked it down on the table, sending drops into the air. "My boy," he said with a smile, "if you think New York is amazing, you must travel to the home country. Amsterdam is twenty times as grand."

"I hope to travel there one day, Father," Samuel said. "It would be an excellent business opportunity."

"I want to go too," Angie said, smiling. "I want to see all the clothing the women wear, and dress like them."

Anna set her napkin aside.

"There's nothing wrong with how we dress here, darling." She spoke softly, not wanting to raise any tension or animosity at the table. "But it would be nice to visit, I suppose."

Johannes listened with fascination as his father and brother spoke of their travels. He ached to leave on his own. Thinking of the amazing possibilities that crossing to Europe or exploring the Americas would unleash, his mind raced with ideas. He just had to establish plans on timing and how to raise capital for his journeys.

As the last family members finished their plates, Albert stood up from the table. "Getting together as a family is always special. But on this very special day, I think it's about time to take a nap, so I'm rested for this evening."

Harmen was not amused. "You will all do your chores before leaving this house. Is that understood?" His children all nodded in obedience. "As for you," he said pointing his spoon at Samuel, "you must tell me more about your business dealings. I'm eager to know more about who you're working with in Albany. It's a rat's nest after all. You can never be too cautious."

"What's so special about tonight?" Arent asked innocently.

Albert rested his hand on Arent's shoulder. "Tonight – tonight is Gunpowder Night."

* * *

The camp's fires were lit at sunset. Jacob Milborne walked along the shore making sure the boats were secured on land. All about him, men moved around, setting about their gear. Some were posted on sentry duty, keeping a watch for threats. With their back to the river, any surprise attack could prove fatally decisive.

Other men, however, were making the most of a short reprieve, to catch some sleep.

He felt alone, even amongst his men. In New York City, he had Leisler and others to turn to for direction. But on the expedition, he was in sole command and he hated that it scared him. Milborne watched his men, knowing their lives were in his hands. Doubt crept over decisiveness. Would he waiver?

No, not while Leisler depended on him.

He swept the thought aside and looked out to the river. The sound of the rushing waters in the dark filled his ears. He ran through his mind. Another four days until he could sleep inside a cozy bed in Albany. The thought offered him a brief comfort.

* * *

If the day's harvest feasts were serene and

orderly, the night's celebrations were anything but that.

On November 5, 1605, an English Catholic – Guy Fawkes, tried to blow up the House of Lords, in London. He failed in his mission, and the Protestants started celebrating the date of his failure.

The celebrations were largely discouraged or outright forbidden for years, under the rule of the Catholic monarch, King James.

For the first time in years, the people living under the crown gave joy without fear of retribution. The bonfires lit up the village center like midday. Kegs were tapped. The violin and fiddle players played their music for all to hear. Effigies of Gunpower Plot conspirators were burned at the stake or in the fires around town. The village of Schenectady celebrated Guy Fawkes night.

Johannes was elated when he found out that Jean Vandervort and his daughter arrived that evening. He wandered through the dense crowds, straining his neck to see over the masses. Amidst the cheering and fireworks and gunfire, he felt a hand grab hold of his arm. He turned and was met by a beautiful figure he recognized instantly.

"Thought I wouldn't find you," he admitted.

"Shhh!" she said, taking him by the arm, leading him away from the celebration. They rounded a corner and hidden from the crowds, kissed and held each other tightly.

"I love you so much, Maria," Johannes said grinning. Maria laughed.

"You are madly in love with me, aren't you?"

"I am so in love with you," he admitted, grabbing her tightly by the waist, and pressing her chest against his. "I want to spend every day and every night with you."

"Then do it," she whispered. His eyes

widened. Maria nodded and smiled. "My father is here, tonight. Ask for my hand. I think he will say yes."

Johannes could scarcely believe her words. "Are you sure?"

"Do it!" she insisted. "Tonight. Please, Johannes. I do not want to be married to another man. I want you."

He pressed his lips against hers. "I will ask him," he said, parting. "I will ask him right now. Where is he?"

She laughed. "Somewhere out in that mess of people."

Gathered around a group of men, both Leislerites, and those of the Convention, Harmen listened inventively to the dialogue. Douw Aukes raised his glass. "Here's to overthrowing tyrants, be they in the citadels of England or the mansions of New York City."

"Hear, hear," said a few of the Leislerites.

The few men who opposed Jacob Leisler merely ignored the bravado and continued to sip on their ale.

"Come join us, father," Aukes said, as Reverend Peter Tassemaker joined the assembly. "What do you think of Guy Fakes Night?"

"I despise it," Tassemaker responded.

There was a murmur among those gathered.

"You, sir?" Aukes said. "How can you disapprove it?"

"It's quite simple really," Tassemaker said. "The Gunpowder Plot was attempted murder. God has many paths, not all of them clear, but one rule was made clear in my opinion. And that rule was 'love thy neighbor as thyself.' I think the plotters forgot that part of God's will.

"They started it, Reverend," Aukes said. "They could have…"

"Could have what?" asked the priest. "You forget that we are all Christians of this new land. Dutch, English, and yes, the French also. Even some of the Wilden have been Christianized. And yet, we kill each other like we are barbarians. Canada has suffered greatly this summer, at the hands of our ally – the Mohawk."

Tassemaker took a long drink from his cup, emptying his beer. "Not many of you remember King Philip's War. I was just a boy, but I remember it. And it was terrifying. Every month, another village was butchered. Every month, more Christians were scalped, and shot, and burned alive by rival factions. I would call it hell, yet that cannot be the word for it. For hell is filled only with the condemned souls, and not the innocent. No, war is something else entirely. A monstrous entity with a mind of its own, that consumes all it touches."

"That was a long time ago," Aukes said. "Nearly twenty years ago."

"You are right," the Reverend conceded. "That war was English colonists versus native tribes. Never, have we directly confronted our mortal enemy – France, on the holy grounds of this new world," he paused, "until now. There will be a reckoning, and my heart weeps for the day it comes."

Johannes and Maria searched the crowd for her father for an hour, only to find him at Van Slyke's tavern, turned over on a table, a puddle of his own making on the floor aside him.

"I guess you won't be asking tonight," Maria said. "I've never seen him passed out drunk before."

"According to my father, it was common a

long time ago. There were taverns that had late-night tappings, tappings on Sundays, dancing, brawling. Then the government cracked down on it for a while."

"You always know so much useless knowledge," Maria laughed.

Johannes shrugged. "I suppose so," he said. "I know the owner; he'll take care of him. You can pick him up in the morning."

"Where will I stay tonight?"

Johannes thought for a moment. "My house. I will introduce you to my mother. My father would have you sleep in my sister's room. He is very strict on that sort of thing."

"What a shame," she whispered, a sly grin flashing across her face. Johannes licked his lips and stared deeply into her eyes, longing to be alone with her for the night.

"Someday soon, I hope," he replied quietly.

They strolled down the street in relative isolation, with most of the celebrations having dissipated into the taverns and homes. Reaching his house, Johannes embraced Maria, and in the darkness, they kissed each other passionately.

As they broke apart, Maria shook her head. "My family has friends who live here, a family. I think I will stay with them tonight."

Before Johannes could change her mind, she kissed him on the cheek, turned and rushed off, leaving him alone outside. He suspected the prospect of meeting his family was too much. A smirk crossed his lips; knowing that he found one thing that she was hesitant about doing. He took one last look at the fading figure who he was so in love with, before heading inside for the night.

Chapter 23

The first boat was spotted on the river just after sunrise. It emerged from the foggy mist as a dark shadow, its gray sail fluttering in the wind. It was followed by another and another, until the small armada of sloops came into full view of Fort Albany. They sailed up the river, the oarsmen mustering all their strength to move the boats along with the greatest possible speed.

A guard atop the stockade wall of the fort was the first to spot the ghostly fleet. He looked down below where his sergeant was quietly conferring with a civilian doctor about the pain in his shoulder. "Sergeant, we have boats on the river."

Sergeant Charles Rodgers looked up. "And?"

"There are men on them, sir. A lot of men."

Rodgers waved off the doctor. "I won't hold you up. I'll seek you out if it gets worse."

The doctor acknowledged and left.

Rodgers climbed up the nearest ladder and walked the defenses until he reached the soldier's post. By now the four boats were clearly visible on the water. Rodgers studied them for a moment before his eyes widened. Though new to the militia, he had a keen sense about him.

"Leisler," he growled. "Sound the alarm. All men to arms; stand at the ready, gentlemen."

The soldier turned and gathered spit in his throat before shouting at the top of his lungs. "Stand to, stand to."

The word spread and in short order, the bell rung from the Dutch Reformed Church steeple. Rodgers leaned on the stockade, watching the boats with interest.

Pieter Schuyler was eating a bowl of porridge, reading through administrative documents when the bell sounded in the distance. Just then a soldier rushed inside the office. "Leisler's men are sailing up the river, sir. I believe they mean to land at the docks."

Pieter Schuyler rushed out from his quarters in the fort and to the east wall, climbing up the ladder to the soldier on guard.

Four boats moved rapidly along the water, the dark shapes of the men aboard scurrying about. As the fog parted in the sunlight, Schuyler could only watch as his small detachment of men on the Albany docks fell back to within the walls of the city.

"We lost the docks," he declared. But even as he spoke he watched in amazement as the four boats sailed right past the docks leading to the city. "What are they doing?"

Jacob Milborne stood at the helm of the lead boat. Behind him, his men readied themselves for the coming battle. They checked the flints of their muskets, made sure their powder was accessible, and their knives were handy. Laying between the oarsmen was a sturdy wooden ladder.

Milborne eyed the docks without care. *They'll be ours soon enough*, he thought to himself. He looked ahead to the shoreline up ahead. *The closest landing point to the fort.* He straightened his stance and turned to his men.

"Head for that spot of flat land," he said pointing. "And prepare to attack!"

About the same time Milborne was readying his force, Pieter Schuyler saw what was happening. "Get the garrison in the city and bring them here. I want every man who can bear arms."

"Where, sir?" the guard asked.

"Here!" Schuyler cried out. "They're not going to take the city. Don't you see? They're going to storm the fort. Go!" The guard rushed off, calling others to man the walls. Schuyler watched the boats approach.

Jacob Milborne called out to his men. "Here we go, lads."

The four boats lined up and headed directly to the shoreline. Milborne checked his own pistol. He stuffed it into his belt and drew his sword. The oarsmen grunted and rowed harder, picking up speed. Those men not rowing, faced forward, crouching down with their muskets at the ready.

Fifty feet, thirty feet, ten feet – the men braced. There was a shaking as the boats touched earth.

"Now!" Milborne yelled.

The men stammered over the sides of the boats, grabbing the ladder and hauling it ashore. The other boats touched down and the men grabbed each of their ladders and the whole contingent assembled on the shoreline, spreading out parallel to the walls of Fort Albany.

"Where's my troops?" Schuyler shouted. Only a handful of men stood at the wall. It did not take Schuyler long to figure out that they were outnumbered three-to-one. "Are those ladders?"

"I believe they are," Rodgers said, rushing over. "Sir, if they attack now, we won't hold the fort."

Schuyler turned around. Men of the militia were arriving in small clusters. "We don't need long to bring in the men. Fifteen minutes at most."

"With respect, sir," the sergeant began, "they can reach these walls in one."

A minute passed, then another. Schuyler grew restless, constantly checking between the arrival of more men, and the threatening force that stood to attack the fort.

"I count fifty men at arms," Rodgers said to the mayor. "We have half that. Most of my men are out on other duties."

Schuyler folded his arms and looked out from the parapets. "If it comes to battle, can we hold them or not?"

Rodgers looked about, making come calculations in his head. Schuyler, not hearing a reply, glanced over. "Well?"

"I cannot say," Rodgers admitted. "I think we can hold them. But that's if they have not infiltrated the city and gathered support inside. If they have …"

"We hold the fort," Schuyler replied. "No matter the cost, no matter their terms of negotiation, we hold the fort. Get word to my brother. He has a number of men in his company."

Rodgers straightened up slightly. "Yes, sir," he said with pride.

Having forsaken peace, Schuyler now set his mind on the reality of winning the coming battle. He moved about the parapet swiftly, checking the readiness of each man on the wall. By himself, he pondered what was about to happen. Would these be the first shots in a civil war that would see the colony torn apart? His conscious tugged at him. When he set Albany on its course several months prior, never would he have imagined it would escalate to such calamities as open, armed conflict. He rested against the defenses. The knowledge that the lives which would soon be lost on both sides, were partly because of his actions, weighed heavily on him.

Jacob Milborne grinned as he received the report he was awaiting.

"Several of the townsmen have assembled inside the city," the scout reported. "Mostly lower class farmers and immigrants who favor Leisler's rule. They will secure the main roads in Albany, then attack the fort from the south, as we attack it from the east."

"Then our preparations are ready!" Milborne replied, his words carrying out to the other militia leaders nearby. "Gentlemen, today is the day we unite New York and bring the failed so-called Albany Convention to its knees. Once again, we will be united for king and country – under the leadership of the commander, Jacob Leisler."

Milborne beamed with pride as he watched the reaction on the men's faces. They were hungry for a fight, and a fight is exactly what he would give them. "Men," he called out, "today will be marked by our victory here and we shall return as heroes before years' end, to our beloved city."

The men of Leisler's militia cheered and rallied, hyping themselves for the charge. On the walls of Fort Albany, the Convention's Albany militia stood silent, unnervingly waiting for the attack. What began as harsh words and threatening speech, was set to spark into open war. Schuyler watched with grim determination. Though he knew the odds were against his men, there could be no other recourse. Leisler's actions were treason.

The usurper had to be stopped.

Captain John Schuyler, younger brother to the mayor, rushed up, nearly knocking into Pieter himself. Pieter grunted. "What is it, John?"

"You're not going to believe this," John Schuyler replied with a grin.

"What's that?"

The soldier's words alerted Jacob Milborne to a nearby hill where a lone figure stood. The man was a little too far to make out his exact features, but he was clearly of the natives.

"Mohawk, I think" Milborne said. "I wonder what he's doing?"

On the hill, Tahajadoris stood tall. His face was hard and emotionless as he stared at the cluster of men from the great city to the south. The time had come. He raised a musket high above his head.

Jacob Milborne held his breath as the hill filled with Mohawk warriors. Dozens of Indians crested the hill, their rifles and tomahawks at the ready. Their faces were painted black and red – war colors of the Iroquois.

The men—who just moments before had been supremely confident of their victory—grew sheepish in their boots. They cluttered closer together, a genuine fear creeping up inside them.

Milborne knew the tides had turned. He found himself outmaneuvered, with the enemy holding strong positions to his front and right flank.

"Should we attack?" one of his men asked him.

"The battle is lost," Milborne answered quietly.

"We have yet to fire a shot," the man said. "How could we have lost?"

"Because it would be our own deaths if we were to attack. It would appear we have underestimated the strength of Pieter Schuyler's alliance with the Wilden Indians. We cannot achieve victory through strength of arms alone – not on this day."

Pieter Schuyler nearly cried tears of joy. The

sight of the Mohawk Indians on the hill brought a sensation of relief and thankfulness that could not be described. Sergeant Rodgers looked out from the wall. "They have to surrender."

"No, they don't," Schuyler said. "They may yet return to New York City without bloodshed. But with the amount of support from the town, I suspect Leisler will push to keep some permanent influence here. Perhaps one or two of his more trusted lieutenants. Perhaps he'll try his hand at politics again."

His brother chimed in. "Or we can wait until the main body leaves, and then arrest those he leaves behind. It won't be hard. All we have to do is …"

"No," Pieter Schuyler said, stopping his brother. "It would ignite a rebellion amongst the lower classes and those who are not landowners. Leisler is more popular than you realize. Even this far north, he has many supporters."

"What would you have us do?" John Schuyler said, trying to conceal his own frustration. "I am not one for politics, brother, but leaving the enemy to fester and grow inside our own city is as dangerous as it is stupid. If Leisler wants a lesson in war, let's teach him what happens to those who invade the north."

Schuyler turned to his brother and the sergeant. "Gentlemen, the real war is to *our* north. The French have not forgotten Lachine – nor must we. They will strike at us with all their might and we must be ready to meet them, or we will surely perish. I will do everything in my power to prevent bloodshed amongst our people, even if that means negotiating with the usurper himself."

His brother thought for a moment, then gave a slight nod. "I understand. For what it's worth, I think it's a mistake. I think bloodshed is inevitable and it should happen sooner rather than later."

"I respect your counsel," Pieter Schuyler replied. "I have a great deal of respect for you as both family and a trusted officer. I pray you are wrong though. For now, we should be thankful that on this day we avoided war."

Chapter 24

Word of the confrontation quickly spread throughout the colony. When it arrived at Schenectady, Johannes Vedder and his brother Albert were at Van Slyke's tavern, taking a break from chopping wood. Myndert Wemp, a well-known Leislerite, burst through the door and shouted the news. The tavern roared with shouts, both in support and opposition to the failed coup.

Douw Aukes was the first to express his anger. "What are the savages doing interfering with the internal business of the colony? Shouldn't they be fighting the French?"

Adam Vroman stood up. "Sit down, Douw. We all know your agenda, sir. The usurper tried to overthrow the legitimate council of Albany, and he failed."

A few men shouted their usual, "Hear, hear!" while others expressed their disproval at Vroman. Aukes and Vroman shouted each other down from across the tavern, as others joined in the debate.

"Nothing good will come from us staying," Johannes whispered to Albert. "We should go."

"You can go," Albert said. "I am staying because it is our duty as men to know what is going on in our country. If Father were here, do you think he would leave?"

Johannes ignored the question. Harmen, he guessed, would calculate that not enough wood had been chopped, and return to the task. But Albert relished any debate, and it was simply not worth the effort. Johannes emptied his cup and dropped a coin on the table. He left Albert to discuss the politics with the other men, and headed out into the fresh, crisp

November air.

Walking home, Johannes felt aggravated, but could not pinpoint the source of his frustration. He knew Albert had a point in that the events going on all around them were important, but he could not bring himself to become entrenched in endless political bickering. It had been ongoing for months and resulted in nothing but increased tension and hostility in the village.

He had seen men refuse to trade goods or services with others, depending on their allegiance to Jacob Leisler or the Albany Convention. He saw former friends shun each other in the streets. Women would gossip about each other and how they were all wrong with their views. Even the children of the Leislerites and anti-Leislerites would hurl insults at each other, until some responsible parent would come along and order them home. The village was being ripped apart at the seams, and it all came down to politics.

The more Johannes thought about what was happening, the more he appreciated his father's actions. Harmen was far from politically neutral, but he kept his eyes on his business, trade, and his family. Those were real, and with hard work, produced tangible benefits.

Suddenly he heard a voice call out for him. He looked up and saw Maria rushing towards him, her face flush with tears. Alarmed, he opened his arms as she wrapped hers around him, crying uncontrollably. He held her tightly, not caring about the looks from men and women walking past.

After a moment, she took a step back. "I am scared," she said.

It was unusual for Maria to show such vulnerability. Johannes gripped her shoulders. "What happened?"

"My father was threatened last night," she

stuttered, wiping away some tears. "Some men came to our house. They said they knew he was French and he should leave before something bad happens to him and me."

Johannes felt his throat go dry. He brought her in, hugging her. "I will not let anything happen to you. Do you hear me?"

She nodded. "All he wanted was freedom to worship and work without fear. If we leave, I don't know where we can go. Johannes, I'm scared."

In one moment of twisted irony, the politics he cared so little about, suddenly became real.

"This is how it happens," Johannes muttered.

Maria looked on puzzled. "What do you mean?"

Johannes shook his head. "It's just – one moment, it's nothing more than old men talking in a tavern about some distant event. The next, it's knocking on your front door. I guess I tried pretending it didn't matter."

"Well it does, Johannes," Maria said. Her temper changed. "Why wouldn't you think it mattered? Do I matter?"

"Of course, you do," Johannes said, moving closer. Maria took a step back.

"Then act like it," she snapped. "I may have to leave the country if my father sees how dangerous Albany has become. Maybe you should take this stuff seriously." She paused, catching her breath. "I have to go," she said suddenly.

"Maria, please," Johannes begged.

"No," she said. "I must get back to my father. He is heading back to Albany this evening."

Maria turned and hurried off. Johannes stood in the middle of the street, unable to decide whether to follow her or not.

* * *

A cold drizzle fell outside Jacob Milborne's tent. Following the failed attempt to seize Albany, and rather than retreat in shame, Milborne had instead elected for a stalemate. His men erected tents and barriers outside Albany's walls. For two days, they waited. Milborne had sent men out to disperse leaflets and try to rally those in Albany to his cause.

Twice so far, John Schuyler and other Albany militia leaders came down to discuss a withdrawal. Much to Milborne's dismay, he was refused an audience with Pieter Schuyler and Robert Livingston, inside Albany. Milborne knew the Mohawk would have to eventually return to their castles to the west and hoped that would put pressure on the Convention to meet him. He was met only with silence.

One of his men opened the tent flap. "Sir, a visitor."

Milborne turned as a man walked inside.

"Nasty weather out here, isn't it?" The man looked to be in his mid-thirties, and clearly a fur trader.

"And who are you, sir?" Milborne asked.

"Excuse me," the man said. "My name is Joachim Staats."

"And what is it you want Mr. Staats?"

Staats wiped his hand through his wet hair and smiled. "Recognition for my service to Jacob Leisler." He paused, checking to see Milborne's reaction. Milborne remained impassive. "Let me explain," Staats said. "I am a signer of the Albany Convention. I thought I was standing up to a tyrant when I signed that document."

"Of what concern is that to me?" Milborne asked.

"Now I can see that I was wrong," he said. Milborne crossed his arms but kept listening. Staats continued, "Since forming their convention, Schuyler and Livingston have commandeered any sense of fair governance. They rule as supreme aristocratic landowners. I myself, am one, and a damn successful fur trader, but I cannot abide by their petty laws any longer. I have not been compensated for the work I have put in to the Convention's work."

Milborne smirked. "So, you're here to offer your services to the revolution? To Leisler?" Staats nodded. Milborne approached him. "Very well. Help me get inside the city and I will name you lieutenant in Leisler's royal army."

* * *

Inside Albany, Schuyler approached Livingston. "How long do you think we will keep them in such a situation? This standoff is not good for business."

Livingston crossed the room to the hearth. He stared into the fire, watching the embers glow and fall from the logs. "I know," he said, turning back to Schuyler. "I thought long and hard about Leisler. I knew he would eventually make a move on Albany, and it would have to come before the snow was too deep. With that in mind, I dispatched a courier with a request."

Schuyler's eyes narrowed. "And where exactly did this courier go, Robert?"

At that moment, a knock was heard on the door.

"Sir, troops approaching."

"Christ in Heaven," Schuyler exclaimed. "Leisler brought more men up."

Livingston glanced at him. "I wouldn't count on it." He opened the door and headed outside, with Schuyler right behind him. "The courier," Livingston explained, "went to Connecticut. I requested reinforcements." They climbed the stairs and looked out the gate. "And we have their answer."

The gates opened, and a column of soldiers marched in. Schuyler stared in awe. "There must be a hundred soldiers."

"The governing body of our sister colony has a vested interest in keeping the peace in New York," Livingston said. "Shall we meet our new friends?"

Schuyler followed Livingston down to where the militia had assembled.

"Welcome to Albany," Robert Livingston said. "Thank you for coming so quickly."

The head officer snapped to and saluted smartly. He was a tall, muscular man with a haircut so short as to be almost uncivilized. He had a stubble across his face, a sign of the hard days of march from their colony to New York. Schuyler, always having a knack for reading people, could see this was a hardened veteran and a reliable officer.

"I am Jonathan Bull, Captain of the Connecticut militia."

"Bull?" Schuyler asked. "As in the son of Captain Thomas Bull?"

"Yes, sir," the man replied, surprised.

"I met him, you know," Schuyler said. "It was a decade or more ago. Long after his service in the Pequot War. He was a good man. I am sure you are as well."

"Thank you, sir," Captain Bull replied. "I understand you have a bit of a situation on your hands. If you don't mind, my men are tired but ready to fight."

Robert Livingston chimed in, "How many men did you bring with you?"

The Captain turned to him. "About ninety, sir. They are the best Connecticut had to offer. All of them are well-trained and motivated."

"I appreciate the zeal, Captain, but the situation has changed. We want to avoid bloodshed if possible. There are two things that we in Albany, and Leisler in New York, agree on. The first is absolute loyalty to William and Mary, King and Queen of England. The second, is that the biggest threat is the French to the north. We have a plan," Schuyler said. "And you are key to its success."

* * *

The next day, Captain John Glen made his way to Albany. The courier from Pieter Schuyler urged him to make for the city with all possible haste. He rode through the gates of Albany and headed straight for the fort. Inside, Pieter Schuyler and the other Convention members awaited his arrival.

"I am glad you arrived in such short order," Schuyler said as Glen dismounted. "I do apologize for the lack of notice. This matter needs to be settled at once."

Glen nodded. "Forgive me, but what matter is that?"

Schuyler turned and held his arm out, motioning Glen inside the blockhouse. Glen took lead with the others in pursuit. Stepping inside, he saw three men standing in the center of the room.

"Captain Glen," Schuyler announced, "this is Jacob Milborne – second in command to Jacob Leisler."

"What is this?" Glen asked. "Why is this man

not in chains?"

Milborne took a step forward. "Guard your tongue before I remove it, sir."

Glen moved towards Milborne before Kiliaen Van Rensselaer stepped between them.

"Gentlemen," Kiliaen barked. "You will conduct yourselves with courtesy in this fort. Is that understood?"

Milborne nodded and stepped back. Glen took a breath and paced backwards. Pieter Schuyler took center of the room. "We are here to reach a peace accord. All of us. Captain Glen," he said, "as I am sure you are aware, a few days ago, Jacob Milborne landed a force on the river's edge, attempting to storm this fort."

"I heard," Glen said, "which is why I wonder again, why he is not in chains."

"War was averted," Schuyler continued, ignoring Glen's question. "Not by diplomacy, but only by strength of arms. The Mohawk arrived and tilted the balance in favor of the Convention."

Schuyler paced over to a table where a map of the Upstate region lay spread out. "Needless to say, this was the closest the forces of Jacob Leisler and the Albany Convention came to open confrontation. We must bring an end to this madness, and unite as a colony, the way the king would want us to."

"It would be easier if you would just yield to Leisler," Milborne stated plainly. "He is more forgiving than you believe, and he wants nothing more but to work with all the leaders of this colony, to bring about safety and equality for all those under the king's laws."

"Spare us your words," Glen fired back. "We know what has happened to the landowners and those of the council in New York City. We will not forfeit our lands, or have our fortunes confiscated and sent to Leisler's personal coffers."

Schuyler raised his hand, steadying Glen. "The captain is right, Milborne. We in the Albany Convention stand by our words. We will not submit to anyone without a royal decree from England. That is non-negotiable."

"Then what am I doing here?" Milborne fumed.

"Making a deal," Schuyler said. "Making peace. Because to our north, we have an enemy bent on our annihilation, and the French do not want peace."

The room was silent a moment. Finally, Milborne spoke. "I am listening. What do you propose?"

Schuyler paced around the room. "We are sending a detachment of Captain Bull's Connecticut militia to Schenectady. That village is vulnerable and dangerously undermanned. It will be under the command of Lieutenant Talmadge, of Bull's company. We are offering the chance for one of your officers to act as second-in-command to the expedition."

Milborne thought about it for a moment. He knew from Leisler that many in Schenectady were supportive of the revolution and opposed to the harsh trading conditions enforced by the Albany Convention. An opportunity could present itself.

"What about Joachim Staats?" Milborne asked. "He is from Albany, not New York City. He will be perfect for the command. What else?"

Schuyler took a breath. "We are offering you a commission in the Albany militia, if you choose to accept. This is a letter of commission."

Schuyler handed Milborne the letter. Milborne read it carefully. He folded it in half and set it on the table.

"This I cannot do," Milborne replied, suspecting the Convention wanted to in effect, keep him as a hostage in the event Leisler marched on Albany. "But I wish to leave behind a few men, men who have family connections. They can serve in the militia and increase the trust between our two parties."

Schuyler knew the men would essentially be spies for Leisler, but that did not matter. War had been averted.

"Very well," Schuyler said. "Do we have an accord?"

Milborne looked about the room. All eyes were fixed on him. When he sailed north, Milborne did not suspect there would be any diplomacy. It was a new and frightful world for him. But in that moment, he thought about what his friend and mentor would do. He held out his hand. "Yes, we have an accord."

Chapter 25

The first major snowfall swept through the Mohawk valley in mid-November. It fell late in the night and continued into the early morning. The people of Schenectady woke up to more than eight inches of a light, powdery snow covering their village. Johannes awoke at the crack of dawn to Angie leaping onto his bed and shaking his shoulders. "Look out the window, Johannes. Look!"

Looking out his window, he saw the snow-covered roofs of the homes and smiled. "Go wake the others," he said.

Angie hugged him and jumped off the bed, to go wake Arent and Corset. Their excitement was justified. As had been family tradition for years now, their mother had promised them that on the first day of lots of snow, after their morning chores, they were free to play outside for the entire day. It was seen as a way to welcome the harsh winter months with joy, rather than bitterness. In a house of five children, it was essential to keep them occupied and happy.

Johannes gobbled down his breakfast and set about his chores. Among the most pressing for him and Albert was to clear as much snow from the roof of the house, stable, and shed as possible. The buildup of snow—if left unchecked—often caused undue stress on the supports and led to collapse. Using hoes, they dragged the snow from the roof. Albert boosted Johannes onto the roof where he knocked the rest of it down. It fell in great heaps, landing with a thud next to the house.

"That's all of it," he called down to his brother.

"Well then, we're done," Albert replied.

"Is it clear?" Johannes asked, peeking down at the snow pile.

"Go for it!" Albert shouted.

Johannes let out a yell and leapt down from the roof, falling into the snow pile. "I'm going to get the others," he said.

"Yeah," Albert sighed. "I'm heading to Van Slyke's."

Johannes threw up his arms. "It's too early to start drinking."

"Just a couple beers," Albert commented as he walked away.

Johannes called after him, "It's never just a couple beers with you." He turned back. *He can waste his life in the taverns*, he thought. *I'm going to enjoy this while it lasts.*

Johannes went back inside until the others were finished with their chores. Angie was the first to finish. "My gosh, Johannes," she said. "The roof over the storeroom was dripping all over the place. Mother had me mop it up and place a bucket that I have to empty when it gets full. I already emptied it three times."

Johannes stood there in silence but with a malicious grin.

"What?" she asked.

Without warning, Johannes reached up and dropped a handful of snow down the back of her shirt. She screamed in shock, jumping up and down. He laughed and opened the door, escaping into the cold.

"I'll get you for that, Johannes."

She threw on her coat and mittens and ran outside. Johannes waited in hiding and ambushed her with a snowball. She bent down and packed a snowball of her own, throwing it but he jumped to the side, letting it fly past.

Arent joined the snowball fight, attacking Johannes from the rear. Corset ran around in circles, falling into the snow, rolling around and laughing. Elsewhere, other children played outside too, taking advantage of the scenic change.

After a time, Johannes distanced himself from his siblings. He left out the south gate and disappeared into the trees beyond. In the forest, Johannes took a breath and admired the serenity of the desolate surroundings. Snow covered the ground and branches. Aside from a few squirrels and birds, it was relatively still.

Leaning against a tree, his thoughts inevitably focused on Maria Vandervort. He regretted not going after her and trying to make things better. It had been over a week and he had no correspondence from her.

Since that day, he had made every effort to learn about the ongoing political affairs of the colony. He talked with Albert and a few of the other men of the village on such dealings. He found several men to be of similar mindset, most notably Adam Vroman and the Reverend Peter Tassemaker. Though not exactly a supporter of the Convention, Johannes found himself unable to reconcile with Jacob Leisler or those wishing him to power.

But he remained focused on Maria. He wondered how he could make things better. He guessed she knew he did not mean any offense, but still, he could not help but wonder if her father had already taken her and fled from Albany. Would he ever see or hear from her again? The questions tore at him.

"What are you doing out here?"

Johannes nearly jumped out of his boots. "Heavens, Angie, you startled me."

Angie approached, struggling through the

snow and clutching her cloak tightly. "What are you thinking about, Johannes? Maria?"

Johannes smiled. "I cannot have a private thought it would seem. I just worry that I've lost her forever. It's killing me inside."

Angie stopped a few paces from him. "She is a very nice girl, Johannes. I cannot imagine she would leave without any notice to you – not unless she had no choice. She adores you."

"I know, but I seemed to upset her when we last spoke. Now, I wonder if she is gone or just needing some time to herself."

"Well, I may not know much, Johannes," Angie said, "but I can tell you this. Every girl, no matter who they are, they all need some time to themselves. They'd go crazy if they had men around all the time." She laughed. "Cheer up, she will write to you, or come back. Just give it some time."

Johannes nodded. "Thank you, Angie. I am glad I can talk to you when Albert just laughs and goes off drinking." He looked around, taking in the crisp air. "We should get back."

* * *

The twenty-four men of the Connecticut Company marched slowly along the muddy road, and the new fallen snow only added to the misery. The men trudged through the slush at a snail's pace, helping push the two supply carts along the way.

At the head of the column was Lieutenant Enos Talmadge. A protégé of Captain Bull, and trained since he was eighteen years old in military affairs, Talmadge was a solid solider. Though Schenectady was presented as a hazardous assignment, Talmadge had volunteered to serve in an instant, as the Connecticut detachment's commanding officer. He was young but skilled, intelligent, and above all, an officer who led by example.

Talmadge jumped down from his horse to help free one of the carts from a rut it had become stuck in. Pushing the rear of the cart, Talmadge slipped, falling into the mud. He cursed and stood back up. Two more men joined in and after a struggle, they freed the cart.

He was still wiping the mud from his clothing when a horse and rider rode up from the rear. "Can you not move them faster?"

Talmadge looked up. Leisler's lieutenant, Joachim Staats looked down at Talmadge.

"We would be moving faster if you weren't in the way," Talmadge replied.

Staats realized his horse was blocking the cart. He yanked on the reigns and moved off to the side.

"Still, an officer should look the part," he remarked, pointing to Talmadge's coat. Staats turned and rode to the front of the column. After a minute, Talmadge climbed back on his horse and joined Staats.

"We do not have much further," Staats commented. "I have traveled this road many times."

Talmadge shook his head. "Let's get one thing clear, Staats. I may have been ordered to recognize you as second in command of this detachment. But I personally detest you, and so do the men, all of whom are all loyal to me, Captain Bull, and the Convention. You signed the Convention, then betrayed it by joining the usurper's forces."

Staats laughed uneasily. "And that means what to me?"

Talmadge pointed off to the woods. "It means I could cut you down right here, throw your body in the trees, and say you fell from your horse and cracked your skull, and nobody would question it."

Staats swallowed his saliva and adjusted his seating but stared ahead.

"These men behind you," Talmadge continued. "They're Connecticut men and they're loyal to me, not you. Perhaps in Albany you have some power. But out here, you have no authority. You will not give my men one order. You won't even talk to them, nor they to you. And when we reach Schenectady, you will remove yourself from our presence. Find a family willing to take you under their roof, and stay there. You may show up at the fort every morning for accountability, but beyond that, I expect to see and hear as little of you as possible. Do I make myself clear?"

Staats paused, his mouth halfway open as if trying to find words to counter Talmadge's not so veiled threat. "The people of Schenectady, if our intelligence is correct, sympathize with the true leader of the province; Jacob Leisler. They won't like your presence there in and of itself, and much less if they find out you have tossed aside the agreement made in Albany and made yourself the sole military commander. I am the only man who can stop an uprising in that town."

Talmadge did not buy Staats' argument for a moment. "The people of Schenectady don't know you. Don't think for a second they would follow you. And besides, look behind you." Staats looked back at the Connecticut men. He turned back to Talmadge.

"So?"

"These are some of the best men of the Connecticut militia. By all means, you can try to raise a force to take us and the fort in the village. After you fail," Talmadge leaned in, "I will personally drag you out to the nearest tree and hang you for treason."

Talmadge saw fear in Staats' eyes. Staats looked away and muttered, "That won't happen," just loud enough for Talmadge to hear him.

Satisfied, Talmadge turned back to the road ahead. In his mind though, he privately relinquished one small fact to Staats, though he would never admit it aloud. If their intelligence was indeed accurate, the Leislerites in the village would far outnumber his own men. He just hoped that politics was not their primary concern.

Chapter 26

"Angie, set the table," her mother said. "Quick now."

"Yes, Mother," Angie replied, going about setting plates and cups. Anna wiped her hands clean and yelled upstairs, "Come and eat, dinner's ready."

The men piled into the dining room and lined up, as Anna poured porridge into their bowls. She divided up some dried meat and set a loaf of bread and butter on the table. Harmen filled his mug with ale and sat down.

"Hurry now," he said. Johannes poured himself some beer and took his seat as did the others. "Let's make this fast," Harmen said. Johannes grinned as he bowed his head to pray. "Dear Lord," Harmen began, "we thank thee for this bountiful meal and your blessings. We give thanks to you, Amen."

He immediately grabbed a slice of bread, dipped it into his porridge, stuffing the entire piece into his mouth, and washing it down with beer.

"Harmen," Anna snapped. "Mind your manners at the table."

"No time for manners," he said, grabbing the meat.

Angie snickered. Her mother glared at her but said nothing.

Albert cleared his throat. "Mother, Father, I have an announcement I'd like to make."

The table grew quiet. Harmen leaned back and folded his arms.

"What is it?" Anna asked.

Albert smiled at everyone. "Well," he said. "I think that come the spring. I would like to find a place in Albany and make myself a home. That way, I can

216

become a fur trapper without the hassle that the *handlaers* have put on us. Once I am settled in, I will find a suitable young lady, and I will ask her father for permission, and I will marry her."

The room was silent. Arent was the first to break the silence. "Congratulations," he said.

Johannes and Angie congratulated him next. Corset looked on curiously and smiled.

His mother smiled softly. "You are ready for a place of your own and a wife. We're all so happy for you. Right, Harmen?" Arent turned to his father.

"Get a strong, healthy woman and you'll do fine," Harmen said half-heartedly.

"Harmen!" Anna said, disgusted.

"No, that's alright Mother," Albert replied.

Harmen leaned across. "Well, what do you want me to say? He's a man now; he can make his own decisions. Doesn't need my help none."

Anna sighed. "It wouldn't hurt to be a bit less calculating, my dear. Marriage is just as much about love as it is finding a good partner with which to start a family."

Harmen conceded and gave Albert a pat on the shoulder. "You made a good choice, son."

"Thanks, Father," Albert sighed. "I wish I could stay closer to home, but there are too many hurdles to being a trapper in Schenectady. Those aristocratic handlaers like Robert Livingston and Pieter Schuyler put them there so they could make a fortune monopolizing the fur trade. Isn't that right, Father?"

"Please, Albert," his mother spoke. "The dinner table is no place for politics."

"But it's everywhere," Albert argued. "It's hurting our own family. The more I hear of Jacob Leisler, the more I wish he were in charge and not the Convention."

"Dear, you tell him," Anna said, looking at Harmen.

Harmen took a drink from his ale. He set it down on the table and wiped his mouth. "He's not wrong," he uttered.

"See what I mean?" Albert said.

"You shut it, boy," Harmen growled. Albert slid back into his seat. "Just because you are right, she is still your mother, and you will show her the utmost respect, or I will beat the sin out of you. We are not a political family. We will do what we always have done. We will work. We will work hard, and the good Lord will be merciful upon us. Is that understood?"

The table sat silent. Johannes looked around. He watched Albert lick his lips, and guessed he was trying to decide whether to apologize or defend himself. Angie trembled slightly, from either the cold air or cold aura around the table. And then there was Arent and young Corset nearly oblivious to the tension in the air. Johannes thought how nice it must be to be unbothered by the troubles of their time.

"I am sorry, Mother," Albert said, breaking the silence. "I love and respect you, and Father, and all of you," he said to his siblings. "I do believe we need to stand up for what we believe. I may be wrong; I probably am." He grinned. "But I cannot shake the feeling that these are momentous times, and we have to choose a side."

"I knew men who…chose a side," Harmen said, staring at his son. "Different conflicts at different times for different reasons. Some were friends, some neighbors. Their reasons didn't matter when I had to lay them to rest. It didn't matter to their wives and children, watching their husbands and fathers die in vain. What matters most is taking care of your family."

"With respect, Father," Albert responded,

"these are not usual times. I will take care of our family. But I will stand up for what I believe. And I believe there is a fight coming."

Johannes eyed Corset. He looked visibly upset. "Albert," he said, speaking up, "no there's not. Don't scare Corset like that. Leisler and the Convention made peace in Albany. The Mohawks sided with Schuyler and the Convention, and Leisler won't attack and threaten that alliance. The Mohawk are the only ones standing in between us and the French. And besides, it's the dead of winter. We're all brothers and sisters here. Schenectady, Albany, New York. We're all in this together. There won't be any civil war."

"Hear, hear," Angie said, raising her cup.

His mother warmly smiled at him. "Well said, Johannes. Albert, your brother is right."

There was a shout from the street. The table quieted. "There's some commotion out there," Albert said.

Harmen hissed for him to be quiet.

Suddenly, the front door shook with a pounding.

"Who would bother us at dinner?" Harmen asked angrily.

"I'll answer," Johannes said, standing up. He walked over and opened the door. Standing tall before him was Adam Vroman. Vroman carried his musket in hand and his voice echoed concern.

"Is your father home?" Vroman asked.

"We all are," Johannes replied. "Is there something wrong, or that we can help you with?"

"There's a whole lot of commotion down at the gate," Vroman said. "Seems there are a whole lot of armed guys heading our way. We need some good men out here."

* * *

The sky had turned a dark shade of blue when Enos Talmadge led his column of Connecticut militia up to the south gate from the Albany Road. Two sentries stood outside with blazing torches, lighting the path for the incoming troops. The march had not surprisingly taken much of the daylight hours and the men were exhausted.

The gates were closed when Talmadge arrived. Several of the townspeople waited outside the gate, eyeing the soldiers with suspicion.

"We ask for entry into the town," Talmadge spoke to the crowd. "By directive of the Albany Convention, we are here for the protection of the town, its people, and its property."

The crowd parted as a man made his way through the crowd. He was tall – a foot taller than all the other men, at least. He was dressed in black from head-to-toe, and wore a tall capotain hat, making his presence that much more visible. As he stepped in front of the crowd, Talmadge edged his horse forward a pace to get a good look at the man.

"Who are you, sir?" Talmadge asked.

The man's voice was deep and commanding. "I am Ryer Jacobse Schermerhorn. I am one of the five trustees of Schenectady. I make the decisions around here." He paused for a moment. "And who, sir, are you?"

Talmadge thought about climbing down from his horse but decided he would look small standing next to the tall man. "Lieutenant Enos Talmadge of the Connecticut militia," he stated proudly.

There was a murmur through the townspeople. Ryer Schermerhorn looked at the man as if he was irritated at the slight of Talmadge not dismounting before him. "You say you're here on behalf of the Convention? Remarkable that they did not inform you."

"Inform me of what, sir?"

"That Schenectady – our village, does not need foreign troops within her walls," Schermerhorn stated. There were a few nods and '*hear, hears*' from the crowd. "We have a fort and a garrison on the north side. I think we are safe enough. I apologize for your fruitless journey."

Talmadge was shocked at the blatant disrespect. "Sir, we are here to supplement your forces. England is at war with France, and there is need to strengthen the frontier settlements."

Schermerhorn folded his arms. "But *we* do not need you here."

The men of the Connecticut militia grew uneasy. It was a town clearly set against their presence. One man whispered that they should leave, to which Talmadge turned his horse and stared angrily at the man. He bowed his head in shame. Talmadge turned back to Schermerhorn and handed him a letter.

"Unfortunately, it is not your decision." Schermerhorn grabbed the letter, as Talmadge said, "This is a directive of the Albany Convention, and by that, it overrules the word of one trustee. We are to be quartered within the town, with sustenance and pay to be provided by the town coffer."

The crowd grew angry and more than one man, unseen amidst the mob, hurled insults at the arriving militia. Talmadge's eyes moved back and forth as he scanned the crowd. He tried to identify individuals who voiced their dissent, but it proved futile as there did not seem to be a single person who was pleased with their arrival.

Ryer Schermerhorn read the letter carefully.

He folded it and put it in his pocket. "The snows have come. The French are on the defensive. So why are you *really* here? Could it be you are here to suppress the people who express dissent against the Albany Convention? If so, you can leave, because we believe in liberty, not oppression."

"Speak for yourself, Ryer," a voice called out. An elderly man stepped forward, with a couple others behind him. He turned to the young lieutenant from Connecticut. "I am another village trustee – Sweer Teunessen. On behalf of the townspeople, we welcome the additional troops to protect us from the French threat." He looked at the Schenectady militiamen barring the gate. "Open it," he ordered.

The troops turned to Ryer Schermerhorn. His eyes remained fixed on Talmadge as he nodded, and the gates were opened.

"Thank you, gentlemen," Talmadge said. He grabbed the reigns and waved his men forward. The column of troops marched through the gate. More villagers appeared from their houses and congregated along Church Street, watching the troops march towards the blockhouse.

Standing along the side of the street, Johannes Vedder, along with his father and Albert, watched the line of Connecticut troops marching through the gate.

"I don't understand," Johannes whispered. "What are they doing here?"

"I told you, brother," Albert said. "The Convention wants to oppress us and keep us bound to their unfair laws. Leisler is right. We need to become free of the *handlaers* and make our own way in this world."

"But this doesn't make any sense," Johannes wondered out loud. "They are here to protect us from the French, not Leisler. I mean unless they suspected the town might turn on the Convention, and rally to …"

Johannes paused, thinking it over. His eyes looked down the line of soldiers marching. He cringed at the possibility.

As if reading his brother's mind, Albert leaned over and whispered to him, "So, little brother, tell me. Do you still believe that a fight is not coming?"

Chapter 27

December 5, 1689

Smoke rose from every chimney in town. The day had been bitter cold, and the coming night promised only to be even colder. But the warmth of children's joy filled the streets. Boys and girls gathered outside the church and sang hymns while many of the adults, along with the reverend Peter Tassemaker, watched and smiled. Other parents were happy their children were out of the house as the mothers busied themselves with baking treats and preparing for the evening's feasts, for it was the eve of Saint Nicholas' Day.

By the church, Hind Meese Vrooman walked around dressed in a dazzling red and white coat, with a tall red and golden miter atop his head. He carried a long crosier and, in the tradition of Sinterklaas, a big, red book; in which was supposedly the names of the children, and whether they had been good or bad. One of his African slaves dressed in the colorful clothing of Sinterklaas' Moorish helper, Zwarte Piet. He dressed in blue and yellow clothing, a white ruff around his neck, and carried a small bag.

The children flocked to Sinterklaas to find out if they would receive a gift this year. The old man smiled through his long, white beard, and his assistant tossed chocolate candies at the children who yelped with joy.

Johannes and Angie took the two boys, Arent and Corset, down to see Sinterklaas. "Go up to him," Angie urged, pushing the boys closer to the front of the children.

"I don't think Corset likes them," Johannes said laughing at the terrified look on his face.

Angie knelt and looked at him. "Don't be afraid, Corset. He is here to give you a present."

Corset nodded and turned back to Sinterklaas and Zwarte Piet. She stood back up. "I cannot believe mother was able to raise us all. It is so much work."

"That's why I want to see the world first, before I settle down," Johannes said.

Angie grinned. "Maria will not be happy to hear that."

"Whoa!" he said, holding his hand up. "She is an amazing girl. I am just not ready to settle down right now. Like I said, I want to see the world first."

Johannes caught movement and looked over. Two Connecticut soldiers were watching the children with Sinterklaas and shook their heads in disgust.

"Why are they upset?" Angie asked.

"They are New Englanders," Johannes explained. "They don't celebrate Saint Nicholas' Day, or many Christian holidays for that matter. They consider it a sacrilege. It's an English thing." He sighed. "Maybe I shouldn't be so eager to see the world. It's such an ugly place."

"Oh, you're so dramatic, Johannes," Angie said with a giggle. "The world is a great and beautiful place, just like the Lord made it. Some, like those men, do not see the miracles all around. We do though, right?"

Johannes glanced at her and then at their younger brothers. "Yeah, I think so. Still," he said, "there aren't many miracles these days. Not a whole lot of good going around."

Angie's smile faded. "We should grab the boys and get home."

By time they reached home, Anna had set the table and the feast began in earnest. Johannes' eldest brother, Samuel, made the trip from his home to

Schenectady to dine with the family. For one night, no one – not even Albert, spoke about politics or the tension gripping the colony. Anna strictly forbade all talk of such matters at the table.

Once dinner was finished, the children placed their shoes by the fireplace in hopes that by morning, they would have gifts inside. Anna then saw them each to bed, before going back to the kitchen to prepare some morning snacks and treats.

* * *

Symon Schermerhorn was awake, reading a book by the fireside, when there was a knock on the door. He grunted as he set the book down. Opening the door, he was surprised to see a familiar face.

"Ryer," he said. "Late night for a celebration, but please come in."

His brother stepped inside as he closed the door. Standing side-by-side, as tall as Symon was, his elder brother stood several inches taller.

Ryer was a serious man. It reminded Symon of his friend, Harmen Vedder.

"What brings you here at this late hour?"

Ryer stood a moment, warming up by the fire. Then he faced his brother. "Symon," he said. "There are great changes coming to this town. To this colony. To this – *country.*"

Symon was a bit unclear but nodded. "Alright," he said, with some pause.

"I want you with me on this."

"On what do you speak?"

Ryer took a breath. "The winds of change are sweeping the colony. Jacob Leisler intends on taking Albany next year, before the snows melt. Before this happens, we will take charge in Schenectady and cut off

Albany from their Mohawk allies."

"So now it's we?" Symon asked, speculatively. "How many more do you have in your enterprise?"

"That I cannot say," Ryer responded. "What I can say is there are many of us. You know I am one of the five trustees of the Schenectady patent. Join us, and I will make sure you become the sixth. We need men of talent, and you are my blood."

Symon folded his arms. His brother was always one for politics, but this was uncharacteristically rash of him. "What happens to the other patent holders who refuse to back you? Are you going to arrest them with the older landowners, the way Leisler did in New York City?"

"These are changing times," Ryer said. "People need to choose to back the one true leader of New York or face the consequences. We cannot let Convention aristocrats like Schuyler, Livingston, and Glen run this colony into the ground."

"Ryer, you know I am a man of business, not politics." Symon took a pause. "I cannot support any side in this domestic strife. It will only bring misery and ruin the lives and fortunes of all whose partake, and many who do not. If blood is shed between neighbors, one of the Convention and one of Leisler, there will be no stopping this colony from splitting into civil war."

"War is here," Ryer said quietly, his voice deep. "We are under occupation by a foreign army. And we intend to cut it out of our town, by any means necessary. So – are you with us or not?"

Symon licked his lips. He stared at the floor for a moment, in total thought. Ryer watched his brother with eagerness. Finally, Symon raised his head.

"No, I am not with you."

"Then I will make my leave," Ryer said, grabbing his hat and heading for the door. As he opened it, a gust of cold wind blew into the home. Ryer turned to Symon. "I pray to God it resolves itself peacefully. But I pray harder that you do not force my hand against you, if you side with the Convention. You have chosen to remain neutral. Do not shift from that."

"And what of thou shall not kill?" Symon asked.

Ryer paused. "Mark my words Symon, this will be a year of harvest for the souls of men. This is the time of the sword."

* * *

It was on the last day of the Christian calendar, when Lawrence came back to the Great Castle at Tionnontogen. The village of the Wolf clan was rife with excitement. The warriors had returned from their successful raids against their mortal enemy of New France and were busy hunting deer and preparing for the feasts.

"Good to see you, brother," Tahajadoris said, embracing Lawrence in a firm hug. "How was your trip?"

"Good, brother," he said. "I have never seen such energy in our people. Their joyful hearts lift my spirits."

"As is it does mine," Tahajadoris said. "In just over two-week's time it will be the midwinter festival. There is much to be done in the way of preparing. We have much to be thankful for this year, and much to look forward to in the year following the new moon."

Lawrence sighed. "You are right about this year, brother. But I cannot help feel that next year the celebrations may not be so warranted."

The sachem nodded. "Walk with me."

The two men walked around the feverous village.

"I had a vision in my dream," Lawrence said.

"Tell me about this vision," Tahajadoris spoke softly.

Lawrence swallowed. "It was our white brethren to the east. They cried out in the winter night. I raced through the snow to save them, but I could not reach them before fire and blood consumed their cries."

"They are a young people," Tahajadoris said. "Their history is new and no matter how well we teach them, they are prone to stumble and fall from time to time. We can only guide them through their troubles as they find their own way in our world."

"They did not stumble," Lawrence replied. "In my vision, they were extinguished. Their fire went out in the world and they moved on to meet their God on their terms." He looked into the sachem's eyes. "I fear a great tragedy will befall them."

"You may be right," Tahajadoris said.

"How so?" Lawrence questioned.

"The white men have angry hearts," the sachem said. "They are consumed by hatred for their fellow man because of a conflict in politics within their own countrymen. Some support one man. Others support another. If they do not heal their broken bonds, and come together as brothers, they will destroy themselves."

Lawrence leaned in. "What can we do to stop this destruction?"

Tahajadoris looked beyond his friend. A group of young boys ran around, playing in the snow. The faintest smile crossed his face. He turned to Lawrence. "We can only give advice to our white brethren, we cannot make their decisions for them. We have our own people to care for."

"But…"

Tahajadoris gripped Lawrence's shoulder. "If the French come at them, I swear to you the Five Nations will light a fire that will burn brighter than any before, and we will bring our enemy to kneel before we ever let such an atrocity happen again. But…" Tahajadoris trailed off. "If they seek to bleed their own brothers after we council against it, we cannot stand between them and let our own people suffer because of their animosity towards each other. It would be the undoing of our people."

"What would happen to us?" Lawrence begged the question.

"A war between the whites could cause us to ally ourselves to one side or the other, fighting men we swore to never raise arms against. Or worse still, suppose the Five Nations disagree on who is right in the conflict. The great peace could be shattered, and war would split the Confederacy into warring factions that would consume our people. That is our fate if we let our people interfere in the affairs of the English. When it comes down to survival, better our people survive than the English. For some day, they may not be our allies."

"You are wise," Lawrence said. "But here and now, they are our allies – our brothers. And I say to you, as I would to any who ask me, when they call on me to help, I will help."

Tahajadoris looked to the sky. "Well, if the Great Spirit chose you to reflect her vision of the future, then they may indeed need all our help soon."

1690

Chapter 28

The new year saw Louis-Hector de Callières in a state of despair. He peered out his foggy window at the scene below. Montreal had been transformed. What was one once a bristling and vibrant trading town along the river, had become a chaotic nightmare for the frozen masses that huddled behind its walls for survival.

Just a month before, over a hundred Iroquois warriors – this time of the Onondaga nation under a chief called *Chaudïere Noire*, raided the farming settlements at Lachenaie, five leagues north of Montreal. The devastating raid effectively finished the destruction of every settlement on the island, save for the town of Montreal itself. The survivors of the bloody year sought shelter behind the last bastion of safety. Across the land, the winter brought forth untold suffering. The snow fell for days, seemingly without pause. Inside, the people starved, died of disease, and prayed for deliverance – a deliverance Callières could not wait to give them.

There was a knock at the door and Nicolas d'Ailleboust de Manthet entered. "Monsieur, I am glad you accepted my request to see you on such short notice."

"Yes, come in," he said eagerly. As Manthet closed the door and took a seat, the governor spoke. "I pray you have some good news for me, lieutenant. We now stand on the brink of defeat. With last month's raid, we lost another forty-two men, women, and children. Our militias are devastated. One in ten men fit for military service have been killed. More are wounded, missing or sick. Last night I prayed to the

Lord that he would grant us mercy. So, tell me – to what do I owe the honor?"

"We have news from the south." Manthet handed Callières a hand-written note. "This has been verified by two others. The information is accurate."

Callières read it, his eyes beaming. He lowered the letter and thought deeply for a moment. "Summon our officers at once."

Manthet nodded and left. It was early morning when Sainte-Hélène arrived. The governor held up the paper. "Thank you for your visit."

Sainte-Hélène was still trying to wake himself up. "What is so urgent, monsieur, that you would call so early?"

"The English are divided," Callières stated proudly. "Now is the time, Jacques."

Manthet turned to Sainte-Hélène. "We march in one week."

"Hold on," Sainte-Hélène said, yawning. "What are you referring to? What has changed?"

Callières held up the scout's report. "There have been a series of rebellions across the English colonies. One in New York and another in the Massachusetts colony. In New York, there are two factions vying for control of that colony. One in New York City, the other at Orange. But there is tension across the territory. Further," he said stepping forward, "the scout reported that the Iroquois have become disenfranchised at the internal bickering and have retired to their castles to the south and west."

Sainte-Hélène's eyes widened. "So, that means the English frontier is …"

"It's wide open," Manthet smiled. "They cannot stop us. But we may not have long. Come spring, the new king in England will have surely sent magistrates to correct the situation. We must take advantage of this disunity while it lasts." Manthet knew Sainte-Hélène was working something out in his mind. "What is it?"

"I want my brother as a commander," Sainte-Hélène said.

Manthet was taken aback. "I thought you had something to say in regards to this news?"

"It is all in regards to this revelation," Sainte-Hélène replied. "Pierre is a professional soldier and a true patriot. And my youngest brother, François, I want him as well. He could use the experience."

"Okay, fine," Manthet said. "I will send word to Athasata. He needs to get his savages ready and meet us here in one week."

Callières looked to his two officers – his two war dogs. "You each are well-trained, highly experienced soldiers. May the Lord God bless you on this endeavor."

* * *

Johannes wandered up and down the snowy streets, looking for his brother. According to their mother, Albert had left early in the morning and had not been seen since. Johannes sensed something was off. Not with Albert. It would not be the first time he disappeared for a day at a time. But with the town itself. There was apprehension in the air. Everyone seemed on edge.

Three Connecticut soldiers walked by him, one of them glaring at Johannes as he passed. It was of no surprise to him. They were told the people of Schenectady were mostly Leislerites, and the people were told the soldiers were there to carry out the will of the Convention.

Johannes passed a group of women who were

expressing what he was thinking. "'Tis an unwatched kettle," one said, "ready to boil over."

"Heavens forbid it," another said. "These men from Connecticut should return to their wives and families. Our boys are capable of handling anything that comes our way." The women seemed to be all in agreement as they faded out of earshot. All around, the village seemed be echoing the same narrative.

Outside of Van Slyke's tavern, a group of men were smoking from their long, clay pipes and discussing the usual politics when Johannes approached. "You looking for your brother?" one man asked.

"Do you know where he is?" Johannes asked.

The man pointed and muttered, "He's around the back."

Without another word, Johannes turned and walked around the tavern. Peering around the corner, he noticed Albert was speaking with Douw Aukes and Myndert Wemp, two well-known Leislerites. They ceased their conversation and turned to Johannes.

"I have to go," Albert said, extending his hand.

Aukes grasped it, shaking. "We will be in touch, Vedder. Remember what we discussed."

The two Leislerites walked past Johannes, with Aukes dipping his head in a polite nod to Johannes. Albert scratched his head.

"What are you doing here, brother?"

"I could ask you the same thing," Johannes replied. Mother was worried. What was *that* about?"

"It doesn't concern you," Albert said. "Remember, the politics does not interest you."

"Albert," Johannes said, stepping forward, "I know you better than you think. Whatever you are planning, stop it. This town is about to explode, and I don't want our family to be caught up in whatever you…"

"We *are* caught up in it," Albert shouted. "What in bloody hell do you think is happening, little brother? Do you think this is a child's game? This is serious – deadly serious. Our rights have been trampled on long enough by Albany." Johannes shook his head, scarcely believing this was his brother's words. Albert finished with, "We have a moral obligation to restore our rights."

"So – is that it? You are a Leislerite now?"

Albert straightened up and adjusted his coat. "Yes, I am a Leislerite. Our father can barely make money from trading furs because the aristocrats in Albany have monopolized the trade. He has to become a farmer, merchant and laborer just to make ends meet. How is that fair?"

Johannes took a breath. "It's not."

"Exactly!" Albert shot back. "So why not do something about it? We are told Jacob Leisler is evil and all sorts of lies. The truth is, he did what no one else was willing to do. He saw injustice, and he acted against it. He is a hero in my opinion."

"This isn't you," Johannes said. "This is Aukes poisoning your mind. I cannot believe my own brother would back that man."

"You are afraid, Johannes. You have always been afraid," Albert said. "It is time to pick a side and get ready."

Johannes was now starting to lose patience. "Get ready for what?" he snapped. "This is not our fight."

"You're wrong," Albert replied. "We are at war."

Johannes snapped, "You are Goddamn right we are at war. But we are at war with France, not Albany. Maria's father was threatened not for being with Albany or with Leisler, but because he is of French descent. The Indians burned half of Canada. The French will retaliate. This bullshit between the Convention and Leisler needs to stop. We have a common enemy."

Albert was taken aback by his brother's rant. "That is the first time I ever heard you care what is happening. Unfortunately, you are still wrong. The colony does need to unite against our common enemy. But why should we make a distinction between the French who want us dead, and the aristocrats who want us enslaved to their unjust laws?"

The two brothers stood in the cold in silence for a minute. Johannes shrugged, giving up. "There is nothing I will be able to say to convince you to go back home, and help out the family, and not get involved in these politics. So, I am not going to try. Father will be disappointed."

"Perhaps," Albert said. "But I hope when I am a father someday, my children will understand and respect me for standing up for my beliefs."

Johannes thought about everything that was happening. All the tension and conflict brewing. "If we make it to that age," he said. "Only if we make it."

Chapter 29

"Rider coming," the guard called out. "Open the gate."

The man approached on his spotted stallion, hardly slowing the beast down as it tore through the north gate and into the village. Mothers moved their young children out of the way of the rider as he came to a stop outside the blockhouse.

Lieutenant Talmadge was administering extra drill to several of the newer men when the rider dismounted. "I have a letter for Lieutenant Staats. Where can I find him?"

There was no politeness in the man's voice and he waited impatiently for a response.

Talmadge approached the man, wiping grease from his hands with a rag. "I am Lieutenant Talmadge, senior officer here. I'll take that letter," he said, reaching out.

The man took a step back, holding his hand up in a blocking motion.

"I'm sorry but my orders are clear. This letter is to be given only to Lieutenant Staats."

"*Orders?*" Talmadge remarked. "I wonder – who gave you these orders?" The rider held firm but did not speak. Talmadge raised an eyebrow. "Do you not know who gave you your orders? That's poor leadership, I'd say."

The man straightened up, guessing that the lieutenant already knew where the message had originated from. "My orders come from Jacob Milborne, deputy commander to Colonel Leisler; commander-in-chief of the New York Militia and acting governor of the province. Now, tell me where I can find Lieutenant Staats or I will give your name to Colonel Leisler when I return to the city."

Talmadge had a passive look on his face, as if the threat passed through him without fazing him one bit. Talmadge studied the man for a moment. "Grab him!" he ordered suddenly. The rider tried to run but was quickly grabbed by two of the Connecticut Militiamen. The rider struggled to free himself, but the soldiers' grips did not give an inch. Talmadge approached to within a couple feet of the man.

"You come into this village and threaten *me*? You dare to mention the name Jacob Leisler as an authority figure in *my* presence?" He looked back at another soldier standing by. "Fetch the irons and the rope." Turning back, the rider could see the rage in his eyes. "What you speak is treason and by the authority of the Albany Convention, I am entirely within my right to drag you out of this village and have you hanged for treason against the Crown," he paused letting his words sink in. "And that's exactly what I am going to do."

The rider begged for mercy as Talmadge headed back into the blockhouse to fetch his uniform and sword. By then, the cries of the prisoner were drawing in crowds of curious villagers, some in support of the Convention and others in support of Leisler. The grumbling of dissatisfaction among the Leislerites reached the ears of the militiamen who immediately called for additional troops. Four more men joined those already outside the fort. But the odds were fast tipping against them.

By time Talmadge reemerged from the blockhouse, he was standing amidst a crowd of angry villagers, and it was still growing. *There must be thirty of them*, he thought to himself as he weighed his options. He eyed the crowds, noting some of the men carried muskets and hatchets, knives and clubs. Then came a shout from the crowd. "What's the charges against this man?" a voice yelled. Talmadge did not respond.

From the crowd, Albert Vedder stepped forward. "What is the charge?" he repeated.

Another chimed in, "They're hanging an innocent man."

The crowd jeered and screamed. A torch lit up in the back of the mob. Talmadge pulled out his pistol and cocked the hammer back. He knew the mob would tear apart his small force in seconds, but at least he could take down one with shot and however many more with his sword, before he was killed.

He cursed himself that he sent half the company out on a patrol north of the river to practice ambushes. They would be occupied for hours and would never get back in time to save Talmadge and the remaining garrison. The other men were scattered about the village and two were down with pneumonia – useless in a fight.

His mind raced back and forth as he tried to think of a plan. If he let the rider go, he and the Albany Convention would lose power in the village. The only way to remind everyone who was in charge was to enforce the law. But as he looked around him, he knew that hanging the Leislerite would mean certain death for the entire Connecticut garrison.

The crowd had nearly double in the last few minutes. Knowing he had no choice, he turned to one of the soldiers. "Find Lieutenant Staats and bring him here immediately." The man nodded and started to head off, but Talmadge grabbed his shoulder keeping him there. Leaning in he spoke in a quieter voice. "After you've done that, get across the river and get Captain Glen. He needs to know what's going on here."

"Understood, sir," the soldier snapped and

pushed through the hostile crowd. They immediately filled back in the void he left, edging closer to the remaining militia, which had formed a semi-circle with their lieutenant behind the line.

Talmadge watched as his militiaman disappeared and hoped to God he would return soon.

Joachim Staats was at the Christoffelse home meeting with David Christoffelse and Douw Aukes when he was summoned. To Staats' surprise, the Connecticut militiaman did not betray any sign of aversion to the Leislerite officer. He saluted properly and spoke only as a professional soldier would.

"Sir, you're needed at the blockhouse – at Lieutenant Talmadge's most urgent request. A mob has gathered when we apprehended a suspected traitor."

Staats shot a glance at the other two men at the table. They shared a common understanding of the situation. Staats, not bothering to get up, turned his body in his chair to the soldier. "Tell Talmadge I'll be there right away."

"Yes, sir," the man said before saluting.

After he left, Staats turned back to Christoffelse and Aukes.

"I think this is the news we've been waiting for."

"And if it is?" asked Christoffelse.

"Then we'll be in charge of this village by sunset," Staats replied, a wryly grin on his face. "Better dress in your finer attire, gentlemen. Today will be a grand day."

The soldier had nearly run all the way from the Christoffelse home, across the frozen river and all the way to the home of John Glen. He banged on the door and was still breathless when Glen's senior house slave, Robert, answered the door. "I – I need to speak to the Captain – right away." He coughed and tried slowing his breathing, his nostrils flaring as he caught his breath.

Robert disappeared into the house casually and the soldier stood outside on the porch for a minute. The door reopened, and John Glen appeared. "What is it, soldier?"

"Sir, there's a mob assembling in Schenectady. We captured a Leislerite rider and Talmadge had arrested him. Then a mob surrounded us. Half the company is out on maneuvers. We need you to bring up your Schenectady men, sir." He stopped to remember the scene around the blockhouse when he left. "We're about to be overrun."

Glen immediately understood the gravity of the situation. Being one of the most talented military officers in the Mohawk valley, he had a keen sense for assessing situations and determining the appropriate course of action. "Has blood been spilled yet?"

"Not yet sir, but I doubt the peace will last much longer."

"Get back as soon as you can. Tell Talmadge not to do anything to antagonize the mob. It will take me a half hour to gather my men. Only the ones readily accessible. We can't wait to gather every man at arms. That would take half the day. I'll march them through the south gate and to the town square. We'll seal the north gate. If the mob tries anything, we'll pin them against the north wall and the fort – and destroy them."

He paused, thinking aloud. "Damn Jacob Leisler for forcing us into this position. This is exactly what he wants; chaos and disunity in the village. It's a dangerous game he plays and one we can't bluff in."

"Sir?" the soldier asked.

Glen refocused his attention. "Never mind,

lad. Get back to Talmadge. Remember, nobody is to push the crowd to violence."

The soldier smiled, seeing the confidence that the Captain displayed, knowing he would not let the situation get out of hand. "I will tell him, sir."

He saluted and Glen returned the gesture. The soldier turned, took a deep breath, and started his run back to the village.

As he closed the door, his wife, Julia, stepped forward. The look on her face needed no explanation. Glen felt a pang of regret. "I have to go, darling."

"Heavens, John, you're going to start a war if you go down to Schenectady. That place is too dangerous."

"I am trying to stop a war," he said. She crossed her arms, glaring at him. He leaned in, wrapped his hand around her hair, and kissed her forehead. "I will be back shortly."

Glen dispatched several servants to carry the assemble orders to the men of the Schenectady Militia. Although some were known Leislerites, he hoped enough would do their duty when the time came.

As he assessed the situation in his mind he knew that that time was now.

Joachim Staats made his way through the cheering crowd whose tone had changed at his arrival. Some of the mob had dispersed, becoming bored at the standoff, but they still possessed the numbers that could overwhelm the garrison with little difficulty. They were the most passionate supporters of Leisler and swore that the rider who was still being detained, would not be punished by Talmadge.

Albert Vedder remained too, and took heart at Staats' arrival.

Coming to the head of the mob, Staats walked

before Talmadge. He knew the crowd was watching. Every word and every movement would be watched carefully. Against his personal contempt for the officer from Connecticut, he saluted Talmadge. With equal distain, Talmadge returned it. They stood face to face for a moment before Talmadge spoke.

"We intercepted a courier for the traitor, Jacob Leisler. He says he has a letter for you."

Staats knew Talmadge was trying to lure him into a verbal confrontation in order to dismiss him from the militia's ranks. He saw the trap and refused to take the bait.

"Have you read the letter yet?" Staats asked, sounding almost uninterested in its contents, partially because he had already guessed what it said.

"Not yet," Talmadge stated.

Staats walked in closer, several of the militiamen parting to let him into their defensive ring. He walked up to the rider and held out his hand. "May I?"

The rider held up his restrained hands and then struggled to open his jacket. Slowly, he produced a crumpled letter, the seal of Leisler clearly stamped onto it. Staats received the letter and broke the seal. As he opened it, Talmadge stopped him.

"Read it aloud," he said. Talmadge knew the letter must be important. Perhaps he could have Staats read some incriminating message; written evidence of high treason with a large crowd as witness. Perhaps he would hang Staats next to the courier in the same tree. The thought brought the slightest smile to Talmadge.

Staats seemed very calm about reading it aloud, a mysterious burst of confidence emitting from his voice. For a moment, Talmadge got a bad feeling that the letter was not what he hoped. Staats cleared his throat and spoke loud enough for all to hear.

"A proclamation of appointment by the acting governor of the province of New York, Jacob Leisler. To the people of Schenectady, I have heard your pleas for new order and justice for your village, neglected and abandoned by the rich aristocrats of Albany. I therefore appoint five men from your village who have shown they are able-bodied and of sound mind, to serve as magistrates and Justices of the Peace until such time as correspondence from the King arrives."

There was a murmur among the crowd. For a moment, Staats thought the crowd was not enthusiastically taking the news. In fact, some looked outright hostile.

Then someone started clapping.

Others joined in and the mood changed in a flash. This time it was Talmadge who grew nervous – and instantly regretted, letting Staats read the letter. But it was too late to stop him. He cursed Staats, knowing he had set this up.

Staats continued, reading off the names of the new appointees. "The men hereby appointed as magistrates and representatives of the people of Schenectady are Douw Aukes, David Christoffelse, Johannes Pootman, Myndert Wemp, and Ryer Jacobse Schermerhorn."

The crowd again cheered. Aukes and Christoffelse stood amongst them and nearby men shook their hands in congratulations, patting them on the back. As Staats finished the letter he folded it into his pocket with satisfaction. The next move was Talmadge's to make and both men knew it.

Chapter 30

Enos Talmadge had been in volatile situations before but never in all his years of military experience had he been in a predicament such as this. Not like this. In his care was a prisoner – a man who had carried a message by the usurper of New York. It was a traitor's deed and deserved a traitor's justice. But his duty was first and foremost to his men. Hanging the prisoner would guarantee none of them would make it back to Connecticut alive.

"Orders, sir?" one of his men asked.

The mob was increasingly restless since Talmadge had not released the courier yet. They started to push on the soldiers, who in turn, shoved the crowds back with their muskets. The move drew more anger and verbal threats from the mob.

Talmadge had played two risky gambles, and both had failed. The first was letting Staats read the letter from Leisler to the crowd. He cursed himself for that. The second had been less obvious at the time. The blockhouse offered relative safety from the mob. He should have retreated inside with the captive while he had the chance. With the crowd having surrounded him, that chance was gone.

Taking in his surroundings, he noticed something peculiar. The north gate had been closed, but who closed it remained a mystery to him.

Douw Aukes, flushed with pride and knowing he had loyal men behind him, stepped up to Talmadge. Talmadge eyed the large knife in Aukes' hand and raised his own pistol. Aukes sneered, "You can kill me, but my fellow countrymen will tear you and your Connecticut bastards to pieces before I hit the ground."

Talmadge remained firm. The time for negotiations had passed and it was going to end violently. There was no other way it *could* possibly end.

"Disperse or I'll send this shot through your skull," he said trying to stay calm.

Aukes hesitated, sizing up his opponent but Talmadge gave nothing away. He thought of backing down, but the calls for blood behind him kept him in a false sense of confidence, even as his inner resolve wavered.

"Run him through!" someone called out.

"Let's rush 'em," another voice shouted.

The crowd grew restless and moved back and forth, men readying themselves for the charge.

Albert Vedder felt the adrenaline rush but was not armed with as much as a club and felt naked in the face of the guns of the militia. The militiamen had seen enough and shoved the crowd back, gaining enough ground to raise their rifles to firing position.

Damn them, screamed Talmadge in his mind. If it was going to happen then they might as well get on with it. Death would come for many of them before sunset regardless. Talmadge raised his free hand.

"Make ready, gentlemen" he yelled out. "Mark your targets."

Some of the mob in the front buckled, and several in the back broke ranks to flee, trying to escape the coming volley of fire. Talmadge knew the first volley would devastate the mob but after that it would be savage hand-to-hand fighting and they were still outnumbered. He wished the bayonets he'd ordered for his men had arrived. They would have helped. It was too late to think of such things at that point. The fight for their lives was on.

Suddenly, there was a great deal of commotion - not from the front of the mob, but from behind it. Screams and shouts could be heard.

"They're behind us," someone cried out.

Talmadge strained his eyes. Through the crowd, he could make out a line of men forming behind the Leislerite mob.

"Form ranks and make ready," snapped Captain Glen as he trotted back and forth on his horse.

To his front, two lines of a dozen men each checked their rifles. They were a mix of Schenectady militia from the village, and Connecticut militia that Glen had rallied to him as he marched from his house, across the river and into the village from the south. The front rank took a knee, with the second standing behind them. He chose his formation to maximize the fire brought against the enemy.

It was a classic flanking maneuver and Glen knew he had caught the mob in between two formidable forces. He beamed with satisfaction at the tactical situation and knew he could defeat the unorganized Leislerites with little trouble.

Joachim Staats raced to the back of the crowd and found himself staring at the firing line. Having never served professionally, he was thrown entirely off-guard by Glen's superior tactical move. Instantly, Staats knew the day was lost and raced to save what he could. He held his hands high and broke from the crowd, stepping before the line of militia.

"For God's sake, don't fire. There has been no bloodshed and we will not start it."

Captain Glen turned the horse's mane, directing it closer to the front line. "What the hell are you doing, Lieutenant? Is this disorderly mob here on your orders?"

"No," Staats replied instinctively. "They're here on their own terms, but I can speak for many of them. They believe a man was wrongly imprisoned and want him to be freed." He slowly lowered his arms, cautious not to make any move that might appear threatening. He could see the fearful look of the militiamen ready to fire. "Sir, we need to examine the consequences here. This man delivered a letter and I read it to the crowd. That is all. Let him go and we can let this situation resolve itself peacefully."

Glen examined the situation. Civil war was brewing, and he knew a show of strength was needed. It was time for the people to be reminded where their allegiance should lie.

Ignoring Lieutenant Staats, Glen raised his sword and called out to the mob, "This is an illegal gathering in defiance of the orders of the Albany Convention and his majesty's government. Disperse now or we will fire. You have ten seconds."

There was a moment of absolute silence in the air. It was as if not a man present drew even a single breath. Albert Vedder was still staring down the barrel of a Connecticut gun. He tightened his fists, but his heart prayed harder than ever before.

Joachim Staats stood frozen in front of the crowd. His mind went white. There was no anger, no sorrow, no plan, just nothing. His eyes glanced up from the frozen ground to the horse and John Glen. He could see it in the Captain's eyes.

There was no doubt. He was going to do it.

This will be a massacre.

It broke him out of his trance. Turning, he flailed his arms wildly. "Everyone disperse!" he screamed as loud as he could. "Get out of here; they're going to kill you if you stay. Go to your homes."

The mob broke into a panicky mess as men scrambled away, some throwing their weapons to the ground. Terror gripped them all, feeling their unbreakable spirit shatter, as the reality of their dire situation sunk in.

Aukes glared at Talmadge. "This isn't over," he said before running away with a small group of men.

For a brief moment, Talmadge considered going after the group if only to run the Leislerite through with his sword. He ordered a general slow advance of his relatively small group of soldiers. They marched at a steady pace, their rifles low and straight to the front.

Within a minute, the militias had cleared the entire vicinity of the blockhouse and the north gate. They immediately reopened it to the general public but kept four men on guard at each gate.

Talmadge urged Glen to order roving patrols around the village in order to keep a show of force and discourage the populace from exploding into open rebellion. After hesitating at first, Glen finally conceded and ordered patrols to walk the village at random.

"This will keep the Leislerites from doing anything stupid," Glen said, hoping he believed it himself.

"What of Lieutenant Staats?" Talmadge asked.

"What of him?" Glen replied. "He read a letter and in no way directly threatened you or your men. I can't touch him."

Talmadge was aghast. "You have got to be kidding me, sir."

"No, I am not kidding you, Lieutenant," Glen snapped. Talmadge stiffened up as Glen shifted his weight towards him. "Do you have any idea how close you came to being butchered like cattle today? What if the messenger never got to me? What if they attacked before I could bring up reinforcements? Not only would you be dead, but they'd have control of the blockhouse, the arms and powder, and therefore control of the village."

Talmadge swallowed his saliva. "I'm sorry, sir. My apologies; I didn't assess the situation clearly."

"You are damn right you didn't," Glen swore. Seeing the outright fear in the lieutenant's eyes, Glen took a breath and calmed down. "Listen to me, Talmadge. The province is a total mess right now. We need to be diplomats as much as soldiers. Jacob Leisler, curse him, has garnered favor with the majority of the village. If we shoot into a crowd and kill innocent men and women, they'll tear this town apart. We cannot be the ones who escalate it.

"If they yell at you, speak calmly to them. If they shove you, block them and only push back if necessary. If they use clubs and blades, use the rifles to keep them at bay. Once the first shot is fired, the men will pour volley after volley into the crowd. And *that*, Lieutenant, is how wars begin."

"But this messenger, sir, carried a treasonous letter."

Glen threw up his arms in despair. "And what were you going to do? Hang him for bringing a letter? Christ, man, use your head."

Talmadge could see the furious look in Glen's eyes. Where had he gone wrong? He was only trying to do his duty.

"Captain, if I acted out of rank I will turn in my commission and command and report back to Captain Bull in Albany."

Glen shook his head. "That won't be necessary. Schenectady is my responsibility and I will report on what happened to the local magistrates."

Talmadge felt guilt which he had not expected. He could only guess how the Leislerites would react when they heard John Glen was responsible for the incident. He gulped, thinking the retribution would be swift.

"What can I do, sir?" he spoke quietly, humbled by the days turn of events.

Glen looked around, noting how quiet the village had become. Few people stirred outside their homes, and the streets bore the resemblance of an abandoned settlement. Only the smoke from the chimneys gave away the fact that people still lived there.

"Stay close to the fort for the next week. Send a rider back to Albany with a report of the incident." He paused, his mind racing in thought at what other actions could be taken. "And pray."

"Sir?"

Glen looked at him, his eyes darker as if some unseen pain gripped him. "Pray this doesn't get any worse."

* * *

Jacob Leisler stood in front of his desk. Standing before him were his most trusted lieutenants and supporters. Outside, the night was black with the light from the moon was being shrouded in overcast. A steady wind pounded against the window. The men looked tired but alert. Being summoned at such a late hour was not unheard of and Leisler had called them in such a manner many times before. But recently, with the onset of winter, it had become rare. They knew something was going to happen – or had already happened.

"Gentlemen," Leisler said. "We're entering a momentous time for the province; it is a time for action. Two weeks ago, I dispatched a rider to the village of Schenectady, a few miles west of Albany. We have significant support there among the poor and traders, those suppressed by the rich aristocrats of the

Convention. The information he carried was insignificant, the mere appointment of five men as magistrates whom we can trust.

"Before leaving Albany, Milborne gave instructions to our officer in that village sealed orders to be opened the day the appointments were received." He paused, watching his men stir with anxiety. "His orders are to seize the fort in that village and capture the garrison."

There was a low murmur among the present officers. Leisler waited until they had quieted before speaking again. "We will outflank the Convention and capture this strategically important town, cutting Albany off from the Mohawk. We will have dominance over the beaver pelts coming from the Indians and use it to replenish our city coffers, pay the men, build our defenses, and cut into the credibility of the Convention. In short, gentlemen, we tried to seize Albany by force and failed. Now, we will cause them to collapse from within and New York will be ours."

Chapter 31

The reaction came swift. It was much sooner than Talmadge could have anticipated. By mid-morning, the crowds were already gathering again. The militias continued their patrols until noon, when persistent threats forced them from the streets. They rallied at the blockhouse, southeast tower, and both gates. The rest of Schenectady effectively belonged to the mob.

Talmadge did not understand it. He watched the village from a window on the upper floor of the fort. The night had been mostly quiet. A few men and women scurrying about between houses after sunset and one drunken fool he had ordered detained until sunrise. There was not a single sign of conspiracy. *Could the village truly be siding with Jacob Leisler?* he thought. Looking around, he knew the answer.

At the guidance of Captain Glen, Talmadge had released the rider at sunrise. The terms of release were simple. Talmadge wanted him gone from Schenectady. Not a word was to be said to anyone, anywhere. The rider took the generous terms and galloped away without looking back. Talmadge hoped that would buy some good grace with the villagers. Looking around at the clusters of angry men, and even a few women, he knew it would not make a difference. The majority sided with Leisler.

"Johannes, have you finished yet boy?"

"Yes, Father," Johannes said, coming around the corner with a stack of beaver pelts, all beautifully cleaned up. "I'm sorry it took me so long. I have no excuse."

Johannes eyed the floor as his father grabbed

the pelts. Harmen examined each of them. Looking over the work, his frustration melted away.

"This is superb work, son. You will make a fine trader, that's for sure."

Johannes was overwhelmed with relief. "Thank you, Father. I just did what you taught me to do."

Harmen betrayed his usual sternness, allowing a small smile. He was taken aback. In recent weeks Johannes had demonstrated real signs of maturity. He was handling himself like an adult. "What gives?" he asked.

Johannes shrugged. "Nothing really. I just want to make you proud, Father. I want to make our family proud."

Harmen set the pelts down. "What do you want for yourself?"

Johannes noted the unusually casual tone his father spoke with.

"I don't know yet," he responded. "I haven't found what I am looking for out of life, that much I know is true. But I won't let my desires block me from ensuring our family's success. I can't continue to follow only my heart. It would be the end of me."

Johannes knew he must sound like a sentimental fool to his father. To his surprise though, he felt his father's hand come to rest on his shoulder.

"It took me a long time to find my purpose as well." Johannes glanced up. Harmen nodded. "It's true. I was like you for a long time. I could have remained in Holland and made an honest living there. But I came here because I wanted the opportunity and the adventure."

"What made you stop?"

"I settled down," Harmen replied. "I found a woman I loved, married her, and laid my roots down.

Life then gets a lot simpler. You wake up in the morning, and from then on, until you lay your head down to sleep, you spend every moment working to ensure your family survives and moves forward in this new world. Right now, that may sound like a burden, but I hope you live to see the day when it becomes a blessing."

Johannes smiled. The thought did excite him; he could not deny it. "We would never have lasted without you, Father. I suppose I never thanked you."

"You can thank me once I am old and fragile. You can take care of me." They both laughed. "You did well. Off with you, go take care of whatever business you have."

The snow fell steadily outside. A thin, fresh layer already coated the roofs and muddy roads. Stepping outside, something felt amiss. His instincts told him something troubling was stirring. There was a feeling of restlessness – or perhaps preparation. He saw a mother grab her two children and move them into the safety of their home. A group of men were gathered by the church. They were Leislerites.

In the center of the mob, stood Ryer Jacobse Schermerhorn. His long black coat and tall, black capotain hat were unmistakable. Next to him were all the prominent opponents of the Albany Convention. Douw Aukes, Jan Potman, David Christoffelse, Myndert Wemp, and even the village surgeon, Reynier Schaets. They were surrounded by dozens of men, all armed with muskets or pikes. Two of them carried torches and the fires glowed like beacons in the cloudy day.

About the time Johannes Vedder spotted the Leislerite mob, word reached Captain Glen. He mustered what few men he could and marched on the church at the center of town. Upon arriving, Glen realized he was outnumbered badly. Ryer Schermerhorn was alerted to the militia's presence.

"Get them, boys!" he yelled out.

With a roar, the Leislerites stormed forward towards the militia. Glen, on his horse, produced his saber. "Form firing line to the front."

A group of militiamen rallied to his front and knelt to firing positing.

"They're on the flanks," a voice cried out. Glen turned to see angry masses moving towards him from both sides. He could see no option but to withdraw. He did not like the decision, but he knew he had to make it fast.

"Fall back, gentlemen," he shouted. "Fall back to the north gate." His small militia broke rank and ran like rabbits, some tossing their arms and scattering. The orderly withdrawal became a route. By time he reached the north gate, Glen only had a handful of men remaining by his side. Just like Talmadge the day before, they were boxed in, but opposing them was a much larger and more formidable foe.

"Let me pass," Ryer Schermerhorn shouted out, pushing his men to the side as he moved to the front of the mob. Johannes Vedder had followed the mob closely behind and edged in closer to hear the exchange.

"Captain Glen," Schermerhorn began, "you have betrayed the trust of the people of this town. You have brought these peaceful and loyal subjects to the brink of war and bloodshed."

"You did that yourself, Ryer," Glen retorted. "When you took up arms against …"

"Silence!" Ryer shouted. Glen, more from surprise than fear, ceased talking. Unlike the elderly Aukes, Schermerhorn had a natural presence that commanded respect. "We are not here to debate you, sir. We have heard enough of your lecturing."

Ryer eyed the people gathered. No longer just the armed Leislerites, but people from all over the village were gathered in witness.

"Captain John Glen," Ryer said, "You are hereby relieved of your position as Captain of the militia. You are henceforth banished from this village." There was a gasp and murmuring from the crowds. "You are forbidden from entering or conducting business of any kind within these walls. Any breach of these decrees will be met with the most severe of punishments."

Inside, Glen grew uneasy, but he tried as best as he could to maintain a proper front to the public. "You have no authority, Ryer," he stated.

"On the contrary," Schermerhorn said, "I have full authority by the people of this village."

There was a cheer and applause from many in the crowd.

"What would be my punishment should I return?" Glen dared to ask. Ryer stood in silence.

"Bind him in a pillory," a woman shouted from the crowd.

"Brand him," yelled another.

The crowd went wild, shouting out various forms of torture. Glen shifted his body in the saddle as they cried out the various punishments.

Douw Aukes stepped forward. "This man is a traitor," he bellowed. "I say we hang him."

The crowd cheered. Glen started to sweat under his jacket.

"No," said Ryer in a low, deep voice. The crowd hushed. "We will not hang this man." He stared at Glen for a moment. "John Glen," he said, "if you enter this village in breach of this decree, you will die by fire. We will burn you at the stake."

This time the crowd was deathly silent. Only the fluttering winter wind blowing around could be heard. Glen stared long at Ryer Schermerhorn. There was no bluff or give in the man's demeanor. Glen was terrified at the prospect. "And my men?" he stuttered.

"They may return to their homes unharmed, so long as they take no further orders from you."

Glen nodded. "And the Connecticut militia?"

"They are here to protect against a French threat, are they not?"

"They are," Glen said.

"Then they may stay," Ryer replied. There was some disapproval from those around him. "So long as they interfere no more with the internal conduct of the business or politics of this village. They may stand post and conduct patrols. Beyond that, they have no authority. Is that acceptable?"

Glen bowed his head.

"It is settled then." Ryer turned to the mob. "No person shall permit John Glen to enter this village, nor conduct business within these walls. Punishment shall be a hundred lashes." He looked to Glen. "Leave and do not come back."

Glen saw that his men were already dispersing, returning to their homes. Without a word, he grabbed the reigns, turned and trotted out the gate.

Johannes Vedder watched the episode unfold before him. It was unreal to see Captain Glen driven from the village at gunpoint and under a death threat. Ryer Schermerhorn and the Leislerites celebrated Glen's departure. There was no longer any debating who was in control of Schenectady.

Chapter 32

January 17, 1690

The early morning sky was a dark blue and the temperature was well below freezing. Jacques Le Moyne de Sainte-Hélène and Nicolas d'Ailleboust de Manthet were summoned to the office of Governor Callières for one last brief meeting. As their horses trotted through the deep snow, Sainte-Hélène and Manthet exchanged glances.

"I was hoping my next raiding expedition would be in springtime," Sainte-Hélène said with a smile. "After Hudson Bay, I could use a break."

"Would you rather carry canoes to cross the rivers in our way? Come Sainte-Hélène, we've been through this before. Even that buffoon Frontenac agreed that winter was the best time to strike."

Sainte-Hélène laughed. "You don't really believe that there were tactics in his consideration of the timing, do you? He wants revenge as soon as possible and although I want them to bleed as much as the next loyal Canadian, I would rather wait until the spring and we have had the time to muster a larger force."

The two men arrived at the governor's house.

Before they dismounted, Manthet grabbed Jacques' arm. "Do you know what it feels like to be pursued by the Mohawk?" Jacques paused but did not respond. Manthet let go, thinking back to his own experiences. "It's a nightmare is what it is. They are relentless – they are cruel. When you stop for four hours, they stop for two. When you walk, they run. And then they find you." Jacques listened, his heart rate steady but clearly Manthet had gained his attention.

"They go for the stragglers first, picking them off in the dark and the shadows. You run faster, not just to escape the Mohawk, but to escape the cries of the men you left behind as they are sacrificed over the fires or are scalped by tomahawk."

Manthet paused, reflecting. "Finally, when the war party believes you've been sufficiently weakened, they strike. The war cries go up and they pour out of the woods and come down upon your men. In some ways, it's almost a relief from the days or weeks of torturous hit and run attacks they've been using. You can finally see and fight your pursuers. Do you know what to do then?"

"Kill them all," Sainte-Hélène responded.

"No!" Manthet said. "You run – you run as fast as you can while you are still alive."

Jacques was astonished. *Run away? Is this man joking?*

"Make no mistake," Manthet continued. "When the Mohawk finally attack, they already know the odds are in their favor. They plan it that way. Standing to fight will get you nothing beyond dead." He dismounted his horse, his feet sinking almost two feet into the snow. Sainte-Hélène dismounted but kept paying attention to Manthet as he continued, "Just remember, the deeper the snow, the slower they travel."

Manthet stepped through the snow and up the steps to the door. Jacques looked down at his feet, disappeared beneath the white. He thought for a moment, realizing that perhaps the timing was right for an attack.

Inside the governor's home, the three men stood by the fireplace, staring into the glowing embers. Outside, the sky was brightening but the wind had also picked up. But inside, the fire kept the men comfortable.

Callières rested one arm on the mantle and smoked through a long, slender, clay pipe. Sainte-Hélène polished his large wood-runner knife on a small stone. Manthet stood silent, his arms crossed, and his gaze fixed on the flames. The brief meeting had stretched out, lasting more than two hours. Callières wanted to leave nothing to chance. He made each of the two Canadian lieutenants go over every phase of the raid against Fort Orange, including contingency plans if the town proved too formidable for a direct assault.

The governor had suspected for days that they would not be able to assault that town and would have to settle for one of the smaller villages, most likely Corlear. Ultimately, he left the final decision to the two men in the room that would lead the raid. Having reviewed their extensive records of service, he could only conclude that they would make the most logical choice when the time came.

Orange was a much larger town, with a full garrison. With reports of a militia from the neighboring New England colony of Connecticut still in the area, the raiding party would run the risk of having any attack develop into a full set-piece battle, in which the Canadians and their allies would be heavily outnumbered.

"Listen to the scouts," Callières said breaking the silence. "Trust their eyes to guide you and for the Lord's sake, don't risk an open battle."

He looked to each of his lieutenants. Manthet straightened up but Sainte-Hélène continued to play with the knife, running his finger along the blade and grinning maniacally.

"Remember, if Corlear becomes the preferred objective, there are certain considerations to be taken into account."

Sainte-Hélène looked up. "Such as?"

"The manor across the river must not be harmed under any circumstance," Callières stated. "He was a friend to the French years ago. And the minister of the village may be useful. Do not harm him either."

"How could we possibly know who that is?"

"The scarlet cord in his window," Callières replied. "As the good book states, it is a sign of trust; not in walls, but in the Lord. That is how you will identify any priest's dwelling."

"Anyone else?" Manthet asked.

Callières nodded. "The savages in the village itself also should not be harmed if possible. We're trying to win them over to our side and slaughtering them in the dead of night wouldn't help sway them to the French side."

"But if they resist?" Sainte-Hélène asked.

Callières grew annoyed, knowing that the Le Moyne brother just wanted to hear him say the words.

"If they attack, then kill them and burn the bodies." Callières put his hand on Manthet's shoulder. "Seal off the village. If any villagers get away, they'll warn Orange and by noon the area will be swarming with militia and Mohawk – all of them seeking revenge."

"We'll be in and out before they know what hit them, monsieur," Manthet stated firmly. "Whether it's Orange or Corlear, they won't have time to do anything beyond bury their dead and collect the wounded."

"Regardless, the journey back will be undoubtedly the most tedious. But I have faith in you two," Callières said with pride. "There is nothing more to say."

He looked at Manthet who nodded. His eyes turned to Sainte-Hélène and he also agreed. The time for discussion was over.

"Go – get it done. The dead of Lachine march beside you."

It was almost eight before the Canadian militiamen began to show up at the gates of Montreal's defenses. Not to anyone's surprise, the native warriors of the Sault people, belonging to the Caughnawaga—Mohawk's who converted to Catholicism by way of the French Jesuits—were already present. The Sault numbered eighty, and for a time, they appeared to be the main driving force of the Montreal expedition. But slowly the Frenchmen gathered until they numbered one hundred and fourteen. Another sixteen natives of the Algonquin tribe also joined the congregation. The Algonquin were far more trusted by the French than the converted Mohawks, but their numbers were also much fewer.

Both militiamen and natives alike clenched their blankets tight. On their feet, they wore soft moccasins further wrapped up in heavy cloths. A few Canadians, mostly trappers, sported fur hats made from beaver or other small mammals. The muskets were slung around their backs with axes and knives dangling from their belts.

Each man carried with him twenty days' rations of food – mostly bread, salted meats, and dried corn.

Most important to the Canadians and their Indian allies were the snowshoes on their feet. The trek from Montreal to Fort Orange and back would be through more than two hundred miles of wilderness, and the snows were expected to be up to five feet deep in places. To make matters worse, the added rations, weapons, and cold weather supplies made the men of the expedition unusually heavy. Without snowshoes, the journey would be far slower and would certainly drain the men's energy, leaving nothing for the raids which they had volunteered for. The snowshoes would enable them to make the march with greater ease and allow their escape with equal haste.

Only a few horses were present to carry the raiding party's leaders. Manthet found Athasata sitting beside some of his warriors in quiet conversation. He gently tapped the great Mohawk chief on the shoulder and signaled it was time to go. Athasata gave a silent nod and arose with his men. With a force of effort, he managed to climb up onto his horse.

At first, he was determined to make the journey in the manner of most of his warriors – on foot. But in his aging years, he found he had not the strength to make such a long, physically demanding trip without the aid of a horse. A few other natives also brought horses as they were acting scouts for the expedition.

The last to arrive were Sainte-Hélène and his brother Pierre Le Moyne d'Iberville. Another brother, François Le Moyne de Bienville stood in the ranks of the Canadian militiamen. The Le Moyne brothers— already of high prestige and having ascertained a degree of celebrity—had a reputation to uphold. François was younger than Jacques and Pierre. He had barely partaken in the 1687 campaign against the Seneca and was lacking in personal accomplishments. While he liked to pretend he had volunteered for the mission, it was his brothers who had practically ordered him to join them.

As his brothers passed by him on their horses François tried to make himself noticed. He looked for eye contact and raised his hand slightly but neither saw him as they rode past. François dropped his arm to his disappointment. Around him he felt the eyes of his fellow countrymen staring down at him, as if they were ashamed to march besides a man of such unimportance that his only fame was that through his family name. All he ached was to achieve his own glory and join his brothers in all their honor.

Sainte-Hélène, Manthet, and Athasata gathered at the head of the column. Manthet turned around one last time and grinned. He had done the final count. Only a few men did not show up for muster and they would be dealt with afterwards. But the total force impressive by any standards, let alone for one gathered at such short notice. Two-hundred and ten men all together, were ready to march. Roughly split down the middle, the raiding party was half Canadian militia and half native warriors of the allied tribes.

The raiding party looked professional but there was a certain barbarity to their appearance. The tomahawks and hunter's knives slung from their belts, and the muskets looped around the back, were stark reminders of the mission for those men. It was not an exploration nor foraging expedition. It was an army assembled to avenge the savage murders of their fellow countrymen. Soon, the innocent men, women, and children of the New York colony would also know the terror and death of frontier warfare.

Manthet signed the cross, and clasped his hands in prayer. His lips moved as he uttered a few words of hope and victory in the endeavor. Sainte-Hélène glanced around, waiting for Manthet to finish.

Though a Catholic like most Canadians, Jacques made no attempt to hide that he laid his fate in his own hands, and nothing else. After finishing, Manthet turned back to the two co-commanders. "We're ready," he announced.

Sainte-Hélène tightened the reigns of his horse and took the first step. Slowly, like a great machine turning on, the line of men began to move. Those on horses kept the pace slow as to not outrun their infantry counterparts. The men, native and Canadian alike, trudged through the deep snow, their snow shoes helping to keep them from sinking in too deeply.

Like a giant snake, the line of men stretched out and picked up their pace as they crossed through the gates of the Montreal settlement. Several older men, women, and children had come out into the freezing morning to wave the expedition off. The young boys looking on in awe had little idea of what fate lay in store for the Dutch settlers of the New York colony.

And with that, the small army of French Canadians and loyal Mohawk and Algonquin warriors left the safety of the walls of the village of Montreal. The commanders had devised a plan and rather than crossing the river immediately, they took the expedition southeast on the island which the settlement rested on – and the surrounding farms and homes which had been burned out by the raiding Mohawks six months prior. Seeing the destruction again enraged the militiamen. They swore under their breaths and clinched their rifles in frustration. Sainte-Hélène saw their anger and grinned. He could scarcely wait to see his men let loose their full vengeance against the people of Orange or Corlear.

Chapter 33

To Johannes, the next few days seemed almost surreal. Schenectady appeared to have nearly returned to a state of normalcy. Since the banishment of Captain Glen, the village had settled into a stalemate between the Connecticut garrison and the Leisler-controlled council. The soldiers, for the most part, kept to the fort. They only occasionally ventured out on patrol, or down to one of the taverns for a few rounds of ale. The Leislerites for their part, stayed away from the fort, and conducted the business of the village as it had been before the ordeal began.

Johannes stopped by the home of Barent Van Ditmars. Waiting patiently outside, he smiled as several young boys and girls raced by him, chasing one another with snowballs and laughing. A fur trader led his two horses through town, presumably on his way to Albany. Each trudged through the snow with dozens of pelts strapped to their backs. The next house down, a husband and wife were busy patching holes in their roof.

Barent's wife, Catharina, answered the door. "Why hello young man," she said. "How may I help you?"

"I'm just here to return this," Johannes said, holding up the book given to him.

"Well come in and make yourself comfortable. Barent is out back and will be in shortly."

Johannes stepped inside. The fire was fading but the house was sufficiently warm. The home had such a comfortable appeal to it. Johannes smiled, thinking of what his own home would look like someday. Catharina came back from the kitchen with a warm beer for him. He politely accepted it, sipping on it until Barent came back in.

"Johannes, what can I do for you?"

Johannes handed him the book. "I just came by to drop this off, and to thank you for letting me borrow it."

Taking it, Barent smiled. "You liked it?"

"Liked it?" Johannes laughed. "I have never read something like that before. The way Adrien Van Der Donck describes the land, and the animals, and even the Natives, is incredible. Having finally been to the Mohawk land and seen their castles firsthand, his accuracy is unparalleled. I want to explore so much more of this land."

Barent smiled at Johannes' enthusiasm. He grabbed a beer and sat down, directing Johannes to bring up a chair and join him. "So, lad," he said, "are you going to stick with the fur trade like your father?"

"Ideally, no," Johannes replied. "There is so much uncharted territory to the north and west. I would love to go see those lands first before settling down. But right now, I just don't see a way around being a fur trader, or perhaps a farmer. I have to make a living, right?"

Barent nodded, leaning back. "There's more than one way to make a living. Look at myself," he chuckled. "I have been a carpenter, a farmer, a trader, a merchant, and many more. There is no decree that you must choose one path in life and keep to it. Do what your heart desires and you will never be disappointed."

"Well with the war coming, I don't suppose I will be doing much traveling at all. From what my father told me, the Albany Convention suspects the French will attack at some point this winter."

Barent leaned back in his chair and folded his arms. "And this unnerves you?"

"It terrifies me," Johannes admitted. "I am not a soldier. Nor is my father, or brother. My father told me stories about King Philip's War and how every other month, there was news of another attack."

"I know, lad," Barent said. "These are dark times. Yet, we must hold on to our dreams. If nothing else can be saved, then save them. Sooner or later, the fighting will cease. And when peace arrives, you do not want to spend your days lamenting over what you lost. Instead, Johannes, you must seek out what is new, and good in the world. Find a woman, get married, raise a big family on a big patch of earth. Explore the world. Learn new skills. That is how we survive." Barent leaned in closer. "We survive by enduring when there is war, and growing when there is peace. For now, endure. But never forget how to grow."

Johannes grinned. "I won't forget." He cleared his throat. "About the book…"

"Keep it," Barent said. "At my age, I doubt I will ever read it again."

"I can't just accept it," Johannes said.

Barent nodded. "Your father's son, indeed. Very well," he said, standing up. "I will sell it to you – for one penning."

Johannes admired the old man's sense of humor. He reached into his pocket and handed over some copper coins. "I'll buy it for two."

When Johannes left the Van Ditmars residence, he headed out the gate to watch the children ice skate on the river. The unusually cold winter had kept the river frozen and strong enough to support full-grown men. Even small pack animals and sleds weighed down in goods were ferried across the ice on skis.

Passing outside the gate, two Connecticut soldiers were standing guard. Surrounding them were several children of the village. The young boys were children of known Leislerites, and were mocking the soldiers, mimicking their movements with sticks as guns. Johannes ignored them and walked down to the frozen river. The blue sky shined across the white landscape beyond the river. The laughter of children was carried by a light breeze. Johannes stood by the river's edge and watched the ice skating for a few moments, before heading back.

"Johannes, look here!" a voice called out. Johannes saw one of the young boys by the gate. One of the Christoffelse boys, Thomas, was rolling up a giant snowball. He picked up the ball and put it on top of a larger one.

"What are you doing?" Johannes asked.

"We're defending Schenectady!" Thomas laughed. "We are making men of snow to guard against the French. Then the aristocrats and their troops can leave us in peace."

Johannes glanced at the two men at arms. They seemed to be a bit annoyed at the children, but more of a nuisance than a threat. "I do not believe your snowmen will be much of a defense," he mused.

Another boy put a third ball on the top. They proceeded to make a face on the head out of small stones and twigs scattered about. Thomas leaned a large stick up against the snowman.

"It's a gun," the boy said. "Now he can defend us."

Johannes smiled, trying to conceal his disappointment that the feud had even made its way into the minds of kids. Nobody, it seemed, was spared from the conflict.

"Go home, Thomas. I am sure your mom has chores for you."

The children kept up the work into the

afternoon, carving and shaping their two snow soldiers. The guards knew better than to knock them down, else they unleash the wrath of a hostile village. With the sun setting, the two Connecticut guards closed the north gate.

Outside, two snowmen continued their vigilant watch.

Chapter 34

Arnout Viele was learning the new meaning of misery. His frozen hands gripped the oar, wrapped only in a thin cloth. His clothes were wet-through, draining the heat from his body. Icy water splashed all around and the wind whipped in circles, chilling him to the bone.

His neck ached as he strained to turn and look forward. To his disappointment, he saw only a thick blanket of fog all around. At the bow stood a Mohawk scout, tall and firm and wearing clothes far too thin for the near-arctic conditions, gazing out as if guiding them by some unseen sense of direction.

"How does he know where we're going?" Viele asked Robert Sanders. The elderly statesman didn't break his gaze, staring off into the unknown. "Mr. Sanders?"

"He knows where he's going, you can be sure of that." The scout called out in native tongue and Sanders rolled his shoulders as if a weight was lifted. "We're here."

Out of the fog, a dark silhouette emerged on the horizon. As they rowed closer, the tall wooden walls of the Onondaga castle came into view. To Arnout Viele, the castle bore a menacing look. Having been the site of many battles and sieges, its walls were blackened from ash and many sections of the palisade wall were in dire need of repair.

The boats were pulled ashore and the contingent of Mohawk sachem and their two Dutch diplomats stepped onto the shore. Two Onondaga warriors stood outside the village's gate. Viele could smell the burning fires inside the village. A warrior walked along the parapet, looking down at the visitors.

"I was expecting a friendlier welcome," Robert Sanders said quietly to Viele.

"Where's the other tribes?" Viele asked. His answer came almost immediately. The gate opened, and a handful of Iroquois elders came out to greet their Mohawk brethren. Their attire was similar and yet in small ways different from the sachem of the Mohawk.

"That's Onondaga." Sanders pointed. "And the muscular warrior - he's Seneca. The darker one is Oneida, and the other guy is Cayuga. If you get them confused, just ask me."

"How do you know them all? They all look the same to me."

Sanders laughed. "I've been a diplomat on the frontier longer than you've been alive. One of the first rules you must learn if you're going to be effective – pay attention to who you're talking to. From appearance, we may look like the English, but Lord knows there's a world of difference between us and them. It's no different among the Natives."

When they entered the castle, Viele was aghast at what he saw inside. The longhouses and other structures inside were in a sorrowful state. Roofs were collapsed in. On one longhouse, a thin blanket filled with holes was draped over a doorway. A medical chieftain, wearing a handkerchief, directed a warrior with a cart to take a body outside. Other men sat by the several small fires, coughing and gripping their fur coats tightly. Expecting a sturdy and impressive castle, Viele found himself in the midst of a dilapidated, disease-infested stockade, housing the sick, cold, and hungry.

A French doctor approached the Natives and spoke in good English. "We had a cholera outbreak a month ago. It has mostly been eradicated but all the same, we have nothing to offer you in terms of food and drink. The small longhouse to the north has been converted into a makeshift hospital for the sick. We only ask that you keep distance from the sick, so as not to spread the disease."

"I did not expect to see any French here," Sanders replied.

"I was invited by the Jesuits and the sachem of the great Onondaga," the doctor replied. "I do the Lord's work. Nothing more or less."

Viele leaned in and whispered to Sanders, "I never knew a Frenchman who cared if a Wilden died, not even a doctor."

"He doesn't," Sanders replied. "It's all diplomacy. Don't accept anything offered by them. They'd like nothing more than for us to carry cholera back to Albany."

Viele nodded. When he looked at the Frenchman again, he started to recognize him for what he was - an enemy. In their efforts to restore peace, the Onondaga had opened the gates to their mortal enemies. Glancing around the village, he stopped at a lone figure, standing next to the central longhouse. The man was not an Indian, nor did he look distinctively French.

"Who's that?"

Sanders looked over. The man was dressed head to toe in black and had a wide-brim black hat. His beard was black and neatly trimmed. "He's a Jesuit." Viele indicated he did not understand. "Catholic missionary – French," Sanders added. "They've traveled as much of this unknown continent as anyone, preaching their religion to the Natives. I hope he's not partaking in the council."

"Why?"

"Because I've heard they are cunning and devious. They use words as their weapons and in the past have used moving speeches to drive the Natives away from alliances with us."

"A priest?" Viele asked, stunned. "What's a priest doing engaging in diplomacy?"

"Remember, the French and English do not have the sort of separation between church and state that we enjoy. Their ministers are as much statesmen as Mayor Schuyler himself. If I had to guess, I would say he's here to make sure the Iroquois remain divided on their allegiances in this war. That has to be his purpose here."

"Does this mean their peace offering was genuine?" Viele asked. "If it wasn't, then why would he bother coming here? Or is this just another ruse to delay our response?"

Sanders beamed with pride inside. "You ask many questions. I like that about you. You should always ask questions; question the unknown and never assume you know the answer. And you are right, this isn't a trap. The peace offering may or may not be genuine - that we will have to determine here. But Frontenac - who is?" he asked, testing the young interpreter.

"He's the governor general of New France," Viele replied.

"Good!" he said with a nod. "He can't hope to attack this village and kill or take us hostage. These Natives represent some of the most respected sachem and elders of the Five Nations. An attack on them would bring the full force of the Iroquois Confederacy down upon Canada. Even Frontenac knows that would be the end of New France."

The cold winds swept around them. The wooden palisade creaked and the sky grew darker as the harsh reality set in; they were no longer in strictly-friendly territory. While the Onondaga were one of the

Five Nations, their neutrality made Sanders uneasy. "I don't see the threat," Viele said finally. Sanders eyed him suspiciously. "I just mean, there's a hundred miles of nothing in every direction. What are we fighting for? There's infinite resources and land."

"You have much to learn," Sanders said. "This war is about keeping our families safe from foreign invasion. It's about not letting the French dominate this continent. It's about our allies," he said pointing to the Iroquois sachem. "They will not forget what the French did to them. Entire villages were wiped out, crops erased, the people killed, scattered, or enslaved. Men, women, children - they spared no one. They've delivered smallpox to the Seneca, killing untold numbers. They use their own Wilden allies as pawns, fighting their wars for them, without care for loss. Make no mistake, they are the true savages, not the Wilden."

"I understand what you are saying," Viele replied, "but I just haven't seen it yet."

"And I pray that you never do," Sanders said. In his mind, he wished there was a way to show the young man what their enemies were capable of. "I fear that this war won't end until either us or they are driven from this new world forever."

Tahajadoris approached Sanders and Viele. "My brothers," he said, his deep voice carrying in the cold air. "It is time to sit down and talk. The Five Nations are all here and the Great Council has assembled. The fire is lit."

Arnout Viele felt a chill run through his body. Not because he was cold. On the contrary, the room he found himself standing in was quite warm. The fire burned hot and the plethora of bodies made it almost too much. But he felt a deeper cold, the kind that comes from the unknown, for that was where he was.

The great longhouse had been converted into a meeting hall for the occasion. The walls were coated in deer hides for added insulation. The women grabbed the children and vacated the building, leaving the men to discuss the volatile situation. Standing about the room were over a dozen Natives from the various Iroquois nations along with two Frenchmen, serving as ambassadors to Frontenac. The only people Viele recognized were Sanders and the Mohawks he traveled with, including Tahajadoris. The rest almost felt threatening due to their mysterious nature.

The Frenchman who had greeted them opened the council with a brief speech about peace and understanding. The words had little effect on Viele as he had come to expect the false courtesy from Sanders' teachings. Next, Tahajadoris stood to speak. Even the quiet whisperers in the back fell silent as they focused to listen to the elderly Mohawk who was respected by all.

"My brothers, we have come to a dangerous place in our time. At stake is the world we leave for our children and their children. We come here in the offering of peace and journeyed far as a sign of our commitment to that peace.

"But we are offered this peace by a man who lies to us; a man who cheats us. What has this man who calls himself Frontenac ever offered that was true of the heart? When has he not offered us food and given us weeds, offered us meat and given us bones, offered us peace and given us war, and offered us life and given us death? This man has cut down the tree of peace before and will do so again.

"I say brothers; we cannot trust this man nor any man that carries his message. I stand here before you today with the word of Brother Quider, of the

Dutch peoples. His people and our people stand as allies against the French threat. Together we are strong and need not listen to lures of peace and safety. We will not suffer the pain of being deceived."

Tahajadoris sat down as the lead sachem of the Seneca nation stood up. His message was even more blunt and hostile to the French than Tahajadoris' speech. The well-built Seneca warrior gestured several times in the direction of the French while calling for war. It was difficult for Viele to make out what the Indian was saying but he could pick out the more basic vocabulary.

While listening to the speaker, Viele noticed that the mysterious Jesuit had somehow made his way into the council room. He was standing in the back, the brightness of the flame not reaching his dark corner, as if he wanted to remain out of sight. Even as the Seneca spoke of the atrocities committed by the French, Viele noted that the Jesuit remained like a statue.

As the Seneca leader sat, the sachem of the Cayuga stood to speak. He was not particularly noticeable in any way. He was neither tall nor broad nor carried himself well. Before speaking he glanced at the Jesuit who faintly nodded.

"The Cayuga nation stands with our brethren of the Five Nations," he began. "We will come to the aid of any who call upon us, and will fight alongside our brethren. But we remain committed to peace and we trust in the peace offered by the French and Father Milet."

Viele looked at the Jesuit. Clearly the missionary was upset that the Native mentioned him by name. Viele started to question whether this man was even a true priest, or just a French spy dressed as one.

The sachem continued, "The hardships that have befallen on our people have also befallen on their people. They do not wish for a continuation of war any more than we. The bloodshed must cease at a point and we must grow a new tree under which peace can once again prosper."

The Oneida was next. Viele watched with apprehension as they too pledged to support the peace deal offered by Frontenac. The sachem did make it clear though, that the Huron were still their enemy, even if they were allied to France.

Viele wondered as much as anyone there about the last of the Five Nations - the Onondaga. With the release of the chieftains who were taken more than a year ago, there stood a chance that they too had been won over by Frontenac's peace offering. The great chieftain of the Onondaga, Sadekanactie, stood up.

"Brothers, I urge you to heed the word of Brother Quider and not listen to the vile French, for they are liars. We must stand against them and urge our Dutch brothers and English allies to fall upon Quebec in the spring, to choke out the liars from those lands."

His speech was quick and to the point. As he sat down, all those who were not Iroquois left the longhouse, so the elders could talk more, in private.

"What are they discussing now?" Viele asked.

"It's now about compromise," Sanders said. "They will either decide to unite in peace, unite in war, or …"

"Or what?"

Sanders shrugged. "Or the great fire will be put out," he said. "At that point, each tribe stands alone. And God forbid, if that happens, the French will come for us all."

Viele swallowed, looking over his shoulder. The Jesuit priest was standing by a fire, clutching a Bible, and looking back at him. Viele turned away, wondering how long the elders would debate.

It would be another hour before the sachems and chieftains exited the longhouse. Sanders and Viele stiffened up when they saw the look on Tahajadoris' face.

"What happened?" Sanders asked.

Tahajadoris, a man who rarely showed emotion, was clearly disturbed. "The Cayuga and Oneida remain committed to the lies of peace. The great council fire is out." He lifted his head slightly. "But know that the Mohawk stand with you."

Chapter 35

François Le Moyne de Bienville gripped his coat tightly, against a draft of icy wind, blowing through the trees. He shivered and wiped his nose. The snow of the mountains in the northern New York territory was deep, and every step was a struggle, only made easier by the snow shoes on his feet. The raiding party was already south of Crown Point.

The sleds that carried them down the frozen Lake Champlain, overladen with food and equipment, were a struggle to drag through the snow-covered hills.

Both behind and in front of François, the column of French Canadian troops stretched out, snaking through the dense forest. All of them were tired and hungry but trudged on relentlessly. Their stomachs ached on the undersized rations each man was permitted for the day and their legs were worn out from the constant marching.

François looked up ahead to his two brothers on horseback. His envy and jealousy were intertwined but each was trivial next to the task ahead. He knew his brothers had done more than their share in service of New France and it was why they were selected for key positions in the raiding force. He had only been on a few expeditions into Seneca land, and not fought in as many battles. The key to advancement, he knew, was through battlefield glory, and he was proud his brothers were setting the example for him and all Canadians.

Seeing the column halting, François continued up to his brother. Sainte-Hélène was climbing off his horse when François approached. "How goes it, brother?" he asked.

"It is a fine day," Sainte-Hélène replied. "How is your strength? Are you finding this march to be fitting?"

François nodded. "How much further south is it? My legs are sore, and I am eager to get this done and head back to Montreal for some warm porridge," he said with a smile.

"Another week perhaps," his brother replied curtly. "Manthet will be calling a council soon. I must get going."

Sainte-Hélène started to turn. François took a step forward. "Jacques, wait."

"What is it?"

"It's just I never talk to you or Pierre anymore," François sighed. "You are my elder brothers and I look to you for guidance. Yet, whenever I approach, you leave or treat me in contempt. Have I done something wrong?"

Sainte-Hélène grasped his younger brother by the shoulder. "It is not that you have done something wrong. It is that you have not done anything."

François' head dropped. "Do I make you ashamed, Jacques?"

"Four years ago, I marched with the Chevalier de Troyes," Sainte-Hélène stated plainly. "We walked for several *months* through icy terrain and cold weather worse than that which is before us now; worse than you can imagine. We nearly starved on more than one occasion. And after that difficult journey, we still seized the English Fort Monsipi on James Bay. From there, we made great haste to Fort Charles and captured that as well. And then," Sainte-Hélène recalled, "we laid siege and captured a third fort – the Quichicouanne.

"I had only a few dozen of the hardest men on this continent with me, and we captured three forts. And now," he lectured, "we have two-hundred and the weather, though harsh, is endurable. Yet, you think I will listen to you bitching like a child because you are in pain."

"I apologize for my gripes," François said. "I know I have not climbed to your heights of accomplishments yet, but this is my chance now."

"Yet?" Sainte-Hélène laughed. "You never will, little brother. You never will."

The council assembled by a hastily-made fire. Nicolas d'Ailleboust de Manthet and Jacques Le Moyne de Sainte-Hélène stood before the assembled officers and chieftains of their Indian allies. "We are having this meeting at the request of Athasata," Manthet said, directing his arm towards the great warrior.

Athasata stepped forward. "My brothers, we seek to know your objective. Do you march for Orange or Corlear, or another location which is a mystery to us? I have asked you in private and you have thus avoided my question. We must know now."

Manthet glanced at Sainte-Hélène who gave a slight nod of approval. "Very well," Manthet replied. "By order of the Governor-General, the Count De Frontenac, we march for the town of Orange."

Athasata and the other Caughnawaga despaired at the news. "Brothers, we may only find peril and defeat if we attack that place," Athasata stated. "The enemy has great numbers there. Corlear would be an easy target."

"Our orders were to act accordingly and seize or destroy what we could, without too great a risk to ourselves."

"Then you have no orders to attack Orange?" Athasata inquired.

"Not specifically," Manthet admitted. "But we will partake in the enterprise to capture Orange."

The Indians were uneasy. "Our people know well what the guns of the white man can do," Athasata said. "To attack that place is a great risk. Since when did the French become so desperate?"

The other French officers were aghast. Athasata's insult was unexpected and bore no shield of friendship. It could only be seen as a direct challenge to Manthet's authority.

Manthet took a step forward and looked at the assembled leaders. "We march to regain the honor of New France – an honor which we have thus far been deprived. And the sole means of us accomplishing that task is to take Orange or perish in that glorious enterprise."

Athasata was still frustrated at the decision but held his tongue.

"There will be no more talk of this," Manthet said to the men. "Our business now, is south."

As the column began to march once again, Athasata approached Manthet in private. "We are still more than ten days from the river of the Mohawk. Perhaps we should revisit the plan at a later date, when we are better informed of the enemy strength."

"I am willing to reconsider the objective," Manthet said, much to Athasata's surprise. "But you must understand what is at stake for us. If we do not seize Orange, we will only wound the English in a way they can easily recover from. By taking Orange, we will wound them critically."

"I understand," Athasata said. "Let us talk later."

It was several days later when the decision was forced upon Manthet and Sainte-Hélène. The Sault scouts, as well as their own trusted scout, Giguiere, reported they were approaching a separation of trails.

"The left trail heads due south," Giguiere said. "That leads to Orange. The right trail," he said pointing, "leads southwest towards the village of Corlear."

Manthet thanked Giguiere and dismissed the scout. He turned in his saddle to Sainte-Hélène, d'Iberville, and Athasata. "Well, gentlemen, here we are. Should we pursue a more glorious path of victory, yet assuredly more costly victory at Orange, or a less risky path and raid the western village of Corlear?"

Surprisingly, it was not Jacques, but his brother Pierre, who spoke up. "While Orange would be a tremendous blow to the English, I think it should wait until we have a more formidable force. I believe we should go for Corlear."

Manthet acknowledged d'Iberville and glanced at his brother. Sainte-Hélène nodded his approval. He turned to Athasata. "Well, we will follow your advice. We march to Corlear." With the question settled, Manthet directed the column down the right trail.

"What do the English call this village again?" he asked.

Athasata looked to him. "They call it – Schenectady."

Chapter 36

February 8, 1690

Johannes stepped outside and stretched out his arms in the morning sunlight. The day was brisk but not freezing, and the wind was gentle. It would be a good day, he reassured himself as he started out.

After several days of working odd jobs for anyone who would take him—everything from home repairs, to taking care of farmstock, to brewing beer—he had amassed a small amount of money.

He set out for Barent Van Ditmars house, to make additional offers for books. After a lot of thought, he decided to invest in his own library collection.

Walking down the road, he passed by Symon Schermerhorn and his family.

"How goes it, sir?" Johannes asked.

"You're Harmen's boy, right?" Symon asked. Johannes nodded. "Thought so," Symon said. He patted the horse and wagon that his wife and youngest boy were on. "Well the boy has taken ill, and Mr. Schaets has too many patients already, so she's taking him to Albany for care."

"Fever?" Johannes asked.

"Not sure yet, but possibly," Symon replied.

"I hope they have a safe trip."

"I would go with them, but I have so much to do here," Symon said. "So, I got my other son here, only five years of age, who is also named Johannes," he said with a laugh. "And my brother, Cornelius and sister, Janet back at the house. Cornelius fractured his leg recently, so he's healing up in bed."

"Where's Ryer?" Johannes asked, curiously.

"Ryer caused quite a stir when he sided with Leisler's men. I don't think the Convention would want him anywhere near Albany. He's out, checking up on the mills. Probably won't be back until Tuesday." Symon paused. "I never cared for his politics, that's for sure."

"With respect to your family," Johannes said, "neither do I. This thing that has descended on the village is decaying it at the foundation. Even my brother has thrown in with the Leislerites."

"So I've heard," Symon replied. "I'm glad you did not. Your father speaks very highly of you. You'll go on to do great things." He looked to his wife and turned back. "Well, they have to get going. Drop by the house, someday. Perhaps we can talk about employment for you when the fur trapping season has passed."

"I will do that," Johannes replied before heading off. His mind ran through the possibilities. Though the thought of working for Ryer Schermerhorn was not appealing, he did wonder at the economic opportunities afforded by the diverse businesses operated by the Schermerhorn family.

Walking up the street, Johannes saw a cart parked outside a house. It looked strangely familiar and he stopped. Just then, the front door opened, and Maria Vandervort stepped outside.

"Maria?" Maria stopped in her tracks, appearing more surprised than Johannes. "What are you doing here? I haven't heard from you."

She walked towards him, slowly. "I had no time to write you," she said. "I'm sorry, Johannes. My father wanted me to stay here for a few weeks until it's safe for me to return. They're family friends," she said, tilting her head towards the house.

Johannes thought to respond but his mind

went blank. He smiled. "It's so nice to see you again," he said. She stared awkwardly at him. "I'm sorry," he said. "I know the last time we met I was …"

"No, it's fine," Maria replied. "Truly, it's okay. I overreacted. I shouldn't have acted the way I did. I just …"

Johannes stepped forward and embraced her in a kiss. She took a step back in shock.

"Johannes, there's people around," she said, stunned, but with the slightest grin crossing her face.

"I missed you so much," Johannes said. "I really did. I don't care who sees us. I love you."

Maria grinned. "I still love you too. Will I see you after church tomorrow, perhaps?"

"Yes, of course," Johannes replied. "You said your father is still in Albany? When he wants you to come back, I will come with you. I'll ask him then."

Maria laughed. "Let's just take it a day at a time for the moment. I need some time to adjust."

Johannes took a breath. "Sorry, yeah take your time. So, I guess I will see you tomorrow?"

"Sounds good," she commented. They quickly hugged again and broke off just as fast, each smiling uncontrollably. Johannes watched as Maria went back inside. He turned and headed off, his heart pounding in excitement.

* * *

The morning silence of the forest was broken by the marching of horses and men. Snow crunched, and dead branches snapped. But the men were silent. It was unlike previous days where the Natives and French Canadians alike would talk amongst themselves, mostly to take their minds off the endless march and bitter cold. In that moment, each man's mind was somewhere else. Whether it was on their loved ones back at Montreal, possibly friends from Lachine, slaughtered by the Mohawks, or on the task ahead, every member of the raiding party dealt with the morning in their own way.

For, that day, they would reach Schenectady.

"Horses!" one of the militiamen out front shouted. Manthet galloped up to the front to check on the disturbance. Looking past the pine trees, he could make out two dark figures on horseback moving fast towards the column.

"Skirmishers to the front," he ordered. At once a line of men formed, stretching out among the forest.

Sainte-Hélène joined the rank of men, producing his pistol from under his blanket. "Make ready!" The militiamen primed their guns with the black powder and cocked the triggers back. "Present!" They aimed in on the two riders closing in.

"Hold!" someone shouted ahead. Manthet took a few steps forward, peering over the horse's crest. He eyed the men closely. A wave of relief swarmed him as he waved off the skirmishers.

"It's Montesson," he said to Sainte-Hélène. Jacques dropped his head. The line of men rose from the snow, their hearts still racing. It was no secret that tension was high among the raiders. Being only several leagues from the village, they were now well within the defined English territory – and worse, the land of the Mohawk.

Repentigny de Montesson and his Native scout emerged from the trees. "Lieutenant," he said to Manthet. "I have seen the river with my own eyes."

"And?"

"It's only four leagues from here – and it's frozen."

Manthet smiled. He turned to Sainte-Hélène and the chief Athasata. "Tonight – we go tonight!"

Athasata nodded stiffly and turned to his warriors. Jacques took a deep breath. He eyed his brother Pierre who remained unaffected by the decision.

Manthet approached Sainte-Hélène. "We'll stop in two leagues. The men need a rest and some speaking with. They're exhausted."

"So we take the village tonight?" Sainte-Hélène asked. Manthet agreed.

"And with luck, we'll carry the day and be back across the river by mid-morning."

The sun was fast disappearing beyond the trees when several scouts reported to Sainte-Hélène and Manthet about a large clearing ahead, void of any disturbance. The two officers led their men into the field and decided at once that it would be the place.

"Halt the column," Manthet ordered La Brosse. The Frenchman directed the militia and Natives to the field and set sentries on the outskirts.

Manthet climbed down from his horse and produced his coveted watch – an heirloom handed down from his father. It was just after four in the evening. As Sainte-Hélène approached, Manthet turned to face him. "Scouts estimate we are almost exactly two leagues from the river opposite Corlear. We'll rest here for a few hours and then get to the village before midnight."

Sainte-Hélène nodded in satisfaction. "That'll give us time to work our way around to the south gate and avoid the sentries."

Pierre Le Moyne joined the two commanders.

"How long will you need?" Manthet asked Sainte-Hélène.

Jacques turned to his brother. "What do you think? An hour?"

"Two – at least," Pierre stated matter-of-factly. "They must have sentries at both ends. It would only take one man seeing us to raise the alert. I don't know about attacking a fortified town with a small garrison."

"You doubt we'll carry the battle?" Manthet asked.

"No but it would make for a much bloodier conflict and with wounded we would be slower on the march back. Mohawk catch us and…"

"Yes, we know," Manthet stated.

"They won't catch us," Jacques said. "Give me two hours to take sixty men across the river and make our way around to the south gate. The attack begins at two o'clock in the morning."

Manthet agreed. "Okay gentlemen, I think we should try to get some shut eye for an hour. We'll have an officer's meeting at six o'clock to go over the plan one last time and finalize the details. Then we march and don't stop until we reach Corlear."

The crackling of the fire woke up François Le Moyne. The sky was black. But the air felt warmer. *Or is it my blood?* The thought shot through him like an arrow. *Tonight's the night. Tonight, I shall prove myself to my brothers and my fellow countrymen.* He stood up, stretching his muscles. His eyes turned to the sky where he whispered a silent prayer into the night.

A group of men gathered around the central fire in the campsite. They were the leaders of the French regulars and Canadian volunteers. Also present was Athasata and two of his senior warriors. The leader of the Algonquin Indians also stood by the fire.

Manthet and Sainte-Hélène approached the fire. The men ceased their conversations and stood rigid as if at attention. Sainte-Hélène allowed Manthet to take the reins and stood off to the side. As Manthet looked around, he felt his blood begin to boil. "Get your men up right this minute. We are finished here. Now – we march."

"GO!" Sainte-Hélène shouted. The leaders dispersed and in the cold night, the shouting of men could be heard. Athasata stood like a statue. For a moment Manthet opened his mouth to speak when he saw that the Sault warriors were already well awake, applying their war paint and readying themselves for battle. He gave the chief a slight nod of thanks.

After a few minutes the officers had reassembled, their men now awake and eating quick snacks or tightening down their gear. Sainte-Hélène stepped up. "Remember Lachine," he stated deeply. "Make your men *remember* Lachine."

Manthet rested his hand on Jacques' shoulder. "We are engaged in a just war. And of the law of just warfare, we make this battle in defense of our flourishing country. We make this battle with the full authority of the king and we make this battle in direct response to the loss we suffered at Lachine. We have the blessings of our Holy Father on this affair. Fear nothing and may tonight make you the sword of God."

"You may take captives at your discretion. The rest be they murdered, by shot or flame – we shall bear no regret tonight. Every man is guilty of the murder of our fellow countrymen. Every woman is guilty. Every child is guilty. But let us not dwell on that now. Sainte-Hélène will go over the details of the assault. Lieutenant?"

Sainte-Hélène walked out into the middle of the circle of men. "When we're in sight of the river and village of Corlear, two men will cross – my brother Le Moyne de Bienville and another of my choosing. They will count guards and find the north gate of said village. When they report back, Messieurs d'Iberville and de Montesson will take sixty men comprising half Sault and half Canadian and move east, cross the river, and make our way to the south gate on the road leading to Orange. Lieutenant Manthet will take one hundred and twenty men and make the main crossing one hour later."

"They will rally at the north gate and at our signal, both parties shall attack. The guards will be shot, men helped over the walls, and the gates opened. We will then surround every home and commence the attack at the same time. If the town is warned, we assault as best as we can."

Manthet took over. "I will lead the attack against the blockhouse on the northwest corner. If the garrison is alerted expect a hard battle and many losses at that place. We burn every home down save those occupied by the Mohawk and that of the preacher in the village. The governor, Monsieur Denonville has expressly forbidden his murder and forbids the burning of his home. Also, forbidden from attack is the mansion on the north bank of the river, that owned by a Captain – Sander Glen. He has been merciful to the French and will be spared along with his relatives in Corlear."

"How will we know?" asked one of the militiamen.

"We'll bring him to the village and let him pick his relatives from the survivors." Manthet turned to Sainte-Hélène. "Are we forgetting anything?"

"I don't believe so." The Mohawk chief did not wait for the others. He turned and left the officers meeting, heading over to his warriors. Sainte-Hélène shrugged. "I suppose that's it then."

"Get your men ready," Manthet ordered. "God be with you tonight."

Athasata called his warriors to him. In the freezing night, he stood beside a raging fire, like a beacon for the warriors to follow. In small numbers, they came to him, circling around the fire until every warrior was present. A few of the Canadian militia who were ready to march also stepped in closer. The fearsome Caughnawaga and Algonquin warriors stood in silence, their muskets and tomahawks, clubs and knives dangling at the side. Their faces were darkened with war paint. By only their appearance, the Indian warriors were truly a frightening sight to any who could see them.

"My brothers," the Great Mohawk cried out in French. He did not speak his native tongue as he spoke a different dialect than the Algonquin. "We are here upon the lands of the English this night. We are here upon the land of the Five Nations this night. We are here upon the lands of our enemies this night. They are our enemies by their choice and not by ours. The Five Nations have aligned themselves with the English who seek to drive all Iroquois and our French allies from these lands. They bring with them the greed of their homeland. They bring with them the sorrows of their land."

As he eyed his warriors, his pride peaked. "The voices of our ancestors cry out from the spirit world tonight. They cry out for us to honor their lives by ending those of the English who have killed so many of our peoples." Athasata raised a war club high in the air. "Tonight, we make just war and do not stop until we have quenched our thirst for their blood."

There was a great shout from the warriors. They let out terrible war cries that echoed through the night air, raising their muskets and tomahawks. The warrior psyche was one of the most powerful forces on a battlefield and Athasata was a master at releasing it in his men. As the cries died down, they joined the main body of militia.

Manthet took one last look around. He raised his arm and then pointed south. Very slowly, the French force began to move, like a snake slithering towards its prey. The dark shadows of hundreds of men crept through the forest. Manthet directed skirmishers to the front. Twenty men, both French and Indian, took the lead, spreading out in a great wedge, ahead of the main column. Their muskets were loaded and at the ready. They acted as a vanguard, preparing to eliminate anyone they came across.

Pride carried them that night. Honor carried them. The promise of plunder and booty carried them. But as they made their way south one thing carried them more than the rest.

Vengeance.

This night, there was a silent war cry.

For Lachine.

Part Two

Chapter 37

Robert Alexander clinched his blanket tightly, the bearskin fur doing little to save him from the frigid cold night. The temperature had plummeted as the cold front moved in from the southwest. He paced back and forth in front of the *chevaux de fries* defenses of the blockhouse. The sweet smell of beef broth leaked from the windows of the fort. Grunting, he cursed the cold.

Alexander checked the guard pocket watch Lieutenant Talmadge loaned him. The watch belonged to Talmadge but he insisted whoever was on guard duty have it on them. It was just over two hours until midnight. "Fifteen more minutes" he said to himself. Knowing he would soon taste the warm broth, he decided to soldier up, and headed for the gate.

Coming up to the open north gate, the wind picked up, blowing icy air on him. Alexander buried his head in his coat and started to head back to the blockhouse.

He stopped.

His head popped up, alerted to something. *What was that?* He clutched his musket and crept forward to the gate. He peered out, looking hard in all directions. He swore to himself he had heard an unnatural noise coming from beyond the darkness. He readied his gun. For the first time in hours, the chills that ran down his body were not from the cold.

For a moment, the world stood still. The wind died down to nothing and the night grew quiet. Alexander realized he had been holding his breath and released it, breathing heavily. He relaxed his stance. Being tense in that weather, even for a brief time, was exhausting. The two snowmen guards that the children had made flanked him on each side. One of their 'guns' lay in the snow, knocked over by the wind.

Alexander picked up the stick and stabbed it into the snow. "Don't lose it now," he said to the snowman, laughing to himself. He paced back inside.

The slightest chill – that eerie feeling he felt just moments ago, returned. He turned to the gate. Thinking for a second, he set his musket against the palisade and grabbed both hands on the left door of the north gate. He heaved, pulling it, attempting to close the village gate. The door barely budged, blocked by the deep snow. He pulled again, but the door only moved inches.

As another gust of wind swept over him, it carried a familiar smell, that of the broth – his dinner in the blockhouse. He smiled, his mind filling with warm thoughts. He looked to the snowmen. "My watch is finished tonight. I leave our lives in your capable hands," he said with a grin. "Don't let anyone in."

He grabbed his musket and took one last look at the open gate. Defeated by a couple feet of snow. He shook his head, almost mocking himself for trying to close it. With his dinner getting cold, he trudged through the snow back to the blockhouse.

Outside the open doors of the north gate, the defenders of the village of Schenectady stood ready to repel the invaders. They watched vigilantly, staring to the north.

Two snowmen. With sticks as guns.

Symon Schermerhorn opened the door and stepped out into his stable. He brought a warm blanket with him. With the dropping temperatures, Symon knew that even animals needed additional warmth. He draped the blanket over his sleeping horse. "Rest easy boy," he whispered before returning inside. He cracked open the door to the cellar. His three slaves slept peacefully on their side of the cellar, their own fire smoldering but emitting a steady heat from its embers.

He returned to the living room to find young Johannes Schermerhorn asleep in his father's rocking chair next to the hearth with its fiery glow illuminating the room. Symon looked at his son with a quiet pride. The boy was going to grow up into a fine man someday, he thought. He thought about waking Johannes and telling him to sleep in his bed but then decided against it. Instead, he dimmed the embers of the fire, and grabbed a great fur blanket, gently laying it on his son, before retiring to his own bedroom for the night.

In the Christoffelse home, David read to his daughter, Gertruy, by the fireplace. Thomas sat nearby but ignored his father's book. He had heard it enough times already. It was the same story every time, but his little sister still seemed to enjoy it just as much each time. He sat silently while his mind drifted away. David's two eldest sons were hard asleep as usual. They bore the brunt of the daily work around the home and David told them until they marry and find a home of their own, he would work them from sun up to sun down. His wife too, was sleeping, not wishing to partake in the nightly reading.

David finished and closed the book. "Now, off to bed the both of you."

"But father," Gertruy pleaded. "I don't want to. It's warmer here next to the fire."

"I'm putting the fire out," he replied. "It'll be warmer under your blankets."

"Why are you putting the fire out? It's cold."

Always asking questions, he mused. *That's my little*

girl. "We have to make the firewood last as long as possible, dear. It's hard to find good, dry wood in the winter." He sighed. "Now off to bed. And say your prayers. I better hear them from both of you. Thomas," he looked at his son. Thomas looked away, at the floor. "Thomas!" his father snapped. "Off to bed, now."

"Yes, sir," Thomas said meekly, shuffling off.

Gertruy gave her father a hug. He kissed her cheek and sent her to bed. He took another look at the book, before setting it away.

Why couldn't I have two sons and two daughters? He asked himself. *That boy is fixing for another whipping.* He cleared the dismal thoughts from his mind and put out the fire before heading to sleep.

Johannes Vedder lay in bed, staring at the ceiling. He had slept for a couple hours, he guessed, but now was wide awake. His mind was a whirlpool of emotions, thoughts, and desires. He ached for it to be morning, so he could see Maria at the Sunday sermon. He prayed that she would give him even the slightest look. He swore to himself. *How could I be so stupid?* He asked in his mind. He thought of all the ways he could apologize to her but with each new idea came a new fear of how she would reject them.

Forcing himself to take his mind off Maria, Johannes sat up and lit a candle by his bed. He picked up the book that Barent Van Ditmars had loaned him. In the dim candlelight, he opened the cover and started to read. The wind batted gently against the window and a cold draft seeped through. He slung a spare blanket over the window to stop the winter chill from entering and immersed himself in the book by the Dutch fur trader.

Johannes marveled over Adriaen van der Donck's description of the northern Hudson River valley with its endless ocean of undisturbed forest and dotted with a thousand lakes and streams. Van der Donck described the route to Canada, in which one could travel for several weeks without ever crossing paths with another man.

The author gave such vivid descriptions of the clear waters and overwhelming smell of fresh cedar and pine, that Johannes forgot the cold and spoiled air of his home, becoming lost in the words. He whispered one more prayer – that someday he would travel up to the mountains himself.

Satisfied, Johannes closed the book and set it on the floor. He blew out the candle, and the room fell into total darkness. He tightened the blanket around his body and fell asleep with a smile on his face and a dream in his head.

Chapter 38

Across the Mohawk River, standing next to a thick pine tree, Jean-Baptiste Giguiere and his Indian companions watched the village. He had stood still in the shadows for over an hour with growing confidence in what he had seen. As dusk had settled into night, he was sure that the north gate would be closed by the garrison. The lone soldier a few minutes before, had confirmed that suspicion, up until the man tried and failed to close the gate, then abandoned it.

Giguiere was thrilled. Never would he have guessed the English would be so careless. Such, however, was their confidence of the vast distance between Montreal and Corlear, that they must have guessed no army could make that journey in the dead of winter. Giguiere half-expected to see the guard return with others and force the doors closed. But as the minutes slipped away, he knew he had to report the good news to Lieutenant Manthet. He whispered his orders that two Indians remain at the riverbank and should any changes occur before the column arrives, to report the change. He took the other seven men with him and started the trek back to the raiding party.

Less than a mile north of the river, Sainte-Hélène passed the order for silence except for passing orders or information. The column continued to move south, the only sound being the crunching of snow and breaking of branches.

"We should not have brought the horses," Sainte-Hélène said quietly to Manthet. "It's one more complication and they could give away our position before we're ready."

303

Manthet nodded. "We'll leave them on the north side of the river and cross the ice on foot. Once the garrison sees us, we'll have to move fast to get over the palisade before they're ready."

Sainte-Hélène reminisced, "When I was seizing all the forts with the Chevalier de Troyes, he always emphasized the surprise and attack. We would never lay a proper siege. We just got over and through their defenses as fast as possible and they would always succumb without much of a fight. Even Denonville said Troyes was the most professional soldier he had ever led."

"What is your point?" Manthet asked.

"My point," Sainte-Hélène said, "is that no matter our differences in how we command, I see a great deal of similarity between the Chevalier and yourself. You have a good head for battle and are one of the most competent officers I've met so far." Sainte-Hélène paused thinking. "It's an honor to serve with you."

Manthet was taken by surprise. He could not find the words to reply and simply said, "Thank you."

Sainte-Hélène looked over the men. "We couldn't have picked a harder bunch of men to carry out this expedition. They're the toughest sonsofbitches north of the Saint Lawrence. I almost think we should've never diverted from the original plan. We should've attacked Orange."

"What's done is done," Manthet said. "No point in trying to change the past."

They continued south with their men, slowly making their way to the river.

"Arrêtez, stop!" The Frenchman sighted his rifle on the dark shadow moving towards him. The figure stopped. Two more French militiamen joined the first man at the very head of the column. "Who's there?"

A man answered. "It's Jean-Baptiste Giguiere." He approached slowly with his hands raised until the men could identify him. "Where's the Monsieur, de Manthet?"

The militiaman pointed behind him and continued onwards. Giguiere hurried along the in the snow until he could see the horses of the officers and the main body of the raiding party.

"Monsieur," Giguiere spoke. "I have observed the village of Corlear."

Manthet leaned down from his horse. "What did you see?"

Giguiere shook his head. "Monsieur, they – they have no guards. Their gate is wide open."

Sainte-Hélène joined the conversation. "What did he just say?"

"The village," Giguiere replied, "it's defenseless. There's nobody guarding it."

Manthet straightened up in horse. "Thank you, rejoin the column," he said to the scout. He looked at Sainte-Hélène. "What do you make of that?"

"It could be a trap," Sainte-Hélène replied. "We enter the village. They're waiting in the homes and catch us in a cross-fire, cut us to pieces."

Manthet grunted in agreement. "That was my thought as well. Nobody can be that foolish to leave their gates intentionally open. The other possibility of course is they truly are not expecting us. Perhaps their Mohawk allies returned to their castles and gave no warning to our advance."

Sainte-Hélène thought about it. "Well Nicolas, we only have one way to find out."

"Indeed!" Manthet kicked his horse, trotting ahead to the front of the column.

The French and Indian war party marched along at a faster pace, the main column splitting and coming back together again, conforming to the terrain, like water running down a rocky stream. The officers pushed the men along, encouraging or cursing them onward. The bitter cold tortured them every step of the way. The icy wind was relentless, assaulting their faces and any exposed skin. It was so bad that some men slung their muskets over their back, so they could stuff their hands under their coats, trying to keep them from freezing.

The Sault and Algonquin Natives fared no better. Preferring to wage war in the warmer months, and never traveling far from their homes, they had never mounted a raid of this distance before. Unlike their Canadian counterparts, they had never known such a long trek to fight a battle. Even Athasata's words had since been lost in the winter night, replaced only by the desire to find warmth in this most desolate of places. Soon though, they knew they would indulge in the spoils of the Dutch village.

Robert Alexander finished his broth and set the bowl aside, wiping his mouth on his jacket. The warm liquid was heaven on earth as it went down his throat, washed down by strong ale. One other man was awake. Ralph Grant, a man of the Connecticut Company sat in the corner writing a letter.

"Who are you writing to?" Alexander asked.

Grant looked up. "My children, back in Fairfield," he said with a smile.

"How many do you have?"

"Three boys and three girls," Grant replied. "I'm glad they're coming of age. My wife Sarah passed away last winter. They had to grow up fast."

Alexander crouched by the small cooking fire,

warming his hands. "Why did you join the militia if they need you?"

Grant shrugged. "I suppose it was my duty. That, and I wanted my children to grow up knowing how to take care of themselves. The good Lord knows I won't always be there." Grant set the letter aside. "Sarah was the best wife I could have asked for and the best mother to those kids. She was a natural with children as her mother before her. I was a loyal husband, but I knew little of fathering. I came here to the colonies as a child by myself, being raised by men on the boat docks and women in the taverns."

Alexander sipped on his ale and stared blankly into the fire, but he listened to every word Grant spoke. Grant sighed. "I think it better that they don't see me as much anymore. Growing up, I taught them discipline. It was all I knew. I guess I should have hugged them now and again." Grant cleared his throat and Alexander saw a tear fall from Grant's cheek. "That's what I shall do first when I return. I will give each of them a hug and remind them that I love them all."

Alexander smiled. To be out of the frigid cold, sitting by a fire, drinking a brew and talking of home was a welcome change of pace. It felt almost serene. "I don't have anyone waiting for me," he said.

Grant's eyed shifted up. "Nobody?"

"Nobody. I was the eldest child in my family. My younger brother died of typhoid. My mother died giving birth to my sister who died a few weeks later. My father was murdered by savages of the Algonquin nation."

"No wife or children of your own?" asked Grant.

Alexander shook his head. "None," he replied. "There was a girl back home, lived two leagues from me. Emma Littlefield was her name," he said with a grin. "Boy was she something else." He leaned in to Grant. "Petite, golden blonde hair halfway down her back, you know that wavy kind of hair. She had these beautiful blue eyes and the most perfect bosom I ever saw."

"Get outta here," Grant said.

"I ain't lying," Alexander replied. "Smart, funny, and caring. She was perfect in every way. When traveling to and from the Crawford farm I would go out of my way just to pass her family's place in hopes of seeing her. When she was outside, she would wave me over and we would talk for hours, till her father came out and yelled at her to get back to work. She'd always give me fresh apples on my way."

"Well she sounds like a darling. You gonna marry her when you get back?"

Alexander chuckled but it was done humorlessly. His smile vanished. "I never could explain my feelings to her. The day before Captain Bull called us up, I passed her house again. She was there in the grove of willow trees with another man. They were laughing and kissing. I didn't know the lad personally, but I had seen him in town before. He was bigger, stronger, more successful, and more handsome than me. It's not someone I could really compete with."

"I'm sorry to hear that," Grant said.

Alexander shrugged it off. "You know; I'm not disappointed that she found happiness with someone else." Grant looked on a bit confused. "I'm truly not," Alexander continued. "She deserves to be happy. What truly disappoints me is that I know she was perfect for me. I would have done anything for this girl and I don't believe she ever knew that or felt the way about me that I felt about her. To her I was just another face and name to talk to. To me, she might just have been the one."

The blockhouse door creaked as the wind pounded it from outside. The image of the beautiful girl from home faded in Alexander's mind. He clutched his musket, looking at it with grief. "Now, I'm in New York Province. The air outside isn't fit for even the most savage of beast or man. I'm locked up here in this fort, in a village that despises our presence, and deciding if I'll die at the hands of the Leislerites, the French, a band of Native savages, or some terrible disease." He tipped his mug back, downing his ale. "I guess we are the watchmen, sworn to fight for the society that has forsaken us."

Grant sat in silence for a moment. He grabbed the ale jug and his own mug. He filled it to the brim and leaned over, filling Alexander's as well. He raised his cup. "Here's to us. A band of forsaken, brutal sons of bitches ready to kill other forsaken sons of bitches in glorious battle, so that the rest of society can die of old age, shitting themselves in bed and forgetting their own names. I say we have the better deal."

The blonde girl from home flashed through Alexander's mind, and for that fleeting moment, he could not even think of her name.

"They'll be forgotten, and we'll be remembered," he said raising his cup.

"Hear, hear!" Grant said, as they knocked their cups together and gulped down the ale.

Chapter 39

Across the frozen Mohawk River, a man on a horse watched the village from the north bank of the river. Lieutenant Nicolas d'Ailleboust de Manthet stroked his horse's crest and looked across at the stockade wall of the village of Schenectady. He wondered when the alarm would be raised. To his rear, the French and Indian war party halted, kneeling in the snow, muskets now at the ready. Several Indians brandished their tomahawks, preparing to silently take out any English they encountered. The men of the column were frozen and weary from the march. Though eager to cross, they relished the chance to rest in the snow and amongst the trees.

Sainte-Hélène had already told them that this would be their last opportunity to rest up for once they crossed the river there would be no pause until the village was stormed and they were back on the north bank with any captives and booty. Several men took the opportunity to piss or eat some dried jerky.

Jean-Baptiste Giguiere joined Manthet at the riverbank. "It's just as I told you, Monsieur."

He pointed to the open gate which could be seen from across the river. There was some light emitting from the open gate, most likely from the fireplaces of the houses inside the stockade. Sainte-Hélène and Athasata rode up beside Manthet.

Manthet wasted no time. "Jacques, take forty men across. Twenty of ours, twenty of his," he said referring to Athasata. "Secure the south bank."

"Here?" Sainte-Hélène asked, unsure. "If this is a trap, we'll be caught on the ice. There's nowhere to go but back."

310

Manthet glanced at the Great Chief. Athasata nodded in agreement. Manthet acknowledged it. "You're right, not here. Take them down the river to the east, two-hundred paces or so. Then cross and secure the south bank. Signal us when that's done, and I'll take the rest across. We'll leave a few men on this side."

"And what of the horses?" Sainte-Hélène asked. "You said we would leave them here."

Manthet patted his horse. He slung his leg over and hopped off and into the snow. "That's right, we leave them here."

Sainte-Hélène grimaced but followed suit along with Athasata. They passed the reigns off and Sainte-Hélène ordered his men to move up. A steady stream of men filed past the officers. Sainte-Hélène turned to Manthet. "I'll see you on the other side."

Manthet nodded silently.

Sainte-Hélène turned to join his men, leading them to the east. Manthet looked to Athasata. "Are the Mohawk in that village?"

Athasata's face was like a stone. He bore no expression of any kind, his arms crossed as he stared across the river, studying the village palisade. "Hard to tell – but yes, most likely."

"Why wouldn't they close the gate?"

"Mohawk are brothers of Dutch," Athasata said. "If visiting your brother's home and he leaves a window open, you do not close it. This was Dutch call, not Mohawk."

Manthet took a deep breath. For a moment, he almost pitied the inhabitants. "They don't have a chance," he whispered.

For the first time since the mission began, he felt a sense of regret. As a professional soldier, he always despised the slaughter of civilians, preferring instead to meet the enemy on an open battlefield in honorable combat. "There's no honor in this."

"No honor at Lachine," Athasata replied, never taking his gaze off the village. "English dogs fight with no honor. Mohawk fight with no honor."

The Chief signaled one of his warriors. The warrior approached from his camouflaged position in the trees.

Manthet looked at the Indian. He was just a boy, Manthet noted. *He must be no older than sixteen years*, he thought to himself. Still, the young warrior looked ferocious. Streaks of war paint crisscrossed the boy's face. He held a musket in his hand. On his belt were two large knives, a tomahawk, and a small war club. The boy's face was stern and angry; ready, if not eager, for bloodshed.

Athasata spoke to the warrior, who then hurried off. A moment later, dozens of Indians started moving, heading to the east for the crossing. Manthet issued the order for his men to follow suit, leaving a small handful of Canadians and Sault Indians in place to watch the horses and other supplies that were left there.

Further down, Sainte-Hélène had already started the crossing. "Disperse," he hissed to his men.

The men distanced themselves from each other but fell in line, keeping in the same tracks as the man ahead of them. Nobody wanted to fall through a weak spot in the ice on the river. The men at the head of the crossing were all skilled men of the coureur de bois. They had experience crossing frozen streams and rivers before. Nevertheless, the darkness of the night made the crossing a daunting challenge for them. They moved cautiously, shifting their weight only once they knew their footing was solid. Any mistake could prove fatal. Not only for the man falling into the river, who weighed down with heavy clothing would surely drown, but the noise might alert someone on shore to their presence and destroy their element of surprise.

Sainte-Hélène was at the forefront, crouched low, a pistol in one hand and his rapier in the other. With a slenderer build than most of his men, Jacques moved swiftly across the ice. He kept his eyes trained on the far bank, only glancing occasionally to keep from falling through. As he closed in on the south side, he turned back. Frustration took over him when he saw that most of his men were barely half-way across the frozen river.

Too late to wait for them to catch up, he decided. He rushed the last few meters, practically falling into the snowy south riverbank. He climbed up until he could see the land around him. Four more men joined him in rapid order.

"Spread out," he told them.

They took up positions behind whatever cover they could find. Sainte-Hélène looked on the stockade, stretching out before him. Finally, he was impressed with the task before him. Never before had he attacked such a fortification. Even the forts he seized with the Chevalier de Troyes were diminutive compared to the palisade wall of Corlear.

Once the last of his men were across, spread out along the riverbank, he slid back down the snow to the edge of the ice. There he produced a piece of flint and lit a small strip of cloth on fire. He waved it for just a few seconds before extinguishing it.

On the other side, Manthet saw the quick flicker of light. While it would be difficult to see such a tiny fire in the daylight, in the dead of night the light shone remarkably bright. Manthet raised his arm and the men braced themselves. He swung it downwards towards the river. Over one hundred and fifty French and Indian soldiers poured across the river. Some men walked at a brisk pace, keeping a low profile. Others jogged across, hoping only to reach the far bank as fast as possible.

The weather was worse on the river. Without the trees to block the wind, it pounded away, blowing icy shards and droplets of water at the invaders. One of the men tripped on the ice, his rifle sliding away from him. He cursed and struggled to get up, slipping and sliding with each step. Another Algonquin Indian took a wrong step, crashing his leg through a small gap in the ice, and into the freezing water beneath. He was helped up and carried on without a single word.

With more men reaching the south side, the riverbank became increasingly crowded. When Manthet found Sainte-Hélène, they knew had to move fast. They were now firmly on hostile ground.

The die had been cast.

Manthet grabbed Sainte-Hélène by the arm. "Lieutenant – it's time. Take your men south and find that gate." He pulled out his pocket watch. "It's exactly one hour till midnight. You have twenty minutes."

"We'll be ready," Sainte-Hélène said. He motioned to his brother, Pierre Le Moyne d'Iberville. "Pass the word down the line. We're going to the south gate."

"Yes, brother," Pierre replied.

"That's an officer you're talking to," Manthet said, through gritted teeth.

"Of course, monsieur," snapped Pierre. "My apologies sir," he said to Jacques, before rushing off to gather the men.

Sainte-Hélène couldn't help but grin. "Was that necessary?"

"This isn't the time to slack on the discipline," Manthet replied. "We can't allow any slip of military order at this point."

Sainte-Hélène conceded the matter.

"God speed," he said to Manthet. He turned to the men nearby. "We go!"

He stood up and motioned them to follow. Athasata waved for his warriors to follow too. A column of men abandoned the relative safety of the riverbank and marched out into the open as they hurried south, using a scattering of trees as concealment from the village stockade. Some eighty men in total followed Sainte-Hélène. Manthet ordered the remaining one hundred and fifteen men to move closer to the north gate. He himself went forward with Giguiere and two Natives.

Advancing until they reached the northeast corner of the stockade, they stayed close to the wall, not wanting to be noticed, if anyone in the blockhouse was awake and looking out the window. As it stood, protruding from the northwest corner and raised above the rest of the village, the blockhouse was ideally-placed to fend off an attack on the north gate. But as they approached, Manthet saw no movement in the dark window and concluded there was no one awake, or at least watching, in that moment.

They stopped just shy of the gate. Manthet stood still, staring in utter disbelief and bewilderment. Guarding the gate were two snowmen armed with sticks. The two Indians stepped backwards, crouching with their guns at the ready. They were more superstitious of the figures than the two Frenchmen.

"What is this?" Manthet whispered to Giguiere.

"I have not the slightest idea, monsieur. Could this be a taunt?"

"A taunt?"

"Yes, like an insult to us. They leave their gate open and guard it with these – snowmen, perhaps saying 'do your worst' to us."

Manthet looked at the guards. He could scarcely believe it but Giguiere was correct. Corlear was completely undefended.

"They'll regret that when they see what we can do at our worst," he commented. "Tell Athasata to bring up the men."

Southeast of the village, Sainte-Hélène's force waited. They dispersed themselves on each side of the Albany Road, barely a stone's throw away from the home of Hendrick Vrooman's family, which lay outside the stockade, seated along the road. Sainte-Hélène and a dozen men moved forward, right under the southeast tower of the stockade.

"I don't see the gate," Pierre remarked. He turned to his brother. "I thought there was a second gate."

"There is," Sainte-Hélène replied. He too was dumbfounded. The snowdrift was deeper along the southern wall of the village. Jacques paced back and forth, looking at the wall. "Or at least there is supposed to be."

"What do we do now?" Pierre asked. Jacques looked at the wall, studying it from one corner to the other. Pierre was impatient. "We could climb over it. The walls are short."

Jacques nodded, acknowledging only the suggestion, not taking the advice. "I have eighty frozen men down the road. Half won't make it over the wall and if this is a trap, those that make it over would be cut to pieces. No, we won't risk it."

"Brother, we…" He stopped himself. "Monsieur, please. We are running out of time. What do we do?"

Jacques thought over his options hard. He knew the chances of ambush were remote. But he could not shake the feeling that this entire operation was beginning to look a bit too easy.

"The northern gate to the town is fully open – and it's completely unguarded," he said finally.

"Sir?"

"We'll double back, reunite with Manthet and everyone goes through the north gate. He pointed to the three homesteads that sat on the road, outside the stockade. Keep nine here, they attack when we attack. Run ahead to Manthet and inform him of the situation." Pierre rushed off, practically brushing against the palisade to tell Manthet. Jacques returned to his men hiding in the woods, passing the homes outside the walls.

Peering out the window of one of those, was five-year-old Lysbeth Van der Volgen. Hearing noises outside her window, she climbed out of bed and went to the window. Looking outside she saw several strange men, including two Indians with guns, rush past the house and disappear. Lysbeth cringed her blanket and doll tightly. She walked to her parents' room.

"Momma, Papa, there's men outside," she said. Her father Claas and mother Maritje barely stirred. Lysbeth shook the bed. "Papa, Papa, wake up!"

"What is it honey?" her father asked wearily, not even opening his eyes.

"There are men outside," she said. Her voice trembled as she spoke. "Papa they have guns."

Claas opened his eyes. "What do you mean? How do you know, honey?"

"I saw them," she said. "I saw Indians."

The words took a moment for Claas to digest. His heart stopped. His eyes shot wide open. He threw off the sheets and crouched down next to his daughter. "Indians, you said?"

"Yes, Papa," she nodded vigorously.

"You are sure? Indians?" She nodded again.

"What's going on, dear?" Maritje said, rolling over in bed.

Claas stood up. He felt his world tighten around him like a noose around the neck of condemned man. He grabbed his pants from the drying line and frantically put them on. "Honey," he said to Lysbeth. "Honey, now listen to me. Papa wants you to go back to your room and put on some warm clothing and boots. Can you do that for me?"

"Okay, Papa," she said. He gave her a kiss on the forehead and nudged her off.

"What's going on?" repeated his wife.

"Get out of bed now," he ordered sternly. "Put on warm clothes and get the hatchet from the storeroom." He threw on his boots. "They're here."

Maritje sat up in bed, still unsure of what to make of Claas' strange behavior. "Who's here?"

"The Indians," he said.

"But the Indians are our friends."

He turned to her. "Not these ones."

Maritje gasped in horror as it settled on her. "Oh my God" she said. She put her hands over her mouth, saying, "No, no, no."

He put on his coat and grabbed her by her shoulders tightly, to the point of causing her to wince in pain. "Get out of the damn bed. We have to head for the stockade." He turned and went to the living room. He made a line straight for the hearth. He stopped cold. "Where's my rifle?" he asked aloud. He spun around, looking all over the room, cursing under his breath. "Where's my rifle?"

Then he remembered.

He had not retrieved it yet from the gunsmith. In the same instance, he remembered another terrifying fact – that the south gate had been blocked by the snow. A cold chill shot through him. In that moment, he realized his best defense for his family was gone. He had failed them, and they would die because of him.

Maritje and Lysbeth joined him in the living room. His wife handed him his hatchet. Lysbeth went to the window, peeking out again. His eyes filled with tears as he looked at them. He could not help but feel hopeless, so much in fact that a very dark thought entered his mind.

He glanced at the hatchet, gripping the handle tightly. His eyes rose slowly, first to his wife, and then down to his daughter. *This would be better than them being captured.* He would not let his family be tortured—or worse—by the savages. His breaths quickened and in his mind, Claas imagined how he would do this terrible mercy.

"Papa, Papa!" Lysbeth said abruptly. "Papa, they're gone!"

His mouth hung open. "Let me see." He cracked the curtain, staring out. "Stay here."

He walked over to the front door.

"No please don't, dear," his wife begged.

"Shhh!" he hissed. Claas opened the door and stepped out. He looked all around. There was not a soul in sight. He returned inside and closed the door. He took a knee next to his daughter. "You aren't lying, are you?"

"No Papa, I saw people out there!" she cried. "There were normal men but with guns, and Indians as well. I swear to you Papa." She started sobbing uncontrollably. Claas grabbed her tightly. His eyes opened. He still clutched the hatchet. He let her go, backing away.

"I have to check the back," he said. He practically fell over himself, going to the back storeroom. He closed the door behind him and stared at the hatchet in horror. He set it down and took a step backwards. He felt sick to his stomach at himself for even thinking of such a heinous act, much less his willingness to see it through.

After regaining his composure, he returned. "We have only one choice," he said firmly. "We can't make it inside the stockade. Our only option is to head for the woods. Grab an extra blanket. We must go now!"

Sainte-Hélène rejoined Manthet outside the north gate. "Your brother explained the situation to me. You couldn't find the gate?"

"No, and even if we did, the gate is closed. This one is open. It makes sense Nicolas – and you know it."

Manthet eyed him, wondering if that was a slight challenge to his authority or a simple statement. But there was no time to go back and forth with either his co-commander, nor the troops.

"Everyone goes through the north gate. You'll take your men down the western side and I'll take mine down the eastern side. We'll meet at the closed south gate. When we meet, we'll know the entire village is surrounded."

Sainte-Hélène nodded. The plan was good. It was simple. He rather liked the simple ones. "What of the blockhouse?"

Manthet paused, going over his options. "Your brother d'Iberville will lead the flank on the east side. I will seize the blockhouse. Is there anything we're missing?"

Jacques shook his head. "I don't believe so. God be with you."

He held up his sword, catching his men's attention. He waved them to follow him. Manthet dropped to one knee and made a fast sign of the cross. He whispered a brief prayer before standing and exhaling deeply. Months of preparation and weeks of travel had led to this moment.

He gave the final signal.

Carrying on in the proud tradition of their family, the brothers Sainte-Hélène and d'Iberville were the first two through the open gates of the village. Manthet and Athasata followed next. Rising like demons from the blackness, ferocious men rushed forward in a swarm. This was it. There was no one to stop them. The French and Indian war party poured into Schenectady.

Johannes blew his candle out. His eyes ached from reading in the dim light. He set the book aside and slid back into his bed. The thought of seeing Maria and what he would say to her was still in the back of his mind but for the moment he had successfully drowned it with thoughts of the untouched wilderness in all its majesty and grandeur. He closed his eyes and slipped into sleep.

Outside, a short distance from the Vedder house, a man passed, then another and another. The jaws of the predator closed in around the sleeping inhabitants. The Le Moyne brothers stealthily maneuvered their two columns down the sides of the palisades.

A short distance from the blockhouse, Manthet had gathered thirty of the best coureur de bois and Sault warriors for the assault. He studied the defenses around the fort. The second palisade was not expected nor considered. The *chevaux de fries* would hamper any attempt to scale the inner palisade. The only way into the fort was through the opening in the second wall, and then through the door itself. Manthet was impressed. He thought the defensive layout was ideal for repelling any attacker.

Jacques reached the south gate first. *So, there it is,* he mused, looking at it. The snows had piled up nearly a third of its height.

He turned back. Stretching to the southwest corner and up the entire length of the western wall, the French militia and Indian warriors stood ready in silence. Some had clustered together to form small groups in front of certain houses. He waited in silence, growing irritated at lack of word from his brother. *Where is he?* He glanced at the men. They seemed impatient, angry – ready to begin.

Another minute passed. Finally, Jacques heard the sound of men on the move. D'Iberville approached the south gate.

"We have them surrounded," Pierre stated. The two brothers stood at the south end of Church Street looking up the road to the north gate.

A French militiaman lit a torch and passed it to D'Iberville. The fire burned brightly in the night. The light reflected in the windows of the nearby houses. Two Indians held torches to the flame and soon theirs lit up as well. They spread out, and more light illuminated. D'Iberville stood in the center of the road and raised the torch.

A small cluster of men stood at the north end of Church Street.

There was a moment of silence. Only the crackling of the fire above his head and the howl of the wind could be heard. Sainte-Hélène stood by his brother's side with his rapier in hand. Then out of the darkness, a light appeared at the north gate. The torch waved side to side in a great arch. D'Iberville mimicked the movement.

The signal had been given.

"And it begins," Jacques said to himself.

A tall and powerfully built warrior of the Sault held up his tomahawk and let out a vicious yell – a war cry that echoed through the night. Other Indians let out war cries too. A shot rang out in the night. Then another. Two Frenchmen yelled and surged forward, crashing through the door of the nearest homestead. Another hurled a flaming torch through a window, shattering the glass. The screams of a woman could be heard inside. French and Indian marauders the length and breadth of the village hurled themselves upon the sleeping inhabitants.

Chapter 40

Johannes shot up in bed at the sound of the first war cry. He looked out the window, but it was foggy, and he could only make out flickers of light coming from somewhere. But the gun shots were unmistakable. Albert woke up yelling. "What's going on?"

"I don't know," Johannes replied, "but I think we're under attack."

More cries and gunfire could be heard outside.

"Bar the door downstairs." Albert ran down the stairs and found the first piece of heavy furniture he could grasp. It was a study oak table. With great effort, he picked it up and braced it against the door. He could hear yelling outside. Suddenly the door violently shook. Albert threw his weight against the table, holding it to the door. It shook again. Someone yelled in what was unmistakably French and he could hear the voices fade away. He peered out the window. A Frenchman and an Indian had abandoned the Vedder house and attacked the neighbors' instead.

Upstairs, Johannes threw on his pants and boots. He grabbed his hunting knife. Without consciously thinking it, he knew instantly what he had to do. He wiped the fog from his window and looked out. With his window facing away from the street, he saw a safe path down. "Johannes, Johannes?" came a shout. He turned. Angie rushed into his room.

"Angie," Johannes said. "Hurry and go find Corset. Then go hide, quickly now."

"Where are you going?" she asked, terrified.

"I have to get to Maria."

"No, please don't go," Angie pleaded. "We need you here."

"I cannot stay," he replied. "Angie, I have to find her. You know I do."

She frowned but accepted it, whispering, "Okay."

Johannes took one last look out the window. The coast was clear. He braced himself next to the window, turned his head away and smashed his elbow through the glass. The cold air blasted through into the room. Angie shuttered, backing away. Johannes knocked away the rest of the glass, clearing the window.

"Johannes," Angie stepped up and hugged him tightly. "Be safe, Johannes. Be safe."

"I'll be safe," he said.

He turned back and climbed out the window, steadying himself on the ledge. He eyed the snow, took a breath and leapt. The lower roof caught his flailing form, and he slid off into the snowy earth. He looked up at Angie peeking out of the window and gave her a quick wave, until she disappeared back inside.

The small yard looked the same. The firewood was stacked the same. Everything was as it should be. He could hear muskets firing and people screaming but for that moment, no French soldiers were in sight. He gripped his knife tightly and set out to find Maria.

* * *

Robert Alexander and Ralph Grant were awoken by the shouts outside. After downing the ale, they each had two more cups and fell to sleep by the cooking fire. But with the sounds of gunfire and Indian war cries outside, they grabbed their guns and alerted the others.

"Stand to!" Alexander shouted to the men of the Connecticut Company. "Stand to! We're besieged!"

Grant checked his musket. "I'm going out there."

"What?" Alexander said, stunned. "Why? Defend the blockhouse, dammit."

But it was too late. Grant unlocked the heavy oak door. Alexander rushed to stop him. Grant opened the door and stepped outside. He stopped. Outside the fort stood a line of men at the ready.

Lieutenant Manthet saw the English soldier appear from the door. "*Fire!*"

A line of musket fire exploded. Ralph Grant felt a thunderous shock and was thrown backwards into the door, falling to the ground. The last thing he saw before his eyes closed were the puddles of blood forming around his destroyed body.

Alexander watched in horror as Grant was gunned down by no less than eight men. He sighted in and took a shot before retreating inside and closing the door, bolting it behind him.

Outside, a letter had fallen from the coat of the dead English soldier. It lay on the snow as the blood seeped over it.

Manthet ordered his men forward. The French and Indians charged, smashing into the door of the blockhouse, beating it with axes and clubs. Others fired at the windows, hoping to keep the soldiers in the fort off guard.

"Get something to knock this door down!"

Inside the blockhouse, Lieutenant Enos Talmadge rallied his men, issuing orders and organizing a hasty defense. "You three, to the windows," he yelled to a group of men. "Fire down on the French bastards."

He ordered the rest to brace the door and hold out.

"Sir," one of the men shouted. "What of the villagers? They cannot defend themselves, sir."

Enos kicked a chair over in anger. "Well, dammit, we cannot defend them if we cannot even defend this fort. Hold the fort, that's an order. Any man tries to leave his post and I'll shoot him myself."

The soldiers of the Connecticut Company acknowledged the order with little protest. Robert Alexander thought of Grant being shot.

"Damn these French," he cursed, sticking his musket out a porthole and firing. The round grazed the shoulder of one of the marauding Indians, sending the man staggering backwards. Inside the fort, the choking smell of black powder filled the rooms. The noise of guns firing and men shouting echoed throughout the night. Each man knew it was a fight to the death and they were determined to see themselves through it.

* * *

Symon Schermerhorn was awake in his bedroom when the first screams went up in the night.

"What was that?" his brother, Cornelius, shouted from the adjacent room.

Gunfire erupted outside.

"We're under attack!" Symon yelled. Suddenly he heard a crash downstairs. "My God, the boy!" he exclaimed, ripping open his door and charging downstairs. As he came to the bottom of the stair, in the darkened living room, he saw a fierce-looking Indian standing over the rocking chair, holding a knife.

That knife was bloody.

With blood in his eyes, Symon surged forward, knocking the warrior to the ground. They crashed over the furniture, grappling and kicking. The

Indian, having been shocked at the sudden attack, stumbled to his feet, and retreated out the front door.

Symon felt a strong hand grip his shoulder. He spun, lifting his fist to strike when he saw the figure hold up his hands.

"Symon, it's me!" Cornelius exclaimed. Symon dropped his hand.

"My son! Where's my son?" He looked around desperately in the darkened room. Then his eyes fell upon his son's body. Symon fell to the floor.

"They killed my son," he cried. "*They killed my son!*"

"Symon," his brother said. Symon turned. Cornelius had a look of terror on his face. "I am so sorry for your son. But we have to get word to Albany. They have to be warned."

"I can't leave my house with my child in it," Symon said. "I need to take care of my boy."

"I can't ride, Symon," Cornelius said, pointing to his leg injury. "Janet and I will take care of your home with the negroes. You have to ride to Albany and warn them."

Symon did not move. His eyes remained focused on his son's body. His brother put a hand on his shoulder. "Please Symon, or others will die too. Please go."

It was the most painful feeling in the world as Symon stood up. He turned to his brother, his eyes filled with tears, and nodded. "Please take care of yourself and Janet. I can't lose any more family tonight."

"We'll be fine," Cornelius said. By then, their sister had come downstairs. She held a dim lamp in her hand and tears streamed from her face when she saw her nephew's body.

"I will ready my horse," Symon said. On his way to the stable, Symon opened the door to side room. The three slaves were huddled together. They shook with fear. "Get out and help my brother." They cringed. He raged in anger. "Get off your lazy asses. Out with all of you from here."

They jumped up and ran to the living room. He headed for the back.

No sooner than the slaves entered the living room, Symon heard a loud crash. For a moment, he thought his slaves had attacked Cornelius. He turned and started to head back. He stepped into the room in time to see the door fall from its hinges in front of the collapsed door. Three Indians and a Canadian of the coureur de bois climbed through the wreckage and into the house. One of the slaves was shot dead instantly. Another tried to escape but tripped. A Sault warrior plunged on him with a tomahawk, hacking the man to pieces.

Cornelius was grappling with an Indian, choking and kicking him. "Get out of here, Symon. Ride hard, brother. Ride!"

Symon had barely the time to refuse as a Frenchman moved in and attacked him, swinging wildly with a musket, using it as a club. Symon fought back, retreating into the kitchen and as far back as the stable door. Grabbing the lid of a pot, he cracked the assailant over the head, knocking the man onto his back. Suddenly another man stumbled in from the living room. It was Gerald, the last of his slaves.

"Go," Gerald said. Symon looked at Gerald. The man had been shot in the gut and stabbed multiple times. "Go!" he repeated.

Symon grabbed the door handle and yanked it open. There was another yell. An Indian charged into the room and ran straight for him. Gerald leapt onto the warrior with whatever strength he could muster. Symon could do nothing as he escaped out the back to his horse. He untied it and leapt on.

He yelled and kicked as he rode the horse from around the back and into the road. The scene before him was surreal. It was a nightmarish hell. All around, French and Indians attacked homes with guns and torches. Men, women, and children screamed, some being dragged out into the street and shot – or worse. He saw two Indians drag a woman he knew, Frans Harmense. She was pulled out by her hair into the snow, still in her night gown, where she was shot and scalped.

From the corner, he saw movement. He turned his horse but was too late to avoid the Frenchman who tried pulling him down from the horse. Symon kicked the man and tore into the horse, galloping away. He could hear the Frenchman discharge his musket, but the round missed.

In his mind, Symon formed his plan. Looking around, he knew Schenectady was lost. But what of Albany? He knew he had to reach the city and warn them of the attack. He galloped down Church Street towards the south gate but seeing it closed, he swiftly brought his horse around and headed north, riding through the chaotic village center.

A few French and Indians took shots at him as he rode through their ranks. He made himself as small as possible on the saddle, peeking ahead as he aimed for the north gate. Suddenly a searing pain shot through his body and his leg jerked violently. He glanced down seeing dark red blood squirt out from his leg. Gritting his teeth, he grabbed the wound tightly, keeping the other on the reigns.

He tensed up as he neared the gate. While still open, there was a cluster of French and Indians surrounding it. They yelled as they saw the horse and fired. Three shots missed but one just barely scraped his arm, catching more cloth than skin.

Galloping through their ranks, he kicked with his good leg, sending one man to the ground. He shoved another back who tried to grab him. All the fear rushed to his brain as he crossed the gate. Heading out into the night, he wondered how he got out with his life. Another shot rang from the dark and Symon's horse stumbled and jerked, heaving. Symon checked. A ball had torn into its rear.

"There's no time for either of us, boy," he said. He yelled and tapped the horse but not too hard as to hurt it further. Struggling, the horse galloped, turning to the east. Symon continuously checked behind him as he rode as hard as he could away from the burning village. He checked his wound. It was still pouring blood, turning the whole of his leg red.

"Come on, boy!" He urged his horse onward, taking one last look at Schenectady from a few hundred meters away. It was now just a small silhouette, illuminated in the dark night by the flames glowing from behind its walls. He could hear the faint screams and cries of the dying. He bowed his head and disappeared along the road to Canatagione.

Chapter 41

The young Mohawk squaw Waneek was the first to hear the war cries go up from across the river. It woke her from her deep sleep, for even though the village was a distance away, the stillness of the night carried the screams far. Scrambling from her cot, Waneek grabbed a fur coat and hurried outside, barefoot into the snow. She knew the war cry at once. It was not Iroquois, but Algonquin.

Then a shot rang out. Then another – and another.

Terrified, Waneek, clenched her coat tighter and watched in horror. She could hear the screams of women, some going silent with more musket fire. She knew where it was coming from but across the river, the village, shielded by the stockade remained dark, save for the occasional flash from a muzzle of a musket.

Standing in the blackness of the night, she remained transfixed in terror at the tragedy unfolding across the great dark void of frozen river. Within a few moments, however, a small glow arose from the village center. The glow started to spread as did the level of screams and gunfire. Suddenly, a flame burst out from behind the stockade; a house having been lit on fire.

Panic struck the Mohawk woman. She turned and fled back to the manor home. Rather than retreating to her quarters, she rushed up the steps to the front door. Summoning all her strength, she pounded on the doors and wailed at the top of her lungs.

"What in Heaven's name is that pounding?" John Glen thundered as he awoke.

"Who's at our home at this hour?" his wife Julia asked him, rolling over in bed. Glen got out of bed, throwing on his trousers and boots. The pounding continued.

"Why does that sound like Waneek out there?" He grabbed a pistol and left his room, hurrying through the corridor and down the stairs to the door. He opened the door. A rush of freezing air and the Mohawk woman crashed into him, nearly knocking him over.

"Get a hold of yourself, girl," he shouted.

"Sir, the village –"

She had no need to say more. Even from his home, Glen could hear the gunfire. He stormed outside, running a few yards from his home. Across the river, the village of Schenectady was bathed in a fiery orange glow. He could hear a woman scream for her baby and then her voice suddenly cut off. Flashes from muskets flickered like a hundred fireworks going off in the village.

But it was no celebration.

When the realization of what was happening dawned on him, grief and dread swept over him. He stood on his lawn, with his eyes fixed on Schenectady. Every muscle and nerve in his body screamed in unison to turn and go back inside but it was like some unseen force was keeping him there, tormenting his soul with the screams of the villagers as they were helplessly slaughtered.

Behind Glen, his family and servants had now heard the gunfire and screams. The slave Robert rushed to Glen's side.

"Captain, what we be doin', Sir?"

Glen remained fixated on the village. It was as if nothing else existed in that moment.

The Mohawk Joseph also came running out.

Waneek stood a few feet from Glen, joining the gathering around the Captain. Joseph turned to Glen.

"I must get word of this to the Mohawk castles." He stared at Glen, waiting for a response. "John!" Joseph yelled.

Glen turned to him. "What?"

"We need to get word to the Mohawk and Albany. I will leave at once for the castle." Glen eyed the burning village across the river. He looked back to his home. Staring out of the second-floor window, he noticed his daughters Catarina and Helena.

"No," he said finally. "I cannot permit you to leave."

"But, John," Joseph pleaded. "They must be warned."

Glen grabbed Joseph by the arm. "Listen to me. That's the French and Caughnawaga there. They will surely come here if they are not already on their way through this darkness." Glen's eyes filled with tears. "Please, you must stay and help me mount a defense of my home. My wife and children are in that home. I need you here."

Joseph gritted his teeth. *Surely, they could not defend this isolated house so far from help?* His mind was made up that the right choice was to get word to bring reinforcements as soon as possible. Suddenly he heard a voice crying. Glen's eleven-year-old daughter, Maria, had run out of the house in her nightgown and rushed to her father.

"Daddy, I'm scared!"

Glen picked up his daughter, holding her as if his life depended on it. "It'll be okay, child." Glen turned to Joseph. "Please, I need you here."

Joseph knew he should have already been on the run, carrying news of the attack. But as he stared at young Maria, stark fear evident in her dark brown eyes, he knew he could not leave that child, or any of them. He put his hand on Maria's head, forcing a smile through his personal anguish. "Alright, John, I will stay."

Glen bowed his head in thanks. "Okay child, back inside," he said, putting Maria down. "I will be back in a minute."

"You promise?" she asked.

"Of course," he smiled back. She ran back to her mother, who was waiting at the front door. Glen addressed Robert and Joseph. "Muster everyone. We have work to do."

* * *

Joachim Staats peered out the window on the western facing wall of the blockhouse. He looked out upon a quiet scenery. It seemed, to Staats, as though the enemy were all inside the village. None were guarding the outside.

He looked back.

Talmadge was shouting out desperate orders to the men. Smoke filled the small fort in the chaotic night and Staats noticed there was nobody paying attention to him. In that moment, he made his decision. He unbuckled his sword and set it down, careful not to make a scene. Then, with a swift motion, he kicked a leg out of the window.

"Joachim!" he heard his name shouted amidst the musket fire. Staats looked back, terrified. Talmadge approached him, pistol drawn. "Don't do it!"

Staats looked down, seeing the far drop to the snow, and back to Talmadge. "I'll take my chances," Staats said. Before Talmadge could respond, Staats kicked his other leg over and disappeared. Talmadge rushed to the window.

Down below, Staats was already up and brushing the snow from his coat. He looked up, staring at Talmadge.

"Coward!" Talmadge roared, taking aim.

Staats did not respond. He took off at a run, never looking back. He vanished into the woods as Talmadge held his fire. As much as he would have liked to kill Staats, turning back at his men firing, he faced a hard reality. They would need every shot they had.

* * *

Johannes Vedder crawled through the snow. His hands shook in terror and shudders wracked his body. But he had to keep going. All around, smoke was rising from homes that were being set alight by the marauding French and Indians.

Foreign voices yelled out so close to him, he thought he had been spotted. He darted up and faced the backs of three Frenchmen, as they took aim and fired at a man who had exited his house. The man screamed in agony as he fell.

Johannes crouched next to a hen house. He dared not move an inch. They were so close, the smell of their gunpowder almost made him cough. He held his hand to his mouth, praying he did not give away his position. More shouting was heard, and the men rushed off.

Johannes squeezed into a dark corner between the hen house and slave's quarters. In his temporary sanctuary, he crouched down, holding his knees. A tear streamed down his face. Every beat of his heart made him want to get up and find Maria, while every muscle urged him to stay in place. He fought his mind, trying to find the will to brave the danger and find Maria. He felt as if his body would tear itself no matter his choice.

And it killed him to stay.

*   *   *

In yet another part of the village, David Christoffelse was gripped with panic. He peeked out the window from his home and was horrified at the sight.

"Lord protect us," he exclaimed.

"What is happening?" his wife Rachel asked, rushing over. Not waiting for a response, she opened the curtains to see.

"My God, woman," David cried in horror. "Close them, now!"

Rachel did not heed her husband's warning. She stared in shock. Outside, there was utter carnage in the street. Two bodies lay in the snow. A band of strange men, both white and Indian, stood around shouting and firing. A woman in a white night gown ran outside from a smoking house. Her sleeve was on fire and she cried in agony.

"That's Alice Janz," Rachel said. "No, please Lord protect her," she sobbed.

The woman in the street fell to her knees, letting out a horrific cry. An arrow had pierced her back, coming out the front. She collapsed to the ground and her hands dug into the snow as she tried to crawl.

A fearsome Indian rushed up, dropping his bow. His face was black and red with war paint. He grabbed her head, and in one swift motion, removed her scalp with his knife. He stood up, screaming and holding it high above his head.

Rachel panicked and tried closing the curtains. The movement, however, alerted the Indian, and he screamed in their direction.

David Christoffelse knew they had been spotted. "Go to the pantry, all of you," he shouted to his family.

"I can fight," Henry said approaching.

"No," David said in reply. "Help me with this bookshelf."

They dragged the heavy oak furniture over, barricading the door. His other son, Andries rushed in.

"Father, they're in the backyard too. I blocked the door."

"Good lad," David said. He retreated to the pantry where Rachel was hiding with Gertruy and Thomas. He saw his daughter crying and held her tightly. "We should be safe." He did not believe his own words, but knew he had to make sure his wife and kids did. "Help will come soon. I am sure the soldiers at the fort will come to us."

* * *

"We can't hold them, sir!" a soldier yelled. His hands and face were red with blood. "We lost two more men."

Enos Talmadge could smell the fires from outside. "They lit the blockhouse, boys. They lit it on fire."

The weary men of the Connecticut garrison were on their last ounce of strength. He knew he had to make a hard choice.

"Gentlemen," he called out. "We cannot stay here." Some of the men nodded grimly. Dirt and ash smeared all their faces. Most of them were wounded in some way. "All those who wish, there is a safe way out the western window. Flee to the woods and live to fight another day. Those who wish to stay with me, we will fight our way out the front and make them pay for attacking Schenectady." He paused, reflecting. "I don't need to tell you we are outnumbered and any man who joins me will be judged by the Lord before sunrise."

He unsheathed his sword. "God forgive our sins."

Manthet was furious. "What do you mean he rode through you?" The three men eyed each other, terrified to be the first to speak. "Answer me, you sonsofbitches. You said you wounded him and his horse, and yet he got away?"

"Monsieur," one of the men finally spoke. "He will surely bleed out or freeze in this weather. We did not think he was worth pursuing."

"You idiots!" screamed Manthet. "He *may* die. And if he does not, and he warns Orange, we lose our advantage. We *already have* lost our advantage." The men did not answer. "Get out of my sight," he said disgusted.

Just then, smashing sounds rang out behind him. He spun around just as the doors of the blockhouse swung open. There was a mass storm of musket fire and shouting as men charged from the burning fort and threw themselves into the besieging French and Indians.

The combat was brutal. After firing off their shot, the men of the Connecticut company used their muskets as clubs or drew knives and crashed into the opposing armies with what little strength they had left.

Talmadge drove his sword into the gut of one Indian. He shoved the man back, crashing into another and taking a blow on his head. He fought off that man too. A fat, bearded Frenchmen with a tomahawk.

Manthet saw the English officer cut down the Indian and charged into the fray. He attacked Talmadge, driving his sword into the man's left arm.

Talmadge cursed aloud and smashed the hilt into Manthet's face. The two traded blows but Talmadge was weak already. He yelled and swung wide.

Manthet blocked the blow and drove his sword deep into Talmadge's chest. While his sword was still stuck inside the Englishman, Manthet reached into his belt, pulled out a small dagger, and shoved it into Talmadge's neck. He stabbed him several more times until the lifeless body slumped down, covered in blood.

Manthet stumbled backwards, checking over his own wounds - which he found to be mostly superficial. Looking around, he noticed that his men were finishing up with the soldiers who attacked them. Aside from the Sault Indian, no one else had perished, though several were severely wounded. Nearly every English soldier lay dead. Only three were taken prisoner. He took a breath and calmed his raging adrenaline, satisfied that he had wiped out the garrison.

Outside Schenectady, several men of the Connecticut company made their way from the blockhouse to the trees. In their desperate final moment, some saw the village that despised them, not worth saving. They would live to avenge Schenectady, but they would choose not to die for it.

* * *

David Christoffelse huddled with his wife and four children in the pantry of their home. They could hear the screams and gunfire from outside. They heard thuds from the door as the savages outside tried to gain entry.

"The Lord will protect us," he whispered. Gertruy smiled up at him and he kissed her forehead.

Rachel gasped. David turned his head. Smoke billowed in. His wife teared up. "The house is on…"

"Shh!" David replied. "We are safe here," he lied.

He pleaded silently with Rachel not to panic their younger children. Both Henry and Andries knew their impending fate and faced it with a grisly acceptance. The smoke continued to pour in and soon they could feel the heat as the fire spread throughout the house. David squeezed his daughter tighter. "Honey, what's your favorite part of the book we read earlier?"

Gertruy smiled. "I like the beginning, Daddy."

He smiled as the tears flowed from his eyes. The walls started to glow red.

"That's my favorite part, too."

He smiled back.

Outside, a group of Frenchmen and Indians shouted and cheered as the fires spread and the roof lit up in a bright, horrific blaze. The voices inside pleaded and screamed, though the language was foreign to the Frenchmen. The screams soon fell silent as flames consumed the house.

Chapter 42

Johannes could hear the screams in the night. That last one made him cringe in horror. It sounded like many voices. They pleaded for God and mercy. Now he could hear them no more. The thought that Maria was one of them struck him in a way he could no longer bear.

He crouched down and inched his way forward until he could see his surroundings. Pillars of smoke rose into the night from every direction. Bodies, many burnt or mutilated, lay strewn on the ground. The snow was mottled red and black with the remnants of blood and ash.

With a clear mind, he could see the house Maria was staying in. So far, it had not been burned. He made up his mind. With terror in his bones and fear gripping his every move, Johannes jumped up and ran for the house. He paused when he moved closer. The door had been smashed inward.

He crept closer and peered inside a window. The place appeared deserted. Cautiously, he made his way through the doorway. Furniture was smashed, and the house looked as if it had been ransacked. But there were no bodies, English or otherwise. Johannes moved about, taking great care not to make a sound. Outside, the screams and chaos still echoed in the streets.

He passed through a doorway and found himself in the storeroom at the back of the house. He checked. The door, though closed, was unlocked. He cracked it open. Suddenly, the door flew open and a girl jumped out swinging a metal pan. Johannes grabbed her wrists, wrestling the pan from her hand.

"Maria," he shouted. "It's me."

Maria paused and stared at him hard. Her knees became weak and she started to give. Johannes grabbed her tightly and lowered her to the floor. "Are you okay?"

"Yes," she trembled. "I am so scared. I don't know what to do."

"We have to leave," Johannes said. "I wish I knew a way out of here, but they're everywhere."

Maria gripped his shirt. "Please don't leave me."

"I will never leave you again," Johannes said, grabbing her hand. "Never." There was a sudden crash from the other room. "They're back," he whispered. She stiffened up. "We have to move – now."

Johannes helped Maria to her feet. "Is there another way out?"

"The window in the bedroom," Maria whispered. "This way."

She peeked around the corner. Standing in the parlor, a tall burly man with a grisly beard, and deerskin clothes poked through the household goods. Seeing he was distracted, Maria tiptoed out of the storeroom and into the bedroom. Johannes followed suit, keeping his eye on the man as he passed. Johannes gently closed the bedroom door behind him.

In the bedroom, Maria grabbed a coat. "Wear this," she said. She grabbed one for herself and headed for the window. "It creeks loudly. He will probably hear."

"Then go quickly," Johannes said. Maria nodded. He leaned in, wrapped his hand around her head, before bringing his lips to hers in a tight kiss. "I love you," he said.

A smile touched her features. "Ready?" she asked. Johannes nodded. "Okay, here we go."

Maria grabbed the window frame and slid it up. As she said it would, the window screeched open. They could hear shouting and footsteps even as Maria climbed out the window, falling into the snow. Johannes rushed to the window as the door behind him flew open. The burly French militiaman stormed in, hatchet at the ready.

Johannes grabbed an iron for the fireplace and swung it hard, striking the man in the skull. The man fell backwards, crashing over a wooden chest. Johannes dropped the iron and ran to the window, jumping out head first into the snow. Before he had shaken it off, Maria was helping him up. He grabbed her hand and the pair ran for cover.

*   *   *

The reverend Peter Tassemaker slammed the door of his house shut. Breathless, he dropped a pile of documents on the floor. They were from the church. He looked out the window. Flames shot up the steeple and sparks hit the roof, setting that ablaze as well. His eyes welled, and the tears flowed as he watched his beloved church burn.

Having already made two trips to save vital artifacts and documents from the church, the reverend did not know if he had the strength or courage to make another trip. Though he lived just across from the church, crossing the street could mean being shot, scalped, or worse.

Suddenly, the door burst open. Peter Tassemaker fell back in horror as two tall Wilden Indians walked inside. They failed to notice the man on the floor just feet from them. One took to rummaging through the shelves. He grabbed a few spoons and a

344

pot and ran out. The second man started forward, looking around.

Peter stumbled to his feet and ran to the door. Alerted, the Indian turned and flung a tomahawk. Peter yelled as it lodged itself into his lower back. He fell in the doorway. "Mercy," he cried.

Outside, a Frenchman saw the commotion and approached. He aimed his rifle and fired, striking the reverend in the shoulder. Peter collapsed back inside. He crawled further inside, and over to the pile of papers collected from the church.

The Frenchman stepped inside the house and eyed the Indian, who had resumed his quest to plunder as much as he could carry. The Frenchman looked down at the bleeding man. Peter looked up and saw his murderer staring back at him emotionless.

"Mercy," he whispered, gargling up blood.

The Frenchman stood before him and calmly reloaded his rifle. Peter held up his hand weakly. The Frenchman aimed directly at the helpless man on the floor.

He fired.

The man's hand fell, his body crumpled, and blood pooled around him. The Frenchman walked outside, grabbed a torch from another, and set the house ablaze.

* * *

While most inhabitants were asleep when the French and Indians attacked, Adam Vroman was not. As the door burst open, Vroman leapt to his feet and grabbed the charging Canadian fur-trader by the coat, slamming him against the wall. The two struggling men traded blows before the stunned Canadian retreated from the house, leaving behind his rifle.

When he observed the repugnant events happening outside from his window, he smashed it wide open, took aim at the first man he saw, and fired. The shot missed, and the man scurried to cover.

"Barent, get over here, son," he yelled. Barent, who was only ten years old, ran to his father's side. "Do you remember how to load a rifle?"

"Yes, Father," Barent replied.

Adam handed the spent rifle to his son and picked up his own musket. "As I fire them, you will reload them. Do you understand?"

Engel came down the stairs with the baby in her arms. "Dear heavens, what are we to do?"

Adam gripped his musket tightly. His heart was still racing with adrenaline. He looked at his wife and baby, then to their son. His voice trembled as he spoke. "I built this house with my two bare hands. They will not burn this house." His voice was unwavering. "*We will fight.*"

Engel took a breath and nodded. She took the baby and ran to the back to hide. Adam peered back out the window and scanned the street. The enemy was everywhere. He took aim with his musket and fired.

Choking gunpowder smoke filled the living room of the Vroman House. Adam fired again and passed the captured rifle to his son, Barent, to reload. Outside, two raiders lay screaming in the snow with blood pouring from their wounds.

Pierre Le Moyne d'Iberville came to see why, among the destruction, this house was still untouched.

"Monsieur," one of the coureur de bois reported, "there may be two or three men inside. They are keeping up a solid fire which prevents us from getting close."

"Get men around the back," d'Iberville ordered. "Smash your way into that house. Put them all to death."

Engel Vroman stood with her back to the door to the pantry. Not able to withstand the baby's crying any further, she undid her night blouse and nursed the baby with milk. The nurturing soothed her, and Engel took the moment for the simple happiness it gave her. She stared into young Lucy's eyes and smiled.

Suddenly the back door smashed open. Two Frenchmen stormed inside as she screamed in terror. One of the men grabbed Engel by the hair. She fought and kicked wildly, still clenching the baby tightly to her breast. He dragged her out the back and into the freezing snow.

Engel raised her hands and scratched at the vicious, bearded man staring back at her. She gouged at his eyes desperately. The Frenchman tried reaching into his belt to get to his pistol. Baby Lucy cried. Hearing her baby's scream renewed Engel's strength. She fought to free herself from the man's iron grip. He yanked her off his arm and finally pulled out his pistol. As he held it to her head, Engel dropped her hand, and in her final moment, rested her hand over Lucy's eyes.

The shot rang out and her head jerked back violently. Her body collapsed where she had stood. The baby screeched, her cries piercing the night. The Frenchman stood motionless. The blood of the woman stained his face and clothes. He stared at the baby as she cried, still clinging to her mother's lifeless body.

He reached down and picked up the baby. D'Iberville had given clear orders. He stared at the infant and gazed into her teary brown eyes.

The orders were clear.

Adam Vroman stumbled back to his feet. On the floor lay the body of a French soldier who had attacked him from behind. The struggle had been hand-to-hand and hard fought. In the end, Adam had taken the man's own knife from him, and ran it through his chest and groin. Pools of blood surrounded the body.

Still dazed, he ignored the warm liquid that streamed down his own cheek. He knew by now the whole of his face was probably painted black with gunpowder and red with blood. During the struggle, he had heard his wife's screaming and a shot ring from out back.

Adam reached into the dead Frenchman's pack and pulled out a short-handled ax. He scrambled over broken furniture and other debris blocking his path, until he reached the back and saw the door wide open. His pulse raced.

Rushing outside, he froze.

His heart stopped and then shattered. Before him, his wife lay, her face so torn apart by the gunshot, he could scarcely recognize her. His eyes then moved over. There, in the snow, was Lucy. He dropped to his knees and took her little body into his arms. The blood spatter on the side of the house and her crushed skull painted a horrifying picture of what had transpired.

Adam laid the baby down. He stood up, the ax gripped so tightly that his hand blistered. He screamed and raged. His eyes saw only blood. He walked back inside, his steps slower than normal. Barent was waiting with both his musket and the rifle loaded.

"Fear not my son," Adam said solemnly. "This will be over shortly."

* * *

The sound of moving furniture echoed through the home of John Glen. Cabinets, tables, and bookcases were set against the windows and the shutters closed and locked. In the main parlor, Glen's wife stripped the dinner table of its tablecloth, and Glen had laid out a small arsenal of muskets and pistols on it. Having hastily thrown on his uniform, he brandished two pistols and his Dutch shell hilt cutlass.

"Robert," Glen called out.

As Robert rushed to the table, the captain thrust a musket into his slave's arms. As Dutch customs still reigned supreme over English law in the northern part of the colony, slaves were considered purely economical and often helped in the defense of homes in dire situations.

"Distribute these other three muskets to the others," he said referring to the other slaves. Glen regularly entrusted Robert, who held a partial freedom, to keep the others in line.

"You think that wise, sir?" Robert asked.

"When the French come," Glen said, "they do not see slaves of the Dutch or English as any different than their masters. When that door comes down, the slaughter will be wholesale, and no man, whether free or slave, should die without a fighting chance to live."

Robert nodded, grabbed the other muskets and went off to arm three more of the male slaves.

Glen gave another musket to his eldest son, Sander. Sander, just thirteen years of age, had proven himself to be a fine shot from his first day hunting.

"Father," Sander said as he entered the parlor. He did not finish his statement as his father turned angrily to him.

"Damnit boy, get yourself upstairs now. I want you at the south window to give fair warning if the enemy approaches. Do not make me tell you again."

"Yes, Father," Sander said, turning and heading back upstairs.

Glen sighed. Although he did want his son to act as a lookout, he was more concerned with keeping him as safe as possible while fighting. Julia had already taken refuge upstairs with the younger boy and their five daughters.

Catarina had heard the ruckus from the start. She slipped into pants, boots, and a fur coat. She tied her hair in a ponytail and slipped down the stairs.

At seventeen, Catarina was Glen's eldest daughter. As she entered the parlor, she saw the muskets laid out on the table, and proceeded to pick one up. Glen, alerted, spun around, pistol at the ready. Startled, she dropped the pistol on the table.

Glen took a breath and lowered his gun. "You should be hiding," he said urgently.

"I can fight, Father!" Catarina pleaded. "I am a fine shot, you know that. You taught me."

"I won't have this discussion," Glen said. "Get to hiding and don't come out until it's over."

Catarina opened her mouth, but her father pointed her finger at her, and she thought better than to continue. She sighed and turned, disappearing back into the kitchen of the blacked-out mansion.

* * *

In the center of the chaotic town, François knelt in the snow and waited. Aside him, his brother d'Iberville and several of his own men, along with a few Indians were gathered.

"This one house has put up quite a fight," his brother said. "But I see no movement now."

François took a breath. "Perhaps they're dead. I will take a man and check it out."

Before his brother could object, François and another militiaman stood and crept towards the house.

At that moment, the door flew open.

Adam Vroman charged out with two long guns in hand. He took aim and fired, hitting an Indian in the arm. He dropped that gun and raised the second one. The raiders, still in shock, barely moved. Adam turned to the two Frenchmen and shot again. The round struck one man in the chest, killing him instantly.

Adam dropped that gun and pulled an ax from his belt and grabbed a young French raider—barely even a man—and held the ax to his neck.

"Enough!" he shouted.

D'Iberville saw his men readying to fire and held them back. Knowing a little English, he spoke. "Do not kill our man."

"You killed my wife," Adam wept, his voice stinging of hatred in its purest form. "You killed my baby."

D'Iberville looked into his brother's eyes. François was terrified. D'Iberville called his men not to fire.

"We can trade," he said. Adam pushed the ax in tighter, drawing blood from his French captive's neck. "Please," d'Iberville pleaded. "What do you want?"

"Leave my family alone," the reply came loudly. "Guarantee you will leave us in peace."

"You have it," d'Iberville replied without hesitation.

"I want your word."

The French officer licked his lips. He glanced to his men. They stood motionless, staring at him. D'Iberville turned to the Englishman. The man's face was terrifying. Blood smeared all over, his clothes torn, yet he stood ready to die fighting. D'Iberville knew what his brother Jacques would do. He would put the man to the sword. Even if it meant their brother François' death. But he was not his brother. He cleared his throat and spoke out. "On my honor and with the Lord as witness, no further harm shall come to you or your family."

Adam Vroman cried. His fury mixed with the deepest sorrow. He hated that they accepted his offer. It would be best to slit this man's throat and rejoin his family in heaven. But through his anger and sorrow there was a finality that peace had to come, even if the price was unbearable.

He released the man and backed up. The young Frenchman stumbled back to his lines. Adam picked up his musket and walked backwards towards his home. His muscles remained tense, expecting an onslaught any moment. To his shock, the French officer kept his word. The marauding French and Indians dispersed, moving on to loot and pillage other houses.

Adam loaded his gun and stood just inside the doorway. There was no describing the way he felt. With his wife and newborn murdered, and his town decimated, he could not come to grips with the fact that his life had been spared. He clenched his gun and waited for the final attack.

An attack that would never come.

Chapter 43

Jacques Le Moyne de Sainte-Hélène moved about the streets, with a sick look on his face that could easily be mistaken for pleasure. Dark blood streaked across his face and shirt from when he had slain an unsuspecting man, who had been dragged outside from his bed.

"Jacques," a voice called out. Sainte-Hélène spun around. His childhood friend, Jacques de Montigny rushed up.

"We have a house that is putting up a resistance."

Sainte-Hélène grinned. "Show me the house."

The two men made their way up the road to the sturdy house. Outside, a Frenchman lay in the street cursing while a comrade held a bloody rag to the man's leg.

"The door is barricaded," an Algonquin stated.

"We shall see about that," Sainte-Hélène said. He turned to his friend. "Are you with me?"

"Until the end," Montigny declared. The two officers charged the house and smashed up against the door. It shook violently but held.

"Again!" shouted Sainte-Hélène. They took a step back and thrust their weight against the door. It gave more. "Again!"

They took a few steps back and charged. The door crashed in, toppling the bookshelf that had been blocking their entrance. Sainte-Hélène fell to the floor and Montigny scrambled almost over him, and into the house.

Inside the house, Reynier Schaets was shocked

when his door caved in and two French marauders fell through. He dropped his pistol and grabbed, what had until then, been a collector's item – an English civil war pike. As the two men scrambled up, Schaets thrust the pike into one of the men. He struck the man's arm and quickly pulled out and thrust again. This time it stuck deeply into the man's abdomen in the side. The man screamed and collapsed.

The other Frenchman—no doubt an officer—surged forward. Schaets tried to pull the pike out but it was too late. The intruder was upon him and Schaets felt a cold sting as the sword blade entered his body. He looked up at the man's bloody face and wondered how many innocents he had slain that night. Schaets tried to resist but the man swung again, this time slicing the jugular. Schaets felt warm as the bright red blood drained from his throat.

Sainte-Hélène watched as the body slumped down. He put his foot forward and pushed the body away. He turned to his friend. "I will be back for you." He moved forward into the house, disappearing up the stairs.

Montigny heard a woman and child screaming from up the stairs. He could hear a clash and then silence. The deep thud of a body hitting the floor was followed swiftly by a quick cry for mercy and another thud. Sainte-Hélène returned shortly after, sheathing his bloody saber.

"There was a woman and boy," he said without pause. He looked over his friend's bloody body. "Let's get you some help."

* * *

Symon Schermerhorn raced forward on his

horse. He fought to ignore the wounds and biting cold as he rode on the Niskayuna road to Albany. He had not bothered to look behind to see if he had been pursued. He guessed, correctly, that the French would have left their horses on the other side of the river.

The road ahead was dark, yet the blinding wind had created such a storm of snow that he could see but a few feet to his front. The deep snow and raging storm would slow any horse, let alone one that was wounded.

"Let's go, boy," he yelled, kicking his heels in and riding hard. His lungs ached from the icy winds that blew all around. His frostbitten fingers grasped the reigns tightly.

Ahead, he saw a dim light. Riding up, he came upon a homestead. "Ahoy!" Schermerhorn called out. The door opened, and a couple stuck their heads out. "The French have besieged Schenectady," Schermerhorn yelled. "They may be on this road within the hour. Hide or take shelter in Albany. I ride on."

He kicked his heels and tore away, leaving the stunned pair in the doorway, in their night gowns.

* * *

Sainte-Hélène had two men carry Montigny to one of the houses that had not been set to the torch. The door was partially open and one of the windows had been smashed. An elderly woman was dragged out by one Athasata's warriors. She wept silently.

"Madam, we require the use of your home," Sainte-Hélène said to her. "In return, we will not burn it."

The woman looked up at him. Her face was pale and her eyes bloodshot. Her hands trembled.

"Do as you will," she muttered.

Sainte-Hélène glanced around. "What is your name, madam?"

The woman cleared her throat. "It is Catelyn Bratt."

"And where is your husband?"

"He passed away many years ago, from the flu."

He nodded. "Children?"

The old woman fought to keep from breaking down. "A son and two grandchildren," she said. "All of them were slain." Sainte-Hélène looked at Montigny who bowed his head slightly. Sainte-Hélène turned to the woman.

"I promise nothing more will be taken from you this night, madam."

She remained motionless. "I have nothing left that you can take. You have taken everything."

Sainte-Hélène sighed. "Very well," he said. He directed the men to carry Montigny into the house. "Remove the dead."

The woman stood as if paralyzed while the bodies of her son and two grandchildren were dragged outside and dropped in the snow. One of the Caughnawaga Indians dropped to a knee, produced a knife, and brutally took the scalp of the son, holding it up as a trophy.

* * *

"I see an opening." Johannes' words brought hope to Maria. "There is a gap in the palisade," he continued. "I think we can make an escape from there if we hurry."

"Thank the Lord," Maria said. "I am beyond exhausted. We have been hiding and running for what must be half an hour. I need to rest."

"First, we need to get outside these walls," Johannes replied. He paused, sighing. "I am tired too." He grabbed her hand, gripping it tightly. "But we have to keep going."

"I know," she said. "Should we go now?"

Johannes took a long look. "Yes – now!"

The pair jumped up and took off like lightning, sprinting to the palisade. There, Johannes saw his mistake.

"I thought the gap was bigger," he stuttered. "My God, I have killed us."

The palisade wall, while appearing at a distance to have a gap, up close was solid. "What do we do?" Maria pleaded.

Johannes glanced up. "The wall is only ten feet high. I will boost you over it."

Maria turned to him. "How will you get over?"

"I will find a way," he said.

"You're lying," she snapped. "I know you are. I want you with me." Her voice shook. "Please, Johannes, I cannot live without you."

"We don't have time, Maria," he pressed. "I will get you over this wall and get out some other way. Maybe I can climb it."

"Please come with me," Maria said again.

"We don't have…" shots ricocheted off the wooden palisade. They turned in terror. A Canadian militiaman and Indian started reloading their muskets. "Run!" Johannes shouted. They fled from the wall as the Canadian and Indian pursued them back into smoky haze of burning houses.

Johannes raced forward, careless of the surroundings, all the while gripping Maria's hand as she struggled to keep pace. The deep snow slowed their run to a crawl.

"I cannot continue," Maria cried.

"We're almost there," Johannes shouted. They turned a corner, running straight into a pack of marauders, both French and Indian.

"*Les saisir*," one of the French said.

Johannes, from a quick glance of the man's coat, guessed he was a regular French Army soldier, possibly an officer. The men grabbed Johannes and Maria, separating them violently as Maria cried. They were led to the town center. In the center of the intersecting streets, a group of French soldiers and Caughnawaga warriors stood guard over a huddled mass of over two dozen survivors. The men shoved Johannes and Maria into the mix and waved their hands downward. They crouched down next to the others.

Johannes gripped Maria. He tried to think of words to reassure her. But none came to mind. He looked around. All about him, homes were blazing in the night sky. Bodies littered the streets. Standing close by was a fearsome Indian with a bloodied tomahawk and a scalp hanging from his belt. Nearer still, a Canadian militiaman wiped blood from his wood-runner knife on the night gown of a woman he had slain.

Johannes took a deep breath.

He never imaged this is how it would all end.

* * *

Angenietje felt paralyzed. Her feet were moving, yet she felt immobile. Her empty hands trembled. Her nightgown and indeed her entire body was covered in dirt and ash. Behind her, fires shattered the windows and flames roared from the collapsing Vedder home.

The assault had come swiftly. After the initial

attackers gave up and moved on, and Johannes had left, the house had been tense, but relatively safe. But after the other homes on their street had been attacked, the marauders returned, this time busting through the windows and setting themselves upon the Vedder home.

Angie was in the living room with her father when they breached the house. Harmen confronted the intruders but had been almost instantly overwhelmed. One Indian struck his shoulder with a tomahawk, sending blood spraying on Angie's face and nightgown. As he fell, she crawled away in terror, fortunate that with her small figure, she could easily hide from the attackers.

More interested in plunder than murder, they ravaged the house, stealing what they could before setting it aflame. Albert yelled viciously, kicking and screaming as he was dragged outside by two Indians. The last she saw of her mother was when Anna grabbed Corset and disappeared out the back, while her father, who had regained consciousness, struggled to contain the fire. When he saw Angie still inside, he screamed at her to escape.

She hated to abandon him, but with the smoke pouring on, she knew she had to leave. Making her way through the smoky interior, she soon found the back door and fell out into the snow. She scrambled away from the house as the fire made its way to the upper floor, shattering the glass on the windows.

She had lost sight of everyone. Her mother and Corset were nowhere to be found outside. Albert, she knew, had been taken captive or worse. Her father, she prayed had escaped, but dreaded the more likely possibility. As for Arent, she had not seen him since before the attack. He had simply disappeared.

Angie had found herself utterly alone. With

the house engulfed in flames, she struggled to her feet and turned away in tears. She walked down the street, her eyes trying not to stare at the mass of lifeless bodies littering the street.

She put a foot forward and felt a stickiness. She glanced down at the pool of blood flowing from a young woman, no older than herself. As she stared in despair, Angie was nearly knocked over by a marauding Indian as he fell to his knees beside the body to claim the scalp as a trophy.

Though at the center of everything, she felt strange that not a single marauder paid her any mind. They seemed more occupied breaking into those houses which were not ablaze, in search of loot they had been promised. The fires had already consumed much of anything valuable, and many of the raiders did not wish to return to Montreal empty handed.

Angie soon found herself standing at the exact center of the crossroads of the village. There she stopped and turned. All about her, the village burned. Fires consumed the great steeple of the church bell tower. Gunfire rang through the village. The terrifying screeches from children, and the war cries of the Indians, echoed in the night. Women screamed as they were dragged outside as captives of the war party. Men were shot and butchered where they lay.

Tears flowed from her eyes as she watched the horrors unfold. Her mind was numb. She could only guess that her family had all been murdered. Her home was gone.

At the end of the world, amidst the blinding snow and raging fires, Angie dropped to her knees, bowed her head, and prayed for mercy.

Chapter 44

Glen turned to the table where he had a crude drawing laid out. He studied his defensive plan from the parlor. Including the slaves, the Mohawks, his son, and himself, Captain Glen had pieced together his army of eight men at arms, plus Waneek who brandished a bow and tomahawk of her own.

Joseph walked in from outside.

"Anything out there?" Glen asked.

Joseph shook his head. "The gunfire from Schenectady has died down as have…the screams."

Glen closed his eyes, resting his hands on the table. "God have mercy on them."

"The village still burns. When I was down at the river's edge, I heard laughs coming from the village. The French must have taken to rape and pillage."

Glen slammed his fists. Rage had replaced sorrow. "They will die if they come here. Every last savage one of them. I will personally cut their hearts out," he growled, touching his cutlass. Joseph ever so slightly nodded, as if acknowledging that it would be no easy task.

"We can fire on them as they cross the frozen river," Joseph said.

"Yes!" Glen nearly shouted. "The river is bare. They have nowhere to hide."

Glen walked briskly to the door, stepping out and looking to the river. "When my son gives us warning that they are on the approach, we'll go down and pick them off, moving back to the house as they approach. Once we're inside, we make our stand."

"And then what?" a voice called out. Glen and Joseph turned. Julia stepped into the room, holding their one-year-old daughter, Annatje in her arms. "And then what, John? They burn the house down with us inside it?"

Glen approached Julia, but she took a step back. He stopped. "My dearest wife, I will not let that happen. I will protect you and our children to my dying breath."

She started to cry. "And then when I'm widowed, what will I do? I cannot lose you, John. And after you are dead, what will happen to the children? Will they become captives of those barbarians?"

John was silent, as if his tongue had been ripped out. Suddenly Joseph spoke up.

"Julia, we have a chance here. The Mohawk – even the Caughnawaga and the Algonquin, respect the most fearsome of warriors. If – if we mount a defense that costs them many lives before they ever reach the walls of this home, perhaps they will ask for terms of surrender. We can negotiate a peace with them that allows your children's lives to be spared as well as yours and any of us still living."

"Well that makes me feel so much better," she said sarcastically.

Glen walked up, holding her by her arms. "My dear, it's the only choice we have. We cannot move the children into the night in this weather. They would track the footprints and run us down. We have to stay and fight." She nodded, still sobbing quietly. "Go upstairs and comfort the children." He kissed her on the forehead.

When she had gone, Glen turned to Joseph. "Thank you for that. You could've said no earlier. Why didn't you?"

Joseph was confused. "I don't understand – say no to what?"

"When I asked you to stay," Glen replied.

"You could have said no and left to spread the warning. But you stayed here, where death is near certain. Why?"

Joseph smiled, this time genuinely. "When I looked at your daughter –"

"My daughter?"

"When I looked into those eyes I realized something John." He put his hand on Glen's shoulder. "Your family is my family. And there is nothing more to that. If this is my time to die, then I die defending my family." Joseph dropped his hand and picked up his musket. He heaped a heavy blanket over his shoulder and headed for the door.

"Joseph," Glen called out behind him. "Will they negotiate?"

Joseph stopped briefly but refused to look Glen in the eyes. He stood motionless for a moment. "I'll go back to the river and keep a watch."

He left without another word.

In the silence of his parlor, Glen interlocked his fingers and started praying, tears streaming from his face.

In the cold, black night, under a thick fur blanket, Joseph sat like a statue among the bushes and rocks of the riverbank. Safely tucked away, he could make out the sounds of the village clearer, but his sight was still obstructed by the village stockade.

More than four hours had passed since Waneek first raised the alarm. While homes in the village itself still burned brightly into the night sky, the sound of gunfire had almost entirely subsided. There was still the occasional native war cry or the laughter of some French militiamen, and for a while they were even engaged in song and drink.

His mind drifted but he dared not close his eyes, for one moment of complacency could mean certain death. He tried to picture the faces of all of Glen's children, but only young Maria's came to mind. He pictured her giggling at the Glen's Thanksgiving table. Suddenly, the giggling turned to a blood-curdling scream. Her face was covered in blood and she was tied above a fire, her arms stretched out to the sides, Caughnawaga surrounding the fire, cheering the sacrifice.

Joseph snapped up, grabbing his musket at the ready. "Maria?" he said, looking around. After a terrifying moment, he regained his composure, realizing it was a dream.

Or was it a foreshadowing?

His mind raced in fear. Sweat dripped from his head.

Suddenly he heard a noise, coming not from across the river, but the shoreline to the east. His eyes darted back and forth until he focused on a single shadowy figure sneaking up to the Glens' house. Joseph steadied his musket, sighting in. The man came within thirty yards. Joseph fired.

The shot rang out in the dark. The man fell backwards, but quickly rose to his feet, sprinting back in the direction from which he'd appeared. Joseph was up and running towards the house. Glen met him at the front door, gun in hand. "What happened?"

"Scout!" shouted Joseph as he rushed inside to reload. "I didn't get him. They'll be back in force."

Glen agreed. For the next twenty minutes, Glen went to Robert, the other slaves, another Mohawk by the name of Atian, his son Sander upstairs, and checked the exterior defenses. Returning to the parlor, he took a breath of relief.

For the moment at least, they were still safe.

* * *

Symon Schermerhorn struggled to stay on his horse. After hours of riding from house to house, every settlement east of the village, at last he had made his way back to the Crooked Road, due east – to Albany.

His body ached. He looked down at his leg. The blood had clotted and no longer seeped through the hastily-prepared bandage, but he could feel the lead musket ball lodged in his leg, its very presence ensuring a constant torture along the journey. His face had swollen in several spots from the blows of the Canadian intruder earlier. The blood had dried up and froze to his face. Fatigue overwhelmed him as he rode on, his mind drifting in and out of consciousness.

His horse struggled to continue, its own wound inflicting unknown devastation as its owner forced it onward through the hostile weather.

While the sun had not yet breached the horizon, the sky was turning to a deep blue. *Dawn is approaching,* thought Symon. *I must hurry. For God's sake, I must hurry.* He kicked his horse and urged it forward with all possible haste. His mind was but a blur, vague images of the nightmare he had left behind playing in his mind. Shadowy assailants in his home, homes set ablaze, the white snow stained red with the blood of his friends and neighbors.

Then another image flashed before him. It was of the lifeless body of his youngest son. Symon's head dropped in despair as he sobbed, tears running down his face, freezing before they reached his grizzly beard.

"My son!" he cried out. "I am so sorry."

His mind thought of his son's birthday which was to be in two weeks. Little Johannes Schermerhorn had not yet seen seven years before he was shot dead by a Frenchman with a musket in the dead of night.

Symon's emotions fueled his resolve to reach Albany, no matter the consequence.

Sunrise was just moments away when Albany's stockade gate came into view. Symon wasted no time, urging his weakening horse onward. The horse stumbled, its wound taking an ever-heavier toll on its strength. It nearly threw Symon off as he grabbed the mane, struggling to stay on. With an almost fanatic strength, the horse kicked back up and trotted faster to the gate.

Atop the gate, a guard paced back and forth with his musket, waiting for his relief to show up. He heard a man call out and looked down. Approaching the gate was a horse with a rider. The man was waving his hand wildly but was bent over as if in immense pain. "Who goes there?" the guard called out.

"I bring news," the man replied wearily. "Dear God, open the gate."

The guard hesitated for a moment, and then turned to several men walking about the street. "You there," he said pointing at two men. "Open the gate and hurry!" The men grunted but rushed over, unlocking the great wooden gate. As they swung both doors open, a horse and rider entered. "Help him!" the guard yelled.

The men helped Symon down from his horse and laid him on the snow-covered road. He was mumbling, dehydrated and greatly fatigued. The horse let out a weak cry before its legs gave out and it collapsed. Its eyes focused on its wounded owner, lying beside it in the early morning. It let out a deep breath before closing its eyes for the final time.

Seeing a small gathering of civilians at the front gate, which was wide open, Captain Bull and a handful of the Connecticut militia hurried over to see what the commotion was all about.

"Out of the way," he shouted, pushing his way through the crowd to where Symon lay, barely conscious. "What happened?"

Symon sat up as much as he could, his strength failing him. "Schenectady burns. French," he paused, thinking. "Indians, hundreds of them. They're burning everything."

He collapsed into the snow.

Terrified bystanders let out shouts. Panic gripped those present. Some rushed off to grab their arms and ammunition. Others ran in fear, back to their homes. Captain Bull looked around. "Close and lock the gate."

"Is he dead?" a man asked, pointing to Schermerhorn.

Captain Bull checked. "No, he lives but he's weak. Take him to the doctor. Get some blankets. And get his horse out of the road; leave it outside of the walls or burn it."

Several men grabbed Schermerhorn and carried him away. Bull stood in the street, looking out upon the Crooked Road, a road which would take the French just a few short hours to reach Albany from Schenectady. As the image disappeared with the closing gates, he wondered how far the French were behind the rider.

He turned to the other officers. "I want men on watch along the length of the entire stockade; every post manned. Shove a gun in the hands of every man you can find and put them on these walls. I don't care if they're with the Convention or Leislerites. We have a fight coming."

Chapter 45

Smoke billowed from burning homes. Others were smoldering ashes, having been torched in the first hours of the raid. The blockhouse had been entirely burned down, and Manthet ordered the remaining stockade sections to be set to the flame as well. Black soot blanketed the snow, as did the rivers of blood from the slain villagers.

Scattered about the village lay the dismembered bodies of the fallen. Many were shot, some burnt, and others with their bloody and bald heads exposed, where they had been brutally scalped. Blackened skeletons, both of adults and children still smoked in the ashes of their homes where they were slaughtered. As the sun dawned, utter ruin stretched out in every direction.

The village of Schenectady had been destroyed.

At the village center, where the roads intersected, nearly sixty men, women, and children sat, huddled in tight groups for warmth; prisoners of the French and Indians. Parents kept the children in the middle, shielding them not only from the extreme cold, but the sheer devastating sights surrounding them. It was a vain attempt, for every villager, young and old, had borne witness to hours of murder and pillaging in the most brutal of fashion. Images of fallen family and neighbors, and the torching of their homes would forever rest with the survivors. They themselves were bound and bloodied; their clothes torn, and their faces scarred.

Some of the more fortunate survivors had been given blankets or coats by their French captors - those wishing to keep their prisoners alive, so that they may fetch a healthy price in Montreal. Others were kept warm only by the body warmth of others or the heat emitting from the charred ruins of nearby homes.

A cluster of Mohawks, men and women, were tied up among the survivors. Their bodies bore the bloody marks of the vicious – yet futile struggle against the French. They were guarded by the Caughnawaga, as Manthet knew he could not trust his Canadian militia, many of whom lost friends at Lachine, to safeguard their mortal enemies. It was a for a larger strategy, and the men simply would not understand.

Manthet approached Sainte-Hélène and his two brothers standing amidst the burnt-out home of the reverend Peter Tassemaker. "We've got some explaining to do to Monsieur Callières," Sainte-Hélène said as Manthet walked up.

Manthet inspected the ruins. The charred body of the reverend was partially visible under a beam from the roof. Melted skin hung from the body's arm like strips of cloth on a tattered shirt. "I thought our men knew which homes to avoid. Was it not marked by the scarlet cord in the window?"

"I guess we will never know," Sainte-Hélène replied, almost in a tone that revealed he cared little for the mistake.

Manthet shook his head. "This is nothing to be proud of Jacques. This man was a man of God. He did not deserve this."

"He was English," Sainte-Hélène said. "He wasn't totally innocent either."

"I don't see it that way." Manthet looked at the village's survivors. "We need to send word to the

Dutch Captain across the river. He may pick out his relatives from among the survivors to be spared. We take the rest to Montreal."

Sainte-Hélène nodded. "I did not like that idea at first, but we have far too many prisoners. They will hamper our return march. I agree to give up some to the Dutch Captain, not out of civility, but rather practicality."

Manthet looked around him. "Send a courier to him immediately."

"We sent him one a few hours ago, and he was fired upon and returned," Sainte-Hélène stated.

Manthet looked to the sky. "It's lighter out." He turned to the other Le Moyne officer, Pierre Le Moyne d'Iberville. "You go. Take Athasata, no weapons. Show him you mean no harm. Let's avoid having to take the entire force across the river to attack his house."

D'Iberville glanced at his brother. Sainte-Hélène gave a slight nod. Iberville straightened up. "I'll go at once."

He walked out of the charred house, brushing the soot from his coat.

Manthet turned back to Sainte-Hélène. "Get the men ready. Once this prisoner issue is dealt with, we're leaving. Do not harm those homes that I ordered spared. Burn all the rest."

Johannes Vedder gripped Maria Vandervort tightly, doing his best to keep her warm. His brother Albert sat close by, holding a wad of cloth to his head, soaking up the blood from the Frenchman's musket strike. Maria rested her head on Johannes' chest. "I'm scared."

Johannes tightened his grip, bringing her in closer. "I'm scared too," he whispered into her ear.

"But no matter what, I will protect you."

She looked up at him and his heart broke at her sorrow. "What will happen to us?"

Albert, overhearing her, leaned in. "The Mohawk tortured the survivors of Lachine, cannibalized them over the fire."

"Albert, shut up!" Johannes said.

"It's the truth."

Maria gasped. "Oh God, please no."

Johannes put his hand around her head, keeping it close to him. "That won't happen." He glared at his brother, shaking his head.

Albert shrugged. "We need to escape. It's that simple."

Johannes turned back to Maria. He knew his brother was right. The French and Indians did not come to occupy the village and the Mohawk River valley. It was no foraging expedition. They came to avenge the slain people of Lachine and the other settlements ravaged by the Iroquois. Little mercy was to be expected.

* * *

The hours passed painfully slow. Glen and the others took turns keeping watch at the windows. They watched as the night gave way to the early morning light. The screams of the inhabitants of Schenectady had subsided, as had the celebratory gunfire and songs of the French and Indians. Joseph sat down next to the Captain.

"What are you thinking, my brother?"

Glen rested his head against the wall. His exhaustion was all too obvious. "They've drunken themselves to sleep," he said. "At least some of them. My guess is that's why it is relatively quiet over there."

Joseph grunted in agreement. "Well," Glen continued, "once they're awake and ready, they'll be back. Maybe we should try to get an hour of sleep on shifts, keep a few on watch."

"You first," Joseph said. Glen laughed.

"No, I'm – I'm okay."

"No, you must rest," Joseph insisted. "You won't be any good to fight if you can't keep your eyes open."

Glen thought it over for a moment. He knew his Indian friend was right. "Pass me that blanket," he said. Joseph reached over, handing him a thick bearskin blanket from a nearby chair. "Just a few minutes," Glen said, clenching it tightly, slouching in the chair. His eyes began to close.

Suddenly Sander shouted from upstairs. "Father, come quick."

Glen jumped up and sprinted up the stairs and to the room where his son kept watch over the river.

"Look, Father!" Sander said, pointing. Glen looked out the window. Coming down the shoreline was a flicker of light – a torch. But what took the Captain by surprise was how many men were marching on his house.

"There's two – only two of them," he said. He wondered what sort of deception was at work. He watched the two men approach, getting closer and closer until soon they were scarcely a hundred yards from the house. "Get ready," he whispered to his son. They aimed in on the men. There was a thud downstairs. Glen looked out the window. "My God!" he exclaimed.

Outside, Joseph slowly approached the two men, a musket in one hand but both hands raised above his head, showing he meant no harm to the two visitors.

"What's he doing, Father?" Sander asked.

Glen shook his head. "I haven't the faintest idea, son." They watched half in awe and half in fear, that he would be shot dead. Joseph stopped within a few feet of the men and seemed to speak to them briefly. He then backed away and started returning to the house.

"Stay here," Glen ordered to his son.

He went downstairs and arrived in the parlor just as Joseph came in from the cold. "What is happening?" Glen asked.

Joseph looked to his good friend. "They want to talk to you, John. They wish you to come to Schenectady."

Glen readied himself. Through the window, he could see the two men with the torch standing outside. Joseph and Julia stood by his side. He double-checked his pistols and made sure they were easy to draw in the event things did not go as planned. He also had his cutlass to fall back on. Briefly kissing his wife, he headed outside.

The cold air hit him once again, breeching his warm clothes in seconds. Walking towards the two men, he saw one was a Frenchman and the other was an Indian. Behind him, Joseph stepped out onto the porch. He was quickly joined by Robert, Atian, and two more slaves – all of them armed. The act had been thought up by Glen at the last moment as a show of force to the French.

Captain Glen stopped a few paces from the men. He could finally see them clearly. The Frenchman wore buckskin clothing and had a tomahawk and large knife in his belt. The man's coat was dirty with soot and something else. Glen knew what the dark stain was. *Blood!* From his looks, Glen assumed he was one of the coureur de bois. The other man was much older. By his looks, he was no doubt Iroquois. The man carried no weapons; only a blue wampum belt.

"Monsieur," the Frenchman said. "My name is Pierre Le Moyne d'Iberville. I am here on behalf of the governor of Montreal, Louis-Hector de Callières. This is the great Mohawk chief Athasata, of the Caughnawaga people."

"Before you speak another word," Glen said firmly, "understand that I am ready to defend my home to my dying breath, and before God almighty, there is no way you will take this house." He half-turned and pointed towards the house where the armed men stood ready to fight. D'Iberville glanced over. Glen continued, "We will not give up this house. Reinforcements are on their way. Turn back to Canada, now."

"Please, monsieur," Iberville said. "I come in the name of peace and mercy, for you and for your kin. We have no quarrel with you or your family."

Glen was taken aback by the Frenchman's words. "You burn our village in the name of peace and mercy?"

"What's done is done," Iberville stated plainly. "The unspeakable tragedy of Lachine *had* to be avenged. But not all the villagers have been slain. We have captured a great deal of men, women, and children."

Glen fumed in anger but decided prudence was the right course of action in that moment. Whether the Frenchman was telling the truth or not, was another matter.

"Go on," he said.

"Monsieur, we have been told of your hospitality you have shown to our fellow countrymen in the past. Governor Callières wishes to repay you for your kindness. Surely, you have relatives that resided in the village. My commanding officer, Nicolas d'Ailleboust de Manthet, requests you to come with us back to Corlear, and pick out those of relation to you among the prisoners we have taken."

Glen could not believe what he was hearing. Were the French truly about to let him pick out his kin and save them from captivity in New France? Or was he to be taken back to be made an example of? Glen considered his courses of action, including drawing his pistols and killing both men where they stood. Yet when he thought of his wife and children, something told him that any way to avoid further bloodshed should be taken.

"What word do I have that my family will not be harmed this night or any other night?"

Iberville took a step forward. "Monsieur, you have my word and the word of the commanding officer, and the word of the great Athasata. No harm nor foul deed will be done onto you, your family, or your property." He lifted his arm in the direction of the village. "Please, we must hurry back though."

Glen stood for a moment, thinking hard. Then he straightened up. "I will come with you. But first, I must speak to my wife."

Iberville agreed. "Please be brief, monsieur."

When Glen returned to his home, Julia, Joseph, and the others swarmed around him.

"I'm going to Schenectady," he spoke out. "They are taking me there."

Julia held a hand to her mouth and gasped in horror. "No, please don't go!"

"It's not as you think," Glen said. "They have survivors – prisoners." He heaved a sigh of relief, the first genuine release of tension since the terrible ordeal began. "They want me to pick out my kin to be spared."

"But why?" Joseph asked curiously.

"It doesn't matter," he replied. "But they don't know who I'm related to. I may be able to save many lives in that haunted place. I have to try."

Joseph warned him. "Be careful," he said. "If you claim everyone as a relative, they'll know you're lying and they may retract on their mercy."

"Save the children," his wife said, still holding their baby girl.

Glen nodded. "I will save as many as I can. But I have to go now." He drew his two pistols, holding them for a moment, before laying them on the table.

"What are you doing, John?" Julia demanded to know.

"I must go disarmed," he said. "I must show them I am interested in peace and not war." He undid his belt and removed the sword, leaving that on the table as well. Entirely disarmed, he looked at Joseph. "If I don't return, defend my family." Joseph nodded. No words needed to be spoken for they each knew what was at stake. "I shall be back soon," he said to his wife before heading out into the morning.

Chapter 46

Each step John Glen took across the ice spanning the frozen river, was a step closer to the horror he knew awaited him in Schenectady. Ahead, the village smoldered. Somewhere beyond the blackened stockade, a fire still poured black smoke into the winter morning.

But what terrified Glen the most was the sound. He could hear not a single voice nor a scream from the village. His heart raced, and his mind filled with horrific possibilities. As he climbed the embankment and headed towards the gate, he prepared himself for the sight of piles of bodies; women and children butchered in their night gowns by the dozen.

Glen passed through the north gate and his heart sank. His eyes immediately fell upon the ruined blockhouse and the bodies of the slain soldiers from Enos Talmadge's detachment. He saw the lieutenant's mutilated corpse, covered in ash, sprawled out on the ground; blood staining the snow in every direction. Other men's heads were sliced red where their scalps had been removed as war trophies.

"Butchers!" he hissed.

D'Iberville ignored Glen's comment. "The prisoners are this way," he said.

Glen followed d'Iberville down the street. In every direction, there seemed to be another poor soul laying still in the snow; men, women, children, freeman, and slave. There was no discrimination in who the French and Indians had massacred.

Johannes Vedder was kneeling and holding onto Maria. His mind had not yet begun to settle on the reality of the situation. It was too violent, too unlike his daily life to be real. He looked around. Albert was with him, but he could only guess where his parents were; where Angie, Arent, or Coreset were. A tear streamed down his face as he guessed they were among the countless dead. He said a silent prayer for all his lost family.

Suddenly, there was a commotion. Johannes looked up to several French and Indians leading Captain Glen of the militia towards them. To Johannes, the captain did not seem to be in bad shape. He was well-dressed, unlike the huddled masses of captives, some still in their evening clothes. Glen bore no scars or marks of battle. But it was his walk that caught Johannes' attention. Glen did not walk in as a beaten prisoner, but seemingly of his own will.

Glen was brought before Nicolas d'Ailleboust de Manthet. "You murderers," Glen said to the French. "There is no law or moral justification for what you have done here. I will make detailed notes of what I witness today."

Manthet took a breath. "I urge you, sir, to guard your tongue. You come before me as a friend, but do not make me change my mind. I extend this courtesy to you by special order of the Governor General of New France."

Glen glanced at the prisoners. Mothers held their children as close as possible. Men sat in deathly silence, dried blood and bruises covering their bodies. One little girl stood barefoot in the snow in her white nightgown. It was smeared with blood and her tiny legs shook as the freezing air blew around her.

"Mercy," Glen said. "I ask mercy for all of them."

"That is not possible," Manthet replied.

Glen took a step towards him. "Why not? Look around, sir. You have destroyed their lives. You have killed more than I can count. If it's vengeance you seek, have you not claimed it this morning?"

Manthet turned and took in the scene of utter ruin before him. "Captain," he said turning back, "when the savages stormed into our village, they carried off dozens of our men and women, and sacrificed them over the fires and feasted on their flesh.

"You must understand," Manthet continued, "that we did not wish this tragedy on you. It was you who sent the savages to raid our lands."

"We did not raid your lands," Glen snapped suddenly. By now, the captives were all listening to the conversation. "We cannot be held responsible for the actions of our allies."

"Oh, but you can," Manthet said. "You are your brother's keeper. By our good graces, I have spared many of the inhabitants of this village. And as a gesture of our mercy, you may pick those among the survivors who are of blood relation to you. They will be freed."

"And the rest?" Glen asked.

"The rest will stay our prisoners," Manthet replied.

There was a low murmur between the dozens of captive villagers.

"We're going to die," a man said quietly within earshot of Johannes. He gripped Maria's shirt tightly.

"I swear I will not let them take you," he whispered into her ear.

"Please don't let them separate us," she said.

Johannes saw the terror in Maria's eyes and silently begged God to give him an answer. Nothing came to him. Neither were relatives of the captain and by the agreement, were bound for Canada.

Glen stared at the huddled masses. In his mind, a plan formed. "I have your word, then," Glen began, "every single one of my kin will be spared."

Manthet bowed slightly. "On my honor as a French officer, every single man, woman, or child of blood relation."

One by one, the Captain picked out survivors. As more and more were chosen from the mass of captives, the French and Indian allies grew uneasy.

Johannes Vedder caught Glen's eye as he grabbed another 'relative' from the survivors. Vedder nudged his head towards Maria. Glen gave the slightest of nods.

"This man has numerous kinfolk," one of the Caughnawaga commented.

"I trust you are not deceiving us," Sainte-Hélène said aloud.

Glen stopped. "Just one more," he said. "My niece, Maria."

Maria's eyes widened. "I cannot leave without…"

"Hush niece," Glen said.

A Frenchman stepped forward, grabbed Maria's arm, and pulled her from the survivors to join the others Glen had declared to be of relative.

"That is all of them?" Manthet mused, eyeing Glen with suspicion.

Glen nodded silently. He dared not take one more soul. Manthet eyed the group. Of the more than sixty prisoners, the Dutch captain had claimed more than a dozen, mostly women and children as relatives. Still, more than forty remained captive.

Glen stepped forward. "And now I beg you, sir," he said, "soldier to soldier, leave the women and children. They will never survive the trip north."

Sainte-Hélène joined the conversation. "Then

we should dispatch them here and now."

He started to draw his pistol. Manthet reached over, grabbing Sainte-Hélène by the arm. "There is no honor in executing prisoners."

"We set out to send a message," Sainte-Hélène argued.

"...and we did," Manthet hissed.

The two officers stood facing each other for a moment. Then Sainte-Hélène tilted his head down and took a step back. Manthet turned to Glen. "Boys of ten years or older will be kept. Those younger, and the women will stay here."

Glen was flushed with relief. "Thank you, sir. Thank you so much. Your mercy will be remembered. As a sign of my appreciation, you and your officers may dine for breakfast at my residence."

There was a grumbling among several of the villagers. Manthet thought over the offer for a moment. "We would be honored, Captain."

"Let me take my relatives back across the river."

"Your kin will stay here," Manthet responded. "At least until my own force is back across the river and underway. Then you may return to the village and tend to them as you see fit."

Glen conceded and directed Manthet and the other French officers to follow him.

Manthet shouted some orders and several soldiers moved towards the captives, picking up the women and girls, and boys who appeared to be under ten, and brought them to those already declared by Glen. After the separation was complete, Manthet gathered his staff by the north gate.

As they departed for Glen's home, the two groups of survivors, just yards from each other, stared at each other in silence. Tears were shed as families looked upon their relatives and friends, some freed and some bound for the frozen north of Canada.

Johannes looked to Maria. Though she was only a short distance away, the space between them felt like an ocean and he ached to have her in his arms again. Maria, meanwhile, only stared with her swollen eyes and she mouthed that she loved him. It was painful as they were so close and yet unreachable. In between the two bodies of survivors, French and Indians slowly walked back and forth, ready to shoot anyone who moved.

All about them, those French and Indian marauders not on guard duty kept drinking and plundering what houses remained. Warriors carried wooden chests outside and dumped the contents into the snow, shuffling through it, seeking anything of value. They smashed open Van Slyke's tavern and took to drinking and eating until they passed out at the stools and tables. Occasionally, another house would be set ablaze and a villager would weep as their home went up in flames. The ashes rained down like a black snow. The carnage was total.

Chapter 47

The rising sun over Albany revealed a scene of true mayhem. All along the ramparts, soldiers hurried back and forth, carrying powder and ammunition to the guards who watched the forest for signs of the enemy that they knew was on its way. Within the city, civilians gathered what food stores and arms they could muster and prepared to barricade themselves in their homes. Though no enemy had yet to appear, Albany was without question, a city under siege.

Inside the fort, the Albany Convention was in equal chaos. Men shouted across the room. Proposals ranged from an immediate counterattack to defending the city at all costs. Captain Bull of the Connecticut militia was also present.

"Gentlemen," Pieter Schuyler shouted, "quiet yourselves."

His voice fell on deaf ears as the other Convention members continued to bicker.

Robert Livingston stepped forward. "Stay your tongues," he roared. The room immediately quieted. "Do not speak unless you are asked to," he ordered. "The mayor has the floor."

Members of the Convention took their seats in silence. Kiliaen Van Rensselaer, who had been sitting quietly in the corner throughout the morning, could not help but grin at Livingston's manner. Letting the past go, he admitted to himself that Robert Livingston most certainly had a way of commanding respect from friend and foe alike.

When the room grew quiet, Pieter Schuyler stood up. "Gentlemen, our defensive preparations are in place. The walls are fully manned and extra guards have been added. All our families have been gathered within the solid defenses of the fort. If the French and allies breach the wall, we have interior defenses all the way back to the fort. We have sent messengers to the Mohawk, requesting they make for the city with all possible haste. We are capable of withstanding a one-month siege if necessary. I can think of no other defensive measures that must be taken. We are ready."

There was a modest applause. Schuyler continued, "Now, I put forth the important question; should we keep to a defensive posture? Or do we ready a company and march to Schenectady, where we will most certainly meet the French in battle?"

There were shouts from about the room, most in the negative on the issue.

"No," Robert Livingston said. "We do not yet know the strength of the French force we are dealing with. We have been getting refugees all morning from that doomed village. Further, there have been scouts sent out in every direction, and the first of them have returned. Captain Bull," he said, turning to the Connecticut commander, "please brief the room as to their reports."

Bull stood up and took the center of the room. "We have reports of three armies on the move. One marched on and destroyed Schenectady. The second is headed south to Kingston. And the third – is headed directly for us." There was a murmur around the room. "Further," Bull said, speaking above the voices, "in total, the enemy forces in the area may number as many as fourteen-hundred men, undoubtedly all French soldiers and Indian allies."

Sheriff Richard Pretty stood up. "We do not know that. The scouts' reports may be wrong. What we do know is that the French are in Schenectady, and that is where our militia should be."

"Hear, hear!" a few men in the room called out.

"I call on the council to have the Convention form a company to march on that village without delay. If the enemy has taken to pillaging the village, their men would surely have given into drink and sleep. The time to attack is now!"

Applause broke out around the room.

Livingston stood up. "From what the refugees are telling us, the French and Indians burned that village and killed every man, woman, and child within its walls. What is there to retake, sir?" Pretty did not respond. Livingston faced the other members in attendance. "For all we know, we lost that village. As a Christian man, may their souls rest in peace. As a member of this convention, I wish for nothing more than retaliation. The French have cast the die. There is no medium left. We must destroy or be destroyed. And yet, the practical man in me says that in times of crisis, we must make logical decisions, not emotional ones.

"Gentlemen," Livingston went on, "we must write Schenectady off as a lost asset." Some of the members voiced their rejection of the notion immediately, but Schuyler steadied the unrest. "What would you have us do?" Livingston asked. "Abandon the city to take back a village, that for all we know, has been obliterated? No! We stay and defend our own city. Once we know the threat has passed, we can send a company to Schenectady and ascertain what has occurred, and how much remains of that village."

Many of the council members nodded in agreement. Schuyler was also in agreement. He turned to the alderman, Livinius Van Schaick. "What do you think?"

Van Schaick saw the look in Livingston's eyes and knew what to say. "It's too soon to send out an expedition to relieve the people of that village."

Schuyler went around the room to the other city council members and asked them. One by one, they agreed with the mayor.

Richard Pretty fumed, scarcely believing what he was hearing. "For God's sake, these are your fellow countrymen. They are your friends and family," he pleaded. "Have you no mercy for those poor souls in that besieged village? Are you so concerned about your land and fortunes here that you would forfeit the lives of your fellow countrymen?"

Pieter Schuyler stood up and faced Bull. "Captain, you will send out another courier to the Mohawk. You will send additional scouts to that village and report back the numbers of French and their Indian allies in said village, and other enemy forces that may be en route to our city. If there are no threats to us, we will march full force on Schenectady and relieve it, pursue the enemy, and destroy them."

The sheriff opened his mouth to protest but Schuyler cut him off. "No more is to be discussed on the matter until we have further information. This concludes this emergency session of the Albany City Council."

Pieter Schuyler and Robert Livingston strolled along the interior fall of the fort.

"Captain Glen and Lieutenant Talmadge are likely fallen at Schenectady," Livingston said. "They knew about the reports of French activity. We can only hope they made some defensible effort before being overran."

"It's those dammed Leislerites and their disobedience to the rule of law," Schuyler replied. "If they hadn't aroused the people, Captain Glen would have properly secured the village, and possibly even repelled the French."

Livingston grunted. "Well, Leisler will no doubt take this opportunity to launch an attack on Albany, while we are in disarray. We have as much to fear from him as we do the French. We must act fast."

"What do you mean?" Schuyler asked.

Livingston stepped in front, halting the pair. "We must delay word of this from reaching Leisler no matter what. He will use this to usurp power and we will be defenseless."

"I agree, but how do we stop him from knowing?"

Livingston felt a breeze and the snow hitting his face. "We seal off the city immediately. Nobody except those dispatched by Captain Bull will be allowed to leave. Shoot anyone that tries to leave. Tell them the weather and the French will prohibit any traveling south. If Leisler finds out, he may seize this city and if he does that, we lose our land, our titles - everything."

"It's a gamble," Schuyler said. "We can only hold such a position for a matter of days at most."

"That's all I will need," Livingston commented. "I must get ready. There is much to be done."

Chapter 48

There was a sudden commotion. Dozens of French and Indian warriors started massing up around their terrified prisoners.

"*Sur vos pieds*," several of the French militiamen were shouting. "*Sur vos pieds*," they repeated. "On your feet," one shouted in broken English.

Slowly – painfully, the survivors struggled to stand up, their joints aching as they had scarcely moved during several hours in the freezing, winter-morning air. Johannes helped Albert to his feet, as he was still a bit weak from the fight.

With a shout from one of the French commanders, the raiding party began prodding and shoving their prisoners forward, marching them up Church Street towards the north gate.

There was a yell from behind. Johannes turned. Laying in the snow and struggling to get to his feet was Robert Hessellng. Blood stained the snow where he crouched and his leg was still bleeding through a crude and ineffective tourniquet that he affixed – a bullet having struck him in the attack. He struggled to his feet then stumbled and fell back to the ground, letting out a painful moan.

"I have to help him," Johannes said. He turned and started walking back to Hessellng. Albert grabbed Johannes by the arm.

"No, don't!"

"I have to," Johannes argued.

Albert shook his head. "It's too late for him."

Johannes looked back. A Sault warrior with a musket approached Hessellng. When Hessellng saw the Indian, he fell to his back and held both arms forward, as if trying to push up on a crushing force.

"Please," he pleaded as the warrior readied his musket. "For the love of God, don't —" the musket shot rang out loud in the morning air as the helpless man went lifeless, his arms dropping to the side.

Several of the survivors looked back briefly before turning forward again and marching to their own impending doom.

Johannes stared at the body of Robert Hessellng, feeling hopeless and saddened.

"Come on," Albert said, grabbing him and pushing him forward, back into line.

As Johannes continued forward he glanced over and saw Maria, her eyes filled with tears. An unimaginable terror swept over him. For the first time since being captured, he suddenly felt that he would never see her again. In that moment, amidst the charred ruins of his village and surrounded by the dead and dying, he felt entirely vulnerable, at the mercy of an enemy who was bent on blood for blood retribution. Maria bowed her head and sobbed.

The French led their prisoners past the burnt-out blockhouse. The charred bodies of Lieutenant Talmadge's Connecticut militia lay twisted in the ruins, their blackened, disfigured corpses a grueling testimony to the savage resistance that had been mounted in that place.

In the village, a small band of Sault Indians rushed around the town with torches, setting fire to whatever homes remained standing, as well as the village stockade. Only a few homes were spared. Adam Vroman held his daughter Christina as he and his children watched Barent disappear with the other prisoners. His home, though shot through and scarred, still stood.

Other homes included that of the widow, Catelyn Bratt. Sainte-Hélène had spared it in return for the use of her home to care for his friend, Jacques de Montigny. Another home had sheltered several of the Mohawk and was likewise spared. The rest were burned to cinders.

The survivors passed through the north gate. Stephen Bouts grabbed his coat, pulling it in against an icy breeze. As he walked through the gate his eyes caught a strange form off to the side. He instinctively looked. What he saw made him sick. The heaped snow in a human-like mound, the coal eyes, and the stick for a gun – the defense of Schenectady stood watch next to its fellow sentinel on the opposite side of the gate, proudly standing in mockery of the devastated village they failed to protect.

Guilt shot through him worse than the knife that had pierced his arm earlier. He bowed his head in shame and sobbed quietly. He thought of that beautiful smile and cute giggle of Antje Janz as they raced the two Christoffelse children in building the snowmen guards. The dying screams of that same family as they were burned alive in their home, rang in his ears. The sight of Antje's body strewn out on the floor of her home was forever seared into his mind, torturing him. The memory of them laughing at the anti-Leislerites as the village gate was propped wide open in defiance, had become a nightmare as the last of the survivors were led through it and it was set to the flame by the invaders – the last of Schenectady to be torched, the destruction complete. In that moment, Stephen prayed more than anything, that he wished he had a pistol. For if he did, he swore in silence, that he would turn it on himself.

The ice on the river was solid in the cold

morning. A string of men, some prisoners, and other guards, snaked its way across the ice to the northern bank. Though some of the French and Indians were no doubt still reeling from the effects of the alcohol, most were keenly focused on their prisoners and plunder. Those who had been the hunters knew only too well that the time of becoming the hunted, was fast approaching.

At the Glen mansion, the French officers were just finishing their breakfast with John Glen. It was tense, but polite.

To Manthet's dismay, Sainte-Hélène had dined with all the blood and grime still present on his face and clothes. Like the rank and file men, the officers too were exhausted. The meal had been an overwhelming relief to many. Glen had eaten in silence, yet every bite made him sick to his stomach at the thought of the butchers who sat at his table.

At last, a courier came in and whispered something to Manthet. He wiped his mouth and stood up. "The enemy will be here soon," he stated. "The prisoners are across the river. I want to put as much distance between us and that river as possible. Let's get moving, gentlemen."

He turned to Glen and extended his hand. Glen reached out slowly, shaking it. "Thank you for your hospitality. I wish you and your family. I hope we do not meet on the battlefield."

Glen nodded in silence, as the French officers readied themselves. Sainte-Hélène turned to face him. "I hope we do meet in battle," he grinned, before turning and walking out.

Glen fumed in anger, watching the enemy walk out his door well-fed and well-rested. As the door closed shut, Glen dropped to a knee and coughed up his breakfast onto the floor in sickness.

"We will make good distance," Sainte-Hélène said. "The English are probably still cowering behind their walls at Orange. I think we have three days at least, before they send out a search party."

"It is not the English that worry me," Manthet spoke in a low tone, to not be overheard by the men nearby. "The Mohawk will receive word shortly, and they will not be so prudent. They will move out immediately."

Sainte-Hélène stared at the long column before them. "I see your point. We cannot stop to wait for them. The only choice is to head back to Canada with all possible haste."

"Precisely," Manthet said. "We are at our strongest now. Make the most of each day. Put as much ground between us and the Mohawk as we can. Once we are across the Saint Lawrence, we will be safe."

* * *

Johannes Vedder looked back upon the smoke across the river with tears in his eyes. It was a painful sight. His mind bounded back in time, when he used to stare across the river so many times before, looking at the beautiful countryside to the north, and knowing home was just behind him.

Looking back south, the once familiar walls lay in ruin and the village beyond was gone.

Just gone.

The yelling of a French officer snapped him back to reality. The prisoners were gathered in a clearing on the north bank. They were huddled into a group, surrounded by their captors.

"What's going on?" Johannes asked quietly, barely above a whisper.

One of the Groot boys, Symon, answered him. "Bet that fella knows the answer."

He nodded his head in the direction of a Frenchman who stepped up in front of the formation. The captive citizens hushed as he held up his hand.

Lieutenant Manthet quieted his prisoners. In broken English, he began to speak. "Lachine is avenged." He stared long and hard at the men and boys before him. Their faces were grim and saddened. "Lachine is avenged," he repeated. "You are now prisoners of his Majesty, King Louis the fourteenth and the allied Indian nations. You will do as we tell you without question or hesitation." He paced back and forth through the snow.

"If you attempt to escape, you will not be successful. The penalty for escape will be death. The penalty for disobedience will be death. Understand that there will be no relief. For just as we have laid waste your town, so too have other magnificent forces of the French Empire, besieged Orange and a dozen other English towns of the frontier."

The prisoners' heads dropped in sorrow. "So, this is it," Albert whispered. "There is no one left."

"There are still the Mohawk," Johannes whispered back. "Maybe they will come."

Manthet turned to Sainte-Hélène. "Okay, move them out." He faced the prisoners. "The sooner we arrive at Montreal, the less likely it will be that you will starve or freeze to death. So, for your own self-preservation, do not walk slow. We have a long journey ahead of us."

Chapter 49

Through the heavy snow, the young Mohawk boy ran faster than he ever had before. The cold bit at him, but his muscles had long since gone numb. Wind kicked up at times, sending blinding snow into his face. He reached the great castle at Tionnontogen by sunset. He had hardly enough breath to call out the friendly greeting to the warrior on guard and was almost stopped by an arrow from his own people before he reached the gates.

Once inside the walls, he ran for the main longhouse of the Wolf clan. He collapsed by the warm fire, his body shaking uncontrollably. His strength had been drained from his marathon and he begged for water. The sudden intrusion had stirred those inside and they closed in around him as they waited.

After a few moments, Tahajadoris entered with several more chieftains and elders. Lawrence also made his way to the front of the pack. He knelt beside the boy and rested his hand on the boy's forehead. It was icy cold like death itself had taken the boy in the cold, and only the fire now restored some life to him.

"Tell us what you have seen," Tahajadoris said, speaking softly to the boy.

The boy needed help sitting up and continued to shake. A woman draped a warm bearskin blanket over the boy and handed him some soup. The boy gulped it down despite the hotness burning his throat. Tahajadoris did not want to appear harsh, but he yearned to know what urgent news had warranted such action. Surely any news could have waited until dawn.

"Evil spirits walk the woods at night. Why have you risked so much to come here? Where have you come from?" he asked the boy.

"Schenectady," the boy uttered finally.

"And what news do you bring from that place?"

The boy stared into the fire, the glow bringing back the fresh memories of the horrors. His eyes filled with tears and he gripped the Mohawk chieftain, sobbing.

Lawrence held the boy, trying to comfort him. After some time, he separated the boy. "What has happened there?"

"The French have come," he whispered. Lawrence leaned back, straightening up. The men and women closest whispered amongst themselves. Tahajadoris remained stiff.

"Tell me more," he said, though he knew from the boy's eyes what had already transpired.

"They came last night," the boy whimpered. "They were on us before we awoke from sleep." His eyes teared up again. "They killed so many," he cried. "Almost every Christian in the village was put to death by the French and the Caughnawaga and Algonquin peoples. Our own people, they spared."

"Spared?" Tahajadoris couldn't possibly see a reason behind such mercy. He thanked the Gods for such fortune, yet raged at the slaughter of so many innocents. Some small part of him angered at his friend Pieter Schuyler and the others for not protecting their people. And yet as allies, he could only stand by their side against their common enemy, not administer their colony for them. "Is there any more news?"

The boy looked distraught. "They killed them. The village was burnt." His head dropped, and his body slumped over. Several women moved in, taking the boy to the nearest bed to be cared for. He would need days of rest before he was strong again.

Lawrence stood up slowly and looked to Tahajadoris. "We must act, brother."

Tahajadoris could feel every eye on him. His heart weighed heavily, and he knew there was only one choice. For him, the blood of his family and friends had been spilled. His eyes raged, and his blood boiled. He gripped his hands, making a fist.

"Blood must be answered," he stated, his voice carrying through the longhouse. "Summon the council."

* * *

Julia Glen chose her footing carefully, as not to step on anyone. Every room in the house seemed to be overcrowded with refugees from the village. She peered out the window and a chill crawled up her spine. The glow of the fires no longer shone as they had the night before, when Schenectady was burning. She knew somewhere out there, her husband was caring for those they could not take in.

A tear rolled down her cheek and she turned from the window, not wanting to think about the horrors that her husband must have seen. She sipped water from her cup, not caring that the warmth had long since dissipated. She looked around the silent parlor where mothers held their children tightly in sleep. After such a day, there were few who were kept awake; exhaustion finally overtaking them. The only real sound came from the occasional footsteps from the two men on guard upstairs. Though Captain Glen spoke with confidence when he said the French had left, he insisted on not being caught off-guard again.

Julia sat on a stool and leaned her head against the wall. Her eyes grew weary and her muscles relaxed. She knew she would have to be up early to prepare food for so many mouths. There would be enough for tomorrow, she thought. But beyond that, she had no answers. She prayed some food stores in the village remained, but from what she heard, the French had been thorough in destroying everything they could not carry back to Canada. Water was plentiful, but food would be scarce.

Her eyes opened at the thought. For the briefest moment, she considered sending them away but dismissed the idea just as fast. Though some of those very people had sworn to kill her husband if he entered Schenectady, so much had changed and they'd become neighbors in need. That answer seemed to satisfy her more than any other, and Julia closed her eyes, falling fast asleep.

In Schenectady, John Glen leaned forward, resting his arms on an ash-stricken wooden frame. It could have been a window, or perhaps a pen for chickens. Who could tell anymore? His body and mind were fatigued beyond anything he had ever felt before. Out in the exposed cold, his fingers were numb, and he strained to move them to keep the blood flowing.

Gazing up from the charcoal ruins, he surveyed the carnage. Of the two homes that remained, both were heavily damaged and overcrowded with the women, children, and elderly. A few men and older boys, those lucky few who had survived and evaded capture, huddled in small groups around campfires. They used blackened planks from homes and blankets, forming makeshift lean-to shelters to protect against the worst of the wind.

There was little civility remaining by nightfall. Though most of the survivors were emotionally and spiritually numbed from the violence of the massacre, it had not taken long for hostility to creep back into the devastated village. As the Glen home took in more and more survivors, and the two remaining households filled, it became clear that there would not be enough shelter for everyone. And once the last food that could be spared had been passed out, there was a certain feeling of abandonment in the mood of those who lost everything.

From that moment, Glen saw what little social order remained, fall apart entirely. There had been several fights as men fought each other for any scraps of food they could. Glen felt his face where he was bruised while pulling a grown man—and known Leislerite—off a small boy. All for a piece of bread and a tiny morsel of rabbit meat. Glen fought every urge to drag the man into the trees and slit his throat. But his own weakness and sense of duty kept him from exacting vigilante justice on the scoundrel.

As night fell upon them and the temperature dropped, fighting over food ceased, and the battle for warmth began. Those who were weaker were often pushed out of the inner circles around fires by stronger men. Glen passed a young boy who sat in the smoldering ashes of a house.

"Where is your family?" he asked the boy, eager to find a guardian for him.

The boy pointed, almost casually and said, "Over there."

Glen turned and saw several blackened skeletons partially buried under what was probably a roof that collapsed. He gasped in horror and immediately took the boy away, to the nearest fire. Producing his sword, he flashed it at the men nearest him. "Keep this boy warm by the fire or I will open your intestines and use them for my own warmth," he threatened. They understood and one boy, a few years older, wrapped a blanket around the younger one and gave him a piece of meat to eat.

Seeing the lack of useable firewood, Glen had ordered a tree felled and chopped up for wood. Soon, small fires lit up the ruined village as survivors huddled in close to the flames.

Finally getting time to pause and think, he leaned against a wooden frame and looked out at the huddled masses, all of them freezing and starving. He wondered how many more would die before sunrise.

His thoughts shifted. "I should have stopped this," he said quietly to himself. "Why wouldn't they listen to me? Why *mock* me? I was not the enemy."

He shook his head. Not in frustration but in utter disappointment and helplessness. It was a feeling he hardly ever experienced. There was always some circumstance that he could change, some force that could be altered by action. But amongst the death and destruction, there was nothing that could be done.

Glen dropped to his knees. "Oh Lord, I pray to thee. Give me the strength and wisdom to help these poor people that you have somehow seen fit to bestow with such misery and misfortune. Help me to understand how this is a part of your plan." He clenched his fists. "Good people died today; good Christians who obeyed your commandments. Why could I not protect them? What must I do to protect those who still live?" He waited in silence, listening to the howl of the wind. "Will you not speak to me?" he pleaded. There was no answer.

Angenietje Vedder shot awake, sweat dripping down her head. "Johannes?" she cried out. "Johannes? Albert?"

She threw the blanket off and climbed over the tightly packed bodies in the house. Having helped survivors all day and into the evening, she found herself too weak to cross the river to the Glen home instead electing to spend the night in Schenectady at Catelyn Bratt's house.

Stepping out into the night, she looked around in panic. Was it a dream? No, it could not have been. They were there. They were *just there*, she thought. Angie looked around desperate for answers but could find nobody aside from a few men sleeping around a fire. She wandered without purpose until unknowingly stopping at the center of the village. Standing in the exact spot where she had witnessed the total carnage, it all came back in a rush. On instinct, she repeated her actions, dropping to her knees and the tears openly flowed from her eyes. It was too painful to imagine living every day like that.

She felt a strong hand rest on her shoulder and raised her own hand, holding it. Slowly she looked up. Captain Glen helped her to her feet. "What are you doing out here, child?"

Through her tears and her voice choked up as she spoke. "I have no home. I have nowhere else to go."

Though, for a moment, he wanted to tell her that she was welcome at this own home; he hesitated, knowing those were not the words she was looking for. What she said was indeed true. The Vedder home was gone – burned entirely into the ground. She had lost two brothers, their fate unknown.

"Do you believe in God?" Glen asked.

"Yes, of course," Angie replied, wiping the tears away.

"Do you believe in your family?" he continued.

She nodded. "I don't understand what that has to do with not having a home."

Glen glanced around and then back to Angie.

"It has everything to do with having a home. A house can be rebuilt. Seeds can be resewn and flourish with every spring. But family and faith are what remains. It's what's important, Angie. I know your brothers. Johannes is as intelligent as any boy, and Albert is as strong as a mule."

"Probably as dumb as a mule too," Angie said, forcing herself to laugh, though he could still sense her pain.

His spirit lifted at seeing her smile. "Your brothers will be safe and will return someday," he said, not believing the words himself but making sure she did. "And your father, I know Harmen. He is the hardest man in Schenectady. He will provide for you and your family no matter what."

Angie looked up at Captain Glen and for the first time in what seemed like an eternity, she felt something almost foreign to her – hope. Glancing over his shoulder, she stared into the clear, night sky. It was filled from horizon to horizon with stars. She watched a shooting star flash across the sky. Perhaps everything would be okay.

She looked back at him. "I know," she said. "But there's so much to do. Where do we start?"

Glen thought for a moment. "The way our Lord and Savior would want us to – by helping someone in need. And then helping another."

* * *

"My brothers, the bodies of our brethren lie in the ruins of their village." Tahajadoris spoke with passion and fury before the war council of the Mohawk. Every chieftain and elder that could be summoned, crowded around the flames and listened to the powerful orator and chieftain. The first sign of daylight had begun to lighten the sky and he knew they had to act fast.

"Where do they march next?" a voice spoke out from the back.

Tahajadoris shook his head. "The plans of the enemy are not known; but they must surely not have the numbers to take Albany or our Great Castle." He paused, thinking hard. "They must return north. So, we must waste no time in sending our warriors to hunt down the French force. We must meet and defeat them while they remain on the run."

A warrior spoke up. "They have two days' head start on us and the snows are heavy to the north. We may not reach them before they cross the great river into New France. There is still greater danger. The French, perhaps, may lure us into a trap, and destroy our war party, and weakening our own numbers. Our women and children will be left defenseless."

A few of the men in the longhouse uttered their agreement with the warrior.

Lawrence stepped forward. "They must be heavy with plunder, and slow with captives. A war party can move fast enough to catch them."

The warrior conceded to Lawrence.

Tahajadoris was satisfied when there was no more opposition. "It is our people who attacked the French settlements. This raid is vengeance for our actions and our Dutch brothers have suffered because of it. We must avenge their dead and destroy the French before they reach the safety of the river to the north, and the gates of their cities. Are there any present of a different view?" The room fell deathly silent as he hoped. "Very well."

"I wish to lead the war party," Lawrence said.

"Should not a more able-bodied warrior lead?" asked Tahajadoris. "You are strong my brother, but the journey will be hard."

Lawrence reached forward, gripping Tahajadoris' forearm in a death-grip. The chieftain could see the tears swelling in Lawrence's eyes and when he spoke, his voice trembled.

"Those were my *friends* – my *family*, whom they killed. Let me lead the attack."

The longhouse was quiet save for the crackling of the fires. Tahajadoris nodded. "Gather a hundred of our fastest warriors. Go first to Schenectady. Let the carnage there light a fire in your hearts." He saw Lawrence stiffen with pride. "Then," Tahajadoris continued, "pick up the French track north of the river. Pursue them relentlessly. When you find them, do not hesitate. Cut them down where they stand."

"I will find them and kill them all," Lawrence said with a vengeance in his voice that shocked the others. Lawrence, being well-known for his overbearing kindness and compassion, revealed a dark side that had never been witnessed before.

Tahajadoris replied with a single word. "Go."

Lawrence bowed his head, then left the council, brushing past the others.

"I shall go to Albany," Tahajadoris said to the other elders and chieftains. "They must be gathering their own men for such a pursuit. I shall tell them of our decision."

The great elder Teeyotago raised his hand and Tahajadoris called for silence.

"My brothers," he spoke slowly and with care. Not a whisper could be heard for all present revered the great elder. "In times long past, the nations of the Iroquois bled each other in war. Divided we walked amongst the earth." His arm shook as he raised it and held up his index finger. "But the great peacemaker,

Skennenrahawi, led us down the righteous path, and united the Five Nations into a brotherhood and confederacy. We have grown strong in the shadow of that mighty peace tree."

Teeyotago lowered his hand. His face was saddened with grief and Tahajadoris wondered if the old man grieved for the past or for the future. Teeyotago sighed and after a pause, continued, "The white man we call our ally, our brothers, fight each other as we have in our own time long past. They too must plant the seeds of a mighty tree and bring peace for their peoples."

The old man's voice shook as he straightened up. It was as if he had a sudden surge of youthful energy. "But that time is not now. Now is the time to cut the tree down and make arrows from its branches and clubs from its trunk." He looked into the fire, his eyes gleaming. "We must answer fire with fire. Since time long past, when two foreign flags were planted on these shores, we knew someday there would be a great and terrible war that would only end when one flag remained. I fear that war is now upon us."

Tahajadoris listened. Though he knew the English and French would never make peace, he thought hard about the events Pieter Schuyler had spoken to him about. With the English colonies divided and weak, as their enemy pillaged and burned their way through the lands, they would surely lose the coming war. He knew what had to happen.

Chapter 50

The first of Captain Bull's scouts arrived back in Albany, in the mid-morning. The first scouts sent out had run straight into a snow storm and were forced to turn back to the city. But they had been dispatched again and returned with the information Bull and the Convention had been waiting on, for many tense hours.

"The French have left Schenectady," the scout spoke directly to Schuyler and Captain Bull. Livingston, as usual, was there in the background, not speaking, but taking note of everything.

"Tell me more," Bull said.

"There are no French forces near Albany. It appears the only army was the one that attacked Schenectady, and they are now north of the river, and heading back to Canada."

"Did you see the village?" Schuyler asked eagerly. "Are there any survivors?"

"I did lay eyes on the village," the scout said. There was a tremble in his voice. "Sir," he hesitated to continue.

Schuyler swallowed hard. "Please, tell me."

"I have never seen such evil and ruin, sir. The entire village has been burnt, only but a few houses remain. The slaughter has been great, and many bodies are still left unburied from the deep freeze. There are survivors there. I passed two women and a man who said they fled during the attack and came back to find their kin slain and home destroyed."

Bull wasted no time; he called for the militia to be assembled.

Within half an hour he had gathered over seventy men at the gates, both of Albany and the

Connecticut militia. Meeting them there was none other than the mayor.

"I am going with you," Schuyler said.

"I would advise against it," Bull replied. "Your people need you."

"Those in Schenectady need me more," Schuyler said, his tone somber. "I must see what has become of that place."

Bull nodded and turned to the column. "Company, forward – march."

The gates opened, and the line of troops marched out of Albany on a westerly course along the snowy road.

*　*　*

"Men approaching!" a man yelled out.

Angie stood up from the fire she had been stoking. A line of men and horses crossed through what had been the north gate and entered the town.

"That's mayor Schuyler," someone commented.

Angie breathed a sigh of relief. "Thank the Lord," she muttered.

The site of the militia was enough to bring tears to many of the survivors. Immediately, Bull ordered some of his men to dispense spare blankets and clothing they had brought with them.

"There is not enough," Bull stated to Schuyler. "We should have brought more provisions and clothing."

"There are more survivors than I imagined," Schuyler said in a low voice. "They must have fled to the woods."

Several dozen survivors and those from the nearby homesteads that were spared, all were gathered in the ruined village. Schuyler grabbed the reigns of his horse and made his way up and down the devastated street, surveying the damage and trying to record in his mind, every vivid detail of the carnage before him.

Suddenly, a soldier approached. "Sir, we have a whole lot of Indians coming this way."

Schuyler eyed the man, but his mind was elsewhere. Captain Bull walked up, hearing the commotion. Schuyler remained motionless. The soldier waited for orders. "Sir?"

Seeing Schuyler in a state of shock, Bull intervened. "Rally the troops," he said. In a few moments, two rows of infantry lined the road. As the first Indians came into view, there were calls up and down the line.

"Stand at ease, gentlemen," Bull ordered. "They're Mohawk."

Tahajadoris and Lawrence led a mass of warriors through the south gate, meeting Pieter Schuyler and Captain Bull at the center of town. They embraced each other in friendship.

John Glen and his wife were also present, along with most of the remaining survivors. Some of the survivors watched the Mohawk with suspicion and anxiety; a side-effect from the Caughnawaga's participation in the raid. Others heaved sighs of relief that their allies had come to their aid.

"I am truly sorry for the loss of your kin, my brother," Tahajadoris said. "We stand ready to go to war with you in vengeance; to drive the French from these shores and seize their lands."

Schuyler nodded meekly. "Thank you for standing with us. My friend," he said, "this is our blackest hour and we are a prayer away from defeat."

Tahajadoris laid his hand on Schuyler's

shoulder, then took several steps back. He climbed a pile of blackened debris and stones, staring out at the gathered English soldiers and civilians, and spoke.

"Now you see your blood spilt, and this is only the beginning of the miseries you face, if not prevented from happening a second time. Therefore, write to your fellow countrymen of Virginia and New England, and tell them to visit this terrible place.

"There can be no peace with the French. There *will* be no peace with the French. I urge you to make yourselves ready, and in the springtime, lead your forces to Canada and make yourselves masters of that land. Use your armies and your great ships and drive them away."

Tahajadoris could see every face focused on him. He chose his words carefully. "You say your king is a great king, and that you are numerous far above the French who dwindle in number. Now is the time to show that strength, or else there is only a greater shame to suffer the French to be masters of this land. We of the Five Nations of the Iroquois Confederacy have suffered at the hands of the French. Your people now, also have suffered. The French are victorious wherever they go.

"Yet, you have told us that if it came to open war, you would stand with us and destroy the French. Now there is war and we come to you asking you if you will make war against those who made war against you. If so, then let us prepare and in the spring, let us destroy our common enemy together.

"Long ago, the Five Nations were divided – and weak. But we made peace with each other. We bound our arrows together into an unbreakable bond, and we prospered under the might of a united people. You Americans are a divided people, and if you brought together your peoples, you can forge, just as we did, a great alliance – united and unbreakable.

"The Mohawk, and indeed the Five Nations, remain ready, with fiery hearts, to join you in pursuing the French, overtaking them, and rescuing your kin and countrymen. May the Great Mother and the Lord guide us and protect us."

Tahajadoris stepped down from the debris. He was met by Lawrence and his gathered warriors.

"We are setting out now," Lawrence said. "We will overtake them."

Schuyler approached with a company of men. "This is Symon Van Ness and Andries Barents," he said, introducing two of the men. "They are able-bodied and ready. They will go with you, to Montreal and beyond if necessary."

"How many men do you bring?" Lawrence asked.

Van Ness replied, "Fifty."

"Split them into two," Lawrence said. "Those fastest with me and my youngest warriors. The rest will follow."

"Go," Tahajadoris stated. "Delay no more."

Without a word, Lawrence, Symon Van Ness, and the army of Mohawk and English set off, leaving Schenectady in an eerie quiet.

Tahajadoris saw Schuyler walk off by himself and step inside a burnt-out home. The chieftain headed over to him, though Schuyler made no recognition of the Mohawk's presence.

"Are you alright, brother?"

"This was the home of the Van Ditmars," Schuyler said. "They were friends of the family. I still remember Barent helping me in the springtime clear out land and helping to build my first home in Albany. They were the kindest people I ever met." A tear streamed from his eye.

"I have seen many battles," Tahajadoris replied. "None have shocked me more than what I have seen this day."

"This was not a battle," Schuyler said, his voice almost a whisper. "This was a slaughter." He sighed. "And now I must write to the Convention about what evils have occurred here. And yet, I am at a loss for what to tell them." Tahajadoris could see the tears in Schuyler's eyes as he spoke. "The cruelties committed at this place, no pen can write, nor tongue express." He bowed his head.

Tahajadoris rested his hand on Schuyler's shoulder. "Say that then," Tahajadoris replied. "Say it exactly like that."

Chapter 51

Johannes Vedder stared blankly into the red glow of the small fire, listening to nothing in the world but the crackling of the fire. Since his body had been offered a small chance to thaw, it was his mind that went numb. No longer was his focus on his physical weariness – a symptom of entire days spent marching north through the deep snow. Instead, he was shrouded with excruciating spiritual pain in his heart and soul.

By his count, it had been one week since he and the other captives had begun their perilous journey to Canada. Though he could only guess at where they were, they were well north of the Mohawk River. He knew his chances of being rescued were rapidly shrinking. Every day they were ten miles closer to Canada.

Ten miles further from home.

Albert kneeled beside Johannes, reaching his arms out to the fire to warm them up. The two brothers looked to each other. "When we get to Canada, stick close by me," Albert said. "You are too weak in the mind and I don't want you to lose hope."

Johannes could scarcely believe it. "Here we are," he said, "a hundred miles from home, and you are still acting like I cannot survive without you. I am stronger than you think, brother. I always was."

Albert was taken aback by the sternness in Johannes' tone. "I didn't mean anything by it," Albert replied. "But I am older and physically stronger than you. We both know it."

Johannes shook his head. "Maybe you were – once. Not anymore, Albert. Either way, I don't plan on going to Canada. The first chance I get, I am sneaking

411

out and heading south, back to Albany."

"Don't be an idiot. They'll kill you if you try," Albert argued. "As you said, we are a hundred miles from home. You would never make it."

"I will tell our father that when I see him," Johannes replied. "I have too much to live for to die in Canada."

Shouting arose and the two brothers looked up from the fire. French soldiers were kicking the prisoners, getting them back on their feet. The fires were quickly doused and the column reformed. The French officer at its head waved his arm and the war party, heavy in plunder and captives, set out once more for Canada.

The French and Indian war party halted by a narrow stream that, fortunately for them, had not frozen over. The men eagerly dropped to their knees and took to filling their canteens and drinking the icy cold—but unbelievably refreshing—water.

Two of the horses, ones that had begun to falter from fatigue and injury, were put down. Johannes and Albert were among five men picked out to quarter and butcher the horses for meat. Johannes resented the notion of killing horses, but took to his task without complaint, as he himself was emaciated. The provisions taken from Schenectady had run nearly dry. It would be only a matter of time before true starvation took hold.

Once over the fires, both French soldier and English prisoner alike, barely let the meat brown before tearing pieces apart and devouring the horsemeat. Johannes grabbed a half-decent piece of meat and sat next to a group of African slaves. Though at first absorbed in his meager ration, his ears soon peaked themselves to the talk among the slaves.

The men spoke in low voices, so low that

412

Johannes could scarcely mark a word. Yet even with their attempt at secrecy, several distinct words struck out at him. The two men stood up, as if stretching. Johannes watched them warily. They made their way, almost casually, over to a patch of bushes, to urinate. Their eyes noted the positions of the French and Indians, seeing few on alert. Most were eagerly gorging down on the freshly butchered meat.

Johannes saw what was happening. He instantly tensed up. With a nod to each other, and no warning, the two black men broke out at a dead sprint, tearing through the trees and bushes, senseless to the scratches from the tree branches. There was an immediate alert. Several Canadian militiamen rushed to the tree line, firing their muskets at the fleeing captives.

With a flurry of orders, several French soldiers and a cluster of Caughnawaga set out in pursuit, tomahawks and muskets at the ready. The rest of the prisoners were pushed into a cluster and surrounded by dozens of French and Indians. There, they remained in total silence.

For two hours.

Just as the sun began its westerly descent, a commotion arose and the howling cries of the Indians filled the forest. Johannes turned to see the pursuing party returning with both black men. Their hands were tied with rope, and their faces bloody from a violent struggle. They were pushed into the clearing, standing in a circle of fierce Caughnawaga warriors.

Two French officers and the Indian, recognized by Johannes as their leader, approached.

"We made it clear when we set out," one of the French officers spoke aloud to the prisoners, "that escape would not be tolerated. The punishment was understood and shall be upheld. Behold our justice." He turned to the Indian leader and nodded. The warrior held up his club and roared a few words in a foreign tongue.

The Indians standing around shouted back and then turned their viciousness to the two black men who dared to escape. The first blows came from war clubs as the men were beaten down to their knees by a flurry of strikes. Then the warriors produced knives and tomahawks and set about brutally carving open the doomed men. The prisoners watched in horrified silence as the sentence was carried out without mercy. By time it had ended, there was a patch of snow entirely covered in blood. The mutilated corpses lay almost dismembered, their skulls bare where their scalps had been taken.

Johannes stared at the scene before him. It had not been a justified execution. It was murder, plain and simple. His mind flashed to the possible fate he could suffer, as he contemplated his own escape. From what he saw in Schenectady and with the African slaves, there was no doubt that the French would put him to a similar death if he tried to run. His heart broke a little as the realization hit him, that he just might never see Maria again. The reality stung him and he gritted his teeth.

There would be little time to reflect on the killings. The French lit torches and declared that they would march throughout the night to make up for the time lost due to the escapees. The plan not only made up the ground they'd lost, but planted a feeling in some of the prisoners, that the fault lay with the two men who attempted escape.

It would discourage further incidents. Or at least Manthet hoped so.

* * *

Lawrence knelt and traced the outline of a footprint. "These tracks are fresh," he said, standing up. "We are gaining on them."

Symon Van Ness came up beside the Mohawk. "I wasn't sure if we would find them."

Lawrence had a stone-cold look on his face. "I was," he said.

Symon nodded. "Very well, no sense in stopping now. From the horse carcasses we came across, they are running out of food and must be getting slower. We should be ready to make contact with them in the next two to three days."

"And then we will make the earth red with our vengeance," Lawrence commented, more to himself than to Symon.

Symon turned around. Behind them, scattered throughout the trees were dozens of Mohawk warriors and a few English men of the Albany militia.

The gap was closing.

* * *

When the order to stop was given, Johannes Vedder collapsed into a snow bank. Albert grabbed him by the shirt and checked up on him. "I'm okay," Johannes replied. "I just am a little dehydrated is all."

Albert asked for water and one of the Canadian militiamen gave each of them a sip from his canteen. Resting on the ground, the two brothers glanced at each other. "We are close to Canada now," Johannes said softly.

"Maybe," Albert said.

"No, we are," Johannes insisted. "Look at the guards. They are getting lazy and complacent. They are not keeping lookouts as often when we stop."

"Brother, don't start this again." Albert said.

"We can escape."

"No, we cannot." Albert took a breath. "I will not."

Johannes shook his head. "Then I will."

Albert grabbed his brother's arm and leaned in. "We are a hundred leagues or more from home. This is an alien world. You do not know any of the landmarks. How would you find your way south? The sun is out maybe an hour every other day. And at night?"

Johannes paused, thinking. "I would have to use what I can," he said. "Go by the sun when it's out and dead reckoning when it is gone."

"You are a fool," Albert said.

"Damn right I am," Johannes snapped. "But I would rather be a fool than a slave or dead. They will kill us in Canada or work us to death. Or we'll freeze. Or catch a disease. I want to go home, Albert. I want to see our family again."

"And you think I do not?" Albert replied. "Toughen up and bear it out." He sighed. "Maybe you are right. Maybe we'll die in Canada. Maybe you'll die escaping. Maybe our fate was sealed at Schenectady. Maybe this whole damn thing is futile."

The brothers fell silent as a Canadian militiaman strolled by, dragging his feet in the snow. "I have made up my mind." He turned to his brother. "Tonight, I am going."

Torches flickered in the forest. The prisoners huddled in masses for the night to keep some warmth. Johannes kept as close to the others as possible, to keep his muscles warm and loose. At times pretending to be asleep, he continuously peeked around to check the coming and going of the French and Indian guards. The Indians, Johannes noticed, were not keen on pulling night shifts, and ultimately it was usually Canadian militiamen, weary and undisciplined, who kept watch over the prisoners.

One such man was only a few yards from Johannes. He was a tall, burly man with a great brown beard and a racoon hat. The night was milder than the others, and the man had discarded his white and brown capote – a heavy overcoat used by the coureur de bois on their long hunting trips. He was occasionally bobbing his head, struggling to maintain alertness.

For more than an hour, Johannes waited patiently, watching like a wolf stalking its prey. At last, the big man stood up and stretched his arms out, yawning. He walked over to who Johannes guessed was the man's replacement. He shook the man, said something inaudible, and then moved closer to a fire and covered himself with a blanket. The man on the ground moved about under his blanket, shifted, and remained asleep.

Johannes leaned back, taking a deep breath. His body trembled, not in fear, but in anticipation. The time was imminent.

The moment he'd waited for, hoped for, and prayed for, was finally upon him.

Now or never.

Shifting around the huddled bodies, he crawled his way to the edge. He peeked around and reached out cautiously, grabbing a firm hold of the militiaman's capote and dragging it towards him. Taking extreme care not to upset or wake anyone, he slid the coat on.

He looked back at the replacement guard.

Still asleep.

Johannes glanced at the men from Schenectady. Amidst the sleeping prisoners he could see his brother's face. "God speed, Albert" he whispered.

He turned and looked one last time before slipping across the last few yards of snow to the tree line.

He took great care to slide his body in such a manner that no traceable footsteps would be apparent in the snow. Even in the tree line, he continued to slide and gently pulled pine branches down behind him, to further conceal his trail. Looking over his shoulder, satisfied at the more than fifty yards of concealed tracks from the campsite.

At that, Johannes stood up and faced what he knew to be south. He took a breath and stepped off. In the distance, he heard the howls of wolves and beasts, the blowing wind cutting through the trees, and the rustling of branches. Each step in the blackness could hold an unseen creek or rock, something to cause him illness or injury. But it did not matter. Every lone step took him further from slavery, and closer to home. And with each one, his pace quickened. The move had been made.

Come sunrise, there would be hell to pay.

Chapter 52

The French camp was chaotic. It started at dawn when the morning count came up one short. Lieutenant Nicolas d'Ailleboust de Manthet immediately summoned his council. Manthet was disappointed not to have Athasata and the other chieftains of the Caughnawaga present. However, it would take too long to summon them, and the problem could not wait.

Manthet laid out his map on a felled tree. "How many days are we to Montreal?" He addressed the question to the group as a whole.

They exchanged glances, waiting for someone to be the first to speak. The scout Jean Baptiste Giguiere spoke up first.

"By my best guess, five days at most, Monsieur."

"We're still too far," Manthet stated, staring at the map. "While using the horses for food has kept us alive, their loss has deprived us of our speed. The enemy must be gaining on us. And what is this I hear of a prisoner escaping?"

Jacques Le Moyne de Sainte-Hélène answered him, his voice echoing his frustration at the unfortunate turn of events. "During the night one of the boys disappeared. We picked up his tracks after some searching. They led due south. I'm preparing to lead ten men to hunt him down."

"No," Manthet stopped him. "I need you here, Jacques." Sainte-Hélène thought to protest but saw that Manthet was planning and held his tongue. "The men are starting to slip in discipline and order. You are needed to push the men along and get them to Montreal."

"And the prisoner?" Sainte-Hélène asked. Manthet did not respond. "If he eludes Athasata's scouts and finds himself amongst the Mohawk, they will know our position and how close we are. They will fall upon us without mercy."

The words struck a chord with Manthet. He looked to the other officers and they shared Sainte-Hélène's worry. He knew the prisoner had to be caught. But to divide his forces was unthinkable with the enemy's location unknown.

"I will go." Manthet turned around as Jean Baptiste Giguiere stepped forward. "I will track down this boy."

"Take my brother with you," Sainte-Hélène said to him. "François has been practicing the art of hunting. He is quite the skilled tracker."

Giguiere glanced at Manthet who nodded in approval.

"Two more men as well," Manthet added. "In case the boy puts up a fight. I want him alive. Examples must be made." He turned to Sainte-Hélène. "Send four men ahead to Montreal. Two of ours and two savages. Inform them of our position so they may ready themselves."

He turned his attention to the others. "We have not had word from Athasata in two days now. I will send a few savages to the rear to make contact and get a report on the situation. It is critical we know the moment they make contact with the enemy."

* * *

Johannes Vedder splashed across the stream and fell into the earthen slope of the opposite bank. He dug his fingers into the snow and clawed his way up, willing his body to continue.

420

His muscles burned from the sudden and continuous strain he forced upon them. His fingers froze, and he had long lost feeling in his feet. Since his mind had gone numb, Johannes could scarcely remember the specifics of his plan. Instead, he focused on the one core element he knew to be true.

Run south to stay alive.

Johannes did not know how long he had been moving. Looking at the light that shone behind the cloud cover, he judged it to be mid-morning. *Five hours? Six?* He could not tell. Every ounce of strength he found, he gave towards putting as much ground between himself and his captors as possible. Instinctively, he turned around to check for any pursuers. He knew they were out there somewhere, bearing down on him; every minute closing the distance.

He clambered along a sloped hill, stumbling like a drunkard, knocking into dead branches, scratching his skin and leaving thin red streaks covering his face and hands. Johannes creased the top of the hill and found a cluster of brush to rest. His legs felt like they collapsed under him as he fell into the foliage.

Resting his head against a tree, Johannes felt unwavering fatigue grip him like never before. His mind was demanding that his body rest or sleep, but he knew sleeping out in the cold could just as easily kill him as the French would.

With his body swelling up, and numbness relieving him of the pain of torn muscles, his mind drifted to Albert and the others still in captivity. He wondered what the French would do to Albert if they learned the two of them were brothers. Perhaps they would retaliate against Albert if they failed to reach him before he made it back to Albany.

421

Johannes cleared it from his mind. It was a waste to think of such things. Perhaps it was the exhaustion of the escape but even the French camp seemed impossibly distant and his mind could scarcely visualize it. He closed his eyes for a moment trying to will himself to…

*   *   *

Jean Baptiste Giguiere traced the footprint with his finger then looked up suddenly. "The steps are becoming more irregular. The path is no longer straight."

François Le Moyne de Bienville took a knee beside him. "He is tiring. Losing his sense of direction. He has drifted eastward."

"And his strength," Giguiere added. "Maybe two hours ahead of us." He stood up and gazed out like a hawk seeking its prey from afar. He scratched his scruffy beard aching to get back to Montreal for a hot bath and shave. "We'll catch him before the sun sets."

François looked over the ground ahead of them. From this clearing they could see for over a mile south.

"Let's say he has holed up to rest," he fathomed. "When he is done, he will see the sun more clearly now and will chart his course due south again. We could run a south-southeast bearing and intercept him faster than tracking his path."

"That is a fool's errand," Giguiere snapped. "You are guessing. There is no way to know what path he will take, and we could lose his tracks altogether. Besides, you are not as experienced a tracker as I am."

François glared at him. "I am one of the finest trackers in Canada."

"Then go," Giguiere said. "Go find him using

your – *instincts*, and we shall see who is the better hunter."

* * *

His eyes opened wide in sheer terror. Johannes moved as if on a swivel, looking around in panic. How long had he been asleep? Minutes? Hours? He looked to the sun and thanked God the clouds had parted enough to give him a clear bearing. But precious time had been lost.

He was up and moving before he knew it. His stride stretched, and his legs were stiff from being still while he had foolishly napped. He let himself slide down an icy slope, desperate to escape the net of savage French and Indian hunters.

Johannes wondered where the relief force was, or if Albany had even sent one. His mind churned up scenarios, each darker than the last. Perhaps Albany did not even know about the Schenectady massacre. Or they felt the village had sealed its fate by siding with Leisler. Though he hated admitting it, he knew that it was not beyond some men of the Convention to abandon them to their fate.

Taking a pause next to a rocky wall, the smaller part of a major cliff, his mind conjured up an even more dreadful scenario. Maybe the French officer was not lying when he said Albany was attacked as well. Johannes felt his pulse quicken as he thought of the idea. All the Dutch settlements along the Mohawk may have been wiped out. That would make the nearest safe-haven being the Mohawk Castle of the Wolves – Tionnontogen.

Johannes ducked down and tried to plan it out. He knew he would still have many days of walking, but rather due south, a southwest course could put him on track to the Mohawk lands. His mind flashed a concern that the Indians may have turned on them, but he dismissed it just as quickly. They were rare allies, true to their word.

The plan was decided. He stood up tall, ready to make the next step in a long and tedious journey. The force that took him from behind was completely unexpected. Johannes tumbled down the slope, catching a mere glimpse of his attacker before the man was again crashing into him.

This time Johannes braced himself just enough to wrap his arms around the man and take them both down, sliding again. They traded blows in a frenzy. In a moment of opportunity, Johannes kicked his legs and the man crashed to a stop, his back smacking hard against a tree trunk. He yelled out in anger but rose just as fast, ready to attack again.

The man was clearly French as his attire matched that of those who had butchered Schenectady. As the man charged, Johannes did what he thought the assailant might expect the least. Or perhaps it was what he simply did not expect of himself. His legs leapt forward and he crashed into the man. This time it was the Frenchman who had the advantage and threw his weight low into Johannes' legs, sending him toppling over the man.

Before Johannes could regain his composure, he felt a powerful shock against his abdomen. The man kicked him repeatedly, trying to soften his opponent. Johannes could do little to stop the beating except cover his face against similar blows. Though his vision was restricted, he heard the shout of voices. They were Indian, though he could not tell the dialect.

The kicking stopped.

He cautiously removed his hands from his face. Staring down at him were two straight-faced

Indians. He strained to move his head to see what had happened to the Frenchman. The pain however was too much, and he could do little more than lay still. Though his body ached all over and he could feel the blood seep out from his many scratches and cuts, staring up at the men he couldn't help but crack a weak smile.

Suddenly he saw a familiar face and his smile vanished. The Frenchman spat blood into the snow and scratched his beard. He looked to his two Indian allies and said something Johannes could not make out. The two Indians reached down, forcefully grabbing Johannes' arms and dragging him to his feet in spite of his cries of pain.

Giguiere ordered the two Algonquin Indians to take the prisoner back to the camp. They dragged him off and he was satisfied to see no resistance from the captive. Alone, Giguiere rolled his shoulders. He knew for certain he had at least one broken rib, several bruises, and a laceration on his arm. He was surprised the boy—who did not appear menacing—turned out to be quite the fighter. He would be happy to see the boy tortured and executed. The lesson would have to be burned into the memories of the prisoners so that none would attempt escape again.

He wondered what had happened to the lieutenant's brother. Sainte-Hélène said François was an experienced tracker. Surely, he would have seen the impracticality of his venture, and swung back around to meet them. Had the arrogant fool gotten himself lost? Giguiere could not help but imagine what their next meeting would be like. He caught the runaway while one of the famous Le Moyne brothers had gotten lost while tracking a tired, underfed boy in the snow. Maybe he had gotten caught by the enemy. Giguiere admitted to himself that François being killed would not bother him in the slightest.

He took one last look south, looking over the endless layer of trees that stretched for miles. Satisfied, he turned to catch up with the two Indians and his prisoner.

* * *

The torches burned bright in the night when Giguiere returned with Johannes. He ordered the Indians to drop him, leaving him in the snow at Manthet's feet. Surrounding him was an array of French coureur de bois and Algonquin Natives. A handful of prisoners, Albert among them, were huddled close by. Albert tensed up when he saw Johannes, laying helpless in the snow.

"Is this him? He's not much older than a boy. Where did you find him?"

Giguiere shrugged. "Further south than I expected." He rolled his shoulder again, grunting. "This one can run for sure. How shall we kill him? I want first go at making him bleed."

Manthet studied the boy at his feet. His face was purple with bruises. His whole body trembled in fear and pain. "And you will," Manthet replied. Giguiere grinned maniacally.

Sainte-Hélène strode up to the scout. "Where is my brother?"

Giguiere faced him. "Your brother has much to learn."

"Where is he?" Sainte-Hélène repeated. He stepped in closer, his unflinching gaze boring into Giguiere.

"I tried to convince him to follow the prisoner's tracks. He insisted on trying for an unlikely path to cut him off. That was the last I have seen of your brother, Monsieur."

Manthet put his foot on Johannes and nudged him to look up. In English, the French commander spoke. Not only to Johannes but loud enough for all the prisoners to hear. "Were my terms not spoken clearly? Did I not prove my clemency and mercy at your village? Did I not make myself clear that any man attempting escape would suffer death?"

Albert clenched his fists and tears streamed down his cheeks. He urged his body to charge the man speaking, but something held him back. One man mouthed a silent prayer.

Manthet stood as if at attention as he addressed the captives. "I hoped you would have behaved as gentlemen and spared us the indecency and—" he paused, choosing his word, "—brutality, of what is to happen next."

He looked to Johannes and spoke to him directly. "You cost us nearly a day of marching, boy." Johannes twitched, gritting his teeth. "Do you think you are in pain now, boy?" Manthet asked. "We will show you true pain before you die."

For Johannes, the words passed through him like a wind that sucked the life from him. He was overcome with despair and could do nothing but sit and wait for the end.

Giguiere stretched, loosening his muscles for the coming retribution. Strapped to his waist was a large wood-runner knife. Some of the Frenchmen laughed and mocked Johannes and hurled insults at him, though they knew he did not understand.

Manthet and Sainte-Hélène stood front and center for the execution. Most of the prisoners stood by silently. Arnout Viele cried out for mercy and was himself knocked to the ground by an Indian with a club.

Johannes knelt with his head slightly bowed. He whispered a brief prayer before rising to face his doom. Manthet turned to Giguiere and nodded, signaling him to start. Giguiere deliberately pulled his knife out slowly, watching the condemned boy tense up in fear. He started towards him and then suddenly stopped.

There was a commotion on the outskirts of the camp. Out of the darkness came several of the sentry guards at a steady jog. In the center was François Le Moyne de Bienville. He was exhausted and struggled to catch his breath.

"Monsieur," François heaved. He stopped to collect himself.

"It seems you found your way at last," Giguiere jested.

François ignored him and the look in his eyes told of trouble. Manthet crossed his arms. "What news do you bring?"

"The savages of the Caughnawaga are gone."

There was a wave of commotion among the French. Manthet raised his hand, willing them to quiet. "Destroyed? I have heard no noises of battle."

"Not destroyed, Monsieur. They have gone to hunt and forage for food. They are headed back to their villages. We have no defensive force at the rear of the column."

Manthet opened his mouth to speak but saw the look on François' face. "Tell me," he said.

François swallowed. "I saw campfires to the south."

Manthet turned to Sainte-Hélène. "Mohawk?"

François took a step forward. "English, Monsieur."

"How many?"

"I could not see numbers. But they are less

428

than two leagues from here. And if they are that close, the Mohawk are surely closer." He glanced at Johannes. "While we looked for him, they have closed the gap. They will be on us by morning."

Chapter 53

Giguiere was furious. "With respect sir, what do you mean we are postponing the execution? We need to make a lesson of this boy who defied your orders."

Manthet stopped from giving orders for a moment. "We have no time. We make for Montreal without delay."

"Night has come. How are we to see?"

"I don't care," Manthet barked. "Use torches, use the stars for all I care. We go – *tonight*. We must reach the Saint Lawrence and cross before the enemy fall upon us. I suggest you gather your things."

Giguiere felt humiliated but he obeyed without question. Having served in the Seneca raids of 1687, he understood the necessity of discipline in the ranks. "I will move around the column, checking for signs of the enemy."

"Excellent," Manthet replied. "I dispatched three savages to watch the rear until we can find a spot to create a more formidable rear guard."

The French column set off in the darkness, with only two torches to guide their way, without revealing their position. The men, most of whom were hunters and trappers by trade, lost some heart on the prospect of marching all night through the deep snow. Each day, the air seemed to grow colder and darker as they ventured north.

The men carried on though, no longer motivated by pride or vengeance. They trekked hard out of fear. Many had fought the Iroquois before and though few men would admit it, not a man present wanted to be caught with their backs to the Indians, for if they were, they would suffer worse than their own victims in the English village they had burned.

And so, with dwindling rations and no sleep, the French raiding party moved steadily away from the campfires of their pursuers, leaving them behind in the blackness. Manthet and Sainte-Hélène urged the men onward, giving encouragement and sometimes threats - any means necessary to add fuel to the pace of the unexpected nighttime march.

Sainte-Hélène turned his horse to Manthet. They had only a handful of horses left, and those were used by the commanders and a few scouts.

"If we keep up at this pace, men will die. We must have marched nearly two leagues. We can afford to slow the pace. The English are sleeping, not chasing us at this hour."

"I would prefer to get within two days of Montreal, by noon."

"That is not possible, Nicolas," Sainte-Hélène stated plainly.

Manthet looked back and forward at the line of men walking. "Then we keep marching until it is." He kicked his horse and trotted ahead to the front of the column.

* * *

The campfires were extinguished an hour before first light. Symon Van Ness made a quick head count and set off as the sun peaked over the tree line. "Pass the word down the line for all men to load their muskets. We may reach the French, and we must be ready to overtake them at a moment's notice."

A young boy who accompanied him as courier hustled down the column and spread the word. Andries Barents scouted up ahead a hundred paces, checking the tracks in the snow.

"There is no maybe," a voice said from behind. Van Ness spun around.

Lawrence squatted beside him. "They are just over the next hill and through a thick patch of forest. One of my men saw several of their force – an Indian contingent. No more than five at most."

Van Ness rubbed his bushy beard. It had been more than a week since he shaved last, and it was starting to itch. "You are certain?"

"I am," Lawrence said without hesitation.

"Then," Van Ness responded, picking up his rifle, "let's go hunting. And may God bless us all."

* * *

The Indians walked casually, dragging their feet through the snow. The three Algonquin warriors had been sent to the rear of the column and resented the task. They took their time in the march, and soon found themselves far behind the rest of the force.

Rather than catch up, they set about creating a small campfire to warm themselves against the cold. The weeks of travel had made them weary, and they felt no danger so far north. One slumped against a tree and was fast asleep. Another tiredly held his rifle and crouched near the fire.

The third, an older boy no more than seventeen years of age, was less relaxed. He grabbed his musket and headed into the nearby woods to stand watch. He was the first to go.

Crawling meticulously through the underbrush, two Mohawk warriors crept up with knives. In a moment of violence, they fell upon him, cutting his throat in silence, and laying his body gently in the snow, the blood pouring out.

Lawrence watched the two careless Algonquin

scouts from behind a tree. He glanced to his side as several men moved into position in total silence. At his signal, they rushed the campsite. The man by the fire had just propped his head up when the first Mohawk tackled him to the ground, wrestling with their knives. The Mohawk stabbed into the Algonquin, spraying blood from his pulsing arteries everywhere. The sleeping Algonquin had no chance either. He had hardly stirred awake when Lawrence drove a tomahawk into his skull.

"We are done with these men," Lawrence said. "We go on."

Rushing past him from seemingly thin air, Mohawk warriors by the dozen swarmed through the trees. They were racing north, with vengeance and wrath in their hearts.

* * *

Snaking through the mountain passes, Sainte-Hélène and Manthet had to force the men forward every step of the way. Having eaten some of the animals, and others dying of weariness, the men soon found the sleds too heavy with plunder. Much to the dismay of the raiders, Manthet ordered four sleds left behind. Grudgingly, they obeyed. Others were relieved to be free of the added weight. With the previous night's report, their concern was not reaching Montreal with riches, but reaching it alive.

And as midday approached, their spirits rose. Manthet acknowledged that the night's march had done the trick. When the English and Mohawk reached their camp, they would find only smoldering fires and tracks headed north. Sainte-Hélène had pushed the men along at a ferocious pace, but the effort paid off handsomely.

By his own estimate, they had put another five

miles between them and their pursuers. "Shall we order a halt and let the men rest an hour?" he asked Manthet.

Manthet looked back along the line of troops and prisoners. Many were close to collapse. He hated losing the momentum, but he had no choice.

"Thirty minutes," he barked. "Not a minute more, Jacques. We cannot afford it."

Sainte-Hélène halted the column. The men shoved the prisoners into huddled groups and rested. Some rested their heads on their musket barrels and nodded off. Others stuffed a piece of cold meat and water in their mouth, savoring the taste.

"Thirty minutes," Sainte-Hélène said to one of the officers at the head of the column before returning to center. The line itself stretched for half a mile. Significant gaps separated small clusters of men and prisoners.

"We should tighten the line when we march again," Sainte-Hélène to Manthet. "We're vulnerable like this."

"Agreed," Manthet grumbled. "Let's give them an hour. I hate it, but they look half-dead." He undid his belt and saber. "I need a few minutes myself."

"Keep it moving, men," Lieutenant de La Brosse ordered the men at the head of the column. They picked up their pace, eager to reach Montreal. The Calvinist officer Le Bert du Chene rode up.

"The rest of the column has stopped. We should wait for them."

"Denied," de La Brosse snapped. "We go now. Monsieur Manthet's order was clear. Reaching Montreal is the utmost priority. We have most of the prisoners with us. They will slow us down and the column will catch up in time." With a swing of his hand, the cluster of men and prisoners set off.

* * *

"Where in bloody hell are the rest of the men?" Sainte-Hélène raged, riding his horse back and forth. The column, once again, was on the move but it had noticeably shrunk.

"They are gone," Jean Baptiste Giguiere replied. "I scouted up ahead. They must not have stopped."

"How many?"

Giguiere shook his head. "Best guess? Forty men-at-arms and over fifteen prisoners."

Pierre Le Moyne d'Iberville rode up. "Brother, Manthet has left the column."

Sainte-Hélène was shocked. "Why would he leave?"

"He is trying to rally the stragglers," d'Iberville said. "Many men have fallen behind."

Sainte-Hélène swore under his breath. "No more," he said. "You beat them, threaten them, I don't care. Next man to fall behind I will shoot him out of hand. You tell the men that. We press onwards."

Turning to Giguiere, he motioned him closer. "You must be our eyes and ears. Scout in every direction. I need to know where the Mohawk are before they discover our own position."

"Understood," Giguiere said. "But, monsieur, I'm quite sure they already know."

* * *

"Eleven men are missing," the scout reported. Manthet waved him away. He took in the surrounding forest, looking in every direction. Having failed to find the tracks, even with the help of several Natives, hope had all but faded for those separated from the column.

Repentigny de Montesson stood next to Manthet. "They may have collapsed and died in the snow, wandered off course, or been captured. We must find them."

"I don't want to leave any man behind. They made it this far, farther than I could have asked." Manthet sighed. "But if they were overtaken by the Mohawk – I don't think we can save them."

"We have to try," Montesson urged.

"I won't sacrifice the entire column for the sake of eleven men." The faint cracks of gunfire echoed through the trees. "They're to our west!" Manthet shouted.

Within moments the gunfire had ceased. Montesson turned to his commander. "Sir, we must move west to engage the enemy with all possible haste."

"No," Manthet replied coldly. "It could be a trap to lure us in. It could be a diversion. Maybe it is our men, but they have taken casualties. Either way, they will not make it back. It pains me to say this, but they are lost." Montesson wanted to plead the case, but Manthet turned to the twenty men he had managed to gather. "We have a long way to rejoin the rest of the column. And we must make it. Our lives depend on it." He turned to Montesson. "Lead them out."

Leaving the stragglers behind left a bitter taste in Montesson's mouth but he obeyed the order. In the very rear of the French column, its commander wondered if they would continue to be picked off.

He wondered if any of them would make it back to Montreal.

Chapter 54

Andries Barents surveyed the carnage, his eyes beaming with satisfaction. Before him the bodies of several Frenchmen littered the snow. A short distance away, four more were huddled together in captivity. Their fear was evident as they stared at their Mohawk captors.

"The main body is not far ahead," Barents said to those close enough to hear. He turned to Symon Van Ness. "You should bring up the men and send skirmishers to the front. We have suffered only minor injuries here – a small price to pay for this victory."

Van Ness gripped his musket. "I have been waiting for this moment since seeing the devastation of our countrymen at Schenectady. They will not escape us this time."

"The gunfire will have alerted them to our presence," Barents stressed. "We must move fast. There are two courses that the enemy may take. They may make haste to Montreal and reach the town before we catch them."

"And the other?"

"They may turn and fight."

Van Ness showed no sign of concern. "If only the good Lord would bless us with such an outcome. We have the numbers. We can take them."

Barents agreed but with caution. "If they find good ground and fortify it, they may make us pay dearly for our advances against them."

"What would you recommend?"

"Make them change their minds," Barents replied. "We need them to stop long enough so that they may fall into route before our very eyes." Barents paused and looked at the prisoners. "I have an idea."

Van Ness sent out orders and soon the forest crawled with lines of men, cautiously moving through the trees, muskets at the ready. For the first time since setting out, there was a feeling of anxiety in the air. Whereas just days before it looked as though the French would indeed escape, now they were jubilant that the Schenectady massacre may be avenged at last.

Johannes gripped his coat and focused on the back of his brother. They were being forced at a brutal pace through the deep mountain snow. Relieved he was not executed, Johannes felt stronger than he had in days; even though his stomach was painfully empty, and he could only beg for miniscule drinks of water from guards or other prisoners.

He, like the others, had heard the brief gunfire. Their spirits sored. They knew half of them had been forced onward and had to be much farther north, but the French commander of this section had allowed them to rest. Now they could hear the sounds of battle, and hope of rescue filled their minds.

Unfortunately, Johannes knew it would still be suicide to attempt escape. The French commander swore at the prisoners in broken English that he would execute any prisoner who fell behind. Johannes walked with confidence, praying that by nightfall, he could be surrounded by the warm campfires of the Mohawk or even with friends from Albany.

* * *

Manthet was reviewing the line of men when there was a cry from the trees. The men readied themselves to face the Mohawk onslaught. Instead a lone Frenchman stumbled out, his face bloody and his clothes torn.

"Where have you come from?" Manthet demanded to know.

"We were separated, sir," the man said through his chattering teeth. "Seven of us together. We stopped to gather our bearings and the enemy fell upon us in great numbers. They were mostly savages, but a few English accompanied them."

"How many?"

The man shook his head. "I don't know, sir. Twenty or thirty at least," the man replied. "The other six men fell by shot or tomahawk. I escaped but only with my life. I lost my rifle, my kit, and was wounded in the process."

Manthet ordered the man to be treated and fed. He turned to the darkening forest. It looked menacing in the growing shadows. It would be dusk in less than an hour.

"We have to go now," he shouted out to the men. "Pick up your feet and don't look back. We are marching at the double until we rally with Monsieur Sainte-Hélène and the main body. Discard all weariness and don't lose heart. We will dine inside the walls of our beloved city by tomorrow night."

Manthet arrived just after nightfall. To his surprise, he found Sainte-Hélène's men digging in on the ridge where they stood. "Why are you not marching north, Jacques?"

Sainte-Hélène pointed south. "Two scouts were spotted not long ago. The Mohawk know our position. This ridge faces south and gives us the high ground. We will dig in and face their attack directly. They will break upon our hasty defense and then we can continue without their harassing presence."

"We're outnumbered two-to-one at least."

Manthet looked over the earthworks that had been turned into a makeshift wall of stone, tree, and ice. "Still, it is a good position. If we must stand to fight, I would agree on this spot."

Sainte-Hélène dipped his head in thanks, knowing that was the closest Manthet would come to praising him. "Besides, continuing at night would risk the column falling apart entirely. We will turn them back tonight."

"Very well," Manthet said. "I will get my men to lengthen the line." For the first time in days he felt his spirit rise. "We'll break them here."

* * *

The glow of fires lit up the forest. All along the ridge, small fires were set up to light the front line. To the rear, the few remaining captives, Johannes among them, huddled by another fire. His eyes constantly studied the rough French soldiers that guarded them. He studied the commanders as they walked up and down the defenses.

"Don't even think about it," Albert hissed. "I know what you are thinking. They won't just kill you," he warned. "If you try to escape, they will shoot every one of us dead."

"I am not planning to run," Johannes whispered. "But if the Mohawk attack, I will escape." An icy breeze blew, and he inched closer to the fire, holding his hands out. "I will not be a slave to these barbaric people. I will not be a hostage to be traded. I will escape."

Albert reached out, gripping Johannes' arm tightly, causing him to flinch. "Stop it!"

"Stop what?"

"Everything," Albert said, struggling to keep

his voice low. "You are here and that's that. If we can escape, that's well and fine. But you better get it through your thick head that we're just as likely to be their prisoners for years to come."

Johannes dreaded the very thought of it. "Not me. I swear I won't."

"Then you will die," Albert sighed. "I tried to look out for you; keep you safe. But I won't save you if you try to be a hero."

He let go of Johannes' arm and edged away, distancing himself from his brother.

Johannes ignored the gesture. He thought of Maria and Angie, Corset and Arent, even his parents. He had too much to live for and would be damned if he was going to be stuck in a cell in Canada for the rest of his life. He looked up, mentally continuing his escape from the French soldiers.

The forest came alive with war cries.

Manthet and Sainte-Hélène jumped up, nailing themselves to the defenses and staring hard out into the black void beyond the light of their own fires. The terrifying war cries of the Mohawk echoed through the trees. The French aimed their muskets at nothing. They could see nothing. But the unseen screams of the Mohawk send chills down their spines.

"My God," Sainte-Hélène said. "There must be a thousand of them out there." He shot a glance up and down the line. The men appeared to be thinking the same thing.

"Steady," Manthet ordered. "Steady the line. They are playing tricks with your heads. There are but a few of them out there, running around."

He knew it was not true, but it only mattered whether the men believed him or not. By the looks on their faces, they did not. Even Sainte-Hélène, known for his reckless bravery, appeared stirred at the enemy presence in the woods.

"This is a new tactic," Sainte-Hélène said. "When you fought the savages in the frontier wars, have you ever seen anything like this?"

"The Seneca taunted us," Manthet replied. "For five nights, they harassed our lines. They butchered our sentries on two occasions, leaving the scalped and mutilated bodies to terrify us. I was with one war party," he said. "We were forty strong. After they picked at us for a week straight, one night they shouted their war cries and came at us with all their strength."

Sainte-Hélène listened but his eyes remained focused on the trees. "What happened?"

"Half tried to form a defense. The other half ran. They wiped out those that stood to fight and cut down many that ran. Only three of us made it to safety. We ran for a hundred leagues before they stopped pursuing us."

Sainte-Hélène let out a deep breath. "We will not survive the night."

Manthet remained like a statue. The cries of the dead echoed in his memory. "Probably not, my friend. But we can take a few of them with us."

Light flickered in the trees some distance away.

"What was that?" Sainte-Hélène asked.

There was a scream in the distance as a fire lit up. This was not the war cry of a blood thirsty warrior, but the pleas of a terrified man, screaming in French.

The screams grew as two more fires lit up – just beyond the range of muskets. The two commanders watched in horror as the realization struck them.

"Those murdering savage bastards," Sainte-Hélène growled. "Those are our men. Those are *our* men!"

Manthet shook his head in disgust and hatred as the three French prisoners pleaded for God and death. The smell of burning flesh blew through the trees into the French defenses. One man dropped his musket and fled in a panic right away. Others backed away or coughed and vomited. Though they had smelled a similar, horrible stench at Schenectady, there was something gruesome about knowing it was their own countrymen who were being burnt alive.

As the cries of the dying quieted, the Indian war cries once again echoed through the trees. Only this time they came not only from the south.

"They're on the flank!" Giguiere yelled. "They have moved around to the east."

The forest lit up with torches. Across the breadth of the French line, the silhouettes of Mohawk warriors appeared. The fur trappers and woodsman had made the raid for easy plunder. Nothing could prepare them for such a foe and one by one, the line started to crumble.

"Get the prisoners," Manthet shouted. In a lower voice, he added, "We will need hostages."

When Johannes heard the first cries of the Mohawk, his spirit soared. Then, as he was lifted to his feet by the French, he knew it was the end. They had all heard the screams of the French who were being burnt alive. Would they too, be burnt as a warning to stay away?

To their relief, they were pushed until they understood to start marching.

"I am not going anywhere," one man declared proudly.

A French officer jumped from his horse and swiftly ran the man through with his sword. As blood leaked from the body, the other prisoners got the message and set off with their captors.

Johannes ached to turn around and see what was happening behind him as the war cries grew. But even such a trivial action might bring the guards down upon him and he knew this time they were not bluffing. They would kill any man who defied them. Suddenly a shot rang out from behind.

The line erupted. Those French troops who remained behind the defenses shouted and opened fire. Dozens of Mohawk warriors surged forward before stopping short of the French line. Several fell in the snow and were carried back by their brothers-in-arms. For a few minutes, gunfire raged back and forth. By time the attack was beat back, Manthet checked over his line.

"I count four dead and many missing."

"The cowards must have run," Sainte-Hélène cursed. "They will pay for their disobedience."

"If we make it back alive," Manthet reminded him. "We still have several leagues to Montreal." He looked back and was satisfied that the prisoners had been led off. "Leave a small rear guard. We are pulling out."

"Are you sure?" Sainte-Hélène asked.

"We have beaten them back," Manthet replied. "They must be gathering for a full strike. I do not wish to be here when they attack."

Sainte-Hélène nodded. "If we light enough trees on fire we can shield our withdrawal."

Manthet agreed. "Get to it, Jacques. If we have any luck left, we just might make it."

* * *

Van Ness and Lawrence watched the fires burn. "It's a ruse," Lawrence said aloud. "We should go straight in."

"The fires are too hot," Van Ness replied. "We will go around."

"How much time will it cost us?" Lawrence asked, cursing aloud.

"Not long, but we must hurry."

The Mohawk and English militia made their way around the disturbance. Some areas were smoldering, and men cautiously made their way through the smoky haze. Their spirits raised when they saw the bodies of several Frenchmen strewn out in the snow.

One wounded man plead for mercy. Van Ness approached him.

"*Eau?*" the man asked.

"He wants water," a Mohawk said. "His wound is not serious."

"I know," Van Ness responded. He looked at the Frenchman. "But he does not remember Schenectady." Van Ness pulled out his pistol. "I do." The single shot rang out in the night. The Mohawk turned and headed forward without another word. Van Ness glanced down at the body. "*That* was for Schenectady."

* * *

Johannes Vedder stared in hopeless realization at the wooden palisade stretched out before him. For four long hours, the French had moved them at a brutal pace through the snowy passes. The sounds of battle had long faded. It appeared the French had

445

indeed outrun the Mohawk. He ached to hear the war cries again or the sounds of gunfire. Anything that would signal there was still hope for the captives.

He guessed that most of the prisoners, those that had continued on the day before, were already inside. He wondered what fate they had suffered and what his own would be. The thought of being tortured, or worse, did not seem to be possible. Yet with every step towards the looming gate, he felt as if he could sense his impending doom.

To his side, the rough Canadian trapper who walked with him felt a different feeling. He was overcome with joy and relief at the site of the walls. The horror of the previous night was only too real, and he ached to eat and sleep in peace. He prodded Johannes with his musket, urging him to speed up.

Johannes resisted every urge to knock the man down and make a wild run for it. Maybe he would make it. Maybe he would be shot down. But his gut instinct screamed at him that he just *had* to try. He eyed the man's belt. A large knife hung loosely.

He glanced up. The man did not appear to be paying strict attention. Perhaps his mind was elsewhere. Johannes rubbed his hands together, going over his spontaneous plan. Suddenly there was a shout from behind.

He turned his head. The man whom he recognized as the French commander galloped out of the trees with a small contingent of men running at his side. They were shouting and waving their arms.

"Get inside the walls," Manthet yelled. "We have no time. The enemy is upon us." The raiders grabbed the nearest captives and hurried them along, one young boy fell in the snow and had to be dragged by a burly, bearded fur-trader.

Manthet glanced back and could just make out some distant movement. He produced his pistol and took loose aim. The shot rang out and several men turned and fired into the trees as well. Having sent Sainte-Hélène ahead to the town to rally defenders, Manthet was the last commander still in the field. The rear guard had long been wiped out, and it seemed the Mohawk had caught his own men.

"Run!" Manthet called out. He trailed his men as they made the last dash to the gates.

Johannes knew the time was now or never. He wouldn't get the chance again. He purposefully tripped and fell into the snow. As the Canadian stopped and reached down to bring him to his feet, Johannes reached for the knife.

He was met by a fury of blows. He tried desperately first to seize the knife, then to protect himself. Two more men had seen the commotion and rushed to the aid of the Canadian. Johannes was helpless as he was beaten and then lifted to his feet. His legs felt like twigs and he nearly collapsed. The two men each held one arm and dragged him the last few feet through the gate.

Through his swollen eye he could see dozens of French militia and Indian warriors moving about. The two men dropped him next to the other prisoners. Johannes suddenly found himself being held. He looked up to see Albert gripping him tightly.

"You don't learn, do you?" Albert said, trying to laugh through the tears streaming down his face.

Manthet was the last through the gate. He jumped off his horse. Sainte-Hélène approached with a fresh contingent of troops – French regulars.

"I thought you could use the backup," Sainte-Hélène shouted as he waved the men forward.

"I am glad you made it safely, Jacques," Manthet replied. "We are not going to launch a counterattack. We will hold at our walls. If they mean to attack, then let them. They will not get through. Get everyone inside and if they come at us, give them hell."

"Yes, sir," Sainte-Hélène snapped.

He halted the troops. Manthet climbed up a ladder to the catwalk on the palisade. He stood beside a militia soldier and watched the tree line.

One by one, he could see the Mohawk fill up the forest. They did not cross the open ground between the forest and the walls. They stood in silence for a few moments. To Manthet's surprise, the Mohawk slowly faded back into the forest, disappearing from site.

After a few minutes, Manthet looked down at Sainte-Hélène. "They're not coming. Close the gates." Several French soldiers put their weight behind the heavy wooden doors and slowly pushed them shut.

Johannes looked on in despair. Having caught a glimpse of the Mohawk warriors, he could sense they saw him inside the walls. His heart sank as he saw them vanish. The last hope died as the gates closed.

Chapter 55

"In short, our provisions are adequate to get us through the winter. We're still short on arms and powder but we can muster a few hundred men-at-arms from the city and surrounding farms and hamlets."

"Thank you, Abraham," Jacob Leisler said to Abraham Gouverneur – the town clerk. Abraham closed the inventory books and prepared to leave. "You have been a tremendous asset these past months and I just wanted to express my…"

The door burst open, jolting the two men. Marshal William Churcher stammered in, out of breath, and holding a letter. "Sir, the French have attacked Schenectady."

"Good heavens," Gouverneur gasped, holding his mouth.

Leisler walked around from behind the table and approached Churcher. "What happened?"

"A force of hundreds of French and Indian attacked them several days ago, coming in the dead of night and entering through a gate that had been left open."

Leisler closed his eyes, gritting his own orders for the villagers to resist the Convention and their Connecticut mercenaries. He took a deep breath and grabbed the letter.

"How bad is it?"

Churcher hesitated a moment. "How bad?" Leisler repeated.

"The village, sir," Churcher said, "the village has been destroyed. They burned everything and killed almost everyone. Some women and children were spared, but most of the men who survived were taken captive."

"My God," Leisler exclaimed. Gouverneur dropped back into his chair and rested his head in his hand. "This is the Convention's fault," Leisler said. "They were supposed to protect Schenectady and they failed. I have no doubt that their failure was intentional. The people of Schenectady supported me. They killed those innocent villagers as much as the French and Indian savages." He turned to Churcher. "Marshal, send word to my staff. We're going to war."

With his staff gathered, Jacob Leisler laid out the plans on a giant map of the territory. "How many men would it take to seize Albany?"

The commander of the militia, Nicholas De Meyer spoke first, "We already have men up there from our November attempt, and we have lots of local support. Another eighty should be enough."

"Double it!"

De Meyer glanced at the others. "Is that necessary, sir?"

Leisler turned to him. "This is not just about seizing the city. It's about making a statement to the whole colony that I am in control. Only a united colony can defeat the Canadian threat."

"I'll lead the assault myself," Jacob Milborne stated. "I have a debt to settle with the Convention."

Captain De Bruyn, recognized by Leisler's entire staff for his strategic intelligence, stepped forward. "Sir?"

"Go ahead, Captain," Leisler stated.

"Sir, it's not just the Convention our men have to fight for control of Albany. The troops from Connecticut are still garrisoned there, and I am certain the Mohawk presence will be reinforced after Schenectady. Even a hundred and sixty men may not be enough when considering."

"I cannot spare any more men, even for an expedition as important as this. We will need to raise more troops for the war. But do not concern yourself with the Connecticut troops," Leisler said with a smile. "I will take care of it."

* * *

Kiliaen Van Rensselaer was busy cutting wood in the front yard of his manor, preparing them for delivery, when two horses trotted through the snow to his front gate. Pieter Schuyler and Robert Livingston disembarked and approached.

"You have a lovely house," Schuyler commented, removing his gloves to shake Kiliaen's hand.

"Thank you," Kiliaen replied. "Tell me, what brings you out here?"

Schuyler glanced at Livingston and back to Kiliaen. "We need to talk."

In the warm parlor, heated from a beautifully-decorated fireplace, Van Rensselaer offered tea and biscuits to his guests. After they were settled, Schuyler began. "Three days ago, we heard a rumor that the usurper's forces were on the march."

Kiliaen nodded. "Christ, and you waited three days to tell me?"

"They were unverified," Livingston chimed in.

"Until now," Schuyler said. "This morning a scout confirmed the report. Jacob Leisler has sent another army up from New York City. They'll be here in two, maybe three days. It's an army three times the size of the one he sent last November."

"We will beat them back," Kiliaen stated

confidently. "We have just as many inside the city."

"Well that's just it," Schuyler replied.

Livingston sipped some tea and set the cup down. "We have sent men to rebuild Schenectady's defenses. We have sent scouting parties in every direction to watch for the enemy. We cannot allow the French to catch us unguarded again. Many of the Mohawk also, have left either to fight in the north, or to defend their own castles. Half of our force is the Connecticut contingent and the other half are mixed with Leislerites."

"I get the picture," Kiliaen responded. "We are in a bad position."

This time it was Schuyler who spoke, "Kiliaen, we need to consider all courses of action here, and decide what's best not for ourselves, but for our country."

"I do not like where this is going," Kiliaen murmured.

"Going to war with Jacob Leisler will be costly in both lives and money. A victory will in-debt us to Connecticut and Massachusetts, will hurt our alliance with the Iroquois, and distract us from the real war to the north. I just want to make sure we consider all options before we decide on a military endeavor."

Kiliaen stood up so fast Schuyler and Livingston moved their chairs in surprise.

"I will not give in to the usurper," he bellowed. "I will raise fifty men and subside them myself. We'll crush them between the walls of the fort and the river." He paced the room, detailing his plan. "I will have Captain Bull's company hold the fort and draw in the usurper's army. Then I, with my men and those of the city, will hit them from the west. They will be trapped and perish. We need to deal them a blow that Leisler cannot recover from."

Schuyler smiled and stood up. "Very well," he said, his hope restored. "You won't have much time to gather your men."

"I am a wealthy man," Kiliaen stated. "I have done favors for every farmer from here to Massachusetts. I will call them all in for this one effort."

Livingston joined them and the three stood in a small circle. "I have friends in Massachusetts, and others who owe me for past loans. I have a lot of favors I can call in. I'll do what I must to bring in reinforcements."

Schuyler nodded. "So, we fight then?"

"We fight," Kiliaen replied.

Schuyler eyed his friend. "Robert?"

The slightest grin flashed across Livingston's face. "We fight."

Chapter 56

Kiliaen Van Rensselaer looked on his men with disgust.

"Barely twenty answered my call to arms," he said aloud.

Pieter Schuyler, who stood next to him, shrugged. "More will come."

"Several of them didn't even bring muskets. They're armed with pikes. It is a dismal display of force."

"Take heart," Schuyler said. "Robert will bring in his men and we'll still be able to hold the city. This is still a battle we can win."

"We need more men," Kiliaen gritted. "Can you send word to the Mohawk? I am sure Tahajadoris would support us against the usurper."

"In fact, I did send a letter to him." Schuyler paused. "But you heard him the other day. They want unity out of us, not civil war. I don't know if they will come. And they're a few days away at least. They may not get here before Leisler's army."

"Then it will come down to sheer will," Kiliaen said, walking over to his small militia force. "Sheer will!" he cried out, as they circled near him. Others too, walked over to hear. "We have enemies to our north, and to our south," he began. "And both are equally dangerous. Dangerous to our lives; dangerous to our liberties. We shall resist them and beat them back from our walls, no matter the cost.

"Neither side has the numbers in the coming fight. The fate of the battle will be decided not by musket balls or pikes or cannon, but courage, ferocity, and honor. We have the almighty God on our side. We shall prevail."

The men roared, cheering wildly and raising their arms. Schuyler publicly applauded the rallying words of Van Rensselaer, but his mind still focused on the numbers. Such a battle would indeed be hard-fought, and though they were sure to win, without their Indian allies, the city would be vulnerable to a French invasion. But there was a sense of confidence and he did not wish to disturb it, and so he retired into his quarters for the evening.

Pieter Schuyler awakened the next morning to commotion outside. Though a light snow was falling, he could hear the rattling of men and horses and equipment. He swiftly dressed himself and walked outside.

The troops of the Connecticut militia were gathering in formation. Not a battle formation, but one of marching. "What the devil is going on?"

"Orders, sir," a militiaman replied as he passed by the mayor.

"Where is your commanding officer, Captain Bull?" shouted Schuyler.

"Reckon he by the gate, sir."

As Schuyler pounded his feet through the snow, he was joined by Van Rensselaer.

"Is the enemy upon us?" he asked.

"I hear no sounds of battle," Schuyler curtly replied. They found Captain Bull readying his own horse, loading it with his personal effects. "Captain, where are you headed? Why is your company forming up?"

"We are heading home," Bull replied, never facing them.

"What do you mean home?" Van Rensselaer asked.

Bull finished fastening his belongings and turned to the two Albany men. "I mean we have been recalled to Connecticut. We march at once."

Schuyler was aghast. "The battle is days, maybe hours away, and you would abandon us? We need you and your men for this fight." Bull stared at them, no empathy slipping through. "Captain," Schuyler said, "get your men back to their posts. You are sworn to our service."

Captain Bull reached into his coat and produced a letter. "No more," he said, handing the letter to Schuyler. As the mayor opened it, Bull spoke, "By order of the Connecticut Assembly, we are to cease coordination with any governing body in the New York colony save for..." Bull swallowed, forcing the bitter words out his mouth, "...save for the *legitimate* government of Jacob Leisler."

Schuyler stared at him, speechless. Bull cringed slightly. "Sorry, Pieter. This wasn't my call."

Van Rensselaer was fuming. "Leisler must have sent emissaries to the assembly. He whispered into their ear and they gave way. He won't get away. Not with Livingston there."

Schuyler grasped the letter, crumpling it. "He already has," he said, his voice no louder than a whisper. "He has outmaneuvered us and negated our best defense." His mind was frozen. He could not think of what to say or do.

"Captain," he stuttered, "please don't do this."

Bull sighed. "There's nothing more I can do. We have received reports of French armies moving south from Canada with Indian allies. They're raiding as far east as the coast of Maine. We won't be drawn into a domestic dispute inside our sister colony, while our homes are burned by the French and their savage allies."

Without another word, Bull climbed onto his horse and called out the orders to his company. The gates of the city opened, and the long column of men started off slowly, trudging their way through the snow.

The company halted briefly at the river, requisitioning every boat they could muster, to ferry them across the river. Schuyler watched from the ramparts in dismay. Though the order to march had come from their home assembly, rumors began to spread that the Connecticut troops were leaving of their own will because of Leisler's advance.

"They're all cowards," one militiaman called out from a small cluster of men.

"They're the smart ones," another replied. "If we had any sense, we'd leave too, or lay down our arms when they come. I'm not dying for these aristocrats."

Others in the group nodded and voiced their agreement with the man. Their conversation spun to open talk of when and where they should leave the city.

Pieter Schuyler heard the conversation from above. He climbed down the ladder and started back towards his quarters. The men quieted and stiffened up as he approached.

But Schuyler passed by them without a word.

Chapter 57

Atop the wooden walls, Pieter Schuyler knew it was the end. In the distance, a dark line slithered its way across the white landscape, inching its way toward the city.

As Kiliaen Van Rensselaer climbed up the steps and joined him, Schuyler tilted his head in the direction of the column. "Leisler is here."

Kiliaen looked out from the parapet and his head sunk. "We still have the militia. We could fight."

Schuyler sat down on a barrel and shook his head. "No," he said. "We cannot."

Kiliaen eyed the man who had for years been a competitor, if not an adversary. He now looked like a beaten dog.

"I know we had our differences, Pieter," Kiliaen, began, "but over the last few months, I have gained enormous respect and admiration for you." Schuyler glanced up. "It is true," Kiliaen said. "You have shown extraordinary leadership through these dark times, despite your own grievous personal losses, to which I still mourn. But while you have led us through this effort, perhaps it's better to let another take the helm. You are tired – I can see it in your eyes."

Schuyler did not speak. The last few months had sapped him of much of his strength. Between the deaths of his wife and child, Schenectady, and then Captain Bull's men leaving, it was just too much to handle.

Schuyler sighed. "We no longer have the support of the people. I won't sacrifice anymore lives in this bitter conflict. Not when we are at war with the French. I have been to Schenectady. So much death and ruin. I would rather a despot lead us, than tear our colony in two, in civil strife."

Schuyler climbed down with Van Rensselaer just behind him. "It was so simple when we started," Schuyler said tiredly. "I thought we would have a royal magistrate here no later than the first of the year. But no one has come. Perhaps there is more pressing matters in London. Perhaps the King has forgotten about us." Footsteps and shouts from Leisler's men could be heard as they approached. Schuyler said it plainly, "I have no stomach for a civil war, my friend. This colony must be united, and Leisler is not a man who will back down."

"Does that mean we must?" Van Rensselaer responded. "We risked everything and set aside our differences to unite against this man. He will take everything from us. You must realize that. Isn't that why we formed the Convention in the first place? To resist tyrants like Leisler."

Schuyler sat on a bench. Kiliaen stared at the man who he had watched age terribly over the winter. "I understand you have suffered," he said. "More than any man should suffer, to lose a child and then your wife. To be falsely accused of dividing the colony and being responsible for the tragedy at Schenectady. But now is not the time to give up what we have gained."

"And what is that?" Schuyler asked.

"Independence," Kiliaen said. Schuyler turned to Kiliaen. "We held Albany against Leisler for half a year. We did that without the approval or guidance of the King's court. We do not need some usurper from New York City, nor anyone else, to tell us what is best for the people who look to us to lead."

"What you speak is treason," Schuyler replied.

"Then so be it," Van Rensselaer snapped back. "Why shouldn't we govern ourselves? Damned any man who says they know better than I, on how I should run my life." He paced back and forth furiously. "What are you going to do, Pieter? You're the mayor. The people will look to you."

Schuyler sat still for a moment before rising. He refused to meet Kiliaen's eyes.

"Perhaps they shouldn't," he said on a whisper. He walked away, a broken man.

The capitulation happened within two weeks. To the surprise of the Convention's members, Leisler's troops bypassed Albany and marched straight to Schenectady. They brought blankets, food, and other vital supplies to the ragged survivors. Most of it was distributed in the village center, but Milborne dispatched men to bring supplies to the surrounding homesteads as well, where some survivors were staying with friends and relatives.

At first, the Convention breathed a sigh of relief that a battle had been averted. It was only too late they realized there was an ulterior motive for Leisler's humanitarian mission. The generosity shown by his men had won a great deal of support, not only among the people of Schenectady, but the commoners of Albany as well.

Van Rensselaer suspected that humanitarian aid was not the only thing Leisler's men were dispersing. Numerous papers blaming the Convention were found to circulate wherever the Leislerites passed by. He urged the Convention to resist and prepare to defend the city.

To his utter resentment, he found few men of similar fortitude among his peers. Pretty, Thomase, and the others all sided with Schuyler. Only a handful of Convention signers wished to hold out, mostly out of fear of having their land and estates confiscated by

Leisler's government.

The exception beyond Van Rensselaer, was Livingston. Not willing to capitulate, Robert Livingston had left for Massachusetts and the New England colonies to rally support for the Albany Convention.

The majority of men, however, knew they stood no chance. The populace was strongly siding with Leisler and demanded the Convention turnover authority to the New York City-based leader. In his final address to the Convention, Schuyler told the men assembled that unity against the French was the most pressing matter and they should pray that the King sent magistrates to right whatever wrongs they were about to endure at the hands of Leisler.

After finishing with Schenectady, Jacob Milborne marched over a hundred men through the gates of Albany and the Convention relinquished the fort immediately. Leisler sent letters of appointment and Johannes Wendell – a reluctant member of the former Convention, was named mayor. Pieter Schuyler gave up the position without protest.

With the winter carrying on longer than usual, Pieter spent the short days taking care of his daughter in peace and quiet. When his brother, Arent Schuyler, returned to Albany with a French prisoner, captured on the way to Chambly, Pieter could only offer a brief praise that he returned safely, before disappearing back inside his house.

*   *   *

With April passing, the snows receded, and the first signs of spring dawned. As the trees began to sprout new leaves and the grass grew green again, the people of New York felt as if the siege they had endured all winter had finally ceased.

The French and Indian attacks had ravaged the whole of the frontier. Untold numbers of settlers had been murdered in New York and the New England colonies. Count Frontenac's savage raids had devastated a dozen towns and homesteads. Disease and starvation also took their toll. Hundreds had died, and spring found the homes of many frontier colonists deserted or burnt to ash.

Angie Vedder walked through the village, holding Corset's arm in one hand and a basket in the other. She kept a smile on her face as habit when she was with her baby brother. Seeing her smile reflected upon him, and he rarely asked questions about his brothers.

Most days her smile was but a façade. But walking down the street with the dust kicking up and the sunshine warming her face, she felt genuinely happy. Scattered about the village, there were survivors and neighbors setting out plans to rebuild their homes.

With the village having been mostly abandoned all winter, the first days of spring were especially hard for those who had lost family in the massacre. They discovered the charred remains of their loved ones, decaying in the ruins of their burnt-out homes. It was painful as many graves were dug in those first days.

Steadily, however, the rubble was cleared out. The militia, now solidly under Leislerite command, had established rudimentary defenses along the riverbank. It was, however, a useless gesture at that point. With the ice having melted, the water flowed and there was little threat the French would be able to mount an expedition of any size to raid south of the Mohawk River. At long last, the people finally felt safe.

The first crops, mostly wheat and peas, but barley too, were already sown. She returned to their home where her father was repairing the chicken coop. Harmen saw her. "Angie, go help your mother in the house. She is scouring the floors."

"Yes, Father," Angie said with a dip of her dress, and hurried inside. "Mother, I took Corset for a walk. He is growing stronger. Father said you need help."

"Scrub the bedrooms," Anna said without looking up. She was on her hands and knees, her sleeves rolled up. With a bucket of water, and a soap and lye solution made from wood ashes, she scrubbed along the floor to remove the ox gall that was set down the previous night. It was bitter work, but necessary to keep the house sterile.

"Mother," Angie said, "I want to hold off on marriage."

"That's fine," her mother said, pausing to sit up. "Angie, I cannot afford to lose your helping hands. Losing Albert and Johannes was bad enough, and I can't…" Anna broke into tears.

"Oh Mother," Angie said, dropping to her knees and grabbing hold of her mother. "They will come back. I have every faith in God that he will see them back to us."

Anna smiled through her watery eyes and nodded. "You are so right, dear," she said, not believing her own words. "They will come back." She gripped Angie's hand and held it tightly. "I pray every night for their safety."

Her daughter smiled. "As do I, Mother. As do I."

Chapter 58

They came from as far Boston, Massachusetts and St. Mary's City, Maryland. Delegates from Connecticut, Rhode Island, and Plymouth also gathered in New York City on the first day of May. Jacob Leisler, having seen the value in colonial unity, took the Albany Convention's idea and pushed it as his own.

Leisler welcomed them all into the city hall. Outside, he paraded his best-dressed troops around to impress and inspire confidence in the other colonial leaders. Inside, Leisler made small talk as best he could with the delegates.

"I hear you had a famous father," he asked Edward Fuller, one of the Maryland delegates.

"My father was William Fuller," Edward stated. "He led the Commonwealth forces in the Battle of the Severn, against a royalist force. It was the last, if only battle, of the English civil war fought in the colonies."

"You must be proud," Leisler replied, pretending to be interested.

"I am," Fuller said. "But I dare say you may surpass him in fame for organizing such a gathering."

"I'm just beginning," Leisler smiled as he turned to address the colonial congress. "My fellow countrymen," he called out, waiting for the room to quieten down as delegates took their seats. "Thank you for coming. I know for some, you traveled far to be here today."

"Indeed," he heard a man beside him, whisper under his breath. Leisler ignored the snarky comment.

"Let us not waste time and get to the cause of my summons for this convention." He paused for effect, letting the tension fill the room. Every eye was on him – and he welcomed the attention. Finally, he spoke, "Gentlemen, I brought you here because it is time we avenge our dead. I propose to invade and conquer Canada."

* * *

Harmen led his wife and children down the street. They were joined by two-dozen more villagers as they rallied near the northwest corner of the village.

"Wow, it is quite a bit larger than the last one," Anna remarked.

"It is indeed," Harmen said proudly.

They stared in awe at the new fort that had risen from the ashes of the old blockhouse. It was a floor taller, with thicker walls, and sturdy foundations.

"And you built it, Daddy," Corset said.

Harmen laughed.

"I helped build it, yes."

Anna smiled. Her husband, always so serious, had turned a corner when it came to Corset. She suspected the reason was because Harmen thought he would never see two of his sons again and wanted to raise Corset with more compassion than he showed Albert and Johannes.

"Will it protect us?" Angie asked.

"It has a full contingent of soldiers and two cannons," Harmen stated. "I think it will do. But there is still much more work to be done. We may be thankful that the war has shifted to the east. There are rumors of French forces on the move in Massachusetts."

"I pray they never come back," Anna said. "They have caused us enough grief."

Angie sighed. "Should I go home and prepare

dinner for…" she paused.

A young man approached them and extended his hand to Harmen. Angie looked over the man. He was tall, and though gritty with dirt, strikingly handsome.

Harmen shook his hand. "It's good to see you, lad. How's your father?"

"He is well, sir," the man replied. "He sends his regards and hopes you and your wife stop by some day for dinner." He turned towards the Harmen's family, mostly towards Anna. "Hello, I am Jan Van Antwerp. I worked with your husband on rebuilding the fort."

"That is very nice of you," Anna said, introducing herself. "And this is my daughter, Angie."

Jan Van Antwerp smiled and took her hand, kissing it. "You have your father's eyes and your mother's beauty," he said with a grin.

Angie blushed. "Thank you," she said, shyly. "Are you new to Schenectady?"

"No," he laughed. "My family lives west of the village. We considered moving to the village for defense, but my father instead fortified our house with a stone wall." He eyed Angie. "But, who knows, perhaps I will move here someday."

Angie smiled ear-to-ear. Harmen rested his hand on Jan's shoulder, leading him away from his family to talk business.

Anna glanced at her daughter. "Are you sure about the whole marriage thing?" she said with a sly grin.

"Mother!" Angie gasped. "Yes, I am sure. Well, I mean, for now I'm sure. Like, maybe someday," she said.

As her mother turned away, Angie whispered to herself, "Someday soon perhaps."

* * *

Jacob Leisler sat by the window. Outside, the overcast sky had doused the sunlight he needed, and it burned him that it was one thing in his life not under his control. On his lap lay an open book, one he had tried to read, before hopelessly giving up.

It was a shame to him; an embarrassment that he had never learned to read properly. Through all the adventures and trials of his life, formal education had never been a factor in his many successes. Since he had become the sole ruler of the province, he felt at a great disadvantage to his more educated adversaries.

And they were everywhere.

He heard a knock on the door. "Who is it?" he growled. A man opened the door and popped his head in. "What do you want?"

"Sir, my apologies, but you are needed at the fort."

"By who?" Leisler cursed, standing up, letting the book fall to the floor.

"The council," the man said. Leisler noticed the man was shaking. Sweat dripped from his forehead. Leisler had never seen the courier before; probably why the man was so nervous.

"I will be right there," he sighed. The man left, and Leisler could have sworn he saw the man smirk before disappearing from of the room.

Leisler stepped out onto the street. The cloudy day cast a dreadful view over the otherwise magnificent city. He walked down the street with a soldier on each flank. Though in public, he proclaimed that all of New York was behind him, in private he heard whispers against him behind every corner.

Only then, they were not just whispers. "Here comes the deacon jailer," a woman sneered at him as he passed by.

"Little Cromwell," another man said, mocking Leisler's own comparison of himself to the great Lord Protector of the Commonwealth.

Leisler's face grew red with anger. He gripped the handle of his sword, wanting nothing more than to run the insolent man through his heart. But as he walked, the feeling changed. The crowds evaporated and those that remained stared at him with cold eyes. The women were all but gone and only angry men remained as Leisler passed by.

He glanced over at a group of men conducting some bartering.

No. They were not trading.

Leisler saw the cart. It was filled with clubs and axes, spears and sticks. Each of the six men standing-by were carrying some weapon and they stiffened up upon his approach. Leisler slowed his pace. The men turned, and Leisler took a step back.

"We need to get out of here," he said to the soldiers. He gripped his sword again as the men slowly moved forward. "We need to go," Leisler repeated. "Now!" he shouted.

In an instant, the six men surged forward and hurled themselves upon Leisler and his two soldiers.

From every alley and door, men poured into the street, clubs and axes at the ready. They surged towards the desperate men in the street. Leisler drew his sword and plunged it directly into the first man he could reach. The man fell back, his blood squirting everywhere. Leisler slashed wildly, slicing another man across his chest, painting the street red.

Leisler heard a scream and looked over as one of the soldiers was overwhelmed by the mob and torn to pieces. The other soldier fired his musket, killing one man instantly. Then as he attempted to reload, he too was brought to the ground by a series of blows. Leisler had no time to mourn as the mob stabbed the soldier over and over, for he himself was assailed by three more men. One man lunged forward with a pitchfork, striking one tine deep into Leisler's side. Leisler yelled and swung his sword, slashing the man's face. Another blow fell on his shoulder.

All around him, men joined the mob in the bloody street, now littered with bodies of the dead and dying.

"So this is how you will end me?" Leisler growled. "Like cowards from the shadows." He spat blood from his mouth. He stumbled to his feet, raising his sword. "Then do it. I am ready."

In that moment, the mob surged forward. Suddenly, an explosion of musket fire riddled their ranks. Men fell in the streets, screaming. Leisler heard Jacob Milborne shout orders and militia troops rushed forward, bayonets at the ready. They quickly cleared the street of the mob and carried Jacob Leisler to safety.

The aristocrats and backers of Nicholson's dissolved government were seen as the perpetrators of the assassination attempt, as Leisler had declared it. That night, Jacob Leisler's supporters flooded the city, and in a display of fire and blood, wreaked destruction on the upper class of New York City and all who opposed Leisler's rule. Normally one to quell such riots, Leisler issued stand-down orders for his troops. Many joined the mobs, looting and burning homes.

By morning, all signs of resistance to Leisler's absolute rule had been stamped out. Smoke filled the sky where the homes of a dozen anti-Leislerites had been burned to the ground. Leisler, bandaged up and walking around with a cane, surveyed the carnage from the safety of the fort.

Chapter 59

January 29, 1691

The warm fire crackled and its glow lit up the damp room. Jacob Leisler sat next to the fire, wrapped in a warm blanket. He reached for his abdomen and rubbed it, feeling the scar. It had healed, finally, though it would remain with him for the rest of his life. After the capitulation of the Albany Convention, he enjoyed a few short months of unopposed rule. There were none in the colony who had the stomach or will to oppose him.

All that had changed on that cloudy day in June. He thought back to the mob that had swarmed him as he walked the streets, inspecting the city. They had come from all sides, first beating down his guards with clubs, and then going after him. They would have killed him that day, had it not been for his soldiers coming to the rescue.

From there, it only got worse. September brought a force of over one hundred armed men from Queens County to march against him. Only his one true friend and subordinate, Jacob Milborne was there to stop the advance. With twice the number of troops, he marched against the Queens County militia and it nearly came to open war before the treasonous rebels withdrew to their homes.

With his enemies around every corner, who could be trusted? Leisler nodded his head, knowing he made the right move by dissolving the governing council last December, and seeking out the Papist Catholics and others who would stand to harm him.

The knock on the door brought him out of his daze. "Sir, two ships have just entered the harbor."

The voice echoed from behind the door.

"What of it?" Leisler growled, irritated at the intrusion.

"They are English frigates, Sir."

Leisler stood up and threw off the blanket, grabbed his sword, and headed out to see for himself. The snow was dirty and sloppy and he silently thanked Milborne for the new pair of cavalier boots. A loyal friend indeed. He made his way to the fort with a company of militia.

Reaching the parapets of the fort, Leisler gazed out upon the harbor. Through the morning fog, he stared in awe. The harbor was filled with longboats. Each had a number of men in red coats on them.

"English regulars," he said to Milborne, as his deputy joined him.

"That's a lot of troops to accompany a governor, don't you think?"

Leisler thought about it. "Could it be an assault force?"

"Why else would you bring an army here?" Milborne replied, folding his arms. "They may be sent by the king, but until we know their intentions, I think we should prepare for battle."

"Nonsense," one of the other officers blared. "They are our countrymen. They are no threat."

Milborne looked to Leisler. "Sir?"

Without listening to the protest of several other officers, Leisler immediately heeded Milborne's advice and readied the fort to repel attackers. By time the first boats of English soldiers touched down on the docks and the men disembarked, they were face to face with a formidable defense around the fort.

At noon, a group of English officers approached the fort. They were dressed in red coats, black pants and boots. They all appeared slim and fatigued from their long voyage across the vast Atlantic Ocean.

Leisler and his staff met them just outside the walls. "I am Major Richard Ingoldesby," the senior officer stated loudly. "I have been appointed Lieutenant-Governor of New York by his Majesty, King William of Orange. I am here to prepare the city for the arrival of the newly appointed Governor of New York – Colonel Henry Sloughter."

There was a low murmur through the militia's ranks. Leisler himself looked at the man with instant disdain. He had known this day was coming eventually, but it bit at him nonetheless. "I am Jacob Leisler – the acting governor and commander of this province. Let me see your papers."

Ingoldesby stiffened up. "I am appointed by the king himself. I do not answer to you or any subject of the crown. My light foot company will take over the defense of the city and the fort."

Major Ingoldesby waved his men forward. To the surprise of the English, Leisler ordered his own men to block their path. "You will not enter this fort, Major. I have seen no royal decree and therefore my duty is to hold this fort until properly relieved."

"You are being properly relived, here and now, sir."

Leisler shook his head. "I do not see your papers. Where is the governor you claim has been appointed?"

There was a tense silence as Ingoldesby tried to explain. "The governor sails on the frigate *Archangel*, captained by Captain Gaspar Hicks. The ship was set to sail for the Bermuda first, and will be here in due time. The royal papers are on that vessel."

There was a low murmur of resentment in the crowd.

"How convenient," Leisler said, "that I give up the fort before getting confirmation from the king. I think my duties are clear. I will hold the fort until the governor arrives."

"Are you mad, sir?" Ingoldesby asked, stunned. "You would defy a duly appointed magistrate and his loyal soldiers from carrying out their duty?"

"I will not give up this fort to you or any man," Leisler suddenly roared. "If you try to take it by force, you will be fired upon."

After a moment of tense silence, Ingoldesby grasped his hands behind his back. He could see that Jacob Leisler was not budging, and it would be a bloodbath to storm the fort. "Very well, have it your way. I shall come back tomorrow for your answer."

Leisler replied, "The answer will be the same, sir."

For the next few weeks, New York City was frozen in a state of emergency. Leisler reinforced the fort with every man he could muster. Three hundred and fifty in total.

Ingoldesby's two companies of English soldiers occupied the city and surrounded the fort. Barricades were set up and several cannons were brought from the ships and positioned facing the fort. Ingoldesby sent agents out to gather the old city council from before the rebellion. They were only too joyous to return and share every incriminating rumor to Ingoldesby and his staff.

The presence of the old council only added fuel to Leisler's paranoia that the English troops represented King James and were part of a greater Catholic conspiracy against him. His resolve stiffened and every night, by candlelight, he laid out battle plans.

As the winter carried on without an end,

supplies ran low in the fort. Milborne was forced to punish several men for stealing food from the storerooms. Men deserted at regular intervals and discipline started to fall apart. The militia, having grown used to peace, were ill-prepared to standoff against a greater number of well-trained, professional soldiers. But Leisler's iron-will was not something to be easily crossed. On four occasions, messengers from Ingoldesby were turned away from the fort at gunpoint.

After the last transgression, Ingoldesby returned to the barricades and ordered the cannons to be loaded.

"They're preparing to attack!" Milborne yelled out. Turning to the artillery crew next to him, he pointed at their own cannon. "Fire the gun."

"But sir…"

"Dammit, that's an order," Milborne snapped. The militiaman hesitated. Milborne pushed him out of the way and set the fuse and lit the spark himself.

The cannon roared, scoring a direct hit on one of the English guns. The explosion sent men and debris flying. Ingoldesby himself was flung to the ground. He stammered up, his ears ringing from the deafening noise.

"Fire!" he ordered.

The fort lit up in a fury of musket and artillery fire. Leisler rushed out from the barracks, leading men to the walls to pour gunfire down upon the soldiers surrounding them. Men fell on both sides. Smoke clogged the field. A cannon from the fort sent a round smashing into a nearby home, knocking its wall down. Civilians scattered, some falling to stray rounds from the fort's militia.

Sergeant Jost Stoll fell from the ramparts, a round having torn through his shoulder. He was carried away, screaming in agony as the blood gushed out.

Captain de Bruyn called out to Leisler.

"Boats on the water," he shouted.

Leisler rushed from one end of the fort to the other, staring hard at the incoming fleet.

"Sir," de Bruyn said, "the royal banner flies from that ship."

Leisler went cold. "It's the *Archangel*," he whispered. A pang of terror shot through him. "Cease fire," he ordered.

Both the militia and the English ceased fire, and gathered their wounded. Over half a dozen soldiers and civilians lay dead on the field outside the fort.

As the *Archangel* docked, Governor Henry Sloughter disembarked to a scene of carnage. With fiery eyes, he stared at the bodies of the slain troops. He had a larger build to him and was dressed in a fine brown overcoat and buckled shoes. His curly, white wig was gray with dust that still hung in the air from the smoke of battle.

Next to him, Major Ingoldesby and the rest of the Governor's assembly waited for orders.

"Delegates from the fort," a soldier cried out.

Sloughter took in every detail of the terrible scene before him. "Send them over," he said calmly.

Sloughter waited until Jacob Milborne and another trusted Leislerite were standing before him.

"My commanding officer and acting commander of New York wishes to discuss the terms of turning over the fort." Milborne tried to speak as soldierly as possible, not betraying any sign of weakness in front of the new governor.

"Does he?" Sloughter asked. "You must be his lieutenant; I take it?" Milborne bowed his head slightly. "Let me enlighten you," Sloughter said, motioning to some soldiers who surrounded the two men. "The king negotiates with his enemies, not his subjects."

Jacob Leisler watched from the walls of the fort as his men were grabbed and taken away into captivity. Sloughter could see the lone figure standing atop the defenses.

"Major, do what is necessary to get them out of that fort," Sloughter said to Ingoldesby. "The crown does not negotiate with its subjects."

Over the next two days more English soldiers arrived in the harbor. With the deaths of civilians by the militia's hand, public support for Leisler continued to fade away. While the English were busy building ladders to storm the fort – inside, chaos reigned.

Jacob Leisler and his senior officers argued for hours about what they should do. He felt his power falling away as men he had led since the beginning, came out against his plan to defend the fort. They urged a surrender as the only option. By the morning of the third day, the debate was over.

The English were stunned when the gates of the fort opened and out marched over three-hundred militia with their arms in the air. Ingoldesby used the old council members including Nicholas Bayard and Stephanus Van Cortlandt to pick out the ringleaders of the infamous Leisler's Rebellion.

Jacob Leisler was bound and shackled along with his entire staff. Understanding the need to quiet the tension, Governor Sloughter pardoned the rank and file of the militia, disbanding them to their homes. The common people and merchants alike cheered the end of the rebellion.

To many, the king's troops were a welcome sight, after the months of worrying about who would be dragged off to prison each night, on the whims of a dictator's order.

For his part, Leisler knew justice would prevail. The people would not tolerate their leader – their champion, remaining in captivity by a despotic governor no different than Nicholson. While his enemies occupied new positions at the governor's council, and there was talk of a trial, he held his head high in defiance. In the darkness of his cell, he smiled. He knew he would soon be free once again.

Chapter 60

May 16, 1691

Jacob Leisler was sitting on his bed in the jail cell in silence when the guards came for him. The scraping metal of the door being unlocked and opened passed through his ears. He could hear the guards commanding him to rise but paid them no attention. He focused on the shouts from the streets above. He could hear those crying for his head, as well as those shouting their support. He could hear the pounding of the rain on the city street. He glanced at the heavy irons that shackled his hands together.

The trial had been a farce; a sham. Leisler entered what he thought would be a fair trial where the people would testify to his great progress in social reform and justice, and his bringing a sense of unity to the colonies.

Instead Jacob found himself struggling to defend himself against both real and imagined accusations. The old council condemned his actions and used his own harsh words against him as evidence that he was unfit for leadership. Governor Sloughter barred testimony from several of Leisler's deputies and never once halted the council from badgering the accused.

Milborne too, was tried, but in a scant one-day trial. After a hate-fueled rant by Milborne, Sloughter declared him guilty and his life forfeit. Leisler's trial went longer but the verdict was the same.

Sloughter sentenced both men to death.

"On your feet," the overbearing guard said in

479

a deep voice. Leisler sighed and looked up. The two English soldiers stared down at him, expressionless and stern. They each held a large pike in their hands. Behind the two guards, a third man—no doubt a magistrate—stood with a rolled-up piece of paper.

Leisler dropped his head in despair, staring at the cell's stone floor. His blood began to boil.

"You're making a terrible mistake," he said quietly, not much louder than a whisper. "The people will not allow for my execution." His words offered more of a reassurance to himself, than a warning to the guards.

The magistrate stepped forward. He pulled out a pocket watch and checked it before snapping it shut. "It's time, my lord."

He looked to the guards and nodded. They reached down and grabbed Leisler under the armpits, hoisting him up with powerful hands. Leisler did not resist as they led him out of the cell and down the hallway to the stairs leading up to the street. He could hear the commotion outside from the masses of people gathered about the jail. The hall smelled of urine, feces and other unknown odors. He stared straight ahead as he passed the cells of other men, most of them common criminals who hid against the far corners in shame and fear. Others – Leislerites jailed under the new governor, stood in silence and watched their leader pass by.

With the magistrate at the head of the procession, Leisler was led up the steps. The heavy jail doors swung open and he found himself on the streets of the city he once dominated with an iron fist. Rain poured down and gray clouds blanketed the sky, shielding the sun. Hundreds of civilians had gathered. They fell silent as he emerged. Directly to his front, two horses waited with a half-cart. Standing in the cart, also

480

in chains, was Jacob Milborne. The two guards escorted Leisler forward and he climbed up onto the cart, alongside his deputy.

Jacob Leisler looked out upon the people. Old and young, men and women, all had gathered to see him. He picked out in the crowds, those people who had adamantly opposed his rule. Their smirks and jesting pierced him like a sword. He swore that once his supporters freed him from the circus, he would have their heads speared to the city gates like a vengeful conqueror.

He could also see the faces of his friends and allies, scattered throughout the crowd. Their arms were crossed, their faces saddened with grief. He looked at one woman who openly sobbed as she stared up at him. Leisler wondered which of his men would lead the crowd to free him. He looked for one of his captains or other officers but could see none.

The cart jerked forward, momentarily catching the two prisoners off balance. Three English soldiers with pikes marched on each side of the cart, with several more to the rear. More still, walked ahead, pushing the crowds out of the way for the horses. The solemn parade made its way up Broadway towards the city wall.

Leisler glanced at Milborne. Milborne stared ahead, his eyes glazed as if in a trance. Leisler thought to speak but held his tongue and turned his head to the front. The street seemed alien to him, as if he had been captured and once again brought to a foreign country. He tried to remember his march down the very same street as his men seized Fort James over a year and a half before, but he could no longer conjure the memories of that fateful day. Instead of torches and flags, pitchforks and muskets, yelling and celebrations, there was a silent audience that stared like shadows as he passed them by.

The city gate opened before them and they crossed under the wall and into the farmland beyond. Many of the fields were still barren dirt, and the heavy rains turned them to mud. Although spring was in full bloom, the land appeared as if death walked about it, for many of the trees had been felled to be used in the city defenses. The landscape was stripped, bearing a likeness to wasteland. All along the road, peasants and aristocrats alike watched the procession.

Then he saw it.

For the first time in what seemed like a lifetime, Jacob Leisler felt something he did not recognize – fear. Ahead of him, on the rising ground, a great platform had been erected, where the gallows stood towering out. They moved closer and he could see two nooses looped over beam, casually hanging there awaiting the condemned. The field was crowded with more than a thousand people amassed around the gallows.

The cart stopped. The soldiers helped Leisler and Milborne down, before walking them to the gallows' steps. All around, the people were rife with emotion. Many were saddened. Others were angry. And still, others were elated at the outcome of the trial and sentence.

A soldier grabbed the back of Leisler's collar and directed him up the steps. Leisler felt sick, like his stomach was turning. His legs shook and he was no longer confident of his rescue. Not once had he seen a rifle or any sign of rebellion in the crowd.

Stepping up to the platform, he looked on in terror at the rope, swinging sinisterly in the rain. Two stools rested under the nooses. A minister in a large gray overcoat, clutching a Bible, stood beside the executioner - a man in English attire, a metal breastplate, and cavalier boots. He had a thick brown mustache, long straight brown hair and he did not seem to be phased by the rain coming down.

The minister stepped up to the two men. He whispered a brief prayer to them. Leisler watched as his friend prayed with the minister. As the minister finished and stepped off to the side, Milborne looked at Leisler. "I had to make peace in these final moments. You should too my friend."

Leisler said nothing.

The magistrate stepped before them. "Jacob Leisler and Jacob Milborne. You have been tried and found guilty of sedition and treason and sentenced to hang by the neck until dead. Do you have any final words before the sentence is carried out?"

Milborne stepped forward. The magistrate saw he wished to address the crowd, and edged back, letting the condemned speak.

"Am I to die today?" Milborne shouted out. "I see many in the audience who followed Leisler to the fort two years ago; are you now too timid and cowed to step forward now in our most dire hour? Will you not stop this injustice?

"This is the work of my enemies," Milborne ranted. "There is no justice here. They fear my very existence and that of our governing. Why not face me directly, rather than hide behind an execution warrant? You cannot pass this judgment on me."

By that point, Jacob Milborne was yelling and spent several more minutes ranting and condemning every name he could think of responsible for his arrest. His final words were a poorly composed burst of barely coherent snipes and threats. The magistrate, growing frustrated, ordered the executioner to push Milborne into position and draped the noose around his head, tightening it around the neck. Finally, Jacob Milborne stayed his tongue.

The magistrate turned to Jacob Leisler, who stepped forward. His eyes fell upon the rain-soaked crowds as they watched him in silence. Some of the men, aristocrats he assumed by their fine attire, smirked disgustingly at him. Others, many of the poorer people, were stricken with grief. Always one for impulsive speaking, Leisler thought for a moment, choosing his words with care.

"I have only acted in good conscience and in the best interests of my God, my king, and my fellow countrymen. I stepped forward to lead, not of my own desire but at your request. I saved this colony during its darkest hour.

"I do not believe the governor was fit when he signed the order for my death. But I accept this fate as it is all as God wills it. I only ask that those who followed me be spared sentence. Let my sacrifice be enough blood to quench this governor and council's thirst for vengeance. I do not wish my death to bring more death to this province. More death will tear it asunder into discord, strife, and civil war. To my followers, in our graves let all malice, hatred, and envy be buried."

The magistrate whispered to him, "Are you ready?"

Leisler turned his head to the man. "I hope these eyes will look upon our Lord Jesus Christ in Heaven. I am ready."

The magistrate nodded and stepped back.

Leisler stared over the impassive crowd. Even though they clutched their coats tightly, as if their only concern was to protect themselves from the rain, he could see sorrow among many of their faces. For Leisler, there was a sense of finality to the affair. His life had been an adventurous one, and yet, as he looked out upon the masses, he sensed it would be his death that would leave the most lasting mark.

The magistrate gave the order. The executioner grabbed Leisler and walked him backwards to his position. Leisler stepped up onto the square platform. It felt strangely sturdy. He watched as the executioner grabbed the noose from above and passed it over his head – the rope blinding him for a brief moment as it passed over his eyes. The executioner tightened the rope around his neck and he could feel the bristles pricking his skin.

The magistrate reviewed both men and then turned to the crowd. "Let the king's royal decree reign supreme, and let it be known that no man is above the law. Let it be known the law must be upheld even when unpopular. Let justice be brought upon these two men who have committed a most sacrilegious crime against his majesty King William the Third, and Queen Mary, and against the Lord God Almighty. May God have mercy upon your souls." He stepped aside and gave the final word.

Milborne bowed his head and closed his eyes as he felt the presence of the executioner walk behind him. His feet were tied together. The executioner kicked the stool out from under him. Milborne dropped and started jerking back and forth violently as the air escaped his body. Leisler refused to look at his friend as he was slowly strangled. He stared out into the crowd, silently pleading to see someone step forward to save him. He saw no one make that choice. The crowd watched in silence.

The executioner then tied Leisler's feet and stood behind him. Jacob Leisler had once heard from a man who had escaped death that a man's life would flash before his eyes before the end. For the longest time, Leisler thought the man crazy. On the stand, with a noose around his neck, and the cold rain washing away any comfort he may have had, he knew the man was right. But then something strange happened. For a time, he felt weightless, like he was standing on air. Then he saw the horizon rise as he fell, stopped suddenly by the rope snapping tightly.

Jacob Leisler had known pain and terror before but never like that. He could not breathe. His eyes widened, and he tried kicking his feet, desperate to find solid footing. Swinging back and forth, his body turned, and he glimpsed his dear friend beside him. He too was swinging but the movements were weaker and Milborne's eyes were closed. Leisler continued to fight, his mind racing with a million thoughts, feelings and memories. He could not hear anything, not even the sound of his heartbeat. He strained to see but everything was turning gray. Soon, he could neither see nor hear anything. But he felt everything. He felt the rain on his face. He felt the muscles in his neck tearing. He felt his lungs twisting and ready to explode. In the final moments, he tried to visualize something, anything that reminded him of a better time. But everything was black. Soon there was nothing to feel – nothing to remember.

The crowd watched in silence as the two men ceased movement on the gallows. People in the audience cried and grieved. Two women wailed openly, horrified at the spectacle. A small group of men nodded their approval and walked away in stride. The condemned men had been put to death, but the sentence was not yet fully carried through. After some twenty minutes, the executioner cut the two bodies down. Soldiers then dragged the bodies off the gallows and laid them before a stone altar. The executioner returned, wielding a great axe. The soldiers propped up

Jacob Leisler's body on the altar with his head sagging over the side. The people watched in horror as the executioner lined up the axe blade to Leisler's neck. With one great swing, he removed Leisler's head. The crowd gasped in disgust. Milborne was propped up and the executioner beheaded him too.

After the beheadings, the bodies were left in the mud. The execution party assembled and marched back to the city gate. Those who supported Jacob Leisler rushed forward and tore pieces of clothing from his body and even lockets of hair from his severed head, not in insult, but as mementos. Others carried the bodies away, where they would sew the heads back on before burying the deceased.

From that moment onwards, there was bitterness throughout the colony. But even the most rebellious of men conceded. There was no dispute that the crown was once again in complete control. Those who disobeyed were promptly put to death or imprisoned. Order was restored as far north as Albany. But the Dominion of New England—which had dominated the colonies before the Glorious Revolution, and dissolved in the Massachusetts and Leisler rebellions—would never rise again. Territorial control remained under the Governors of the individual colonies. The position of Governor General was permanently absolved, along with all other related positions. While the people debated whether Leisler was right or wrong, one thing remained painfully clear.

The king would not let his colonies go without a fight.

Chapter 61

June 4, 1691 – the Borderlands of Canada and New York

Athasata stood up in the boat and took view of the flat grounds around the mouth of the approaching river.

"We camp here tonight."

He turned to his French counterpart, Lieutenant René Le Gardeur de Beauvais of the Troupes de la marine and signaled him to make camp. The French officer nodded, and in total silence, signaled the other boats to follow their lead.

The force of French Marines and Caughnawaga warriors turned their boats in from the vast Lake Ontario and sailed up the mouth of the river to make their camp for the evening. The campfires soon roared to life and by sunset, the men were filling their bellies with cooked salmon from which the river was named after.

As the fires died out and sky turned black, Athasata walked down to the mouth of the river and sat. He looked up at the vast night sky. Stars filled the blackness from horizon to horizon across the expansive lake that appeared like an ocean. He sat for some time in total isolation, meditating, before finally heading to sleep.

The morning calm erupted with the hysterical screams of charging Indians. Athasata woke up in a daze. He looked over as his warriors and the French fired blindly into the woods. The forest seemed to return a hail of arrows and musket fire. The thought of being under Iroquois attack so far north was shocking to the great chief. He stood up and rushed to rejoin his men.

Suddenly he saw a flicker of black heading in his direction. The piercing arrow embedded itself in his flesh. He reached down and felt his gut where it had hit. A violent force smashed into him as a second arrow plunged into his heart.

The warrior known as the Great Mohawk fell dead instantly. Within moments, there was a call to ceasefire. From their shrouded cover of trees, the attackers emerged. Confused Indians of the Caughnawaga and Abenaki tribes stepped out, holding their weapons high. They had been on the warpath when they saw the campfires of Athasata's war party. Believing them to be Iroquois – they attacked.

The distraught warriors wept upon the body of their mighty chieftain, the shallow water from the river washing over his torn body. All present bowed their heads and mourned for their loss.

* * *

August 11, 1691 – La Prairie, Canada

Rain pounded the earth in the foggy summer morning. Not a foot of dirt, nor a piece of cloth remained dry. It was terrible weather to be outside and worse still for battle.

But for Pieter Schuyler, the weather was perfect.

The men emerged from their positions and charged the sleeping French and Indians. Many were still asleep in their tents. The guards were swiftly overrun, being cut down by pikes and bayonets of the raging English colonists and Mohawk Indians. Those in the encampment closest to the perimeter had no chance. They were slain before they could rise from their blankets.

Even as the attack commenced, Schuyler could see he had miscalculated. The French encampment was far larger than he had thought. And they were responding faster than he had anticipated. A line of French soldiers formed up and fired a volley, dropping several of his men as they surged forward blindly. But the French line soon broke under the weight of the English charge.

Amidst the chaos, Schuyler rushed back and forth, shouting orders to his men. He fired his pistol at a charging French soldier, hitting the man in the leg. The wounded soldier was cut down with a second shot from a Mohawk. "Forward!" Schuyler howled to his men. The troops pushed forward as the French troops scattered, leaving behind their arms and many of their comrades' bodies in the mud.

After some time, Pieter Schuyler withdrew his men. The ambush had been an astounding success. Only a handful of his own men were killed or wounded. He guessed they had inflicted four or even five times that on the French and Algonquin allies. They had devastated the enemy camp, but he knew better than to press his luck. They had been fortunate the French were caught off guard, else their superior numbers would have overwhelmed the much smaller English force.

"The men are marching with high spirits," Schuyler stated proudly to his captain.

"They would follow you to Montreal if you asked, Major," the captain responded. "You are a terrific commander, sir, and if I may add, you would make an even better governor if such a position were offered."

Schuyler smiled, more at the rain splashing off his face than his deputy's comment. "Not anymore. I came up here to avenge our fallen countrymen and I have achieved that. From now on, I shall take a quieter role in life. I have no political ambitions." He looked at his men. "Sadly, for some of these boys, they will not live a quiet life. This war is not over yet, and I fear more is yet to befall us."

The downpour carried on throughout the morning and into the afternoon. Schuyler turned his men down a road towards the Richelieu River. A young corporal rushed up to the commander.

"The road narrows up ahead," the boy said to Schuyler.

"Very well, Corporal," Schuyler stated. "Take a detachment ahead and make sure the way is clear."

No sooner had the boy turned than the sound of gunfire erupted up ahead. The corporal fell in an agonizing pain, blood spewing from his mouth and chest. The tree line on both sides of the road exploded in a fury of musket fire. Schuyler watched as his men fell screaming and bleeding in the muddy road.

An unseen voice shouted something in French from the woods. Dozens of men charged from the trees and were instantly on top of the English. A quick volley by Schuyler's men sent several French troops tumbling into the mud.

Schuyler watched some of his men attempting to fire. The rain had dampened the powder and many muskets failed to spark. He produced his sword.

"Forget the bloody shooting and take these bastards by steel."

He led his men directly into the surging

French. The fighting became hand-to-hand. Men grabbed at each other's throats, stabbing wildly into each other with knives, and bashing each other with rocks and whatever else they could lay their hands on. French, English, and Indians from both sides, slaughtered each other in the downpour.

It was not a fight for land or strategic gain.

It was not a fight for honor.

The men hacked and stabbed at each other, bodies piling up in the mud. They ripped at clothes, gouged at eyes, and drowned each other in muddy puddles.

It was a fight for blood.

Schuyler had his side pierced by a knife, before lunging his sword into the man's chest. The man fell backwards, tripping over a body half-submerged in a lake of blood and mud. Schuyler pushed his men onward down the road, all the while fighting back the French who continued to attack from the woods.

"Sir, we must withdraw," an officer shouted to Schuyler. He paused from the butchery to take account of his forces. Exhausted and bloody, his men looked on the verge of total collapse. Without pause, he gave the order to fall back, keeping the men steady as to not cause a rout.

The French, Schuyler noted, fought with incredible – almost reckless, courage, constantly pressing the attack. It was only after an incredible feat, that Schuyler's force broke contact with the pursuing French. He led his battered troops south. Victory was claimed by both sides and the war continued.

Chapter 62

Spring, 1692

Johannes Vedder lay shivering in the fetal position on a crude bed of hay and wool. The room was dark and hot. His skin was pale, and his eyes were bloodshot. The pain in his abdomen and consistent coughing kept him from getting a full night's sleep in over a week. Sweat dripped from every pore. His clothes were rags, torn and dirty. Next to him lay a dish of half-eaten porridge. What little food was offered to him, he could not keep it down. Three times he threw up that day, and twice the previous one. Each day was worse than the day before. As he drifted in and out of consciousness, Johannes could think of only one thing – the end was not far away. It was in these final moments that his thoughts drifted back to the start of his captivity…

February, 1690

The heavy wooden doors closed behind him. Johannes turned around and watched as two French militiamen secured the doors with heavy planks. The snow swept around his feet. His legs shook in cold and fear. Though he was afraid to look around, he could catch glances of not just armed militia, but regular French soldiers in full uniform. They were in the heart of New France and there was no escape.

Johannes stayed close to Albert as the prisoners were marched through the muddy streets, towards the center of town. Curious women and children peered out from their windows or stood in their doorways, watching the somber parade of prisoners. Others huddled together in hastily-built shanties, refugees of Lachine and the other nearby hamlets that had been destroyed.

The town was in appalling conditions, the likes of which Johannes could have scarcely imagined. The residents appeared horrifyingly thin under their heavy clothing, and their faces bore tales of sickness and disease. Looking at them, he envisioned how the survivors of Schenectady must look, however few were still alive.

In the town square, they were halted. On the far side of the square stood a two-story brick building, larger and sturdier than any other in town. Atop the roof, was a blue flag, with 3 golden fleurs-de-lis – the royal banner of France. Johannes felt a shiver at seeing the flag fluttering above them. Curiously, as he glanced over, he witnessed a French militiaman who had raided Schenectady, wipe away tears of joy as he stared up at the banner.

The door opened and a man, flanked by two soldiers, headed towards the prisoners.

"Who is that?" Albert whispered.

As if hearing the question, Manthet announced, "His excellency, the Governor of Montreal, Louis-Hector de Callières."

Johannes awed at the smartly-dressed governor. He wore tall black cavalier boots, black pants and jacket, with a white and blue sash, and saber hanging from his belt. His face was serious but not menacing like the brutal men he had sent to ravage Schenectady.

Expecting Callières to speak, Johannes was surprised when the governor looked over the prisoners for a moment, turned to Manthet, nodded, and headed back towards the brick building. Another man stepped up – a magistrate. He began speaking, addressing the militia and townspeople.

Johannes edged closer to Arnout Viele. "What is he saying?"

"He is telling the people that we will be gifted to the warriors who raided, and others will be sold at the highest bidder to the villagers." Arnout glanced over. "We are slaves."

Jacques Le Moyne de Sainte-Hélène and a powerfully-built Indian approached the magistrate. They conversed amongst themselves for a bit and Sainte-Hélène pointed towards David Burt, a man of Lieutenant Talmadge's Connecticut detachment. The magistrate stepped forward and spoke.

Arnout Viele's eyes widened in terror as he heard the magistrate speak.

"What's happening?" Johannes begged to know.

Two Algonquin Indians pushed through the prisoners and grabbed Burt as he pleaded for mercy. They dragged him towards the other Indians who shouted, raising their muskets and hatchets. "What are they going to do with him?" Johannes asked. "Arnout?"

Viele took a deep breath. "The Iroquois captured several French and Indians during the pursuit and burned them to death. The magistrate is giving him to the savages for vengeance for the lost.

Johannes closed his eyes and tried to drown out the man's screams as the torture began. The soldier had an ear and several fingers removed and was burned on the face by a hatchet blade heated, to a glow, by fire. After he passed out, the Algonquians dragged him away.

"They are going to burn him alive," Viele whispered. "Please God, have mercy on us."

The gifting and auction started in earnest. Almost immediately, the Indians snatched up three more men and boys including Arnout Janse. They begged for mercy as they were carried off.

The weather deteriorated quickly and by noon the auction was called off. The prisoners were herded into a large barn and given a few blankets and their first ration of food in nearly three days. They gorged down the stale bread and cold soup like it was a feast. Afterwards, they joined together in small clusters for warmth and dozed off to sleep. There was no need for guards. Escape in the storm would mean certain death.

In the cold darkness, Johannes listened to the howling winds outside. His mind thought of home and his family. He wanted to smell his mother's cooking, and see his father's face, and hear Angie's high-pitched voice. He wanted to hold young Corset again and play in the meadows.

But most of all, he missed Maria Vandervort. He closed his eyes and pictured her white teeth shining in the warm sunlight as she smiled; a gentle breeze blowing through her hair and her soft skin as she touched him. He allowed himself to wish so much to be with her that he could swear he heard her whisper to him, professing her love for him. In the grim, desolate place he found himself in, in his moment of tranquility, Johannes smiled.

It was the last happiness he would know for a while. The next morning, the prisoners were immediately put to work. It was treacherous and back-breaking, digging trenches, chopping wood, and assisting in the overall fortification of Montreal. The first few days were the worst. Rumors persisted that the French would work them to death in retribution for those murdered by the Iroquois. Though the rumors eventually proved false, the lives of those taken from

Schenectady remained inhospitable for even the most wretched creatures.

Their lives became a daily routine of hardship and misery. At dawn, the prisoners would be led outside into the freezing cold to be counted and fed with stale cornbread and on every other day, a parcel of meat, usually caribou, deer, or fish. They would then be dispersed for daily work which would mostly entail hard labor such as fortifying the stockade walls or clearing land for future homes. Injuries were prevalent as the tools were often crude and the French masters cared little for the well-being of their prisoners.

They would be fed once more in the evening, a mixed soup of peas, grains, or meat depending on what could be spared. Only once, on a special occasion of unknown importance to the prisoners, they were fed Canadian habitant pea soup – a warm and hearty meal. They devoured the soup and licked their bowls clean.

The first three months of captivity were fraught with uncertainty and fear. Several of the men were taken away as slaves, rewards for those who fought well at Schenectady. David Burts and Arnout Janse had only been the first to be taken. Six more were taken within a fortnight, most leaving Montreal for either Quebec or the hard life at a frontier fur-trading post.

The threat of slavery and the cold were not the captives' only enemies. Disease ran rampant through the prisoners that winter. One of the five Groot brothers, Claes, came down with a severe case of pneumonia. The Canadian guards took no notice until one of the men Johannes recognized as a leader from the raid, ordered them to take Claes and Dyrck Groot to a home in the town to recover. The other brothers would stay locked up. Others suffered from dysentery, fever, and common colds. Jan Baptist injured himself, having a pick axe strike his leg, cracking his tibia and putting him on permanent bed rest for the winter.

In late March, a severe blizzard struck the town. The prisoners who remained were herded into a basement dungeon where they stayed confined in the bitter cold and darkness for the next two weeks. There was little to do in the basement except converse quietly with one another. Politics was the usual choice for discussion and quickly the conversation collapsed into a blaming match between the Leislerites and anti-Leislerites.

John Webb, a man of Lieutenant Talmadge's Connecticut militia, was always the most forceful. He would debate any man who dared to accuse the Albany Convention of incompetence, instead resting blame squarely on the Leislerites who left the gate opened. This regularly drew rebuttals by several of the men who supported Jacob Leisler. They stuck to their claim that the militia and the Convention failed to defend the village, despite their promise to keep them safe.

Johannes sat in the corner quietly. With the atrocities that he witnessed at Schenectady burned into his mind, he could not help but think blaming each other would not help their present situation.

"It's done!" he shouted one day, finally tiring of the debates. "We all lost family and friends, it's too late to pass guilt on who's responsible. The French are responsible, nobody else."

The men quietly broke apart into their factions of friends and changed the subject. Occasionally someone would glance over their shoulder at Johannes, eyeing him with distrust.

Johannes ignored the looks and kept his mind focused elsewhere. He wished they could all be reminded of their true enemy.

And then one day, they were reminded.

The April rains had washed away much of the snow from winter. Though the nights remained frigid, the days were starting to warm and the coming spring brought a sense of hope to the prisoners.

That all changed one cloudy morning.

After their morning count, the prisoners were not assigned to duties. Instead they stood in increasingly uncomfortable silence.

"They're going to execute us," whispered a voice from behind Johannes. He did not want to believe it, but there was a noticeably larger presence of militia.

There was a sudden commotion. The prisoners turned their heads. Marching in at gun point were more prisoners, six in total. They were herded with the others and all were led back to the basement. There, Albert Vedder and the others questioned the new arrivals. One man decided to speak for all the newcomers. He was middle-aged with gray hair and appeared strong and healthy, compared to those from Schenectady.

"Who are you, sir?" Albert asked.

"My name is Ryck Van Vranken," said the man. "I am from Niskayuna."

"Albert Vedder," Albert replied. "This is my brother, Johannes."

"Vedder?" Ryck asked. "You would not be the sons of Harmen Vedder?"

Johannes' eyes lit up. "You know our father?"

Ryck nodded. "He sold me my plot of land that I raised my house upon." His eyes dropped. "It's not there anymore," he said. "The French and Indians raided Niskayuna. They came at night like they did at Schenectady. They killed eight and captured us, burning every house they could find."

"I am sorry," Johannes said.

"You?" Ryck replied. "I feel sorry for the lot of you." He looked around. "You have been living in these horrid conditions since the burning?" Johannes nodded. "Good heavens, these people are savages."

"What news from Albany?" asked John Webb, one of Talmadge's soldiers. "Did the French attack Albany?"

"No," replied Ryck. "But the failure at Schenectady was placed on the Convention. Leisler sent an army up and seized Albany."

There were some mutters in support and others in distress at the news.

"Where is the Convention now?" Johannes asked.

"Gone," Ryck said. "They capitulated entirely. The colony is under the complete authority of Leisler." As he saw the prisoners start to bicker he cleared his throat and they quieted. "It does not matter. I hear Leisler and the leaders of the other colonies will soon assemble. They have all vowed retaliation for Schenectady." He took a breath. "Make no mistake, the real war is coming."

Chapter 63

In late May, worse news arrived. It was Arnout Viele who brought it, after overhearing a courier speaking to the governor of Montreal. That evening when the prisoners gathered for their meal, he announced what he had heard.

"The French attacked Falmouth."

The conversations ceased.

"My God!" Isaak Switts exclaimed. "The people?"

Viele's face bore a deep sadness. "They're dead. The French and Abenaki allies wiped out the town and fort, along with its inhabitants. The courier said over two-hundred were taken prisoner. Everyone else was slain."

John Webb set his bowl aside and stood up. "War is raging amongst the colonies. Our fate is far from certain and staying here in these miserable conditions invites inevitable death."

"What are you saying?" Albert Vedder asked.

"We must plan an escape," Webb responded. "The weather is improving, and the snows are now melted. If we make a concerted effort, I am confident that many, if not all of us, can escape south."

"This is foolish," one of the Groot brothers commented.

"Listen to me," Webb snapped. "We can overtake the guards. I see the way they carry themselves. They have become complacent. One good effort and we are free. We cross the river by any means available. Several hard days' march and we will be back in Mohawk territory. From there we can make our way back to Albany."

501

Albert turned to Johannes. "What do you think, brother?"

Johannes looked around. All eyes seemed to be fixed on him. "You all know I tried to escape. Somehow, for reasons I do not understand, I was kept alive. And after one goes through that, normally they may become a voice of caution against such actions." He sighed. "But I think I have had more than my fair share of Canada. It will not be an easy task, but sooner or later, we will die if we stay here." He looked around the room at all the men and boys gathered. Johannes cleared his throat. "I vote to escape."

For the next three days, a dozen of the prisoners, led by Webb, plotted their escape. The factional rivalry of Jacob Leisler and the Albany Convention was forgotten. Leislerites and those of the Convention came together for their own survival. For those plotting their freedom, they forbade all political conversation as to not cause rivalry.

Arnout Viele taught them a few basic French words and pressed to gain as much intelligence as possible from listening in on the guards. Johannes, while serving on a working party south of the town, learned the places where boats were kept and what times the fishermen would arrive each morning. Isaak Switts and his son, Cornelis, borrowed small planks of wood and spent an hour each night sharpening them into makeshift blades – weapons to be used when the time came. Ryck Van Vranken managed to smuggle rope and a sack that could be used to steal food for their journey. Day-by-day, the plan became evermore real and the anticipation of escape began to stir.

John Webb and Johannes Vedder called together the conspirators.

"June the first is our night," Webb finally

announced. "That is the night we escape."

"Three days," Vedder added. "May God bless us on our enterprise."

The morning before the escape, the prisoners were assembled as usual, for their work assignments. The French magistrate called out Arnout Viele to translate. As the magistrate began to speak, Viele knew something was wrong.

"There has been a request for additional labor," Viele said, translating the official's words. "Those called will be dispatched to the west to the fur-trading posts being built. Step out when your names are called."

Johannes' heart beat faster as they called Johannes Teller, the son of Myndt Wemp, and one of the Groot brothers. Then Viele spoke another name.

"Albert Vedder," he called out.

Johannes turned to his brother. "You take care of yourself, Albert."

"You too, brother," Albert said, briefly hugging him before departing with the others.

There was little emotion in either of the brothers. They both accepted the new conditions and as they left, Johannes knew Albert would do whatever he had to, in order to survive. He thought of himself and wondered if he too would do whatever it took to get back to Maria.

After the party of four departed with a few militia and fur trappers, Viele cleared his throat. "For the second post, Stephen Bouts, Barent Vroman, and Johannes Vedder."

The world stood still for Johannes. He felt his hope of escape disappear before his eyes. The three prisoners stepped out from among the remaining prisoners. Stephen was roughly the same age as

Johannes, though Stephen confessed he himself was not sure of his exact age, having been adopted when he was a toddler. Young Barent was only ten years old and surprised everyone that he survived the harsh winter in Montreal.

Without time to collect any belongings they had, they were led out the gates and turned west. Traveling with six coureurs de bois, they moved swiftly through the deep woods of Canada. One of the men early on had warned them that if they attempted to escape, the trappers would hunt them down and kill them.

The warning was not necessary. Johannes had decided from the beginning, that he would have had better odds of escape at Montreal. Out here, on the Canadian frontier, there was little hope to flee, or be rescued. These men were experts at surviving in the wilderness, scouting, and killing.

Aside from that, Johannes picked another reason to stay. Though he hesitated to admit it to himself, there was an alluring nature to the wilderness. For days as they traveled to the post, he saw more of the wild country than he had ever imagined. By day, they hiked up and down forest-covered hills, or walked alongside crystal-blue, flowing streams. By night, they stared at the star-filled sky. The Canadians knew the importance of healthy labor and fed their three captors well, living off the land.

After two weeks' journey, they arrived at the post. It was little more than two log cabins and a work shed, surrounded by a hastily-built, wooden, split-rail fence. The interior was littered with wood chips, scattered scraps of animal carcasses, and fire pits.

Without delay, the three captives from Schenectady were put to work. They mostly carried out the dreary day-to-day tasks of the post, but on occasion they would spend hours quartering up the captured beaver, deer, moose, and other large game caught by the traders.

The coureurs de bois were impressed by Johannes' skills with skinning the animals, and preparing the pelts to be ready for trade. By summer's end, he soon found himself relieved of normal post duties and relegated almost solely to processing the pelts. The weather soon grew colder, and each morning, frost covered the ground.

One day as Johannes chopped wood by the shed, Stephen Bouts approached him.

"Winter is coming. If we are going to escape, we must go soon."

Johannes was taken by surprise. Stephen, Barent, and himself had grown fond of each other in their months at the post, developing a close friendship. But Johannes only ever saw both following his own lead, which was to conduct themselves with prudence and obedience to the fur traders.

"Where would you go?" Johannes asked. "Do you know your way home?"

Stephen looked exasperated. "Surely, you cannot want to stay here for the winter? We're not in Montreal anymore. I heard the snows out here on the frontier are twice as deep and stay for twice as long. We wouldn't be able to leave until next May."

"Stephen, I want nothing more than to leave this place and go home," Johannes replied. "But we are a hundred, maybe two-hundred leagues from anything resembling civilization, French or English. It would take us months to make the trip back to Albany, providing we could even find our way. I don't want to die out there. My family would want me to do what I have to do, in order to survive. I know your mother would as well."

"I don't think I'll last all winter here," Stephen sighed. "You really mean to stay?"

"I do," Johannes said. "I hate to admit it, but I have learned much from these trappers. They are more experienced and knowledgeable than my father and many others from the village."

Stephen leaned in. "They are still the enemy. Have you forgotten about…"

"Of course I didn't forget," Johannes cut him off. His tone grew harsh. "I will never forget what they did to us. But what is done is done. I am here now. Alive. If I can learn from them and when the time is right, return to my family, having gained more experience and skill, then that is what I am going to do."

Johannes set the ax down and sat on a tree stump. He took a breath. "Stephen, I was a dreamer all my life. I wanted to go out and see the world, explore unknown mountains and rivers, and come back to write about my adventures." His head dropped slightly. "I like to think I still am that person. But my father taught me something I will never forget."

"What was that?"

"He taught me not to let my dreams interfere with reality. That family was the most important thing, and keeping them safe and happy should be my top priority. I like to think someday I can explore the world, but all that is secondary to ensuring food is on the table and coin in my pocket."

Johannes stood back up. "I am a fur-trapper like my father. That is my trade. I am going to keep myself alive and learn what I can of my trade. When the opportunity presents itself, I will be free. Whether it is a ransom paid, I am freed by a raiding party of Mohawk, or I escape of my own accord, I will be free someday. And when I return home, I will keep dreaming, but I will go on with my life."

Stephen took a moment, then nodded and walked away silently. Johannes knew it must hurt Stephen and Barent to be so far from their loved ones, as it hurt him as well.

A snowflake touched his face and melted. He looked up as the snow started to fall. Picking up the ax, he resumed chopping wood for the long winter that approached.

Chapter 64

The winter was darker and colder than Johannes could ever have imagined. Conditions at the trading post were Spartan. The men had a plentiful supply of meat but little else in the way of nutrition. The water had to be brought from a local stream as ice blocks, then melted over the fire before drinking.

Johannes despaired at how little sunlight he saw. The days were noticeably shorter at the higher latitude, and what few hours of daylight there were, were usually marked by overcast clouds and gentle but ceaseless snowfall. He marked a period where he saw no sunlight for six days straight.

During the long winter, the coureurs de bois scarcely bothered or even spoke with their captives. Johannes made warm blankets for himself and the others, using spare pelts that were not fit for trading. They mostly stayed in one of the cabins while the trappers lived in the second, larger cabin. The trappers knew it would be suicide to attempt an escape and some days they did not even bother to count all three prisoners.

It was during this time that Barent fell sick with pneumonia. Johannes kept the young boy under close watch, cooking up a soup mixed with whatever he could scrounge up, and spoon-fed Barent. The boy just laid in bed, pale-faced and sweating.

Upon seeing the sick boy, one of the trappers took Johannes and Stephen outside.

"The boy does not have long left," he told them. "There is a spot in the woods, not far from here. It's clear of underbrush. I would start digging a grave now. The ground is frozen and it will take a while to…"

"I am not giving up on Barent," Johannes snapped back. "He will recover."

"Please man," Stephen urged, stepping in. "Johannes, you saw him. He's as good as gone. Even if it were possible to traverse the land, which it's not – we're hundreds of miles or more from anyone close to a doctor, and he's too sick to travel anyways."

"I wouldn't give up on you," Johannes said, "and I'm not giving up on Barent either. I will care for him until he either passes or recovers."

The Frenchman eyed him for a moment, contemplating whether the young prisoner was either a fool or desperate to save what little civility was left in him.

"Well," the man said, "faith is something few have on this frontier. But if I may suggest, dig it now so if his time comes, he can have a Christian burial. Otherwise, his body will stay frozen above ground until the spring."

The air was still when Johannes ventured outside. Shovel in hand, he headed out to the spot suggested by the trapper. When he arrived at the clearing beyond the tree line, to his dismay, he saw why the man suggested such a location. Half-protruding from the snow was a stone with a name scratched onto its face. Beside it, were two crudely-made crosses with no names.

As he was about to start digging, he heard a long high-pitched call from above. He looked up to see a bald eagle calling out from its nest high in the trees. It raced its head back and forth, as if seeking out prey or watching for intruders. Johannes watched it for a moment before the eagle leapt from its nest, extending its massive wings, and flew off in search of food.

Johannes took in the scene before focusing back to the grim task at hand. He drove his shovel into the ground and a somber thought crept into his mind. Looking at the three graves, Johannes wondered how many more would need to be dug before winter's end.

But to Johannes and everyone else's surprise, no grave was needed. Against the odds, as the first signs of thawing dawned, Barent recovered. The fever broke, and he could soon feed himself and go for short walks outside. In two months, he was as strong as ever. The long winter had passed, and life was blossoming back into the world.

The Canadian spring rains were followed by a sweltering summer heat. Johannes soon departed the camp for Montreal. The coureurs de bois were recalled to Montreal to aid in its defense against the summer raids. Word had spread that the Mohawk were already on the march.

When the trading party finally reached Montreal, Johannes was awed by the sight. The town had been transformed into a veritable fortress. Trenches and *chevaux de fries* crisscrossed the landscape. New blockhouses had been constructed, surrounded by sharp stakes and muddy ditches. French troops, not just militia but regular soldiers in their long, gray or white overcoats and blue cuffs, marched past to the beating of a drum. Nearby, several men readied a cannon.

Governor Callières met the prisoners personally. "Who among you is Barent Vroman?"

"I am," Barent said, stepping forward fearlessly.

Callières looked him over. "Very well," he said. "You are free to go. A ransom has been delivered by your family." He pointed south. "I can spare no escort in this time of war. If you get started now, you should be home in two weeks." Callières turned to the others. "Report to the magistrate of labor for assignment."

Johannes had scarcely time to say goodbye before Barent Vroman disappeared out the gate. Johannes was relieved that his friend was free but crushed to be left behind.

Chopping wood in the hot sun, he tried to force it from his mind, but could not help but cry. His mind raced with thoughts. *Where was Albert? Had their father forgotten about them? Was a ransom on its way? Would he ever be freed?* He tried to fight the suspicions but that day they were too strong.

* * *

The snows came early that year. Johannes shared a barracks building during the winter with dozens of other prisoners. There were men and boys from Massachusetts, Plymouth, Connecticut, Maine, New Hampshire, and New York. They were the spoils of war, and the ones fortunate enough not to be captured by the Algonquians or other Indians allied to the French.

The one consoling bit of news he heard came from one of the prisoners. The night after Barent, Stephen, and himself parted for the frontier, John Webb, Issak and Cornelis Switts, and Ryck Van Vranken, had all escaped. Just like the plan called for, they had snuck past the guards, acquired a boat, and made it across the river. Word later came that they had made it back to Albany. Though it made Johannes happy to learn that his friends had escaped, one captive was put to death as a warning for the others. There would be no more escapes.

And for those who remained, a new definition

of hell emerged.

The barracks were cold and wet. Clothing shortages meant a lack of blankets, and those that were offered, were foul and often carried lice. The food was fair enough to be sustainable, but meager in portion. Disease ran rampant. At night, Johannes lay with his eyes open, listening to the coughs and groaning of the sick.

It was a darker, worse hell than he had ever conceived. Even the fur post the previous year was tolerable, compared to the misery at Montreal. Out there, he could take a stroll outside, embracing the fresh air. Imprisoned in Montreal, it smelled of death, odor, burning food from the furnaces and forges, horse manure, and human waste.

Johannes caught pneumonia in early April just as the temperature began to turn. He fought for weeks, trying to keep up with the work, before finally collapsing one chilly afternoon.

"He doesn't have long," one of the French soldiers commented to the other captives near him. "Throw him in the cellar until he makes peace with the Lord."

As ordered, two men from Massachusetts picked up Johannes and carried him to a cellar, laying him on a pile of straw. They heaped a blanket on him and fed him some lukewarm soup, and then carried on with their work. The next day he was visited by a physician. He quickly left and returned with a dry blanket and food more suitable for consumption. Over the next weeks, his condition failed to improve. Fever eventually took hold. The physician gave up and stopped visiting him, believing it more appropriate to call for a priest.

Johannes Vedder lay shivering in the fetal

position on a crude bed of hay and wool. The room was dark and hot. His skin was pale, and his eyes were bloodshot. The pain in his abdomen and consistent coughing kept him from getting a full night's sleep in over a week. Sweat dripped from every pore. His clothes were rags, torn and dirty. Next to him lay a dish of half-eaten porridge. What little food was offered to him, he could not keep it down. Three times he threw up today, and twice the previous day. Each day was worse than the day before. As he drifted in and out of consciousness, Johannes could think of only one thing – the end was not far away.

"Johannes?" a voice called out from the blackness. "Johannes, come back to me."

He recognized that voice.

"Maria? Where are you?" he stuttered. "Please get me out of here, Maria."

The voice repeated itself. "Come back to me, Johannes."

This time the voice was unknown. He blinked and opened his eyes, squinting at the man's face.

"Arnout, is that you?"

"Yes," Arnout Viele said with a smile. "Welcome back, Johannes." With extreme effort, Johannes leaned up. "Whoa, take it easy," Arnout said. "You have been out of it for three days. We thought you were about dead. I think the fever broke."

Arnout lifted a pouch of water to Johannes, and he gulped it down, coughing as he pulled it away. "There you go," Arnout said. "You're definitely looking better. Some color has returned to your face."

"What day is it?"

"The tenth of May," Arnout replied. Johannes nodded and laid his head back down. "You need to eat," Arnout said. "You need to build up your strength.

The Governor wants to see you when you are better."

Johannes' eyes widened. "Why? What for?"

"Don't know," Arnout shrugged. "That's just what one of the soldiers told me. So, get up, let's go eat, and when you're ready, I will take you to see him."

The next day Arnout led Johannes to the Governor's house. To Johannes' surprise, there was no guard. "The French trust us not to run off?"

"Not us, me," Arnout replied. "I've been doing their translating since arriving and they treat me well enough in exchange for my services. The Governor treats me fairly. I think these long years of war have taken their toll on him. Someday I'll be free. Until that time, I will keep doing what I am good at," he said with a nod. "Okay, here we are."

The house was beautifully decorated. White vases with blue flowers sat atop mahogany shelves. Paintings with fine borders lined the hallways. Drapes of blue and red were pushed aside, letting light flood through the windows.

It was unnervingly quiet as they walked down the hall to the governor's study. Arnout knocked and a voice called out. He opened the door and showed Johannes in.

The governor was still very much the same man Johannes saw when they were marched through the gates over two years ago. Callières stood up, pushing his chair back, and extending his hand. "You are Johannes Vedder, the son of Harmen Vedder?"

Johannes cautiously shook his hand. "Yes, sir."

"Very well," Callières said. He picked up a letter from his desk. "Payment has arrived for a ransom. Monsieur Vedder, you are free to go."

Chapter 65

Johannes took a moment to take in the governor's words. "I am free?"

"Yes," Callières replied. "You are free to leave."

Callières went back to his daily work. Johannes stood still, hoping his presence would be noticed. When the governor failed to recognize him, Johannes spoke up.

"Sir," he said meekly. "My brother was captured too. At Schenectady. Is he to be released as well?"

Callières set his pen down and looked up. "What is your brother's name?"

"Albert – Albert Vedder," Johannes replied. "He's taller and bigger than me."

"Yes, I know now," Callières said. "He was standing in the very spot you are now – two months ago."

Johannes leaned back. "He was here? My brother?"

"Yes. Your brother's ransom arrived, and we released him in March. I suppose you didn't receive word."

Johannes shook his head. "We lost contact after they split us up."

Callières nodded knowingly. "Escape was always a concern," he said, standing up. "But that is in the past. You may return to your quarters and gather whatever personal belongings you have. Like I have told many such freemen, due to the ongoing war, I cannot afford you a military escort. Though we may share different beliefs, I trust you will go with God."

Stepping outside the governor's house, Johannes took a deep breath. He looked at Arnout who smiled. "Is this real? Am I really free?"

Arnout nodded. "It is real, my friend. I suspected that was the reason he called you in, as I saw your brother's release. But I didn't want to get your hopes up in case the situation was different. But you are free. Get out of here."

Johannes smiled faintly. "What about yourself? When are you getting out of here?"

"I don't know." Arnout shook his head. "Maybe my family thinks I am dead. Or they don't have the funds to arrange my release. Hopefully soon," he mused. "We shall see."

Johannes gripped his arm. "When I get home, I will do what I can to get you out of here. I promise."

Stepping out beyond the gate, Johannes took a deep breath. It was as if a veil had been lifted. The sun shone brighter. The air smelt cleaner. Though he had eaten very little at breakfast, his stomach felt full. He looked south, and as he started his long walk home, his legs felt strong enough to carry him a thousand miles.

He made his way down to the pier. A brief note signed by one of Callières' magistrates granted him free passage across the mighty Saint Lawrence River. A grisly Canadian merchant ferried him across, murmuring a hymn under his breath. For his part, Johannes leaned over the edge, watching the current splash and roll off the bow.

Landing on the southern bank, Johannes thanked the boatman in what little French he learned, picked up a small satchel that Arnout gave him, and stepped off the boat. The feeling of freedom was surreal. He hiked up a nearby hill, peering out at the summit in awe.

Ahead of him was an endless forest as far as his eyes could see. It would be an arduous journey, and a dangerous one at that. French patrols and Algonquian warriors still roamed the lands in the north. Though he had a letter from the Governor that would serve to get him past any French, the natives were bound by no treaty. Beyond the human threat, black bears, coyotes, and the unknown landscape would serve as a deep reminder to exercise great caution.

Perils aside, Johannes stared at a scene of unparalleled beauty. The late spring was in full blossom and thick green foliage covered the landscape, dotted with crystal blue streams and lakes. Birds could be heard chirping away and flying in the distance.

He was struck by the irony. Years before, he had traversed the very same landscape when it was snow-covered and barren. At the time, he thought there could be no worse place on earth. Looking at the lush green forests of the great Adirondack Mountains of New York, he thought there could be no place as perfect.

The long journey south was everything Johannes had expected. His days were spent climbing over rocky crevices or forging the seemingly endless number of small tributaries and streams that dotted the forest. On occasion, he stumbled upon a cliff or rocky face that was impassible and would have to backtrack around the mountain.

Combining the trade skills learned from his father with those of the coureurs de bois, Johannes set up several snares, catching two rabbits for eating. By night, he cooked his food over a fire under the star-filled sky. The first few nights were spent without a fire as he did not want to draw attention to himself. But with each passing day, he extended his distance from Montreal and felt ever safer.

On the eighth day, Johannes heard voices while following a stream. He was overcome with joy. He stepped out into a clearing where a scouting party was busy starting their midday cooking fires.

"Halt!" came a shout.

"I'm English," Johannes yelled out as the soldiers grabbed their muskets and sighted in on him. "I'm English," he repeated.

"What are you doing out here? What militia are you with?"

"No militia," he responded. "I was captured at Schenectady. My family paid for my release. My father is Harmen Vedder."

One of the soldiers stepped forward. "Lower your rifles, men. He's telling the truth. I know his brother."

"Albert?" Johannes asked.

"No, Samuel," the man replied. "I am Symon Van Ness. I was on the scouting expedition that attempted rescue of those taken at that village." His head dropped slightly. "My deepest regret is that we didn't succeed. Please," he said motioning to the fire, "I am guessing you are hungry. Join us."

Never in his life had Johannes tasted such delicious food. Though Symon apologized that the bread may be a bit hard, Johannes wolfed it down without hesitation. He savored every bit of venison and fish that had been cooked over the fire. One of the other soldiers even had a ration of beer he gave to Johannes, who gulped it down in pure satisfaction.

"What news of Schenectady?" Johannes asked, finishing the beer. "What is happening there?"

"They're rebuilding the defenses," Symon said. "The blockhouse is finished. The palisade will be bigger and stronger than before. Numerous river defenses were built on the south bank of the Mohawk River. All over, troops are now pouring in from New York City and the southern colonies."

"So, the war will continue?"

"Indefinitely," Symon admitted. "Neither side has gained a decisive advantage. But the colonies are uniting, and we'll continue this war until these French bastards give up." Symon smiled. "You might know that some justice has been given for Schenectady."

"How so?" Johannes asked.

"While we were turned back at Quebec, word reached us that we killed one of the commanding officers of the raiding party sent against your village. One of the Le Moyne brothers— Saint-Helene—was killed in action."

Johannes nodded. "A small bit of justice," he said. "So where is the line between the French lines and our own?"

"You're two days from the southernmost French force." Johannes' eyes lit up when he heard the news. "You're safe and sound in the middle of Mohawk territory."

That night, Johannes slept easy. His mind was flushed with relief. For the first time in years he felt at rest. The following morning, he thanked Symon Van Ness, and parted south. Though he had more than a week's travels remaining, he walked easy, taking more time to rest and catch food. Symon had given him two days' rations of bread for his trip.

Coming out of a patch of forest, Johannes found himself amidst a field of flowers. Yellow daffodils, pink hollyhocks, tulips of every color, and white snowdrops scattered throughout the tall grass, gave a magnificent sight. He thought back to the book loaned to him by Barent Van Ditmars that described the New Netherland region. Seeing it undisturbed by the ravages of war, and miles from any settlements, the land was peaceful and quiet.

He crossed back into the forest, looking at the spruce and fir trees, sugar and striped maple, and of course the mighty oaks and pines. Some of the older pine trees had diameters wider than he had ever seen around Schenectady, with their leaves towering over the forest. He could not help but wonder how old they must be.

By the numerous streams and creeks, everywhere were dams built by beavers. Johannes viewed several fallen trees with their shaved trunks – a clear sign of a large beaver population.

"Father will be pleased to know this," he commented to himself. The land was rich with resources beyond any trappers' wildest dreams.

On the whim of an idea, Johannes stopped for the day, and set about making traps. Using some of the techniques taught to him by the Canadian coureurs de bois, the following day he emerged from the forest with a clean beaver pelt and a sack of beaver meat. The pelt was one of the largest and finest he had ever caught, and he beamed with pride when he thought of how his father would react when he saw it.

With another two days walking, he came upon the most welcome sight imaginable. Before him stood a ferry, and on the other side, Fort Orange.

Albany.

He smiled and walked down to the boat.

"May I cross? I have nothing to pay you," he said to the elderly man running the ferry.

"Ha, nice try," the man replied.

"Please, I can pay you back once I return to Schenectady."

The man glared at him. Suddenly his eyes opened. "You're one of Harmen's boys, ain't you? My god boy, you're alive. You look so much like him."

"Johannes Vedder," he announced to the man. "I've been gone a while."

Without hesitation, the man offered to ferry him across free of charge.

"Don't you worry about payment, boy," he said. "It's good to have you home."

Johannes walked through the gates of the city. Like Montreal, Albany too was armed, and its defenses built up in preparation of attack. Everywhere, Iroquois war parties and English troops moved about, hauling supplies, drilling, practicing loading. Albany was one giant fort.

"Excuse me," he said to a woman. "Where is the Vandervort residence?"

The woman directed Johannes to a small white house on a side street. He took a breath and knocked on the door. There was silence. He looked about, then knocked again.

A voice called out from the neighboring house. "Can I help you, sir?" a man asked.

"Yes," Johannes eagerly said. "Where is Jean Vandervort, or his daughter, Maria?"

The man looked at him suspiciously. "Mr. Vandervort left some three weeks from yesterday. Nobody has heard from him. Some say he went to the city."

Johannes heart sank. "And his daughter? It's important I see her. Is she with him?"

The man shook his head. "No, his daughter went to Schenectady. Apparently, she had a man there, who was taken years ago, during the massacre. She wanted to help secure his release. Might be the best …"

"Thank you!" Johannes shouted, already

running down the street. His heart was pounding. It was already sunset, so Johannes chose to stay the night at the inn, though he could scarcely sleep.

The next morning, he rose early, headed down to a tailor shop, and after some negotiating, emerged with a fresh shave and set of clothes. After a hearty breakfast, he headed out the gate and started on his way down the King's Road to Schenectady. It was the same dry, dusty road he remembered from two years ago, walking alongside his sister.

Two whole years.

To Johannes, it seemed so distant as to be from a different life entirely. But with each step, a certain familiarity came back to him. His memory conjured up images of him reading by the river, listening to the crickets and watching the boats sail back and forth between Schenectady and Albany. He thought about Angie and laughed aloud thinking about how she was always so cheerful and careless. He thought about young Arent holding their baby brother, Corset. Dear young Corset. Did either of them survive the attack?

He tried not to think about that night – the night of February 8th, 1690 – the night of the Schenectady Massacre. A tear fell from his cheek. Though the hardships endured since that night were terrible and tested his faith to its limits, nothing was worse than the night the French and Indians came to Schenectady. He closed his eyes and for a moment, the icy cold, black night returned in its horrid ferocity. He could smell the gunpowder from the muskets and see the snow run red with blood. He heard the screams of those loved and lost, and felt helpless.

He opened his eyes. The road stretched out before him and the sun beamed through the trees, illuminating the dirt. The warm sunlight hit him. He wiped his face and smiled. With renewed energy, he walked the last few miles until at last it opened into fields outside of the village. Carpenters were busy constructing new homes. Farmers tilled the fields. Soldiers patrolled the shoreline.

Johannes knelt, grabbed a handful of dirt and stood back up. He looked around at the village. Everything had changed. It had been a dark and painful journey. More than a few scars had been picked up along the way. And yet as he rubbed the dirt through his fingers, he could not help but feel everything had fallen right into place. After a long journey, he was finally home.

Historical Note

As far back as Homer's *The Iliad* and *The Odyssey*, which spoke of the legendary Trojan War, to Michael Shaara's *The Killer Angels*, which detailed the epic clash at Gettysburg in 1863, historical novels are among the most precious works of fictional writing in our world.

Unlike traditional fiction novels, which may merely use history as a backdrop for a scene, historical figure or event as a reference point, historical fiction makes the history itself the key component to the story. The historiographer's duty is to present an accurate portrayal of historical events, based on the facts available, but in a way which allows the reader to follow those events as they would any other fictional novel; with all the tension, conflict and understanding of events from the perspective of those who lived through the story.

With *Crucible Along the Mohawk*, I set out to tell – in my own words – the story of the Schenectady massacre of February 8, 1690. I picked this event for several reasons. The first is Schenectady, New York is where I grew up, and local history has always fascinated me. Secondly, in reading through the details of that event, I concluded that the Schenectady massacre is one of the most pivotal moments in American history; an unknown link between the world of the English colonies in America, to that of the American colonies in revolution. No event between 1620 Jamestown and the fall of Quebec in 1759, shaped the political theater of the colonies as much as King William's War, and the Schenectady massacre was among the most transformational moments in that long and bitter conflict.

Finally, when I dug through the people involved in the massacre on both sides of the war, and unraveled their complex histories, I uncovered men and women who were not simple characters to be manipulated by an author but real people who, for better or worse, shaped our current world, and I believed that they each had stories worth telling.

What surprised me most in diving into the research, was the abundance of historical documentation and prior information from a multitude of sources, available to begin my work. When I began my research, I knew next to nothing about the event, save for the small inscription on the "Welcome to Schenectady" sign outside of Schenectady County Community College (the old Van Curler hotel).

But I didn't let that deter me. I started with a thorough search of all documents kept at the Schenectady County Historical Society to form a basis for the overall story. Then I read *A Description of New Netherland* by Adrien Van der Donck, who described in superb detail, the lives of the Dutch people, the Iroquois, and even the nature of the beaver trade. It was a solid foundation to build upon. Much of the research into the key events and mentality of those involved, such as Jacob Leisler, Pieter Schuyler, and Robert Livingston, I obtained from various historical books, too numerous to list here.

Genealogy information was another key area of research, and I cannot overstate how helpful the Internet was in mapping out the families of Schenectady and Albany. Even the historical documents that name the victims of the massacre often only listed the husband/father, and referenced several children, yet a thorough genealogy search revealed their children's names and sometimes even their ages.

It never ceases to amaze me, the amount of research available at the click of a mouse with the Internet. I could cross-reference different accounts of key events, to determine accuracy, and provide a clear, concise timeline of events, to not cloud the novel with out of place actions. Many books are digitally scanned, and valuable information was obtained by simply reading books straight from search engine websites.

Now that I have spoken about how the information was obtained for the novel, I will speak to how it was used in the historical fiction context. Let me first state that I kept as much to the facts, the truths, and the legends as possible in this novel.

What's the difference between the three? Facts included the casualty lists of those killed and captured during the attack. This can easily be proven as all records of their existence cease after February 8, 1690. This also included genealogy references with the families, names, and even ages of those who lived in the region. These are usually primary references, written in the late 17th Century, or information gathered over the years by professional historians and genealogists.

Truths are based on historical writings but may not be strictly based on fact. A truth would be that the French and Indians spared Captain John Glen and his family because of his kindness towards the French in the past. While this has never been proven, there are no conflicting reports that he was spared for another reason, so we can rightfully assume that this was indeed the case.

Legends, I took care to review. Ultimately though, I included ones I believed could be historically plausible and added to the story's strength. Most famous of all of course, is the legend that on the night of the attack, the north gate of Schenectady was open and only guarded by two snowmen, made by some children in the village. The story goes that this was done in mockery of the anti-Leislerites who insisted on the village strengthening its defenses against attack - a move not favored by the Leislerites. The evidence of the time supports the truth that there was great mistrust, even hatred, almost to the point of violence, between the two factions in Schenectady. So, while it is impossible to know whether snowmen guarded the village or not, it certainly is believable, and being that it is already part of the legend, I decided to include it in the story.

Another (much less known) legend, and one I just barely touched on, is that Robert Livingston and Alida Schuyler had a romantic interest, while she was still married to the elderly Nicholas Van Rensselaer. Upon Nicholas' death, Alida almost immediately married Livingston, and a bitter feud ensued between Livingston and the Van Rensselaer family over the massive Van Rensselaer patroonship. Though we can never know what happened between Livingston and Schuyler, their youth, proximity, and swiftness of marriage suggests there would have been at least some cause for gossip in the aristocratic class.

Which brings me to the politics. *Crucible Along the Mohawk*, for better or worse, is a highly-politicized book. Not in the contemporary sense, but in that politics, from the local taverns of Schenectady, to the longhouses of the Iroquois, to the high courts of England and France, played a key role in how events of the story unfolded. These were revolutionary times, and (possibly the one connection to our contemporary national politics), the rivalry between factions were at times so strong, that people felt more hatred for those of the other side politically, than that of their common enemy. It was this rivalry that led to Schenectady's destruction. Perhaps there is a lesson in this for those in today's world who would seek to divide rather than unite our nation.

On the matter of characters, I've taken notice that many historical novels often have fictional people as their key characters. Often these people are not of any historical significance and act essentially as the "man on the ground," who shows what life was really like for someone in that place at that time in history. In *Drums Along the Mohawk*, author Walter D. Edmonds makes use of this method, with Gilbert Martin, a fictional character who joins the New York militia in resisting the 1777 British campaign into western New York. This method is used extensively by authors as a way to blend a fictional novel with accurate historical facts, and I must add that it is an entirely acceptable method for authors of historical fiction.

For this book, however, I didn't follow that method. I had no need. There is a very accurate breakdown of persons who lived in and around Schenectady or were somehow connected to the events of 1689-1690, such as the French military commanders or the leaders of the Albany Convention. Using historical references, I could as reasonably possible, create accurate descriptions and understand the personalities of many of these people. Therefore, the characters in this book can be broken down into three categories.

First are those who are portrayed by name, as accurately as possible, including most of the main characters. Their ages, where they lived, occupations, all are as close to the truth as I could make them. One small note is on the story's main protagonist, Johannes Vedder. I encountered several documents which put his age at both six and eighteen at the time of the massacre. Although the majority of the documents seemed to agree that six was the greater possibility, I found it hard to believe such a young boy would survive the brutal trip north to Canada, and so for the sake of the novel, I decided on the age being eighteen.

Several of Johannes Vedder's family members have also had their names changed for the sake of making the story easier to read. Johannes' mother's name was Annatje, not Anna. His eldest brother's name was not Samuel, but rather Harmanus. I figured their names were too close to Angenietje and Harmen Vedder, and so changed it for simplicity's sake.

I wanted not just the characters of historical significance like Frontenac or Pieter Schuyler to be accurately named and portrayed, but even the common people. Those killed at Schenectady were not nameless entities, faceless humans who I can just give any name I wish to. They were real people, with real names, and each had a real story to tell. In naming them and bringing them to life in the story, I hope the reader can truly understand that *Crucible Along the Mohawk* isn't just a story about the massacre, but a story about the people who lived it and some who died in it.

Second, are those characters who existed per the historical record, but were not specifically named. Among these would be several of the Mohawk who, according to documents, were in Schenectady at the time of the attack but were spared for political reasons. We know these people existed, but their names were never recorded so for the novel, I created their names, but not them. Another example would be the slaves kept by some of the villagers as well as Captain Glen. Again, we know they existed, some being killed or captured, but due to their status in society at the time, no names were ever recorded.

Finally, there are some characters that are not specifically referenced in historical documents, but rather they represent a person, group of persons, or some abstract element of the story. An example would be the Mohawk Joseph. As far as my research could find, there is no evidence to support a close friendship between a Mohawk Indian and Captain Glen. However, we know from the historical documents that the Mohawk and Dutch were very close allies, to the point where they lived, worked, and fought side-by-side for decades. Characters like Joseph represent that partnership and bond between the Mohawk and the Dutch settlers.

On the matter of settings, this one is very straight-forward. I depended as much on research as I could to portray each location as accurately as possible. The most difficult part in this process was the "rebuilding" of Schenectady itself. There are references that give clues as to the whereabouts of each home in the village, but they remain just that – clues. A French account of the attack claims the village had some eighty homes, a number no doubt that is greatly exaggerated. But recreating the village was a challenge in that it had to stay consistent throughout the story.

Daily life among the Dutch was another great hurdle to overcome. By the mid 1700's, colonial life in America was becoming well-documented. In 1690 it was much less so. Although, there are enough documents still in existence to give details of events like Thanksgiving or traditional meals. I tried to capture the hardships of frontier life as best as possible, by including even trivial matters like laundry washing and scouring of floors – two tasks that were always difficult and time-consuming.

An often-overlooked tragedy occurred in Schenectady the night of February 8th in that many of the village's documents of every type imaginable were lost in the minister Peter Tassemaker's home. Just like the fire which destroyed the Great Library at Alexandria, there is no record of what documents were lost in the burning of Schenectady.

One of the interesting side-notes in the setting is the dates. The Schenectady massacre occurred on February 8, 1690. That is the date we all know. However, that is according to the Julian calendar. The Gregorian calendar was not adopted in the English colonies until 1752. Technically, the massacre occurred (per our current calendar) on February 18, 1690. But for the contemporary sense of the story, I decided to stick with the Julian system in use at that time (the French at the time were using the Gregorian calendar).

There are a few points throughout the novel that may be eligible for contention among historians. Though I tried carefully to tell the story from the perspectives of the Dutch, English, Iroquois, and French, it could be argued that my own background does lend a slight bias to the Dutch side and does not adequately tell the story of the devastating raids on New France prior to their 1690 offensive (or counteroffensive from their view). The backstory to include the beaver wars would span back decades and I did not believe they could be reasonably included within a single novel.

Another key point, and one that is debated to this day, is whether Jacob Leisler should be portrayed as a hateful, power-hungry usurper, or a champion of the common people. The contemporary articles on this matter are almost entirely biased to one side or the other. The legality of seizing Fort James and the city council itself can be argued in a book of its own, let alone Leisler's decisions once in command.

His government was without a doubt, one that rapidly turned against Leisler's personal enemies, as documentation from both sides clearly presents. One personal conflict that I barely scratch the surface on is between Leisler and Robert Livingston, who Leisler believed (correctly) was the architect behind the resistance in Albany. Though I could find no written documentation as to who came up with the plan of the Albany Convention, it was Livingston who predominantly organized the logistics of the Convention. The animosity was so great that when Leisler seized Albany, Livingston lived in exile for months while Leisler's government seized the Livingston manor and estate.

This brings up the last point – missing plot points. Quite simply, the events of King William's War were so numerous that they cannot be told in a single novel, especially without diminishing the role of several main characters. The Battle of Quebec in late 1690 had to be omitted for purposes of length and again, it would take away from the key storylines of the novel. It was nonetheless decisive, and the English failure to seize Quebec, emboldened the French into further raids, devastating both the English colonies and the Iroquois nations.

In closing, for me personally, the research into the events surrounding the Schenectady massacre was as fascinating and gripping as I hope this novel is for the readers. It's one thing for an event to be listed in the annals of history. But it's another to dive into their daily lives, their politics and wars, who they hated and who they loved, their adventures, and ultimately – their stories. That's what I hoped to accomplish with *Crucible Along the Mohawk*. It's not so much my story. I like to believe it's me telling you *their* story.